BATTLE CRY

Book Two

Loki's Wolves

by

Melissa Snark

BATTLE CRY
Series: Loki's Wolves

ISBN-10: 1-942193-03-3
ISBN-13: 978-1-942193-03-6

Nordic Lights Press
First Edition

Cover Art: *Ravenborn Covers*

Contact Information:
Email: admin@nordiclightspress.com
Nordic Lights Press
P.O. Box 1347
Pleasanton, CA 94566

Published in the United States of America.

The author respects trademarks and copyrighted material mentioned in this book by introducing such registered items in italics or with proper capitalization.

This book is a work of fiction. Names, persons, places and incidents are all used fictitiously and are the imagination of the author. Any resemblance to persons, living or dead, events or locales is coincidental and non-intentional, unless otherwise specifically noted.

DEDICATION

Over the two years I spent working on Battle Cry, both of my grandmothers passed away. My grief and loss have been invested into the pages of this book.

I'm dedicating this novel to the memory of two women who are so inspirational to me. Grandma Florence was an independent and strong-minded lady. Grandma Grace was a source of compassion and kindness to everyone she met.

Wherever you are, please know you are both missed.

ACKNOWLEDGEMENTS

A great many people helped me bring Battle Cry to completion. I'd like to start by thanking the beta readers who provided constructive criticism which helped shape the story: Rissa Watkins, Richard Decker, Kirsten Hale, and Gabby-Lily Raines.

Thank you to Reba Rhynland for all her help in heading up my street team. Her support has been amazing and is much appreciated.

I also owe an extra shout out to my dedicated critique partners, Lisa Rayns and Sheryl R. Hayes. Thank you for helping me through the process! I can't count the number of times I turned to my friends for feedback and support. Or to seek a sympathetic ear so I could vent!

I owe Jennifer L. Carson big time for deconstructing my first flawed draft. Her feedback provided the structural framework for the story before you today.

Thanks go to Sharon Pickrel from Words Done Well.

Thank you also, Joe and Helen Nazzaro from One More Time Editing

Special thanks to Michelle Devon and Lynn Hunter who have been instrumental in the development of my world-building. Upon many occasions I've turned to Michy for sound advice and benefited from her wisdom.

CHAPTER ONE

There stands an ash called Yggdrasil,
A mighty tree showered in hail.
Thence come the dews that fall in the vales.
It stands evergreen 'bove Urd's Well.
From there come women, very wise,
Three from the lake that stands 'neath the pole.
One is called Urðr, another Verðandi,
Skuld the third; they carve into the tree,
Each child's life and destiny.

~Völuspá or "The Insight of the Seeress", Poetic Edda

Urd's Well at the roots of the World Tree

The white wolf ran along the trunk of the great ash tree. Her claws dug into the silvery bark while she descended toward the bottom of the Nine Worlds. Thick gnarled roots radiated from the tree's immense base and then grew thinner. Just beyond, the dark waters of the Well of Urd formed a vast lake spread outward into eternity.

There, destiny awaited: her future and her unborn child's.

Upon reaching the sandy soil, Victoria shifted from

her wolf to her human form and walked naked to join the women gathered about the shallow shore. The Norns, the Sisters Wyrd, personified Fate. One a maiden, one mature, the last a crone: *Verðandi, Skuld, and Urðr.*

At the lakeshore of the Well, the three sisters filled crude wooden bowls with water that nurtured the tree. The youngest sister, the beautiful maiden Verðandi who personified the Present, smiled in greeting. "You visit us again, Victoria Storm."

"As you predicted I would." Victoria spoke with deference. She sought guidance from the Norns and needed to curry their favor.

Skuld, an imposing woman in her middle years and the Future incarnation, labored in ominous silence beside her older sister, Urðr, a gnarled old woman and the Past aspect of Fate.

Without a word, wizened Urðr thrust the bowl she gripped in her bony fingers into Victoria's hands. The vessel, hewn from weathered gray wood, had shallow sides and a broad, flat bottom. Securing a firm hold, Victoria stepped into the lake and grimaced when the frigid cold bit into her flesh. She placed the lip of the bowl to the water and then filled the container to the brim.

Old Urðr said, "The man you loved has died."

Victoria winced. "Yes."

Verðandi's tone softened. "His soul is tormented."

Victoria's foot snagged on a stone, and she stumbled. Water sloshed over the brim and doused her hands. She lost half the contents of the container before she recovered her balance. Her throat worked in a convulsive swallow. "No, you're mistaken. I was there when he died. I saw Daniel's soul cross over."

"I am not mistaken," Verðandi said with genuine sorrow. The youngest Norn stepped away.

Mouth open, Victoria rushed after her, determined to demand the Present Fate provide her with a satisfactory explanation, but the old woman got in her way.

Urðr's lips pulled thin over cracked and yellowed teeth, an expression more grimace than grin. "Your mate has also died, as have so many others. You leave a trail of death in your wake."

"Also true." Fuming with frustration, Victoria followed the Norns to the base of the tree. She walked slowly, placing each step with precision, taking care not to spill another drop.

The three sisters each took a turn watering the roots of the tree. Verðandi acted first, followed by the silent Skuld, and finally Urðr. The eldest persisted in taunting Victoria. "Your love and your mate were not the same man."

Scowling, Victoria bent and poured water on a root until her bowl was empty.

"The past is the past. There is nothing I can do to alter it," she said with determined pragmatism. "I've come to see you because I am pregnant."

Youthful Verðandi clicked her tongue against the roof of her mouth. "You doubt yourself. You drown in sorrow and anger."

Ancient Urðr cackled.

"True enough." Victoria bobbed her head once. Her temper roiled beneath ironclad self-control. She had no patience for delays, no use for games. She wanted answers.

Shadows enshrouded Skuld, and her voice manifested upon the air, thick and oppressive, closing in from all sides. "Your daughter will not grow to adulthood in Midgard."

Victoria's heart slammed against her breastbone. Her breath expelled in a horrified gust. The bowl dropped from her hands which flew to protect her abdomen. "What do you mean?"

"Your daughter will be taken from you on the eve of her third birthday," Skuld said. "The one you trust most, a member of your own pack, will give the child over to your greatest enemy."

A growl trembled in Victoria's throat, and her entire body shook under the dual assault of fear and rage. The suggestion of betrayal from within her own pack filled her with disbelief to the core of her being. It was unthinkable. Gritting her teeth, she sought a solution, refusing to dwell on it. "How am I to prevent this?"

"We speak of what will come to pass," Verðandi said in a sympathetic tone.

"Your predictions are not carved in stone," Victoria said. Arguing with Fate was a foolish endeavor, but she refused to accept their prophecy.

The old woman, Urðr, smiled with a frightening gleam in her eyes. "Predictions, carved into the trunk of the World Tree, carved into the spiritual fabric of the world."

Stubborn determination settled over Victoria like armor. Her mother had taught her there was no absolute fate, just as there was no absolute free will. Life consisted of a wide range of possibilities between the two extremes. She refused to allow her daughter to die at three years of age. She would move worlds, alter fate, slay gods.

Whatever it took.

"Do you wish to save your child?" Skuld asked.

Victoria answered without thought. "Yes. I'll do anything. Tell me. Please."

"The final days are upon us," Verðandi said.

Skuld took over speaking. "To save your daughter, you will side with Loki against the Aesir. You will use your enchanted dagger to cut the binding of the great wolf Fenrir. You will be responsible for freeing the beast that kills Odin."

Victoria's stomach turned. Her head shook in automatic denial. "When the gods imprisoned Fenrir, my people pledged fealty to the Aesir. We have served them loyally ever since. Even when we were driven from the homeland, almost a millennium ago, we remained faithful. I will never cut Fenrir's bonds. To do so would end the world we live in and doom us all."

Skuld's gaze held steady. "You will."

Victoria snarled her denial. "No. I will never become the servant of the Trickster or willingly take part in bringing about Odin's death."

Skuld turned her head and pinned Victoria with one black eye that rolled in its socket like a liquid marble. "To save your daughter, you will."

CHAPTER TWO

Sessrúmnir, Freya's hall in Fólkvangr

The rumble of a throat clearing filled Freya's bed-chambers. Eyelids fluttering, the goddess turned her head toward the sound and rolled onto her side. Her gaze settled on the intruder. Her mouth opened to alert her sleeping companion, but her alarm faded. The young man was unarmed.

His lustful gaze wandered her lush curves, full breasts, and ample hips, instead of centering on her face. The scent of his arousal curled about him like fragrant incense. Well-accustomed to such reactions, Freya accepted his blatant admiration as her rightful due. At the same time, his masculine beauty astonished and pleased her.

He wore the uniform of the modern male: jeans, a t-shirt, and the odd footwear with the swoosh rune—garb the goddess found ugly. However, this brash young male had the brawny physique of a god, attractive enough she found any covering too much. He would prove interesting enough to bed if she chose not to slay him for his transgression.

"How did you sneak past my Valkyries?"

"Shhh." He held his finger to his lips, beckoned with a crooked hand, and then stepped from the room past the heavy velvet curtains that enclosed her sleeping area. In his wake, he left the irresistible allure of adventure.

Midgard

As a man of prophecy, Jake Barrett foresaw his own death. He perished between the gaping jaws of a monstrous black wolf. His blood-curdling howl thundered around the world. Flames burned in his eyes, smoke curled from his nostrils, and leathery lips drew taut over glistening white incisors.

Always, the beast swallowed him whole.

Boots pounded on the hard-packed dirt. The lone hunter sprinted toward the pack of enormous wolves. He reached across his torso to claw at the stylized dagger inked on the back of his forearm: his tattoo weapon, indestructible and always with him. The intricate artwork had rough edges that overlaid scorched scar tissue like a brand. Dark tendrils of energy surrounded the knife, arcing beneath the surface of his skin.

When his palm covered the hilt, sharp pain radiated through his arm. The stench of burnt flesh filled the air. The tattoo vanished from Jake's arm, and a dagger appeared in his hand. The knife had a thick, wide blade aglow with a halo of molten steel.

When he neared an outcrop, he halted briefly and studied the pack. A great red wolf ran at the head of the group. Several dozen wolves followed in a loosely spread formation. They were no mere beasts. The shifters were the descendants of Fenrir, the son of Loki, and several times larger than their animal kin in size. Claws dug into the stony terrain, casting a spray of dirt and jagged rocks in their wake. The Alpha's piercing howl split the sky, carrying for miles across the Santa Catalina

Mountains northeast of Tucson, Arizona.

A half mile distant, Skinner and the hunters loyal to Jake fought in grim desperation for their lives. The enemy army emerged from an old mine shaft in a steady swarm, seemingly endless and without any discernible source. Jake wanted to be with his men at the heart of the fight, not defending their flank alone against the new threat.

The radio transmitter Jake wore buzzed with static, but he clearly made out his second-in-command's voice across the airwaves. Skinner sounded understandably worried. "Is that old Fireball Finn?"

Chuckling, he reached up to adjust the fit of the earpiece. "No one calls Finn that to his face—"

"—and lives," they finished in unison.

"What do you think, friend or foe?" Skinner rasped.

Across the radio, a burst of machine-gun fire blasted Jake's hearing. He winced and grimaced. He infused his voice with confidence. "Friends."

"Twenty bucks says they're going straight for our unprotected flank."

"I'll take that bet, and our flank isn't unprotected. I'm here. Hold the line, soldier."

"That's exactly what we're doing, *sir*. Tho', I'm thinking now's a great time to take the time off I'm owed."

For all Skinner's sarcasm, he would do exactly as he said. They'd served together in the Marine Corps prior to forming their own private paramilitary organization, and they'd had each other's backs in countless confrontations.

Jake trusted no one more.

"What the fuck are these things?" Heavy breathing, grunts of exertion, and the occasional muttered swear word accompanied Skinner's question.

"They're called *draugar*," Jake muttered. "Incredibly rare." They were an obscure breed of vampire from Northern Europe, and they were a problem. Not only were they noted for their strength and intelligence, but they could walk in sunlight. Individual *draug* usually operated as solitary predators found in cool, watery environments.

"Fucking great!" Skinner said. "Vampires on the critically-endangered species list."

"I'd like to reduce that to extinct." Chuckling, Jake resumed his journey to intercept the pack. He adjusted his path to skirt around an area where the rough terrain looked too dangerous to cross at a full run in poor light.

When the Alpha wolf neared, he howled again. The pack echoed the call, blending their voices into a chorus to produce a ferocious battle cry. The sound boomed across the landscape.

Jake's heart thundered in his ears while he ran straight at the charging wolves. The red werewolf stood as high as a horse in the shoulder, taller than Jake at full height, which was impressive even for one of the wolf shifters. His size, combined with the distinctive ginger hue of his fur, left no room for mistaking the Alpha's identity: Fireball Finn. He led a war party from the White Mountains Tribe, perhaps thirty in number.

They were far from their territory, but he didn't have time to consider the possible reasons. He had to deal with what fate put in front of him. It meant regarding them as a direct threat until proven otherwise. The wolves weren't the sworn enemies of the hunters, but neither were they allies. A bitter conflict and many gruesome deaths had undermined trust and destroyed their cooperation.

Skidding, Jake slid into a defensive stance, his dagger poised to strike. He focused on Finn, ignoring the other wolves. In a challenge, the Alpha alone mattered. A bellow tore from his throat, a primal shout of aggression and dominance. He beat his chest with his fist. "Finn, face me as a man!"

The great red wolf broke stride, head and front

quarters jerking up in surprise. The heave of his breathing rumbled the air. His long claws struck bedrock, throwing a shower of sparks. His stride shortened. A perceptible ripple spread through the war party. The remainder of the pack transitioned from a gallop to a jog. They scattered to both sides to avoid colliding with one another.

Finn underwent a swift transformation from wolf to man. His muscles rippled, flowing like water beneath his thick fur. Bones cracked. Tendons crunched, breaking and altering. His spine straightened, and his hind legs restructured. He stood upright. Fingers grew from his front paws. His muzzle shortened to allow speech. He halted the change midway, a form reminiscent of the classic movie wolfman. On his hind legs, the werewolf towered over twelve feet tall, covered in shaggy ginger fur.

Skinner sometimes likened werewolves to living tanks, mounds of muscle with deadly teeth and claws that obliterated everything in their paths. They could be hurt by fire, drowning, or steel weapons, but their real vulnerability was silver. Still, a full-grown male was typically an even match for many undead.

The Alpha's eyes cast a golden glow upon his face. His sharp canines glistened when his lips peeled back in a grim parody of a smile.

Jake strode to meet the wolf's advance. "State your business, Finn."

Finn's sides heaved a huff of laughter. "Are you challenging me, Hunter King?"

"Alpha Finn, if you come to settle a debt of honor, then fight me alone in personal combat." Jake's voice rose to a shout. He brandished his burning dagger to add emphasis to his challenge. "Act with dishonor, and Odin shall know you as a coward!"

"Impressive that *you*, a nonbeliever, have Odin's ear." Animosity replaced the amusement in the Alpha's gaze. He snarled, slyly mocking. "Why should I question your honor, huntsman? It's not as if your hunters participated in the slaughter of an entire pack."

Annoyance frayed his self-control but Jake refused to acknowledge the snide jibe. His eyes narrowed, and he offered a flinty stare. "Do not test my patience, Finn. Are you here for me or the undead?"

A ripple tugged the red wolf's neck and traversed the length of his body, terminating in a tail twitch. His mouth opened, and a snarl rolled from his throat. "Our fight is not with you, Barrett. We come for the vampires."

"Then don't let me stand in your way." Jake lowered his dagger.

Finn's thick muscles bunched as he launched into a standing leap. The hunter's arms jerked, hands tightening on the grip of his weapon. He aborted the impulse to take a swing when the Alpha flew overhead.

The red wolf's paws passed close to Jake's head, so close he could have used the long claws to shave his beard. He stood his ground, refusing to duck or give an inch before the test of his nerves. Even the slightest sign of fear would make him look weak. Following their leader, wolves swerved left and right, flowing about the hunter like a river around a rock.

Torrential relief drenched Jake. Then instinct took over. Whirling, he lurched into a dead run toward the thick of the battle. He kept pace with the pack for a short distance, but even the slowest wolf possessed superior speed when traveling on all fours.

Ahead, Fireball Finn reached the tightly packed wall of hunters who fought against the undead. The unit was dug in on a narrow shelf, located midway along the side of a mesa, facing uphill toward the opening of an abandoned mine. A steady river of undead streamed from the entrance, an army of reanimated corpses—bloated, big, and brutish.

Standing shoulder to shoulder against the overwhelming odds, his men maintained a tight formation. They fought as one. Each man trusted his brother. They lived and died together.

Jake's breath hitched, and the blood in his veins froze. His men were wide open to attack from the rear. They trusted him to protect them. For a paralyzing second, he doubted himself. Doubted the wolves. Doubted instinct and integrity. Without a treaty, Finn had no duty to treat Jake as an equal, no obligation to accept a challenge to personal combat.

A howl swelled from the Alpha's chest when he launched into the air. The rest of the pack echoed their leader's primal song. The first wave also leapt straight at the wall of pinned hunters.

The red wolf slammed into a vampire, and his claws sank into its swollen chest. Sudden pressure distended the gray flesh. Thick fluid burst from the gashes. The pair toppled and vanished from sight behind the sea of animated corpses. The great red giant rose out of the grayness and held the vampire aloft. Roaring his rage, he ripped the revenant's head from its shoulders. Both body parts flew high, disintegrating to ash that was carried away on the hot desert wind.

Battle produced its own sort of music. The rat-a-tat-tat of machine gun fire. The draconic roar of flame throwers. The pops and booms of firearms. The primal shouts of soldiers. Jake took pleasure in the composition.

The agonized scream of one of his men destroyed the harmony. Through the magic that tied all hunters to him, he experienced the agony of his follower's injuries: *A sharp, stabbing pain near his heart... Lungs burning as he labored for breath...*

Their connection cut off.

He added another name to the steadily mounting fatality list: Ron Buckley—a loyal friend, loving husband, father of three, and grandfather of ten. A man who had complained constantly about his bum knee, slurred the letter S when he spoke, precisely mimicked over a hundred unique bird calls, and possessed an uncommon obsession with lacrosse.

Jake sprinted up the slope toward the front line.

"Cease machine guns," he ordered so the wolves wouldn't be hit by friendly fire. "Kill the flame throwers, and switch to small-caliber firearms and melee weapons from here on out."

Ahead, Skinner repeated the orders. He extinguished his flamethrower. He dropped to a crouch and yanked a machete from a belt sheath. The other hunters did the same while more wolves passed overhead.

Arriving in groups of three and four, the rest of the pack rushed and leapt above the defensive line. Midair, they tackled undead. With bloodthirsty howls, they charged straight into the thick of combat.

A steep incline marked the last ten feet. He dislodged dirt and debris that sent a shower of pebbles down the slope. Once on the shelf, Jake hurried to rejoin his soldiers.

With the last of the wolves having completed their overhead jumps, the hunters stood upright. Following his orders, they fought hand-to-hand or fired handguns.

"You owe me twenty," Jake said, coming alongside Skinner. "They are the cavalry."

He swung his dagger and struck a vampire's neck with a decapitating blow.

The stench of seared flesh filled the air. The revenant fell to ash. His remains fed the thick cloud of dust that rode the scorching wind. Sooty grime crusted the hunter's nostrils and mouth, clogging his airways. A harsh cough wracked his lungs.

Jake caught another vamp in the throat then rammed the molten steel at an upward angle toward the brain. Dead flesh sizzled, and its face ballooned. Escaping gases rose to the surface of the skin and formed swollen bubbles that expanded and burst, releasing rivulets of necrotic sludge. The skull exploded. Coagulated blood and bits of carrion rained down on him.

"Never thought I'd be happy to see a bunch of flea-bitten werewolves." Skinner barked his laughter. His machete flew in a wide arc. The blade embedded deep in a vampire's forehead. He spared his leader a curious glance. "How did you know they were friendly?"

Jake flashed a toothy smile. "I didn't."

"The hell you didn't." Skinner edged closer, tightening their defensive stance. He bore cuts on his face and arms. Blood stained his shirt, but none of the injuries appeared to slow him.

The dagger tattoo on Skinner's dark brown bicep glowed white hot, signaling active magic that granted him augmented strength and speed. Every hunter had the same mark, the symbol of their brotherhood, a spiritual bond to the Hunter King.

While the werewolves created a new front line, the beleaguered unit seized the much-needed reprieve, reloading firearms and attending to their wounded. Finn's initial attack appeared to be turning the tide in their favor, driving the vampires back.

The advantage couldn't last forever.

"Where are these bastards coming from?" Skinner shouted.

"There's a magical portal in that mine head," Jake said. "I can feel it. We've got to blow it shut."

"That's a tall order." Skinner swung around, shouting, "Kincaid, what's the status on that repair?"

Crazy Cali Kinkaid crouched over a MANPATS, a man-portable anti-tank system. Greasy brown hair stuck out in every direction from the female hunter's helmet. "It's busted, sir!"

"What the fuck is that supposed to mean?" Skinner demanded.

Glancing up, Cali's eyes glittered. "It means this

piece of equipment is tits up, sir! I don't know if I can fix it."

A colorful spray of curses flew from Skinner.

Jake slapped his friend's arm. "There's another MANPATS in the back of my truck. We'll have to fetch it."

"You." Skinner grabbed Jose Ortiz's shoulder. He issued the orders, sending the young man off at a sprint.

"We need a backup plan." Jake tilted his head back, gazing uphill toward the mine entrance. Impassable rock formations arose on either side of the narrow ravine. Flanking the enemy was impossible. He'd have to swim against the undead current to reach the mine. "Where's the C4?"

"Over here." Skinner dashed to Bobby Edwards's dead body to retrieve a sack. The young man lay face down in a pool of muddy blood upon the rocky ground.

Sorrow twisted in Jake's gut. Bobby had been an orphan. When he was ten, vampires had killed his parents, and he'd escaped thanks to blind luck. It looked like fate had finally caught up with him. Now his adopted family would mourn him.

Skinner tossed Jake the backpack. "Are we going to set charges to blow that entrance?"

"*We* ain't. I am. Fortify the line and evacuate our wounded to safety." Jake performed a cursory inspection of the contents of the bag, confirming it contained detonators and explosives. He closed the fastening and threw the straps over his shoulders.

"You're gonna get yourself killed." Skinner's flinty stare drove home his disapproval, but he didn't argue.

"Better me than you," Jake retorted. "Once I have the charges set, I'll give the signal. Have the men fall back to the vehicles. I'll warn the wolves."

Skinner slapped him on the back. "Good luck. It's been good serving with you, sir."

"You too, Hal." Full-blown laughter tore from Jake.

Skinner must have said the exact same thing to him a hundred times. It was their private joke for the nearly forty years they'd fought side by side, made all that much richer for the irony. One day, inevitably, would be the last time the words were spoken. No retirement in sunny Florida, not for them.

Jake dropped his shoulders. He charged straight through the thick dust, slamming into a revenant and knocking it aside. He pressed onward, picking his way through the combat, evading confrontation rather than seeking it. Hands grabbed for him, but he knocked them aside. The business end of his blade harvested an arm at the elbow, another at the shoulder. He didn't slow to finish the job.

An ice-cold hand caught his sword arm. Elongated nails dug deep, gouging his skin and rending muscle. Blood flowed freely down his forearm. Pain burned. The unbreakable grip stopped him in his tracks.

A cultured male voice asked, "In a hurry, hunter?"

A snarl curled his lips. "As a matter of fact, I am."

Jake grabbed the vampire's wrist with his free hand and bore down with inhuman strength, crushing bones. A pained snarl burst from the revenant.

Over their locked arms, the malformed face of the vampire confronted him: solid black eyes set in a soggy mass of flesh, jaws spread wide, needle teeth formed a tight spiral that covered the inside of its mouth. The stench of death clung to the creature.

The revenant's head cocked. His tone conveyed surprise. "You smell human, but you stink of magic. Who are you?"

Jake's heart roared in his ears. Sweat drenched his entire body. The excruciating pain in his arm fed his anger. Conjuring his magic, he bolstered his physical prowess, pitted his strength against it. Slowly but surely, the tip of the dagger turned toward the *draug*.

"What are so many *draugar* doing in the desert?"

Jake demanded. "You're a century and a continent misplaced."

He called down even more potent magic so the dagger's molten halo blazed brighter.

As if hypnotized, the revenant stared at the weapon, mouth hanging open. His hand dropped from the hunter's arm. "We go where we are summoned."

"Who summoned you?"

"The necromancer summons us."

"What necromancer?" Jake asked.

A brutal impact from the rear knocked Jake off his feet. He lost his grip on the vampire and dropped his dagger. As soon as it hit the ground, the blade vanished and the tattoo reappeared on his forearm. He landed on his back, and the impact forced the wind from his lungs.

A snarling werewolf and four vampires tumbled toward him. The grizzled gray wolf was about the size of a Siberian husky. No doubt, a she-wolf. Male werewolves were usually twice as large as the females.

Jake scooted aside to avoid being crushed. Head reeling, he scrambled to regain his footing. Glancing around, he spotted the *draug* he'd been interrogating. The vampire was headed downhill, still close enough to catch. He stormed after the vamp. A gut-wrenching moan erupted from the she-wolf. He hesitated, bloodlust warring with his humanity. The diversion cost him precious seconds.

With a grimace, he twisted toward the wolf and her assailants. The she-wolf whimpered, struggling weakly beneath one of the enemy while the others circled, looking for an opening. The *draug* held her by the throat, its greedy mouth pressed to her jugular. The feeding created a revolting noise, like a plunger working a clogged drain.

"Ah, hell." With a savage shout, Jake abandoned his target and charged the skirmish.

The three revenants blocked his path. The closest

was an obese female. Her stone-colored skin formed thick folds; swollen breasts hung to her navel. She latched onto his arm and shoved her face toward his throat.

Jake caught the bony gray skull between his hands, immobilizing her. He gazed down into the gaping maw. Writhing maggots squirmed along the gum lines, feeding on rotted danglers.

His lips curled over his teeth in a sneer. His heart thudded. Magic pulsed at his core. His tanned flesh grew translucent. Runes appeared beneath his skin, each symbolic of the most powerful forces in the cosmos. He'd sacrificed much in their acquisition, endured enormous torment to make the arcane magic integral to his being.

From a word to a word I was led to a word,
From a deed to another deed.

Stout frame straining, sinew popping, Jake threw back his head and a primal shout tore from his throat. A transformation swept through him and turned his body from flesh and bone into a statue chiseled from glossy obsidian. His pitch-black flesh smoldered, wisps upon the desert air.

He crushed the vampire's skull between his hands. Her body exploded outward in a shower of ash and bone, a billowing cloud thick on the air. Before the haze cleared, Jake veered through it. He squinted to shield his eyes from the grit.

Another *draug* appeared before him. His body throbbed while he channeled more magic. Striding steadily toward the undead, he punctured the leathery hide with his fist and buried his forearm to the elbow in its chest cavity. Carrion squished. Rot flavored the air.

The vampire howled.

Severe pain lanced through Jake's gut. Hand still embedded in the vamp, he staggered on the verge of collapse. A jagged wooden spike protruded from his stomach, the entry point in his lower back. Bright blood coated the end and gushed from the wound.

Braced against the pain, Jake's fingers closed on the hunk of meat that was the revenant's heart. Grimacing, he yanked his arm from the corpse, ripping the organ free. Worms and maggots writhed within the muscle, slithering against his fingers. Closing his fist, he pulverized it like hamburger. The vampire perished, reduced to ashen remains.

Jake encountered resistance from the other end of the spear when he pivoted. He reached for the protruding weapon and gripped the front and back. Wrenching the shaft, he snapped it in half, and then yanked both ends from his body. A searing jolt of agony ripped through his innards, an injury to fell a normal man. Magic sustained him.

He confronted the final *draug*, a stout and shaggy creature. The undead stood with her mouth agape, staring pie-eyed, oblivious to the battle raging around them. She stumbled backward, and then whirled and sprinted downhill. Hefting one of the wooden halves, Jake hurled the weapon with all his might. The spear impaled her clean through the heart.

Dust on the wind.

Returning his attention to the she-wolf, Jake lumbered toward the intertwined pair. He landed atop the feeding male vampire. The hunter's knees dug into the vampire's spongy flesh, and an overpowering wave of decay hit his nostrils. His dagger wasn't an option. He couldn't risk injuring the she-wolf with the magical weapon.

He yanked his boot knife free. His hand wrapped around the vampire's chin where its slick lips connected with blood-soaked fur. Grimacing, he pulled back with all his strength and forced the enemy's head aside. The *draug* growled and bucked, attempting to dislodge him.

A pitiful whimper escaped the gray wolf. Her

greenish-gold eyes were full of misery and anger. Sympathy grabbed him. His stomach muscles contracted.

Well, fuck all. Talk about getting soft in your old age.

"Let's get this leech off of you." He positioned the tip of the knife at the hinge joint where the vamp's mandibles attached. Delivering a precise downward stroke, Jake thrust, and the blade severed muscles and bone. He wrenched the vampire's head. Bones snapped with a crisp crunch. The *draug's* lower jaw tore away from his face, exposing pulpy flesh and yellowed bone. Thick necrotic fluid oozed from the wound. The stench was worse than a septic tank. He gagged and breathed through his mouth. It didn't help. With surgical precision, he jabbed with his blade and skewered the spiny tongue.

Yowling, the vampire let go of the werewolf's throat and rolled, attempting escape. The sudden shift upset the hunter's balance. He pitched forward and dug his knees in, which prevented the pinned enemy's escape. His free hand caught a fistful of plush fur, softness against his skin.

The gray wolf rumbled.

As he fell, the she-wolf lashed out with her claw but missed the *draug's* head. Those wicked claws caught Jake's eyebrow and raked down, gouging his left eye socket. The orb burst and released a flood of hot fluids.

Agony exploded throughout his head. An awful shout tore from his throat, and he jerked away. Blind on that side, he threw all of his weight backward and grasped for his tattoo weapon. Blood and sweat oozed into his good eye so the world blurred about him. He dodged a shadow, swinging, but missed.

A body struck him, knocking him flat on his back. Decay flooded his nostrils. A wolf thundered her displeasure. He rolled and surged to his feet, brandishing the burning dagger before him. Another frontal attack hit his leg and shattered the kneecap. The wave of pain sucked him inexorably toward oblivion.

He fell.

Jake thrust with his dagger, taking a blind stab, and hit a solid target. The blade sank deep. The resulting moan contained a plaintive note. His heart sank and a terrible sense of wrongness filled him. Nothing undead produced such a sound. The odor of singed fur and flesh filled the air.

"Oh, no." Hissing the denial, he extended a groping hand and encountered wet, matted fur. His gut twisted with grim acknowledgement. Full of awful regret, he crouched on the ground, listening to the wolf's dying whimper, focused completely on her suffering. The battle raging faded from his awareness. Disbelief swamped his mind.

He never harmed innocents, never slaughtered allies.

Sickened, he yanked the dagger from her side. A terrible yowl wrenched from the she-wolf. In the grip of despair, he stroked her fur. His men's lives were still imperiled, and the loss of his sight could cost them the battle, especially if they couldn't get the MANPATS to work. Given time, he would heal. Just not soon enough. He shifted his grip on the dagger's hilt, accepting there was only one thing left to do.

Incanting the ancient runes beneath his breath, he summoned all of his remaining power. Sheer willpower and raw magic mingled. Reality bent and distorted. Within his mind, the second sight he kept sealed off behind a heavily warded doorway swung open.

His perception shifted to the spiritual plane. His altered vision showed him ghostly whorls: light and darkness, swirls of energy, splashes of color. Nothing physical, nothing solid.

His awareness in the mystical realm expanded further. An aurora. Streams of light. Great sweeping patterns. The she-wolf's life thread, terribly short, connected to so many others. The future that should have belonged to her and her children grew fainter with each passing beat of her failing heart.

He had slaughtered countless monsters. He killed without regret or compunction, and sometimes for the simple pleasure of the hunt. But not like this. *Never like this.* He lacked the ability to heal her, or he'd have done so in a heartbeat.

The vortex aura of a *draug* rushed toward him. A dim spark burned at the center of the vampire's dead pattern, the trapped soul that resided in his heart.

In an act of desperation, Jake grabbed for more energy, siphoning from his men. Not just the hundred present but the far-flung thousands scattered throughout the world. A volcano erupted within him. Magma rising. His skin burned. His body pulsated with unchecked power, threatening to annihilate his mortal vessel. The sting in his good eye cleared and allowed him to see.

Rage filled him.

He stood on his ruined leg and towered over the battlefield. His dagger transformed into a spear. He braced the end against the ground to angle the weapon. The head struck dead center, impaling the *draug* through the heart. The revenant's momentum drove it further onto the shaft. The body turned to ash, scattering on the hot wind.

Grasping the spear, Jake slid heavily to the ground. The weapon fell from his clutches, clattering before it vanished.

Skinner's voice buzzed in his ear. "The MANPATS is operational."

"Are the wolves clear?"

"From the looks of it, but you're too close."

"Fire it," Jake commanded.

"Yes, sir."

Gathering his strength, Jake crawled to the dying

she-wolf. With heroic effort, he gathered her warm body into his arms and settled her across his lap. Covered from head to toe in blood, he stained her plush fur everywhere he touched

"I'm sorry." Stroking her head, he leaned in, whispering into her rounded ear. "I didn't mean to hurt you."

The muscles at the base of her ear tugged, and she whimpered. Her tongue lapped his arm with a single swipe. A gentle voice touched his soul. *I forgive you.*

Shuddering, he placed his palm against her side in time to feel the last breath leave her body. Her heart stopped. He choked on denial. His heart wrenched in his breast. "No! I don't—"

Murder innocents. Not ever.

"Heads up. The MANPATS is in the air," Skinner's voice announced across the com just as a rocket passed overhead, trailing fire.

The missile entered the mine and the detonation released an earth-shattering boom. A plume of fire shot from the shaft and the explosion filled the sky. Jake ducked his head and leaned over the she-wolf to protect her with his body. Burning debris and chunks of rock pummeled the battlefield. A thick cloud of smoke and dust blanketed the area.

The remaining *draugur* rushed downhill and escaped into the desert.

Jake sat with the wolf's body across his lap and watched while her pack chased down and destroyed the fleeing undead. He thought it funny how Finn and the rest of the White Mountains Pack appeared unaware of their pack mate's death. Or maybe she wasn't important enough for them to care. Their indifference filled Jake with righteous indignation. Then, he spotted the body of a fallen wolf twenty yards away. Another corpse, and then another. They'd lost a lot more than one member.

The realization gutted his anger.

Ravens descended out of the sky, their coarse

craaing heralding the arrival of the unkindness. Lighting amidst the carnage, the shiny-eyed birds picked through the bodies.

The wolves and the birds worked their way across the steeply slanted battlefield. A raven strayed too close to one of Finn's people, and a claw arced through the air. The bird squawked once, and the body flew. The hot wind whisked away black feathers. Thereafter, the ravens kept their distance.

During the battle, Jake's crew had retreated to the base of the mesa. It would be a good ten minutes, minimum, before they reached him. Through his magic, he sensed the absence of fourteen of his own men. An aching wound filled his soul. He mourned for them. Holes in the unity all hunters shared. Fourteen dead. More suffering.

It could have been so much worse.

His sight remained altered, his portal to the mystical world open. In fading shadow, an averted future lay before him. His entire unit annihilated. They all would have died if not for the wolves.

Always, he wondered, *Why can some futures be altered but not the one that mattered most?*

His gaze dropped to the dead she-wolf on his lap. He held her close and cradled her body and soul against his chest. He considered the absolute insignificance of her demise. In the grand scheme of things, her life and death, her very existence, meant nothing.

They were all doomed in the end.

The futility of everything staggered him. He should close the second sight before apathy overwhelmed him. Yet, he gazed out upon the whole of the universe, unable to look away.

He desperately missed his wife, Sarah, the mother of his four sons. She had kept him balanced, held the apathy at bay, and served as his connection to humanity. Without her, he was lost in this mortal nightmare.

A white-hot halo approached him and broke his fugue.

Jake blinked and looked up. In his mind, the foresight portal slammed shut.

Beautiful young women wearing cloaks of cream, hunter green, and burgundy walked amongst the fallen. *Valkyries*. His men had died honorably, serving him and his cause. Valhalla awaited those worthy dead. Ultimately, all companions in life would be reunited in the great halls.

A shield maiden with golden-blonde hair bent over the body of a fallen werewolf, gathering his soul for transport to Valhalla. She straightened and approached the she-wolf he'd tried to save and accidentally slaughtered.

Sarah had always insisted that every life mattered. If someone cared enough to give a damn. His arms tightened around the wolf's body. His fault. His terrible mistake. The stubborn determination to do right by her set him on his course.

"No. You will not have her." Baring his teeth, he tilted his head back and peered out of his good eye, looking up at the blonde warrior woman.

The Valkyrie paused, gazing at him with curiosity. Her brow knit. "You can see me," she said. "How is that possible?"

"I can see you, Skeggöld."

"How do you know my name?" Even as she asked, she studied his face. His ruined eye. His fierce stare. Her mouth opened, dawning realization on her face. "I must bring the wolf's soul to Valhalla. It is my duty."

"Not this one," Jake rasped. "Not this time. Heal her."

He clung to consciousness with stubborn tenacity like a man denying Death to steal one last breath. Even so, dusk closed about him, shadows closing on his waking mind.

Confusion crossed her face, alongside fear.

"Why not you?" she blurted out, daring to challenge him. "You do it."

Jake allowed his mask to drop, revealing his true face. "I cannot. Not that I owe you explanations. Now do as I command, Valkyrie."

Skeggöld gasped and lowered her gaze. In a show of obedience and submission, she sank to her knees before him. Her trembling arms extended, and she touched her fingertips to the she-wolf's side. A brilliant flash emanated from her hand, so bright he shielded his face and looked away.

"I have done as you commanded." The Valkyrie straightened and vanished, perhaps fleeing before he issued some other command that would put her in conflict with her sworn duties.

Jake allowed the wolf to slide from his lap. He lifted her to the ground and set her gently upon her side. Then he scooted away, wincing when the effort jarred his injured knee. Blood roared in his ears. His consciousness spiraled downward.

With a startled huff, the she-wolf rolled to her feet. She pranced, clearly confused, and turned in a circle, chasing her own tail.

A bark of laughter rocked Jake. No longer holding tight to wakefulness, he let go. Darkness crashed over him in a great wave. He succumbed to oblivion.

CHAPTER THREE

Sessrúmnir, Freya's hall in Fólkvangr

Without a word of explanation, Freya's mysterious visitor disappeared down the corridor that led to her private bath. He strode upon graceful steps, as stealthy as a cat.

Intrigued, she sat up, and the silken cover slipped aside to reveal the unrivaled splendor of her beauty. She wore only the magical Brísingamen, an elegant filigree necklace of gold and gems, which rendered her irresistible to all who gazed upon it. She stood and glanced at her sleeping lover, admiring his powerful shoulders, strong arms, and dark head. Drained from hours of lovemaking, he remained blissfully oblivious to the world. A smile fluttered upon her lips, and she decided not to disturb him. She, Freya, a goddess of war as well as love, was more than capable of coming to her own defense.

She stepped past the curtains and found her visitor lounging against the sculpted fountain that fed the steaming bathing pools. He bent with one hand trailing across the surface of the water. As her footfalls echoed across the marble floors, he looked up. He carried no weapons and presented no immediate threat.

He smirked. "I see you've already thrown a thigh

over your new general. Have you taught him to heel yet, Freya?"

A gasp escaped her lips. The audacity! The thrill of outrage aroused her. She scowled, and her spine stiffened as she stood straighter. She considered rebuking him for his insolence, but something in his furtive attitude struck her as intimately familiar. She held her tongue, considering him.

That naughty gleam, that infuriating smugness. Could it be?

No.

His snicker removed all doubt.

Her mouth dropped. "Loki?"

Midgard

"Hey, I hate to wake you, Sleeping Beauty, but the Arizona governor is on the phone. He's pissed 'cause we didn't include the National Guard in our 'unsanctioned military exercise'."

Skinner's sarcastic voice impinged on Jake's slumber, but it was the pointed kick to his foot that jolted him awake. The Hunter King opened both eyes, blinking to confirm his vision was fully healed, and sat up. He glanced left and then right, registering the injured men to either side. They were inside the personnel transport that served as their mobile field hospital. The medical crew buzzed about like frantic bees, treating and tending their patients.

"Did you tell him to fuck off?" Grunting, Jake climbed to his feet and tested his knee. He found the joint to be sound. At least an hour had passed since the battle. Stretching his awareness, he performed a headcount and then sighed in relief upon discovering he hadn't lost anyone else.

"Of course I did." Skinner's mouth twisted in contempt, an expression he reserved for the animated dead and politicians. "He's deploying a unit. They'll be here in ten."

Fuck. Just what he needed—the government. Bursting with frustration, Jake strode to the back of the transport and dropped to the ground. He glanced around, assessing his surroundings. The sun had long since set, and the waxing moon was a pregnant disc over the mountains. His own men were present, tending to their duties, but none of the White Mountains Pack remained.

He scowled. "Did the MANPATS close the portal?"

"Sealed up tighter than a drum," Skinner said. "But we've still got no clue what opened it in the first place."

"Figuring that out is at the top of my to-do list." Jake rubbed a finger over his upper lip. "What happened to the wolves?"

Skinner flashed a grin. "They lit out of here like someone had set their tails on fire once they found out the government was on its way."

"Damn, I wanted to speak with Finn." Jake dragged a hand through his hair, thinking about that she-wolf and what she had seen. Worse, what she might say. How much had she grasped about what had happened?

Skinner stepped closer, thrusting a cell phone at him. "Oh, and Sawyer's holding on the other line. He's got Victoria Storm cornered again."

A sudden, lancing headache threatened to split Jake's head wide open. Striving for patience, he sucked air between his teeth, closed his eyes, and counted to three. He cursed vampires, werewolves, politicians, civilians, and his second son, in that order.

Opening them again, he accepted the phone. Family first, always.

"What's my hotheaded boy gone and gotten himself into now?" Jake asked Skinner, wanting as much information as he could obtain in advance. When dealing with Sawyer, he needed every advantage.

His friend scowled. "He's going after her alone."

"Well, ain't that just dandy," Jake muttered. Desiring privacy, he marched toward his SUV, parked further up the road.

"What should I tell the gov?" Skinner shouted after him.

"Don't tell him anything. Let him cool his heels."

Once situated comfortably inside the cab, Jake turned on the radio to provide background noise. He hit the unmute button and put the device to his ear. "Sawyer?"

His boy's voice emerged amid a burst of static. "Dad."

Jake lost his temper. "Sawyer, what the hell are you up to? You promised me that you'd stay away from Victoria."

Sawyer snapped out an angry retort. "I didn't promise. I just said I'd think about it. Well, I thought about it."

"And decided to do the exact, dumbass opposite," Jake snarled.

"Yeah, pretty much."

"Son, if you're committed to killing that bitch, then take a crew of experienced hunters." Over the phone, Jake Barrett's voice was as hard as steel. "I'm not comfortable with you going after her alone."

You'll get your stupid ass killed, or worse.

The last part hung in the air unsaid, but Sawyer's mind filled in the blanks. He stifled a sigh. His father never failed to make him feel inadequate, always the disappointment. His birth order as second son may have contributed to his rebellious tendencies, but none of his brothers ever clashed with his father to the same extent.

"Dad, I'm not going after Victoria again," Sawyer

said, striving to sound reasonable, biting his tongue against any inflammatory statements that he'd regret as soon as he spoke them.

"*Victoria?*"

Sawyer huffed. "*Miss Storm* sounds a little pretentious, considering we've been on a kill-or-be-killed basis for the last six months."

"Don't get smart with me, Sawyer."

"Sorry, sir." He apologized out of ingrained respect for his father's authority, but it pinched his pride. Always, Sawyer's independent spirit warred with his desire to attain his dad's approval. More often than not, communication went poorly between them. They argued. They fought. They banged heads. Their relationship was never easy or peaceful.

Sawyer shifted his grip on the cell phone and wedged it between his chin and collarbone. A stabbing pain throbbed between his shoulder blades, radiating throughout his entire back from too many nights spent living on the road. When he slept, it was in his car or on cheap beds in sleazy motels. He used his free hand to massage the ache at the base of his neck.

Appearance-wise, all of the Barrett men shared the same tall, broad-shouldered build. His father and three brothers had dark brown hair and chocolate eyes, but Sawyer took after his mother. He wore his dirty-blond hair to his shoulders in pointed defiance of his father's insistence upon a military cut. His clothing hung looser than usual, and he suspected he'd lost weight over the last few months.

At just after eight in the evening, most of the businesses in the commercial complex were closed. Only the grocery retailer that served as the anchor store remained open and well lit. The smaller stores had their lights turned off, so darkness covered the recessed sidewalks connecting the L-shaped plaza.

He held his shotgun with the shortened stock cradled in the crook of his arm, the sawed-off barrel resting against his chest. His black leather trench coat allowed him to conceal the modified weapon in public. For the moment, the cold concrete pillar at his back provided cover. However, his telephone conversation introduced an element of risk in giving away his location. Some creatures, beasts of myth and magic, possessed superior hearing.

Across the parking lot, the glass door of the dance studio opened and women spilled out—fashionably thin mothers toting designer purses with daughters clad in pink leotards and fluffy tutus. He tracked the stream of humanity but failed to find the white-blonde head he sought.

Despite the cool April evening, a warm flush touched his skin. The long shadow of guilt hung over him. Lately, he didn't have much to be proud of, and lurking outside dance studios filled with little girls didn't make him feel any better about himself.

Jake cleared his throat. "Do you have feelings for her?"

"What? No!" Sawyer's voice hit a startled spike. "Damn it, Dad, it's not like that."

"What exactly is it then?" Jake asked. "I understand you believe you saw your brother's spirit—"

"Not believe. *Know*. I saw Daniel. He spoke to me." Sawyer jerked away, turning his back on the parking lot as he ran an agitated hand through his long hair.

The memory of his brother's visit remained as fresh and as vivid as if it had happened yesterday. Danny had looked straight at him and said, *"There's been enough killing."*

Sawyer's throat closed. He swallowed convulsively in an attempt to clear it. His brother's plea had eviscerated his rage, leaving him mired in guilt and grief. Robbed of his drive for revenge, he was lost.

"I believe you, Sawyer. But I want you to stop and

think. The last time you confronted..." Jake hesitated.

"Victoria."

Jake snorted. "Victoria. She almost killed you. You're alone—"

His father's lecturing hit a sore spot, and Sawyer's temper snapped. "I've got a plan."

"Care to share it so we're on the same page?"

Sawyer hesitated, deliberating on his choice of words. The faint sound of a static-filled AM sports talk show crackled in the background. Even though the old man's SUV had satellite radio, he insisted upon an old-school approach to entertainment.

"I want the two of you to agree to a face to face meeting." His neck ached, so he transferred the phone to his hand again.

"Is Victoria pushing for a meeting?" Jake asked.

"No, I expect I'll have to convince her. At this point, she probably doesn't want anything to do with us."

"I don't know what you hope to accomplish with this, Sawyer. The Storm Pack has left Arizona, and I'm not interested in pursuing this further. Not after what happened in Albuquerque. But you keep pushing..." Jake's tone remained reasonable. Too reasonable.

Sawyer's grip on the phone tightened, and his teeth ground together. He hated being humored. "I can't let this go."

"Why not?"

Restless, Sawyer shifted and quelled the desire to pace. He opened his mouth to explain, but couldn't find the right words. The feeling of being confined aggravated his frustration. "I have an obligation to fix this thing."

A harsh bark of laughter escaped Jake. "Son, this *thing* isn't a broken toy."

He clung to his resolve with grim determination. "Don't talk to me like I'm a kid, Dad. I know what I'm doing."

He didn't. He had no clue, but sheer cussedness had

to count for something.

"You're obsessed, and it's not healthy. Listen to me, Sawyer. I'd like to set things right with Victoria's pack too, but not at the risk of your life. Let this thing go and come home."

Sawyer gritted out his answer: "I can't come home. I won't."

Jake's voice rose to a shout. "God damn it, Sawyer. Pull your head out of your ass! Think about other people for a change!"

Shock rocked Sawyer back on his heels. "What the hell is that supposed to mean?"

"You always do whatever the hell you want without considering the consequences to anyone else. You're determined to chase this she-wolf until she kills you. I've already lost one son. I don't want to lose another."

Sawyer snapped out an instant denial. "I'm not—"

Jake ignored him. "Have you considered what your death would do to your family? To your brothers? They've already lost Daniel and your mother."

He was so angry his hands shook. "Leave Gage and JD out of this."

"Normally, I would." Jake's volume dropped, and he sounded tired. "Why can't you see reason, Sawyer?"

"Dad, I—" Sawyer bit off a sharp retort. Struggling to get a handle on his short temper, he rested his open hand against the cool concrete pillar, leaning with his head bowed. The burden of responsibility weighed heavily on his shoulders, and he regretted always being at odds with his father. He didn't want to hurt his younger brothers or cause his old man grief.

The scent of rotted flesh filled his nostrils.

Blurred motion caught his peripheral vision. Sawyer jerked his head around. Light glanced off a wide blade gripped in a skeletal hand. His mind registered his attacker's face as an eerie white skull juxtaposed upon brown skin.

Before he finished turning, excruciating pain shot through his hand that was pressed to the column. An agonized shout tore from his chest. His eyes fell on the steel blade as it impaled his flesh and sliced through his pinky and ring fingers. The middle digit dangled by a filament. Blood spurted from the injury.

"Look at that. There are pieces of hunter all over the place." The speaker had a stilted, formal accent—not Mexican but Spanish.

Disbelief and anger surged through Sawyer. He doubled over in agony, and his phone smashed against the concrete. Gasping, he twisted fully toward his assailant. The Spaniard towered ten feet tall with unnaturally long limbs stretched too thin. The tattoos of chalk white bones covered his exposed skin, including his bald scalp which made him look like a walking skeleton.

Jovial laughter rolled from two other men beyond Sawyer's field of vision.

"I am disappointed," the Spaniard said. "Barretts are renowned as fearsome opponents. Yet, you are as easily defeated as your brother. He, too, died by my hand."

Sawyer's mind reeled. *This* skeletal vampire was the bastard who'd murdered Daniel? His blood roared with the song of the hunt, drowned their mocking voices. Rage overruled reason. Lightning flashed. Thunder rumbled. The pain of his injuries dulled in comparison to the roaring fury building within him.

"This one is unworthy of my attention." The Spaniard addressed his minions. "Carve him into pieces. We shall send him to his father in a box."

Sawyer flung his body sideways and seized the stock of the sawed-off shotgun. The familiar weapon became an extension of his arm. "Wrong hand, asshole. I'm a southpaw." He pulled the trigger, firing point blank into the Spaniard's face. The gun boomed, unloading both barrels.

The twin slugs blew out the back of the Spaniard's

skull. Bone shards and fleshy chunks splattered every-where. Not a kill shot, but enough to fuck him up for a while. His oral cavity yawned wide open. A thick barbed tongue dangled through the hole in his face. He swayed and then crashed to the pavement, landing with a heavy thud.

Feminine screams echoed the shot, girls and women from the parking lot creating a terrified chorus.

Off-kilter, Sawyer careened into the front window of a yarn store, and his shoulder collided with plate glass. The bone-jarring impact jolted his entire body. The shotgun only held two rounds, so he released the stock and drew his .45 from his shoulder holster. He tucked his injured hand to his abdomen, staunching the bleed-ing against his shirt.

A couple paces distant, the shadowy figures of two men stood side by side. More vampires. Sawyer didn't recognize the breed. They choked on laughter and stumbled into silence. A flickering light cast their ghoul-ish features into surreal relief. The Spaniard's blood painted their brown skin. Thick rivulets ran down their faces.

One of them opened his mouth, revealing glistening fangs. His thick tongue snaked forth to lave across his lower jaw, greedily gathering the fluid.

Berserker frenzy cast a crimson patina upon Saw-yer's vision. He felt no fear, no pain. Only blood lust. The song of the hunt burned in his veins, pulsing louder with each beat of his heart. He fired, hitting the undead to the right in the shoulder, but his second shot went wide.

With enraged growls, the revenants launched to-ward him. The injured vamp charged faster than his companion, grabbing a slight lead. Regular ammunition did little to slow undead. Fire, holy water, and bladed weapons were effective. Killing one required the de-struction of its head or heart.

Sawyer got off another shot, striking him in the chest just before the vampire tackled him. His skull and shoulders collided with the plate glass window, forcing the breath from his lungs. He threw his injured arm out and caught his attacker across the throat. The revenant's jaws gaped wide. A forked tongue and dozens of needle-like fangs filled his vision. The fetid stink of decay fogged the air.

He dropped the .45 and groped for his belt knife, a heavy bayonet with a guard. His hand closed on the hilt, but he wasn't able to draw it. The weapon was trapped between their bodies.

Snarling, the second vampire jumped on the first's back. Under the combined weight of two assailants, Sawyer's legs collapsed. He crashed to the pavement, landing on his back with the revenants on top. He lost his grip on the bayonet.

The injured vamp swung on his companion. "Back off!"

"I want a piece of him."

"He's mine."

The squabbling vampires shoved at one another, rocking the dog pile. The weight on Sawyer's torso shifted, freeing his good hand. He kept his injured arm raised to shield his throat. Gritting his teeth in anger, his fingers locked around the hilt of his bayonet, and he yanked it from the sheath.

"Boys, boys, he's a big guy." Lilting female mockery cut through the growls-and-snarls argument. "Can't you share?"

Rumbling in their throats, the revenants swung toward the woman who remained beyond Sawyer's field of vision. A glimmer of recognition penetrated the haze of his rage — *Victoria*.

The wounded vampire cranked his head toward her. With the blade angled toward the brain cavity, Sawyer rammed his knife into the vamp's exposed throat. It sank to the hilt.

The vampire gurgled. His mouth fell open, and thick sludge gushed forth. He groped for his throat while his tongue lashed wildly, seeking a target. Needle spines hooked on the sleeve of Sawyer's coat but failed to penetrate the leather.

Gathering his strength, Sawyer shoved his attacker off and over. The revenant landed on his back. Sawyer straddled his chest, yanked the knife free, and sawed at the stocky neck, going for the spinal column. From behind him, a wolf's growl preceded an undead's hiss. The exchange of heavy blows and shifting feet made a commotion that ended abruptly with a heavy thunk.

Steel connected with bone. Lips peeled back in a fierce grimace, Sawyer bore down, throwing his weight behind the brutal assault. With a jarring crunch, vertebrae shattered, and the blade slid clean through to the other side of the vampire's neck.

The decapitated revenant's insides liquefied within the rotted hide. Coagulated blood gushed from the body's natural cavities, the trickle too slow to relieve the pressure as decay accelerated. The corpse swelled and then burst, releasing festered fluids across the pavement. The stench billowed outward in a fetid cloud.

Only newly turned vampires died so messily.

Nausea turned Sawyer's gut, and his eyes watered. His rage lessened, and clarity returned. A distant cacophony of sounds assailed his hearing—the wails of frightened women, car engines being gunned, and tires squealing.

Bright agony slammed him. A glance at the bloody stumps and his dangling middle finger churned his stomach. *Fuck. Oh fuck, it hurts.* He'd never be able to use his right hand again. Being left-handed offered cold comfort.

His throat worked, swallowing convulsively to be rid of the bile filling it. The stench from beneath him made it worse. Covering his nose and mouth with his arm helped a little. Gripping the bayonet, he retreated until his back collided with a wall.

Victoria Storm occupied the same spot where the two vampires once stood. The petite blonde wielded a magical dagger, a blade like moonlight shimmering on water. At less than five feet, she appeared less imposing than any one of the undead, except her eyes cast a golden glow and her lips twisted into a feral grimace, revealing wicked canines. The bare skin of her arms rippled, precursor to the transformation that turned her into a more ferocious predator.

"Unbelievable. Vampires in my territory. The whole neighborhood is going to hell." Victoria glared murder at him. "This is your fault, isn't it, Sawyer?"

"Victoria, I didn't come here to fight you." Tightening his grip on the hilt, Sawyer braced for her charge. He preferred to face another revenant over an angry werewolf. The one silver weapon he carried was a four-inch dagger strapped to his wrist. The stiletto lacked a guard, but its precise balance made it perfect for throwing.

She snorted. "You don't look like you're in shape to fight anyone."

His gaze dropped to his hand. Weakening spurts of blood pumped from the finger stumps. His head spun.

"One left," he gasped.

"Sawyer?" Lovely features drawn to a taut mask, she advanced a menacing step toward him. Her blue eyes glittered as she contemplated killing him.

A shadow twice her height arose directly behind her. Long, sinuous arms spread wide to either side. The vampire's lower jaw and cheek bone were gone thanks to the point blank shotgun blast. His head hung on a stalk of intact vertebrae, bloody gristle attached to exposed bone.

The Spaniard.

A shout tore from Sawyer's throat. "Duck!"

Her brow knit. "What?"

A whip crack split the air. A thick black appendage covered in barbed spines wrapped around Victoria's throat. The oily black muscle undulated, and its coils tightened so the spikes punctured her skin.

A sharp snarl arose from the she-wolf. She grabbed for the tentacle. The mystic dagger fell from her hand. It struck the ground and vanished. Employing his tongue, the Spaniard reeled Victoria toward him. Those vicious barbs pulsated, sucking blood from the werewolf.

Sawyer lurched and stumbled. Pain made his head spin. His awareness of his body zoomed out to a distant point.

Victoria reached behind her and grabbed the Spaniard's arms. Bending, she hauled him over her head and threw him to the ground, but the tongue lassoing her throat dragged her down. Clutching at the coils, her mouth opened in a strangled moan as she sank to her knees.

Face twisted in a grimace, Sawyer swung the bayonet in a stroke aimed at the vampire's neck stalk. He missed and hit the shoulder, cleaving a deep gouge into the collar bone and shoulder.

The vampire bellowed. His tongue slackened, and Victoria wedged her fingers between the muscle and her throat. Struggling to be free, she forced the garrote to loosen further. With a huge gasp, she sucked air into her starved lungs.

The Spaniard's flailing arm pummeled the side of Sawyer's head. Pain exploded behind his eyes, and his spine compacted. Crying out, he crashed to his knees, still clutching the knife with tenacious determination.

Distantly, the song of the hunt resounded through his mind, echoing the blood surging in his veins. His resolve to fight was strengthened through pure tenacity and raw willpower. Wedging one knee under his chest, he gritted his teeth and pushed upright.

Victoria freed her arm and thrust an open hand into the Spaniard's face. Her voice emerged as a raspy croak.

"In Freya's name, be gone!" Nova brilliance radiated from her hand, bathing the vampire's face in light. The meaty strands dangling from the revenant's shredded cheek burst into flames. Exposed muscles scorched to burnt crust and then dissolved to ash.

Wielding the bayonet, Sawyer staggered after the vampire, fully intending to take another swing. He raised the weapon high overhead.

The Spaniard jerked his head aside. Swifter than human eyes could follow, the vampire sprang to his feet and fled. His long form blurred, stretched like pulled taffy toward the parking lot.

The Spaniard vanished from plain sight.

Blinking, Sawyer stumbled. "Did he just turn invisible?"

"That's what it looked like." Victoria's voice contained enormous tension.

Her proximity startled Sawyer. Drawing up, he looked toward the werewolf. "That was the son of a bitch who murdered Daniel."

Through narrowed eyes, she shot him a scornful glare. "I was there. I know who he was."

"We have to go after him." He tried to take a step, but his feet refused to cooperate. The world swayed.

"You're in no condition to go anywhere." Victoria reached with hands still transformed into deadly claws.

Distrust screamed through him, and his survival instincts kicked in. Sawyer dropped the bayonet and grabbed the hilt of his silver weapon. Yanking it from its wrist sheath, he brandished the stiletto, his last resort.

Victoria pulled up short. Her mouth fell open, and she took a step back. "What the hell? I was trying to help!"

"Your eyes." The colored parts of her eyes eclipsed the whites, and the pupils contracted to black points.

"What about my eyes?"

"You have on your angry eyes." His heart throbbed in his ears, and his consciousness narrowed to a distant point. Gasping for breath, Sawyer used the last of his strength to remain upright. "You're still pissed."

His father's voice echoed through his memory: "*Son, there's not many things in this world more deadly than an angry werewolf.*"

"I've been pissed since the day I met you, Sawyer. I haven't killed you... yet."

It was the 'yet' that worried him. If the she-wolf wanted to take him out, he made for easy prey in his current condition. "The last time I trespassed on your territory, your mate promised to kill me if I came back."

Victoria huffed, closing her eyes, and when she opened them again, they appeared human. Her hands flexed. Bones ground and crunched as the fur and claws disappeared. "But here you are."

"Here I am." He attempted sarcasm, but a wet cough ruined the effect. The last of his strength kept him upright.

Victoria retreated and bent, retrieving something from the pavement. When she straightened, she held his phone in one hand, and a pinky and ring finger in the other.

The sight of his severed digits resting upon her open palm sent a fresh wave of nausea through Sawyer. He shoved the silver knife into its sheath and clutched his injured hand to his chest. The world was a million miles away. His father's voice impinged on his awareness.

"Your father sounds upset." Victoria stabbed at the touch screen of his phone, switching on the loudspeaker.

Jake Barrett's frantic voice roared from the device. "Sawyer, what the hell's happening?"

"Dad," Sawyer croaked. "Calm down. I'm fine."

"What the fuck has that bitch done to you? I'm going to kill her if she's hurt you."

"Standing right here." Victoria scowled. "You know, I really wish you Barretts would stop calling me *bitch*. Can't you think of an original insult?"

Sawyer forced a chuckle. "It's really more of an accurate descriptor."

Jake fell silent, and Sawyer easily envisioned the stoic mask that settled over his old man's face, the cold calculation in his eyes.

"Sawyer, report," Jake ordered.

"Vampires jumped me, but I'm fine." Sawyer's voice sounded weak to his own ears. Exhaustion sapped his strength, threatening to drag him under, and he leaned his shoulder against the building to remain upright.

"You don't sound fine," Jake said harshly.

"I'm a little cut up."

Victoria snorted. "That's one way of putting it."

Urgency gripped him. Shaking so hard the phone repeatedly struck his cheek, he wheezed the words. "It was the vampire who murdered Daniel."

Jake grated a curse. "Are you sure?"

Without warning, Victoria seized Sawyer's hand, securing his grip on the cell phone. "Barrett, your son has lost two fingers on his right hand, and the middle one is dangling... He's going into shock."

"*Sonofabitch.*" Jake's voice contained a hollow note of horror.

Sawyer cringed, humiliated at the stark summarization of his failure as a warrior. He grabbed for his phone, determined to end the conversation, and Victoria surrendered it to him. "There were shots fired and witnesses. Someone must have called 911. I need to get out of here before the police arrive."

Victoria jerked her head in automatic denial. "Let me heal you."

"No, there's no time." Sawyer didn't trust her. Not entirely. He couldn't even say why, but his suspicion ran bone-deep.

"Damn it, Sawyer. Stop being a stubborn ass. You need medical attention." Jake hesitated, and then asked, "Victoria, can you heal him?"

The blonde she-wolf pursed her lips. "Maybe."

"This isn't up for debate," Sawyer said. "I'm—"

Victoria cut him off. "Jake, order your son to cooperate and allow me to heal him. If he waits too long, there are no guarantees the fingers can be reattached."

Sawyer opened his mouth to argue, but his father beat him to the punch.

"Can you make guarantees, Victoria?" Jake asked.

Sawyer would have sworn he could hear his father's mental wheels turning, suspicion vying with practicality. His old man possessed an unparalleled ability to parse even the most charged matters down to cold calculations.

Victoria bent, taking a closer look at his injured hand. She swiped her lower lip with the tip of her tongue. *Her tell.* She wasn't completely confident his fingers could be saved even with her magic. Oddly, Sawyer found the fact she didn't offer immediate assurances actually reinforced her credibility.

She cleared her throat. "I can definitely heal the middle finger. I'd say I have better than fifty percent odds of reattaching his fingers without any adverse side effects. No guarantees."

"The cops," Sawyer protested

"Better arrested than maimed for the rest of your life," Jake grated. "Sawyer, do as Victoria says."

His back stiffened, but he swallowed the instinctive protest. "Yes, sir."

"Good." Jake's exhalation conveyed marked relief. "Call me afterward to let me know you're okay."

"Will do." Sawyer ended the call without saying goodbye. He shoved the phone into his pocket and stared at Victoria, stuck in a quagmire of suspicion. The impending threat of being arrested compounded his paranoia. Victoria had plenty of reasons to hurt him. He'd tried to kill her several times and invaded her territory. Sneak attacks and subterfuge weren't her style though.

A cold trickle of sweat ran down his back, and a shudder shook his body. He hadn't been so scared or alone since he was a kid.

"Sawyer," Victoria said sharply.

He looked up and found himself snared in her blue eyes. His breath hitched, and his heart thudded hard in his chest. She captured his gaze, compelling and commanding, and he was unable to look away. She extended her hand, palm open.

"Please let me heal you." Her voice embodied a powerful skill possessed by truly dominant wolves, and the hypnotic melody created a marked resonance deep in his chest. Her will pushed against his mind, attempting to subdue him as if he were one of her subordinates. She promised a haven of security and comfort.

"I—" Words failed him. For a second, he wanted nothing more than to succumb, to surrender to her authority and fall into safety. His stubborn streak rebelled, fighting her influence. His resistance throbbed, spreading outward and fracturing her hypnotic spell.

A snarl trembled in his throat as if it were the most natural response. He asserted his will, turned her aside, and drove her out. "No. Knock it off."

"You're just like your brother." Victoria flashed a sheepish smile but spoke with a morose moodiness that indicated she didn't necessarily think the similarity to be a good thing. However, her attempt to sway him ceased.

"Did you try that mind trick on Daniel?" he asked, driven to satisfy his curiosity about her relationship with his brother despite his weakness. He'd spent months thinking Victoria had murdered his brother, and just as long hunting her. Their killing dance had ended in a burning warehouse with a visit from his brother's spirit, but a whole lot of people—hunters and wolves—had died along the way.

"No. It's an Alpha's trick. Not to say Daniel and I didn't have our fair share of contests of will." A sad smile flickered across her lips, but she didn't elaborate. She glanced away as if to conceal her grief. Her hand remained extended in offering, the other cupped protectively against her stomach—a chilling reminder that she held his severed fingers.

A chuckle resonated through Sawyer's chest, but the vibration reduced him to shaking. Sweat poured from every pore in his body, leaving him drenched and freezing. In vivid contrast to his weakness, he noticed how the injuries to her throat had already healed; leaving only flaking bits of dried blood on her skin. Lucky for her, werewolves were immune to the necrotic properties of a vampire's bite.

Victoria bit her lower lip. "Sawyer, please let me help you. I understand that you were trying to avenge your brother's death, and I swear on Daniel's soul, I don't harbor any malice."

He didn't know why, but her choice of words convinced him when nothing else would have. Before he changed his mind, he thrust his injured arm toward her, trying to ignore how it trembled.

CHAPTER FOUR

Sessrúmnir, Freya's hall in Fólkvangr

"Loki?"

"The one, the only. Back by popular demand." He presented a shallow bow, rolling his hand in a flourishing mockery of deference.

"But you were bound—" The goddess swept her arms across her body and summoned a midnight gown to cover her nudity.

Loki snickered. "False modesty hardly becomes the whore of Asgard."

Freya seethed, fire in her heart. "You are a mange-covered cur who has been bred as a mare and fornicated with filth."

His brow waggled. His smirk spread. "It's true. I've fornicated with you."

She sputtered and refused to acknowledge his jibe, however true. "How is it you are here? You are supposed to be imprisoned."

He tilted his head, eyebrows lifting. His cocky demeanor cracked, and she caught a glimpse of the smoldering fury burning in his soul. "Bound at the bottom of the world tree while the serpent's fangs dripped venom onto my face?"

She exhaled sharply, shocked at his vehemence.

"Yes."

He scoffed. "They lied."

Midgard

"Why are you helping me?" Sawyer asked in a raspy voice.

"Isn't that a question for a burning building?" Victoria snapped off the sarcastic reply because she didn't really know why she was going out of her way to assist her sworn enemy. As a rule, her people used their magic to benefit their own kind. Not outsiders. However, he wouldn't be the first hunter she'd healed, and she doubted he'd be the last.

"You didn't explain why you helped me then, either." Tremors shook his entire body, and sweat beaded his forehead and upper lip. He stank of pain and fear.

His suffering engendered a deep tug of sympathy in her heart. She'd seen Sawyer mad with grief and anger, curious and bewildered following a visit from his brother's spirit, annoyed and impatient for answers. But never vulnerable.

"It's going to be okay, Sawyer," she said, adopting the soothing bedside manner she'd acquired from her training as a nurse and a healer. Catching his proffered limb in a firm grip, she pushed up the sleeve of his coat and revealed a sheath strapped to his forearm. The toxic aura of the silver knife overpowered her perception of his spirit.

She unfastened the first strap holding the sheath in place, and his arm jerked in reaction. "I'm taking this off so I can heal you."

He grunted, but offered no further resistance.

Once she had the straps undone, she allowed the weapon to fall to the ground and stroked her palm across his furry forearm. Bending her head, she took a closer look at the injuries. His pinky and ring fingers on his right hand had been amputated with a single clean slice. His middle digit dangled by a few strands of sinew.

Her stomach kicked into her throat, and she gagged. Swallowing, she turned her head and breathed deeply. Normally, she wasn't squeamish. At six weeks, she wasn't showing yet, but nausea had been her ever-present companion since she'd become pregnant.

"Don't hurl," Sawyer gritted out from between clenched teeth.

"I won't. My stomach is a little upset."

"What's wrong with you anyway? Werewolves don't get sick."

She ignored him. As Victoria summoned her healing magic, light radiated from her hands, and their spirits connected, allowing her to perceive the damage to his body. She still held the severed fingers in her cupped palm, doing her best to shield him from the sight. She positioned the middle finger so the bone would set properly, and then directed the spell to mend the break at a vastly accelerated rate.

The hunter exhaled and relaxed as the pain eased. "You didn't answer my question," he said. "Is something wrong?"

"Nothing's wrong." *Damn the man.* Persistence was his defining characteristic, and also his most annoying. She didn't owe Sawyer any explanations, but relief washed through her when a police siren wailed in the distance, conveniently diverting the hunter's attention from her nausea.

"The cops." His arm jerked, forcing her to tighten her grip.

"Don't panic. I need you to remain still." Proper healing required proficiency, patience, and power. If she rushed, she risked leaving him with nerve damage.

Victoria pulled his hand toward her chest, curling

her hands around his so the severed fingers were held in proximity to the stumps. She bent her head to pray. As Freya's Valkyrie and priestess, she shared an intimate spiritual connection with the Norse goddess of love and war. "My Lady of the Vanir, please, I need your help."

"You're praying," Sawyer muttered. "That can't be good."

Victoria's eyes popped open, and she reprimanded him in a sharp tone. "Show respect."

Sawyer's mouth hung open for a second and then snapped shut. Victoria nodded and scowled, hoping he had the good sense to keep quiet.

A brilliant flame ignited within her second sight. Freya's golden voice filled her mind. *Victoria, what do you ask of me?*

"Help me heal this man."

A hesitation ensued, leaving Victoria sweating. At last, Freya replied: *This man attempted to kill you. He set the fire in the warehouse and led the ambush that killed Rand.*

Victoria winced. "Yes, he is wretched. Goddess, I know he isn't worthy, but as you have instructed, I must show compassion to my enemies."

A delicate snort preceded Freya's reply. *Those weren't my exact words.*

Siren blaring, lights flashing, a police vehicle turned into the parking lot. Panic lanced through Victoria. "Goddess, please. I beg of you—"

You are my priestess, Victoria. Against my better judgment, I will heal the hunter. I hope it is not a mistake.

Divinity flowed from Freya into Victoria, manifesting as white-hot light like the sun, radiating from her palms, her eyes, and her mouth. The power touched Sawyer, jolting the hunter. Victoria's firm grip kept him from toppling.

The brilliant flare lasted several seconds and then faded, leaving Victoria momentarily blinded, blinking while her vision returned to normal. Intent, she listened, absorbing Sawyer's harsh breathing and racing heart-beat, the sudden silence of the siren, and then a cacophony of many voices all talking at once.

Her eyes focused enough to make out Sawyer's bulky form across from her. She dragged his hand close to her face for inspection. All five fingers appeared to be intact.

"What happened?" he asked, sounding stunned.

"My goddess consented to heal you." Victoria traced a fingertip over where the injury had been, searching for a scar, but she couldn't find as much as a scratch.

Sawyer inhaled sharply. "Tell me—"

"Yes?"

"Will I ever play the piano again, Doc?" He maintained a deadpan expression, but the mischievous glint in his eyes gave him away.

"If I had any respect for you, it's gone." Groaning, Victoria quelled the impulse to smack him upside the head. She let go of his hand. "I hope you don't mind the fingers being reversed too much. It's not pretty, but at least it's functional."

With an alarmed squawk, he bent over his hand, scrambling toward the pool of light cast by a lamp. A second later, he muttered a curse. "Very funny."

"I thought so." Chuckling, Victoria recovered Sawyer's bayonet and the sheathed silver knife from the pavement. She stepped beside him as he snatched up his .45 and holstered the handgun.

"A county sheriff's car just pulled into the parking lot."

At the news, her spirits took a hopeful upswing. She crossed her mental fingers that Sheriff Mike Trash was among the first responders. Glancing about, she performed a quick inspection of the area. A gory mess covered the pavement. Once morning came, the remains of the vampires would turn to ash, leaving no trace.

"Get these out of sight." She thrust the bayonet and

the sheathed silver dagger toward the hunter.

He accepted the knives, tucking them out of sight with quick, efficient movements. He cast a sideways glance in her direction, his eyes lit with sudden curiosity. "What happened to your dagger?"

"What do you mean?"

"No way you're hiding anything in *that* outfit."

Victoria glanced down at herself. She'd forgotten she wore a dance instructor's clothing—a skintight, rhinestone-studded black leotard with lacey sleeves and fingerless gloves. The shorts hit mid-thigh, showcasing her shapely bare thighs and calves. She had on black ballet slippers, and her long, blonde hair dangled down the middle of her back in a French braid.

"The dagger is magical, and I didn't have time to change *and* save your sorry ass."

"I didn't need saving. I had everything under control."

"That's rich." Victoria peered toward the police car in the lot. On the far side, two uniformed officers stood amid a swarm of frightened women and girls. She recognized all of them as either her students or their mothers.

She sighed. "Why didn't they get the hell out of here when the gunshots started?"

Sawyer grunted. "Sheep. People are sheep."

"No argument here. We're in luck. One of the officers is my brother-in-law."

Technically, the relationship was a bit more complicated, but she didn't have time to explain how Sheriff Mike Trash was the brother of her dead mate's murdered wife. Or was it easier to say he was her brat stepson's uncle? She and Arik had never married, so none of the legal terms applied, but in the world of wolves, kin was kin.

"Great." Sawyer's tone said the opposite. "The young guy or the bald guy?"

"The bald guy. His name is Mike Trash." She toed his shotgun toward him. "Wouldn't a Super Soaker filled with holy water have been more effective in a vampire fight?"

Grunting, Sawyer stooped to retrieve his weapon and shouldered the strap so the weapon disappeared within the folds of his coat. He chewed his lower lip, and his pensive stance was reminiscent of the hunted instead of the hunter. "I didn't know I was going to be fighting vamps, or I'd have brought different weapons. I assumed your territory would be clear."

She bristled at the implied insult. "My territory is clear. Or it was..."

Damn him. Anger percolated beneath her ironclad control. Had the hunter led the master vampire to her? Or had the monster already been stalking her when he happened across Sawyer? Either way, the safety of her entire pack was in jeopardy.

Sawyer scowled. He exuded supreme confidence, but she scented the sweet note of fear underlying aggression. "You're right. From what little he said, the Spaniard was after me. They got the jump on me because I got careless. It was stupid."

His recrimination was aimed at himself. Victoria relaxed and allowed her defensiveness to slide. She had no reason to believe he'd lured the undead into her domain on purpose. Forewarned of the threat, she could prepare and warn her pack to be on their guard.

She was surprised when she offered the hunter consolation. "Don't be too hard on yourself. He got the jump on me too—" Her lips compressed. Her failure had meant the death of her lover...

From beneath a furrowed brow, Sawyer looked at her. Reluctant realization tempered the warrior's brooding gaze until it was no longer vicious with accusation.

She pitied him, but his understanding gladdened her also. Clearing her throat, she asked, "How does your hand feel?"

He stilled, flexing his fingers, staring as if seeing the appendage for the first time ever. A genuine smile tugged at his lips, and his eyes shone with gratitude. "It feels good. Thank you."

Her breath hitched, and her unaccountable rush of pleasure rendered her embarrassed. The man made her feel caught in his crosshairs. She turned her head so he wouldn't see her bemusement, but her voice warmed. "You're welcome."

Awkward silence descended.

Victoria cleared her throat. "I want to talk to the sheriff alone. This will be easier to explain if I don't have to explain *you* too."

Sawyer chuckled. "I'm going to call my father and let him know I'm still alive."

"Good. The last thing I need are more hunters trespassing in my territory."

Sawyer shot her an odd look but said nothing. He retreated, fading into the shadows. When he wasn't fucking up, the hunter was a damned scary opponent, proficient with guns and knives, a skilled tracker who moved like a cat.

Victoria stepped into the open, standing beneath the circle of light cast by an overhead lamp. She waited a couple seconds before the officers spotted her. They talked for a moment, and then Mike Trash approached her alone. Relief suffused her when he kept his sidearm holstered.

"Victoria." The sheriff appeared to be in his late-forties to early fifties with a rectangular face, ears that stuck out a bit, and a receding hairline. His piercing, intelligent brown eyes were his best feature. He stood a handful of inches taller than Victoria and appeared fit. He was good-looking, not quite handsome, but cute. He was human and also a medium able to perceive spirits. His awareness of the supernatural and his law enforcement position made him a powerful and influential person.

"Hi, Mike." Victoria tipped her head in greeting and mustered a polite smile. She hadn't spoken to the sheriff in weeks, not since Arik Koenig's funeral. Victoria's mate of one day had died battling a Norse winter witch, leaving her pregnant but not alone. She still had her pack mates.

"I-ah, wasn't expecting to find you here." Mike rubbed his finger across his upper lip. His gaze strayed past her to where a pool of vampire blood congealed on the sidewalk. "The witnesses are reporting multiple gunshots and growling. And then a brilliant flash of light."

She followed his gaze. "Vampires—three of them. They've been dealt with."

His head swung toward her, eyes and mouth agape. "Vampires?"

"They're all dead," she repeated. "There's no cause for concern."

She hated lying, but she refused to tell him about the Spaniard. The master vampire would annihilate any human who got in his way. Mike and his officers wouldn't stand a chance.

The sheriff produced a sound of disagreement in his throat. "There haven't been vamps in Sierra Pines in decades. Arik—"

Victoria flinched at the sound of her mate's name spoken aloud. "I've slain the undead and fulfilled my duty as Alpha to protect this territory."

More lies. Her honor reduced to tatters.

Mike looked away, scratching an itch behind his ear. "I'm sorry. I didn't mean to..." He trailed off and then asked, "Are you all right?"

"I'm fine."

"What about the gunshots?"

"There's a hunter—" Her hands rose to stay his sudden alarm. "It's okay. He's only here to talk, and he helped me destroy the vampires."

Pursing his lips, the sheriff glanced toward the scene of the fight again. "What about the light?"

She exhaled. She'd hoped he'd let things slide once he found out the threat had been dealt with, but it appeared she had no such luck. "The hunter was hurt, so I healed him."

The sheriff stared at her. Dark swirls flickered through his aura, and his scent took on a sour tinge she associated with distrust. "Victoria, you saved my life. I don't want to seem ungrateful, but this is difficult."

Victoria closed her eyes, struggling with an unpleasant combination of weariness, nausea, and grief. "Look, Mike," she said, opening them again. "I'm tired, out of sorts over finding vampires in my territory, and I still need to deal with the hunter. If you could please cut me some slack and write this up without arresting or shooting me or him, I'd really appreciate it."

As Alpha, she would have been within her rights to make demands and order the sheriff to cooperate. Technically, Mike was her kinfolk through her deceased mate. However, their relationship was already uneasy at best. The last thing she wanted was to cause further hostility with a man she desperately needed as an ally.

Surprisingly, Mike nodded quickly. "Sure thing, I understand. Go ahead and take off. I'll see to it this gets cleaned up and provide a reasonable cover story for the papers."

"Thank you. I appreciate it." She smiled in gratitude, incredibly relieved. At the same time, she wondered if it could be that easy. Nothing, but nothing, ever went her way, so she had trouble trusting the break.

He cleared his throat. "Later, you and I really ought to get together and talk about stuff."

What stuff? Uneasy, she hesitated before she agreed to his request. "How about next week? Do you want me to come into the station?"

"I'll come by the house if that's all right. I'd like to meet the rest of your pack," he said.

The sheriff was out of his element, but Victoria gave him points for trying. She smiled. "That sounds good. We'll grill steaks. I'll call you to set something up."

The awkward exchange of pleasantries ended, cut short by the urgency of the situation. Victoria left Mike and his deputy to deal with the few remaining civilians. She avoided coming into contact with any of the girls or their mothers, hoping she hadn't been recognized or linked with the incident.

Leaving the shopping center, Victoria headed away from the crowd of people, sticking to the shadows. Close to the edge of the complex, she caught Sawyer's scent and tracked him to the park across the street. He stood in plain sight, leaning against a lamppost as though he were waiting for her.

Sawyer's eyebrows lifted as she approached. "That was fast."

"It pays to have connections." Victoria stopped three full paces from him, unsure of the polite social distance to maintain when speaking to one's former enemy, recently turned... Her mind stuck on the right word. *Ally* implied trust. *Friend* connoted familiarity. *Dead lover's vengeful brother*—accurate, but not catchy.

"I guess so." He stared at her, expectant, but she had no idea what he wanted from her.

"Did you talk to your father?" Victoria asked.

"Yeah, it's squared away."

Victoria's impatience aggravated her already short-temper. "What are you doing lurking outside a dance studio full of little girls, Sawyer?"

He flushed. "Put that way, it sounds downright perverted."

Victoria cocked her head, and pinned him with her gaze. "I'd hoped maybe we were past the point where you thought it was okay to stalk me."

He cleared his throat. "You were supposed to call me. It's been six weeks."

She looked down and sighed. "I know. I'm sorry. The last six weeks have been... hairy."

His lips curved in a smile. Laughter danced through his aura.

Victoria had no idea what he found amusing about the current situation. Either his brain was addled, or his sense of humor was seriously skewed. Maybe both. Either way, she wanted nothing more than to wrap up their conversation and send him on his way so she could go home and soak in a hot tub.

"Did you kill the witch?" Sawyer asked.

The unexpected question blindsided her, opening the floodgates to her dammed-up grief. Stunned, she blinked back tears and inhaled sharply. "Yeah, we killed the witch," she said, her voice hoarse. "My mate died in the fight."

Sawyer's mouth opened, and a slight growl rumbled in his throat. He took a quick step, fists clenched, and then halted. Brilliant hues painted his aura, and he stank of anger and regret. Thankfully, he held his tongue and kept whatever smart remark he'd been about to make to himself. He must regard her taking a mate mere months after his brother's death as a betrayal of Daniel. He wasn't wrong, but desperation had driven her decision. Arik had offered security and stability for the surviving members of her small pack. Theirs was a union rooted in practicality—a modern marriage of convenience.

Sawyer grimaced, and his scent altered as he lied. "I'm sorry to hear that."

"Thank you." She let the deception slide away unremarked. Social niceties required white lies. At least he had enough courtesy to acknowledge the proper forms. "Sawyer, can we just cut to the chase? Why are you here?"

His voice grew flinty. "I need to know what happened to my brother. You're the only witness."

Victoria rubbed her temple, seeking to alleviate the pressure building in her head, the beginning of a headache. For a moment, she considered telling him what the Norns had said about his brother's soul being tormented. But she had no proof and plenty of doubt, so sharing such an inflammatory possibility with Sawyer served no practical purpose.

"I explained how the Spaniard murdered Daniel. What more do you want from me — graphic details about how he died?" Victoria asked.

His gaze smoldered. His posture bristled with pent up aggression as if he were spoiling for a fight. "Daniel's death must be avenged."

She arched her brow and pinned him with a pointed stare. "A lot of people, mine and yours, have died because of your bloodthirsty quest for vengeance."

He glared. "Are you saying that you don't want to rip out the heart of the evil bastard who murdered Daniel with your bare hands?"

Anger shot through her, scorching hot, and she surged closer so they stood toe-to-toe. She flashed her teeth just to remind him her bite could shred a throat. "I want his death. I thirst for it with my entire being. But I have responsibilities, people who are counting on me to keep them safe."

His jaw jutted. "Daniel was counting on you to keep him safe."

Victoria punched him square on the chin. The blow sent him staggering backward, but he kept his footing. Fist poised to throw another blow, Victoria strode toward him. "Say that again. I dare you."

Sawyer rubbed his jaw with one hand, and the other rose in a staying gesture. "Damn, you hit like a linebacker."

Confused, she stopped and lowered her fist. "You

provoked me on purpose."

"I needed to be sure you want that vampire as much as I do."

Her teeth ground together. What was it with aggravating males who refused to listen? "That was stupid. You can't go around provoking wolves and expect to live long."

He shrugged. "If you'd intended to kill me, you'd have done it in Montana."

He made a valid point, but she didn't have to like it. Her lips compressed with displeasure. "I have a duty to my pack. I can't just take off on a vengeance quest."

"The way I see it, you don't have a choice."

"How so?" she spat out.

"The Spaniard got away, and he knows you and your pack are here. He'll be back with more minions..." His head adopted that stiff-necked tilt Victoria associated with Daniel at his most stubborn. "If you want real safety, then we have to end this war and repair the alliance."

"What are you proposing?"

"Meet with my father. Tell him everything you've told me."

"Hell no."

He blinked and paused, then his brow arched. "Why not? We can restore the treaty. We can avenge Daniel."

Victoria laughed, a broken sound. "There can be no alliance. My pack is all but gone. What's left are females—an old woman, a teenage girl, a mother wolf and her pups. Rand and Paul are dead. My mate..."

Prior to her arrival in Sierra Pines, Sawyer and two other hunters had ambushed her pack in a Montana warehouse. Rand Scott, her second-in-command, had died in the confrontation. Her comfort was Rand died a warrior's death, making it possible for his soul to reside in Valhalla with her parents and many of her other deceased pack mates.

Sawyer had too much blood on his hands to ever wash clean. She'd never forgive him, nor forget all he'd done.

The hunter's head bowed, and his shoulders slumped. His scent took on the sharp taint of guilt. Anguish coalesced in his aura like broody storm clouds. "Victoria..."

She held up her hand. "Don't say it, Sawyer. I really don't want to hear it, especially from you."

"Don't you want to end this? To have revenge?" he asked in a hollow voice.

Heat flushed her body, and she braced for violence. "Of course I do, which is why I can't meet with your father. Do you remember the boy who died in Albuquerque? Jasper was only fifteen years old, and he was my responsibility."

"Oh." His mouth snapped shut.

Unable to stop the flood of words, Victoria kept talking, determined to make him understand the vast depths of her grief and rage. "If I came face-to-face with your father, I'm not sure I could stop myself from killing him. Or from trying to anyway."

Certain death awaited any foolish attempt to kill the unkillable.

She winced and continued, "Even though I know that I can't without dooming the few surviving members of my pack. Your father is too powerful. He has too many allies who'd avenge him." Her eyes narrowed, and she pointedly stared at Sawyer, leaving the "including you" unsaid.

He didn't correct her.

"If what they say about him is true, he wouldn't stay dead anyway," she muttered. "Seeking revenge on him is the same as committing suicide."

"My father didn't kill Jasper," Sawyer said, his tone brusque.

Her heart thundered, and her mouth went bone dry.

"I know he didn't pull the trigger, because we were talking on the phone when it happened. But I hold him responsible. He took a child hostage. He allowed it to happen."

"You're blaming the wrong man."

Victoria rushed toward him. She placed her hand over his mouth, silencing him before he said anything else. Her voice dropped to a soft hiss. "Think really carefully about what you say next, Sawyer. If you feel any loyalty at all to the man who pulled the trigger, then keep your mouth shut, because I won't hesitate to kill Jasper's murderer. Do you understand?"

He swallowed so his Adam's apple bobbed, then nodded.

"Good." She removed her hand. "Still want to tell me?"

A cold stone mask settled over his face. He remained silent for a full minute before he spoke. "A lot of people are dead because of me. I just want to fix this awful mess." He ran a hand through his shoulder-length hair, shoving it back from his face. "I *need* to make this right."

As impossible as it sounded, she believed he meant well. Pity swelled her heart to aching. "I know you do, Sawyer, but some things can't be fixed." With a sad smile, she raised her hand and brushed his wrist, a feather light touch, seeking to offer some degree of comfort.

Energy buzzed in the air, building as a single harmonious note, creating indescribable sensations—warm sunshine on bare skin, music in color, a moment of perfection—the manifestation of her pack bond. She caught a glimpse of his emotions—enough guilt, grief, and rage to drive a man insane.

Victoria snatched her hand away. Simultaneously, Sawyer gasped and took a step back. To her immense relief, the rudimentary link between them fizzled.

Sawyer's tone hardened to steel. "You have to meet with my father if you want this to end. This affects more than just us. It's crossed state lines. Other packs are openly hostile or refusing to cooperate with us. And there are still a thousand hunters out there who consider it open season on the Storm Pack."

An ironic smile twisted her lips. "Of course there are."

"Be practical. It's for the good of your pack."

She sighed. "Isn't it always? Fine, I'll think about it. Can you give me a day or two?"

His jaws clamped, but he grunted. She interpreted his posture as one of begrudging resignation. "Yeah, I can hang out, but don't take too long. I'm not going to wait around for you forever."

A genuine smile lit her face. "Yeah, yeah, that's what all the hunters say."

CHAPTER FIVE

Sessrúmnir, Freya's hall in Fólkvangr

"They lied."

"They are not the ones well known for their lies. Thor himself boasted of your capture." Freya watched him with narrowed eyes, attempting to discern even a fragment of truth from the Trickster's expression. Loki was darker than she remembered. Before his punishment, the Trickster had been more mischievous than evil. Now, his manner oozed menace.

Loki clicked his tongue. Despite his studied casualness, coiled anger defined the lines and plains of his muscular form. "Don'tcha just love the irony? Tell me, did Thor also boast of how he murdered my sons? Both my boys were innocent of any wrong doing, but he killed them anyway. He used my children's intestines to bind me to that rock and left me helpless for centuries while the serpent's venom dissolved my face. Until my flesh melted from the bone."

Her stomach heaved at his vivid retelling. Such momentous rage... A shiver of dread clawed at her gut. Had he come to her seeking revenge? Did he blame her in some twisted miscarriage of reasoning?

"I had nothing to do with your punishment, Loki."

Midgard

Beneath the fluffy cloud of fragrant lavender foam, the water level reached the rim of the clawfoot tub, so Victoria twisted the faucet off. With a contented sigh, she settled her forearms and hands on the copper sides and sank to her chin. Her long hair, freed of her customary braid, floated about her, and the crackle of tiny popping bubbles filled her ears. Weariness overtook her, and she closed her eyes, luxuriating in the soothing heat on her sore muscles. As soon as she'd returned home, she'd alerted her pack to the new dangers. All members were safe and accounted for.

Leaning back, her mind drifted, releasing the pent-up stress of a day filled with shrieking six-year-olds and overbearing dance mothers, murderous vampires and relentless hunters. As a registered nurse, she was an overqualified ballet teacher. To obtain an appropriate position, she would have to put in an application at the local medical center. However, she had delayed doing so.

Sylvie, her best friend and pack mate, said Victoria was scared to put down roots for fear of losing everything that mattered to her again. Maybe the older woman was right, maybe not. Victoria preferred to regard her caution as good, old-fashioned common sense. The last several months of her life had been transitory, always on the run, always looking over her shoulder for the hunters hot on her heels.

Now she had vampires trespassing in her territory! Until the threat resolved, she needed to keep her options open and have an exit strategy ready.

Truth be told, she thrived on the conflict and preferred the onslaught of violence to little Tammy Turner's mother's constant complaining about why her daughter should be taught to dance *en pointe* years in advance of the child's training.

Victoria's mother, Katherine, had always called her a "danger junkie." Her mom expressed dismay when Victoria had given up years of ballet to learn how to fight and hunt, competing head-on with stronger and larger males. Katherine argued that Victoria's preoccupation with combat delayed her development as a priestess and a healer.

Looking back, Victoria acknowledged that her mother had been right, but she refused to regret her unorthodox choices. Without her skill in battle, she would not have been chosen to become one of Odin's Valkyries. Her pack might not have survived those arduous months on the run from the hunters. Even her mistakes were fundamental to the woman and the Alpha she'd become.

"Victoria."

"Mmm?" Victoria turned her head toward the sound.

"Victoria."

The man's strained whisper penetrated her sleepy mind. Her eyelids fluttered, rapidly blinking as she groped her way toward consciousness.

"Victoria, wake up. Please. I need you."

There it was again. Harsh, pleading, and chillingly familiar.

Alert, Victoria sat up straight in the tub, searching the spacious ensuite bathroom for the intruder. She found nothing. No one. The water had grown cool, and she had no idea how long she'd been asleep.

A thick, eerie fog filled the bathroom. Her hot breath condensed into a visible cloud as she exhaled. When she rose from the water, a chilling blast of air struck her wet, bare skin, raising goose bumps.

Shivers coursed through her body. Her right hand rose, seeking the mystical dagger that hovered over her shoulder, invisible until drawn. A warm welcome, a murmur rather than distinct words, whispered through her mind as her fingers closed on the silken hilt.

The weapon appeared in her hand.

Vanadium—as light as a feather, as swift as the wind, as bright as moonlight on water. A product of Dwarven craftsmanship, a sword of prophecy said to be able to cut through anything.

The blade was a piece of *Gleipnir*, the ribbon that bound the great wolf Fenrir, made from six impossible things. A gift from goddess to priestess, Victoria wielded the weapon the same as her mother and her grandmother, going back over many generations. Someday, she would pass *Vanadium* on to her daughter.

"*Victoria,*" the voice in the mist called to her, louder and edged with desperation.

Following the sound, Victoria approached the vanity mirror with careful steps. A thick layer of ice covered the polished surface. Raising her hand to the edge, she placed her palm on the glass and swiped a diagonal swath from top to bottom.

"Daniel?" Victoria called, peering into the mirror.

"Victoria? I need your help." Daniel's voice emerged clearer and stronger, but he still sounded as if he were shouting over a great distance.

She tensed, preparing to shift. Her wolf rose, muscles flowing beneath her skin, and her eyes cast a golden light. The strange mist glowed. She hesitated, naturally suspicious, expecting a trick or a trap. Even so, concern overcame caution, and she leaned closer.

"Daniel, is that really you?"

Spectral tentacles crawled from the mirror, oozing from the opening, reaching for her like the appendages of a sea creature. There were a dozen or so, wriggling like Medusa's hair, and they varied in size from millimeters to several inches thick. They rooted in a thick mass of blackness at the base.

Heart racing, she took an instinctive step back before stopping, angry with herself for succumbing to fear. Her face set in a determined frown, she advanced again, reclaiming the ground she'd surrendered.

The rotten odor of death and decay permeated the bathroom, upsetting her ever-sensitive stomach. The fresh bout of nausea irritated her further. As a Valkyrie and priestess of Freya, she didn't suffer from nightmares. She *caused* them.

With a huff, she flicked her fingers. Bones crunched, a pleasurable pain replaced her unease, and her hands shifted to claws. A bloodthirsty anger filled her, the savage desire to inflict pain and destruction upon her enemy.

Victoria reached for one of the tentacles, intending to rip it out by the root, but the tendril evaded her grab and whizzed toward her face. The end split into two wishbone fine filaments, and lanced for her nostrils. Ducking her head, she parried with *Vanadium*, severing the appendage with the blade. As it fell, the entire thing dissolved to a wispy finger of fog.

Summoning her power, she cast a pulse of divine light from her free hand. The beam sliced through the gloomy fog and struck the necrotic force. The writhing fingers retreated before it and a long, thin window appeared in the mirror, revealing a terrifying abyss on the other side.

Her unwilling mind perceived grotesque things within the blackness, and she shuddered. Nightmare imaginings full of apparitions and abominations that were darker than the darkness. Daniel stood at the center of a point of light on the other side of the horrific void. Even across the great distance, there was no mistaking his dark head or athletic form. Nor the arms that had held her or the voice that had whispered her name.

"I'm here." Daniel reached for her as if seeking to escape the confines of his prison. "Victoria, can you hear me?"

Her heart leapt in her chest and slammed against her breastbone.

"I can see you. Where are you?" Victoria shoved her arm through the reality rift, desperate to save him, but he was just out of reach.

"I've been imprisoned by the vampire who killed me. He calls himself Vildivia. Self-important asshole if you ask me."

Her suspicion hardened. Daniel's back had been turned to the vampire who murdered him. So how could he know? Her breath hitched. "He's short and covered in tribal tattoos?"

"He's tall and covered in skeletal tattoos." He paused, and his lips compressed. She wasn't close enough to see his eyes, but her imagination supplied the wry gleam in their depths. "It's really me."

She swallowed an instinctive apology. She had to ask and Daniel would understand why. As lovers, their trust in one another had been a difficult, drawn out process. A werewolf and a hunter. Their star-crossed romance had seemed doomed from day one, and yet he defied his father to be with her. They had dated for a year before his murder.

"Vildivia has my soul," Daniel's manner contained marked reluctance and distress. He clearly despised his helplessness. "I need help."

"How long have you been trapped?" Horror squeezed the life from her, the crushing coils of a serpent. She couldn't breathe. The knowledge he suffered alone, imprisoned by their enemy, sickened her.

"Since I died." With each passing second, he drew further away from her, his voice fainter. "Listen to me, baby, this is important. I've been trying to escape for months, but I can only leave this prison when he allows it."

With the use of his pet name for her, her doubt regarding his identity vanished. The only man who'd ever dared *baby* her—and lived—was Daniel. "When you appeared to stop Sawyer and me from killing each other?" she asked. "You're saying Vildivia sent you?"

"Yes."

"Why didn't you ask for help?"

"I tried, but he stopped me somehow."

"He has you under a *geas*?"

He hesitated. "Is that like a curse?"

"Sort of," she said. "Yes, especially if he compels you to do something against your will."

"He controls what I can say, and he's got to be allowing me to talk to you now. There's no way I suddenly broke through after all these months of failing."

Victoria swallowed, trying to free her constricted throat. She gasped for air as tears streaked her face. "So this is a trap."

Daniel shouted across the vast distance now separating them. "Yes, exactly."

Her heart grew stout; her entire will turned into a razor point of determination. "I'm going to free you, Daniel. I'm going to find that filthy creature and rip him to shreds."

"No!" His volume swelled to convey the command. "Don't come after me alone. Go to my father—"

The rift closed, silencing his voice.

Victoria gulped a breath, instead of inhaling a lungful of water. She choked, limbs flailing. Fluid rushed down her throat, into her nose, and pressed against her eardrums.

She kicked and thrashed her arms, struggling against the horrifying discovery of drowning. Her foot broke the surface and then her hand. Panicked, Victoria shot upright. Gasping for air, she grabbed for the side of the tub. Her frantic motion sloshed a wave onto the tile floor.

It was a nightmare. Not real. She clung to the tub for support, coughing up water from her lungs. Once they were clear, she inhaled blessedly cool air while her mind raced. *Had the dream ended?*

Gathering her strength, she slithered over the side and landed on her hands and knees atop the drenched bath rug. Panting, she crouched on wet memory foam while her heart raced. She had no idea how to interpret her dream about Daniel's soul being imprisoned. *Or was it a vision?* She couldn't leave it alone. She wouldn't. She needed answers, and she'd stop at nothing to obtain them.

A sudden, violent wave of nausea sent her bolting to the commode. She lost what little her stomach contained, and then the morning sickness abated enough to allow her to brush her teeth. She cleaned up the water on the floor.

Faint daylight filtered through the frosted bathroom window. A glance at her phone showed it was past seven a.m., causing her another faint shock. How could she have fallen asleep in the tub and spent the entire night there? The prune-like appearance of her skin suggested that was the case. In the master bedroom, she dressed in a short-sleeve blouse and skintight jeans, deciding to wear and enjoy them while she still could. She dried her hair and styled it in a neat French twist.

Victoria padded barefoot through the lakeside Craftsman-style house. The vehicle and property belonged to Arik Koenig, her recently deceased mate. Or, technically, everything now belonged to his son, Logan. Arik had died before they were legally married. The law did not recognize the existence of werewolves, let alone the validity of a mate bond.

Over twelve hours had passed since she'd spoken with Sawyer, but he remained at the forefront of her thoughts. Following their meeting, he had texted her with the address of his hotel, a shabby establishment right on the southern edge of her territory. The courtesy extended surprised her, since it implied a degree of trust she considered impossible between them.

The delicious aroma of fresh-baked bread led Victoria to the kitchen where she found Sylvie Thornton. The Native American woman had a tall, strong stature. Her gray hair was pulled back into a neat ponytail. Victoria's second-in-command, Sylvie held the rank of Beta within the Storm Pack. She also acted as their Skald, the keeper of tradition, and was a devout follower of Freya.

"Good morning! How did you sleep?" Sylvie asked with a smile of greeting. She wore a flour-covered apron, and stood at the center island kneading a ball of dough.

"Okay, I guess. I fell asleep in the tub." Victoria glanced around, looking for other members of the pack. Emptiness echoed through the house. Curious, she extended her awareness through the pack bond and confirmed they were the only ones present. With an effort, she had the ability to reach farther, but it was easier to ask. "Where is everyone?"

"Morena took Sophia and the pups for a run along the lake. Those youngsters are growing like weeds and just bursting with nervous energy." Sylvie paused, pursing her lips. "You look tired."

Victoria took a seat at the kitchen table. "I'm okay, although I'd forgotten how rambunctious ten six-year-olds can be."

Sylvie cast a knowing look and smiled as she lovingly used her friend's nickname. "Victory, you've never known what any six-year-olds are like."

She laughed. "Well, I'm learning."

"Isn't that the truth? Are you hungry?"

"No." She crossed her arms over her uneasy stomach. Despite having lost the contents of her stomach, the queasy sensation in her gut persisted.

"How are you feeling?" Sylvie asked. Soft, nurturing hues suffused her aura.

Her Beta's gentle concern soothed her tension somewhat. Relaxing a little, Victoria mustered a wry smile. "Sick."

Sylvie chuckled, pounding out the dough. "Don't worry, it will pass."

"Yes, but when? I'm six weeks along, but this feels like it's been going on forever."

The smile lines crinkled about the corners of Sylvie's hazel eyes. "I can't wait to have another baby to coddle. Are you sure you're having a girl?"

"So the Norns said." Absently, her hand pressed against her flat stomach. Her emotional turmoil agitated her nausea. The prophecy plagued her with dark thoughts and doubts, and now nightmares troubled her sleep.

At the kitchen island, Sylvie grew still and alert. "That's the first time you've spoken of your visit to the Norns since your return."

Victoria licked her lips, debating how much to reveal. As a Beta, every potential threat to the pack concerned Sylvie. At the same time, Victoria worried about sharing the dark prediction for fear of endangering her friend.

"Is it that bad, sweetie?"

Victoria forced a smile. "Worse."

Sylvie covered the dough with a cloth and then set it aside. Wiping her hands on her apron, she rounded the island to sit at the table across from Victoria. "Have you decided yet whether to meet with Jake Barrett?"

Victoria huffed in exasperation and perched her elbows on the table. "I told Sawyer that I'd consider it because he wouldn't take no for an answer."

"So you've put him off for another day. The man is nothing if not persistent. He'll keep coming until he gets the answer he wants."

She succumbed to an irrepressible grin. "Then I'll school him. Someone needs to teach that man what no means, and I'm just the woman to do it."

Sylvie chuckled and shook her head. "I know you will, but danger is closing in on us from all sides. The vampire who attacked you last night is a threat to us all. This meeting with the Hunter King may be the opportunity we have prayed for to end the awful violence. We have a duty to consider our living children."

The reminder stung her pride, but Victoria depended on her friend's steady temperament to keep her on an even keel. Sylvie told the truth even when Victoria had no desire to hear it.

"Maybe you're right," Victoria said. "Maybe I'm putting pride before the good of the pack."

"It is difficult to maintain a sense of perspective." Sylvie's shoulders relaxed, and she waved a dismissive hand. "You are young, ruled by your heart. I am old, and my heart aches. I long to be reunited with my mate in Valhalla, but until that day comes, I will share what little insight I possess with you."

Her friend's melodramatic statement made her smile. At the same time, Victoria ducked her head in sheepish acknowledgment of her own stubbornness. "You know I honor your wisdom, Sylvie. Do you think I should meet with Jake Barrett?"

"I think you must do whatever is necessary to restore the peace. Our pack is few, and we are weak."

Victoria's temper sparked. "I am not weak."

Sylvie smiled. "No, you are not weak. You are the mightiest of us, but it does not change the fact that you are with child. As the pregnancy advances, it will sap your strength, and you have no mate to defend you. All of our men are dead. Even your mate's son, that shiftless excuse for a wolf, has abandoned us."

"That's not entirely fair. I told Logan we didn't need him."

Sylvie snorted with derision. "His head was full of nothing but selfish concerns, or he wouldn't have believed you."

Victoria sighed. "He provided the roof over our heads and enough money to cover our bills for some time to come."

"Without a male to defend our territory, our situation is worse than precarious. Vampires boldly trespass on our lands, and we are living on borrowed time until another pack decides to drive us from our territory."

Victoria bit her tongue. Her defense of Logan died. Her numerous concerns and obligations dictated she focus her energy. "I can't help it. I don't trust Jake Barrett."

A pause ensued while Sylvie composed her thoughts. Victoria waited patiently.

Eventually, Sylvie spoke: "Victory, I have known Jake Barrett for almost thirty years, and I have observed him to be honorable in his dealings with us. He is not the sort of man to bring a bomb to peace negotiations, or to murder a child."

The memory of the events in Albuquerque still haunted Victoria. During December of the prior year, Jake Barrett and his people had captured fifteen-year-old Jasper. The hunters held the teenage werewolf hostage, and murdered him in cold blood. The pain of having lost a child of the pack who was under her protection fueled her smoldering anger.

"But he is exactly that sort of man," Victoria said in a tight voice. Conflict divided her heart. In her dream, Daniel had told her to go to his father for help. "The hunters ambushed our pack and slaughtered our people in a vicious act of revenge because they believed I murdered Daniel."

Sylvie's hand cut the air in a forceful gesture. "That's what we assumed, but that explosion wounded many people on both sides, and the fighting broke out afterward. Do you really believe Jake Barrett would kill his own people?"

"I don't know. I just don't know." Victoria's teeth

gnashed together, and she shook her head in frustration. For a moment, arrogance defined her. She considered ordering the older woman to drop the subject even though a Skald must always be free to speak her mind.

"The question of the man's character must be resolved."

Victoria sighed. "I agree, but I can't help feeling we're dishonoring all those who have sacrificed their lives by initiating peace talks."

Morena cleared her throat. "Hey, guys, what's up? Whatcha talkin' about?"

Sylvie and Victoria traded a glance and then turned in unison toward the kitchen entrance. The teenage werewolf stood with her arms across her chest, obviously trying to look nonchalant, but she fooled no one.

"Hi, Morie, how was your run?" Sylvie asked. The Beta's apprehension bled into the pack bond. They both tried, though often failed, to shield Morena from life's grim realities.

"Great. I covered about ten miles with the pups. They should be nice and worn out." Morena headed straight for the fridge and pulled out an energy drink. Curls of damp hair clung to her face, and perspiration gave her brown skin a glossy sheen.

Victoria refused to play games. She pinned Morena with a direct gaze. "What did you hear?"

"Oh, was there something to hear? What did I miss?" Morena bounced on her heels and wore a wide smile, the very image of innocence.

Victoria grumbled indistinct words beneath her breath, but she gave credit where it was due. Morena possessed exceptional skills of deception. The girl lied through evasion and wordplay designed to manipulate the truth. She stole from those outside the pack without compunction, and her lawless tendencies were getting worse as she got older. Their people admired cunning and guile, but a question remained whether her talent would ultimately benefit the pack or become a serious liability.

Victoria exhaled, formulating a reply, but Sylvie saved her the trouble. "We were talking about Victoria's baby. She's having a girl."

"Too bad." Morena waved her hand in a flippant gesture. "Boys are better."

"Girls are the same as boys, but then girls turn into incorrigible teenage brats." Victoria smothered a smile, and then adopted a stern expression instead. She enjoyed bantering with Morena. The girl more than held her own in most verbal skirmishes.

Morena grinned and rolled her eyes. She downed her energy drink in a single long gulp and then belched in satisfaction.

"Manners," Sylvie snapped.

"Excuse me." Morena assumed a repentant air.

"I need to get my bread into the oven." Sylvie rose from her chair.

"I can't wait to have a baby." Morena sighed with longing, a dreamy smile on her lips.

"Oh, goddess." Sylvie collapsed onto her seat with a solid thunk.

Victoria's mouth opened. Her mind went blank. She traded a panicked glance with Sylvie.

"Morie, enough of this nonsense," Sylvie said, wagging a scolding finger. "You're too young to be talking about babies. You don't even have a mate!"

The girl's dark eyes flashed, and her chin tilted at a defiant angle. "I'll be seventeen in a month. I'm old enough to take a mate. If I choose a man from another pack and ask him to join us, it'll make us stronger. Besides, it's not like I'm doing anything important right now anyway. I'm not in school. At least if I start having babies, I'll be contributing."

"That's enough," Victoria said, snapping out of her stupor. She didn't want to admit it, even to herself, but

Morena's words worried her. Any male coming in from the outside would instinctively seek to take the rank of Alpha from her. She squared her shoulders and glared at the teen. "First thing Monday we're enrolling you in high school."

Morena's eyes widened. A smile curved the corners of her mouth as she rocked back on her heels, bouncing excitedly. "Really? Do you mean it?"

"Absolutely," Victoria said.

"Cool!" Morena flipped the empty bottle into the recycling container. "I'm going to grab a shower. I stink."

Like a shot, the teenager departed without waiting for a response. Victoria stared after her, brow knit. "She played me for a fool."

Sylvie chuckled and patted her shoulder. "Don't feel too bad, Victory. That girl has the devil's tongue."

"I hope it doesn't get her into any more trouble." Victoria placed her hands on her knees, head bowed. Nausea churned her gut. Misery rode her.

"Perhaps this meeting with Jake Barrett is an opportunity for you to begin training Morena to assume greater responsibilities," Sylvie said as if the matter were already decided. "Someday soon, she must take her place among the adult females of the pack."

"Right—all three of us," Victoria said, bitterness coloring her voice. Where the Storm Pack once boasted many members, the war with the hunters had reduced their numbers to seven.

"She may be premature in planning for offspring, but Morena may attract a fine male to our ranks when she chooses a mate. There will be many young men who will recognize the opportunities to be had by joining our pack."

"Every last one vying for leadership." Victoria scowled, and her frustration mounted. In general, male werewolves outweighed females, and Victoria was smaller than the average she-wolf. The chances she could take even a mid-sized male in one-on-one combat were slim. To make matters worse, strict cultural taboos forbid pregnant females from fighting.

A heavy sigh escaped her.

Sylvie's footsteps approached, and the older woman pressed an ice pack wrapped in a towel to the back of Victoria's neck. The cold alleviated her nausea.

"Thank you." Victoria looked up.

"You're welcome." Sylvie smiled, and the women traded a commiserating glance. "I don't know what to tell you, Victory. Arik Koenig was a noble man. It's unlikely you will find another male of his power who will treat you as a partner rather than chattel. However, you must—"

"Act in accordance with the best interests of the pack," Victoria said with a sharp stab of bitterness. Her independent spirit balked at the obvious choice—find and take another mate powerful enough to protect the pack and defend their territory.

"I will not suggest you accept another mate. You have suffered too much already."

"I don't think I could survive losing another lover." Victoria looked away. The last several months had been pure hell, on her heart as well as her pack. But as Alpha and expectant mother, she needed to put the past behind her and look to the future.

"We will face external challenges. There are many other packs more powerful than our own," Sylvie said. "Our territory is rich. Desirable. It is a measure of Arik's power that he controlled so much with no other pack to help him defend it."

"You've obviously thought this through." Her lips formed a wry smile. "Go ahead. Tell me what you're thinking."

"The Barrett family is powerful," Sylvie said. "They are feared and respected by our kind. If the alliance could be restored, other packs might be discouraged from attempting to take what is ours. It might buy us breathing space. Time to recover."

Despite her reservations, Victoria smiled. She had to hand it to Sylvie. Her wily friend's reasoning was sound. She sighed and swallowed her pride. "All right. I'll talk to Sawyer and have him arrange a meeting with his father, but it will be outside Sierra Pines in a neutral location."

Sylvie's hazel eyes gleamed. "A wise precaution."

Victoria rose to her full height and squared her shoulders, mentally gathering her strength for the coming confrontation. Her spirits took a turn for the positive.

Extending her awareness, she drew on her mystical connection with the natural power inherent within the earth, lake, and sky. *Arik's land.* Hollowness echoed within her soul for the space her mate had filled too briefly. She missed his strength, his steadiness, and his stubborn willfulness. But Freya had chosen him to serve as her general, so Victoria persevered alone as the sole protector of the pack.

"Stop worrying, Sylvie. Two months ago, we were starving and homeless. I promised I'd find a way to improve the situation, and I've delivered." She sounded strong, but her conscience reminded her that three members of her pack had died along the way—Jasper, Rand Scott, and Paul Thornton, Sylvie's mate.

"Yes, you have." Sylvie's kind expression shone with warmth and gratitude. "Our bellies are full, and we have a safe haven here in Sierra Pines."

"I'm going to resolve the situation with the hunters. I'll protect our members from any external threat, and if another pack tries to grab our land, then I'll stop them. I'm going to prove that an Alpha female is every bit as capable as any man."

A smile split Sylvie's face, easing the worry lines. "I know you are, Victory. I have every confidence in you."

"Thank you." Grim determination locked Victoria to her chosen course. The Spaniard had better be counting his remaining days on one hand. If she didn't catch him first, then she'd bet her soul Sawyer or Jake Barrett would hunt the bloodsucker to the ends of the earth.

"Will Morena be accompanying you?"

Victoria's lips tugged into an involuntary grin. "Yes, I'll be taking her along."

Victoria shifted her hold on the bulky cardboard box she carried, freeing her arm. She knocked once and then waited.

Through the closed door, she detected a soft rustle and the sound of a book closing. Then Morena's voice called out a soft, "Come in."

She twisted the knob and pushed the door. Stepping inside the dimly lit room, she carefully navigated the piles of clothing which were strewn across the floor.

Morena rested on her stomach atop a pile of pillows, her head close to the foot of the bed. At sixteen, the whip-thin teenager was already taller than Victoria. She had flawless, brown skin and black hair, the product of an ethnic heritage more Hispanic blood than Norse. She wore her short tresses in several ponytails bound with multi-colored bands. Gold piercings studded her earlobes and cartilage. Her appearance was foxlike, but her pedigree was one-hundred percent pure wolf.

"Hi," Victoria said, setting the box by the door.

"Hi, Vic, what's up?" Morena flashed a too-cute smile, but her dark eyes were wary. Sitting up, she shifted her position and scooted around to face her pack leader.

Victoria winced. "Don't call me that," she said. "Please. It's bad enough when Logan does it."

"Shouldn't that be past tense? Logan's gone." Morena averted her gaze and spoke in a flat tone that failed to hide her disappointment. Dark swirls of depression tinted her youthful aura.

"He has a cell phone, Morie. You can always call him."

"We text." The girl shifted the pillows in a further attempt to conceal the book. For the first time, Victoria noticed a tattoo of a half-moon on the inside of her wrist.

Victoria's brow lifted. She indicated the tattoo. "Is that new?"

"No," Morena said, an obvious lie. She fidgeted, covering, then uncovering the tattoo with her hand. A look of defiance settled on her face. "Yes."

Victoria smiled. "I like it."

"Really?" Morena beamed, and her pleasure perfumed her scent even as her aura brightened.

"Yes, really."

Victoria experienced the teenager's happiness through the pack bond, and it shocked her that such a little thing meant so much to the girl. But then, maybe it shouldn't have. Morena lost her parents in the Phoenix massacre. A couple weeks later, Jasper's death left the girl devastated. Yet, she never cried, and she never complained.

"Whatcha reading?" Victoria darted closer, then seized the corner of the book concealed beneath the pillow.

"Nothing!" Morena squawked and grabbed for the book but not fast enough to prevent Victoria from reading the title.

"*My Broody Vampire Lover*?" Acid threatened to burn a hole through her stomach. She stared at Morena in disbelief.

The teenager stuffed the book beneath the covers once again and sat up straight, shoulders squared, eyes bright with defiance. "It's just a book," Morena muttered.

"It romanticizes *vampires*," Victoria said, struggling

to maintain her composure and remain calm.

"Look, I know the difference between fantasy and reality," Morena said. "I don't need a lecture."

The pressure in Victoria's temples increased, throbbing, the beginning of a world-class headache. "Vampires aren't romantic, Morena. They're monsters. They murder people."

"It's not like I'm dating one." The teenager fidgeted, obviously embarrassed.

Victoria's heart ached. "That's not funny, Morie. A vampire murdered Daniel."

Morena's eyes widened. She gasped and sprang off the bed to hug Victoria. Apology replaced the insubordination. "I'm sorry! I didn't think! I didn't mean to be a bitch."

Victoria embraced the girl, reaching up to wrap her arms around the teenager's shoulders. "It's okay, Morena."

"I'll get rid of the book. I'll burn it."

"You don't have to do that," Victoria said. "Just remember, it's a fantasy, okay? Once you fight vampires, I doubt you'll ever want to pick up another vamp romance novel again."

They separated. Morena went to sit on the bed again. Victoria remained standing.

A gleam entered Morena's eyes, and she bounced on the mattress. "Are you taking me on my first vamp hunt?"

"Not quite yet. You need to learn to fully control your shape shifting before we go after undead."

"Oh." Morena's face fell. The teenager still lacked the discipline necessary to perform even a partial shift on her own. Such control required patience and practice.

Seeing the teen so excited and then disappointed served as a sharp reminder of how the girl had been neglected for the last several months. Guilt cast a long shadow over Victoria. High time to correct the injustice.

"What we're going to do is even more dangerous."

Morena perked up. "Yeah? What?"

Victoria met her gaze. "I'm going to negotiate with the hunters, and I need a wingman. Do you think you might be up for it?"

Morena's mouth fell open. She sat upright. "No shit! You're kidding? You are kidding?"

"Not kidding." Victoria shook her head. "I won't lie. It'll be dangerous. You might have to fight. There's a chance you could be hurt. You might have to kill someone."

"Wow, I can't believe you're asking me." Morena gushed excitement. "Are you sure Sylvie's okay with this?"

She huffed with exasperation, willing to play along with the girl's impression that Sylvie disapproved. "I am Alpha. At least, the last time I checked. It's my call. The question is, do you want to come with me?"

"Yes! Absolutely!" Morena burst to her feet, bouncing with hyper energy. After a couple of enthusiastic seconds, she calmed and her expression grew earnest. "I mean, yes. I want to go with you. I promise. I won't let you down."

"But there's one condition," Victoria said. "If I say that something smells funny, then you get the hell out of there. Run, and don't look back even if I stay. Do you understand?"

Morena stared at her with wide, round eyes. "Yes, I do."

"Good. Grab your coat and put on your shoes."

Morena squeaked. "Now?"

She nodded. "Now."

Victoria headed for the door, intending to fetch her car keys and notify Sylvie of her plan to visit Sawyer.

"Victory?"

Hesitating, she glanced over her shoulder. "Yes?"

"What's in the box?"

"Oh, right." Victoria stooped and picked up the cardboard box which she tossed underhanded to Morena.

The girl caught the package with both hands and examined it with open curiosity.

"It's a new laptop. I ordered it last week. I figured you'd need one for school work."

Morena sputtered, "You knew?"

Victoria smirked. "Of course I knew."

Pleased at having the last word, she exited the room before Morena recovered her wits and returned one of her sarcastic remarks.

CHAPTER SIX

"I had nothing to do with your punishment, Loki."

A chilled smile settled on his lips. "True enough. You didn't participate in my persecution, but neither did you lift a finger on my behalf."

She drew a sharp breath. "What would you have of me? We are not friends."

"No, but we were supposed to be allies. Or have you forgotten?" Swiftly, he stepped toward her, serpentine in movement, wolf in his eyes.

"I have not forgotten." Heart throbbing, Freya turned her head to summon her Valkyries to her defense. This older Loki lacked the playful mischievousness she remembered from his youth. He frightened her far more than she cared to admit.

Loki waved his hand. "Relax. I'm not angry with you. You've kept your word and honored our deal. I noticed you're still bringing my wolf children to your hall when their deaths are worthy."

She tipped her head. "Half, as we agreed. One of the wolf shifters even serves as my new general."

"You mean your new stallion," he said with a snide jeer.

Midgard

"You want *how many* bricks of plastic explosives?" Andy Chart asked in an incredulous drawl.

"Ten bricks," Sawyer repeated, curbing his impatience with the veteran hunter who acted as the primary supplier of firearms and other high-grade weaponry for every hunter in the southwestern United States.

"Fuck, Sawyer. That's a lot of firepower. Are you hunting or planning to rob Fort Knox?"

"Can you get me the stuff, or should I call Juan Jarvis?" Sawyer asked with a hard edge as he dropped the name of Andy's fiercest competitor.

"Don't get your panties in a wad," Andy snapped. "Sure, it'll take me a few days, but I can do it."

"Just get it done."

The call ended, and he set the phone on the dresser where it landed amid a clutter of coins, knives, and firearms. A shotgun cartridge rolled across the surface and dropped to the floor. Sawyer bent to retrieve it, nose wrinkling in reaction to the moldy odor from the soiled carpet.

While not luxurious, his apartment on the MIT campus had been small and clean compared to the Fireside Inn which served as his temporary residence. The cheap motel was located off the main highway and consisted of a main lodge, a row of solitary cabins, and a pockmarked parking lot. The exclusive alpine community of Sierra Pines offered little in the way of affordable lodging. As a hunter, he shunned the more luxurious bed and breakfasts in favor of anonymity.

He retrieved a bottle of water from the mini-fridge and twisted off the cap. Pulling on his trench coat, he grabbed a hardcover book and headed for the front porch to do some reading in the fresh morning air. As he reached for the knob, a solid rap sounded on the other side of the door. He set the bottle aside and tucked the book beneath his arm, then drew his .45. With the barrel of his gun, he eased back the curtain of the long, rectangular window to the left of the door.

Victoria stood on the porch. She looked straight at him, a smile playing on her lips. She wore her hair drawn back from her face, so the flickering porch light cast dancing shadows on her fine features.

Bursting with impatience, Sawyer allowed the curtain to drop. He holstered his firearm and yanked the door open. His thoughts had dwelled on the she-wolf since the night before. The wait for her answer had been a pins and needles affair.

As he stepped onto the porch, his lungs expanded, filling with cool morning air scented with fresh pine and moisture. He occupied the last cabin on the row, surrounded by thick copses of trees, which offered privacy. Two vehicles were parked in front, his classic muscle car and a black SUV.

Victoria stood turned toward the red Chevelle convertible. At the sound of his footsteps, she glanced back, and he caught a glimpse of immense sorrow in her blue eyes. Her mouth bowed down in an unhappy curve and her eyes were suspiciously watery.

Approaching Victoria, Sawyer absently removed the book from beneath his arm. "Hey. Mind if we talk outside? The smell inside gives me a headache."

"Sure. I know *exactly* what you mean." Victoria flashed a cheerful smile, apparently amused. She cast a quick glance down. Her eyebrows arched, and her hand caught his wrist, turning the cover so the title could be read. "Algebraic Geometry? Doing some light reading?"

Her touch caused a warm flush on his skin. Pleasant. No, fuck pleasant. Fantastic. Deliberately, Sawyer removed his wrist from her grasp and stepped away to set the heavy textbook on a bistro table.

"Just brushing up on the basics. I took a semester off to hunt you."

Mock contriteness crossed Victoria's face. Her pretty mouth formed an O. "Gosh, I'm so sorry to have put you out like that."

He chuckled. "You should be. I was supposed to graduate in May."

She nodded. "You're working on your Master's degree?"

He frowned, wary. She knew a lot more about him than he about her. As always, the reminder of his brother's duplicity gnawed at him. "Yeah, that's right."

Sorrow crossed her face. Then she glanced away and adopted a polite smile. Her head turned toward an area off the porch. Victoria's hand rose, and she tweaked two fingers in a beckoning gesture. "Morena, come over and say hello."

His spine stiffened as he spotted a tall figure lurking beneath a pine tree. His hand flexed, mentally wanting his gun, but he curbed the impulse to reach for it.

Victoria stepped between him and her silent companion. "It's okay, hon. He doesn't bite."

Sawyer chuckled. "I do too."

She shot him a sharp glance, scowling, and a bright flash of gold glimmered in her eyes. A burst of energy, hot wind on his skin, slapped his body. His muscles tensed.

"Not right now. Save the biting for when we're alone."

He flashed a quick grin. "I prefer knives, thanks."

The dark-haired girl stepped onto the far edge of the porch. Sawyer recognized the teenager as a member of the Storm Pack, although he wouldn't have remembered her name if Victoria hadn't said it.

"Morena, are you okay?" Victoria whispered.

"When you said we were meeting someone, you didn't say it was *him*." A low growl accompanied the words. Morena skulked against the porch railing, looking anywhere but at Sawyer. She held her limbs tightly against her body, and her shoulders slouched. Even though the girl stood a full head taller than Victoria, she seemed smaller.

"It doesn't matter who we're meeting," Victoria said, severity coloring her tone. "Do you need to wait in the car?"

The teenager stiffened. Her head jerked up, and her face set in pure determination. She stared straight at Sawyer and edged around her Alpha to face him.

Victoria remained where she stood, allowing the younger wolf to confront him on her own terms. As much as he disliked being turned into a lesson for an adolescent werewolf, he understood the dynamics of what was happening.

His hunter's instincts warned him to remain still, since even a flicker of muscle might set the wolf girl off. Instead of reaching for his gun the way he wanted, he held her stare and waited. Tension thick enough to taint the air gathered, a frozen moment in time.

Morena tilted her head back so her chin jutted. Her bright eyes were full of anger and accusation. "You murdered Rand."

"It was war, not murder." He strove to keep his voice neutral, free of any inflection that might allude to the bloodthirsty wrath that had driven him then or the regret he carried in his heart. Victoria's people understood the rules governing battle in black and white terms. He now regretted leading the ambush that had taken the life of the werewolf, Rand Scott, and two of Sawyer's fellow hunters, but nothing he did could change the past.

"Liar! I hate you!" An angry howl escaped Morena before she launched a clumsy attack, stabbing at him with her fist.

With a nimble step backward, he evaded her attack.

She took another swing at him. Her movements were slow and unpracticed, and he suspected she was too young to change shapes without a dominant wolf's assistance. He caught the girl's wrist in his hand and yanked her off-balance, so she stumbled.

Arms wind milling, Morena crashed into the cabin's wall and slid to the porch. He reached for his gun, but Victoria's hand brushed his, firm but gentle. Scowling, he looked at her.

Victoria bent to intercept Morena as the teenager struggled to her feet. As she caught the girl's elbow, a blast of cold air hit the porch, a gust of wind that seemed to come out of nowhere. Riding the gale, a big black raven descended from the sky and landed on the low-hanging branch of a nearby pine.

Sawyer pulled his coat closer, sparing a precious second to eyeball the bird. Morena's attack hadn't surprised him. She had plenty of good reasons for holding a grudge, but that didn't make him any happier with the current situation.

"If Sawyer were that easy to kill, I'd have done it months ago," Victoria said with an easy smile. "You have a lot to learn before you're ready to take on an experienced hunter."

"I don't understand why you don't kill him." Eyes bright with unshed tears, Morena shot him a hateful glance. "He murdered Jasper in cold blood! He set off the explosion that killed your mom and dad!"

Color drained from his face, and the accusation hit like a sucker punch to the gut, leaving him gasping for breath. Self-hatred and guilt had been his constant companions for months. The weight of his sins sapped his strength. His choices were resignation and damnation, or to keep fighting and hope for an impossible absolution.

"Look at him!" Morena shouted. "It's on his face! He reeks of guilt!"

Fine features frozen in shock, Victoria looked at him with glittering eyes. Her irises expanded, eclipsing the whites, and a wolf stared back at him.

He could tell by her expression that she was considering the girl's words. His hand closed in a death grip on the stock of his pistol. It required all of his discipline to keep the .45 holstered, but he placed shaky faith in Victoria. She didn't want a lethal confrontation any more than he did... Or so he hoped.

Victoria fixed her unwavering gaze on him. "Sawyer, did you kill my parents?"

Looking into her eyes, he believed her perfectly capable of killing him despite their fragile truce. His pulse throbbed against his eardrums. His heart pounded his ribcage. Sweat trickled down his back, but he forced himself to calm. He relaxed his tensed muscles, opened his hands, and released his hold on his gun.

Wolves smelled lies. He had to tell the truth. Of course, if she asked the wrong question and he gave a truthful answer, she would kill him anyway, but it might be very well what he deserved.

He swallowed against a tight throat. "I regret all of the death I've caused, so yeah, I'm sure I smell guilty. The responsibility for your parents' deaths resides with me, but I didn't kill them."

"He's lying." Morena hiccupped, tears coursing down her cheeks.

"He's telling the truth." A warning growl rolled from her throat.

The girl dropped her gaze and fell silent.

"What about the explosion?" Victoria asked.

"I wasn't at the airfield that day," Sawyer continued. "I didn't have anything to do with the explosion. Neither did my father."

Victoria's expression softened. She blinked, and when her lids lifted, her features were human once again. "I believe you. But why weren't you there?"

His pride balked at disclosing the truth. The words stuck in his throat. He remained stubbornly, stupidly silent.

Victoria stepped closer to him, studying his face. She rose on her toes and reached for him, index finger extended. Her fingertip brushed his chin and traced a slow path downward along the carotid artery. Her touch was gentle, sensuous, not remotely threatening. A seductive lie. In the blink of an eye, her human hands could become claws tipped in nails sharp enough to slice his throat clean open.

"Sawyer?" Victoria coaxed, low and seductive.

Abruptly, he realized she'd been playing with him, and anger replaced his hesitation. "My father called me a *loose cannon*, all right? He kicked my ass to the curb for shooting at you instead of listening to find out how Daniel died. He arranged the meeting on neutral ground with your pack and told me I had to sit it out until I could get my head on straight."

"He smells guilty," Morena protested.

Victoria turned to stare at the girl and spoke harsh, clipped words. "If guilt is any measure of culpability, then I deserve to be drawn and quartered for what happened to Daniel."

"I didn't mean to imply—" Horror contorted the girl's face, and she flinched. She looked away, closing her mouth.

"It's okay, Morie." Victoria approached Morena and settled a comforting arm about the girl's shoulders.

Once on the gravel, Victoria turned to face him. "Tell your father we'll talk, but I want the meeting to take place outside Sierra Pines. The last time your father got too close, a child of my pack paid with his life. I don't want hunters in my territory."

The reminder made him wince. "How far?"

"Say, fifty miles."

He considered for a few seconds. "Truckee is fifty

miles as the crow flies. We have a contact up there who owns a dairy farm."

She stared at him as if trying to see into his soul. After a hesitation, she said, "That'll be fine."

"What time?"

"High noon?"

"All right," he said. "I'll arrange it. I'll text you the address."

"Sounds good," she said in parting.

Sawyer waited until the women were gone before he went inside. Gathering his belongings as he prepared to leave, he reflected on volatile emotions, explosive tempers, and the potential for further bloodshed between wolves and hunters. His father would call the situation classic FUBAR. Fucked Up Beyond All Recognition...

Sawyer would have agreed.

Sawyer parked his 1970 Chevelle SS 454 at the farthest corner of the lot to keep one of the many pickup trucks and SUVs occupying the gravel parking area from banging its doors into the convertible. The classic muscle car was red with two black racing stripes down the hood, and it had a white leather interior.

His father had rescued the Chevelle from a junkyard when he and Daniel were just kids. For years, the painstaking restoration had been the weekend and evening project of father and sons. Sawyer had spent just as many hours in the hot garage as Daniel.

Yet, on Daniel's sixteenth birthday, Jake had handed him the keys. "*She's yours now, Son. Take good care of her.*" Sawyer still recalled the sharp sting of jealousy, the bitter taste of burning envy.

After Daniel's funeral, Jake tossed Sawyer the keychain. "*Take good care of her, Son. She's yours now.*" Except she wasn't his, and never would be. She'd always belong to Daniel, and he'd give anything to have his brother back.

Sawyer followed the dirt path toward the main concentration of buildings. The whole dairy farm stank of cattle, dung, and dirt. His steps stirred up a cloud of dust that left him sneezing.

Sawyer located his father on the front porch of the main house along with two of Jake's men: Henry Hedford, AKA Skinner, and Andy Chart. Skinner acted as the Hunter King's second-in-command and right-hand man.

The three men faced each other in a loose circle, speaking in hushed voices. A dozen paces distant, five more experienced hunters gathered. Sawyer recognized every man present as trusted members of his father's organization.

The thud of his boots on the wooden steps announced Sawyer's arrival. The other hunters turned toward him. Jake dipped his head in a slight nod. "Son."

"Dad." Sawyer tipped his head toward the men even though the unanticipated presence of Andy Chart grated on his nerves. What the hell was the man doing here?

"Sawyer," Chart said in a grim voice.

"Hal, how've you been?" Sawyer stepped toward Skinner and offered his hand. "How's Tonya?"

"We're good, but I hear you've gone bat-shit crazy off the deep end, boy." Skinner grasped his forearm and pulled Sawyer off balance, dropping a slap onto his back. The burly African-American man had a shaved head and many intricate tattoos. Despite being on the high side of fifty, he was one tough SOB who outstripped Sawyer in both height and weight.

The blow staggered Sawyer. He missed a step and recovered, accepting the nonverbal reprimand as what he had coming for running off halfcocked on a wild werewolf hunt. "Thanks for that."

"Any time." Skinner's laughter boomed.

"I'd like to speak with my son." Jake, who had reached the rank of colonel in the Marines prior to retirement, snapped out the command with the air of a man accustomed to being obeyed.

Without a word, Skinner and Andy both vacated the porch.

Jake turned his impenetrable dark-eyed gaze on his son. "You're early."

"I couldn't sleep." Sawyer propped an elbow against the white rail, gazing at the grassy front yard ringed by tall trees, the barns beyond, and the stockyards full of cattle. He sniffed, unable to breathe properly thanks to his allergies. As pretty as it was, he hated the country. The dirt, stench, and pollen were everywhere.

"Gage and JD are at home?" Sawyer's younger brothers, fraternal twins, were seniors in high school, so they normally accompanied their father on expeditions during the summer months.

Jake's head bent in a curt nod. "I have Winnie keeping an eye on the boys while I'm gone."

Uneasy, Sawyer surveyed the assembled hunters. He'd expected his father to come alone or with a couple men, not a whole crew. His gaze swept the assembly again, noting that most of the men carried shotguns and rifles, which he assumed contained silver ammunition, the weapon of choice when hunting werewolves.

"Why did you have to bring a unit, Dad? Victoria will spot your men and assume this is a trap. Hell, from where I'm standing, I'd assume the same thing."

A full minute of silence reigned. Sawyer resisted the urge to glance over his shoulder. His father's face would reveal nothing.

At last, Jake said, "These are my top men. They fought beside Daniel and they've grieved for him. They deserve to hear what she has to say."

"Are you sure you're not feeling excessively paranoid?"

"Victoria is a priestess of Freya and a werewolf, Sawyer, and the last time I checked, she was very pissed off for good reasons."

Sawyer took his father's paranoia as further evidence Jake placed no faith in his son's judgment. Heat burned through his chest. "She's going to turn tail and run."

"That might be for the best," Jake said. "I don't know what you think's going to happen..."

His hands curled into fists, and tension rang throughout his body. "I intend to put things right."

Jake snorted. "You're fooling yourself, Sawyer. Too many people have died. I've tried to minimize the bloodshed, but you went off guns blazing—"

"I know what I did." Guilt was the noose around his neck.

"Then you know that I haven't killed Victoria, even though I'm capable of it. I've held back out of respect for her father—"

Sawyer's fist struck his palm. "The alliance—"

"Our alliance with the wolves has been destroyed. Hell, most of her pack is dead, and she's going to be out for blood. It's in her nature."

Sawyer swung back to his father. "She's better than that. She could have killed me in Montana, but she didn't. She's had other opportunities since then..."

"She's exerting too much influence over you, Sawyer." Jake directed an unrelenting stare toward his son. "She's an Alpha. She has real power. I knew her father well. I've seen what a dominant wolf is capable of."

There it was—his father's unremitting disapproval—because his rebellious son failed to live up to expectations. Sawyer gave a shake of denial and glared. "If that's what you believe, then why the hell are you even here? You've obviously got no interest in peace."

The older man's expression softened. "I'm here for

you, Son. Because you need me."

A red haze of anger clouded Sawyer's vision. One thing was certain—Victoria and his father were cut from the same cloth. Both wolf and hunter seemed to share the stubborn insistence that current wrongs could not be righted. Anger fed his determination. The she-wolf and Jake would sit down and talk even if he had to force them at gunpoint.

Silence descended. Not an uncomfortable quiet, but a familiar one. His mother's death from breast cancer two years before robbed the Barrett family of conversation beyond the minimum necessary for survival. All the joy and laughter in their lives passed with Sarah.

Jake seemed to take Sawyer's reaction as a rejection. An expression of sorrow crossed his weathered face, making him look years older than his actual age.

Sawyer's throat hurt, but he had no comforting words to offer. Instead, he glanced out over the yard, surveying the assembly of ruthless men, busy with firearm maintenance and gear preparation. He had trained and hunted with them for years. Every man present would kill or die on his father's word.

"I'm taking this seriously, Sawyer. I pulled Skinner and these men from a post in Tucson to be here," Jake said.

The change of topic made him take a step back and refocus his priorities. "How bad are things in Arizona?"

"Bad," Jake said in his no nonsense way. "Things have never been worse. The undead are overrunning Tucson and Los Angeles. We're fighting a losing battle."

His teeth ground together. His knowledge of events on the front lines came through hearsay. For the last several months, he'd been absent from the trenches, chasing after werewolves, and the one particular she-wolf who'd become his obsession.

His father made no accusations. Aloud. He didn't need to because Sawyer harbored enough self-recrimination for them both.

"We should withdraw," Sawyer said, "and regroup. Draw new lines."

Jake's brow rose. "So you're giving me tactical advice now?"

"I'm just saying—"

"If we do that, then we've lost southern Arizona. San Diego. Los Angeles." Jake's dark brown eyes remained impervious.

"Those cities have already fallen," Sawyer said, because someone needed to say it. "Dad, how many more people have to die before you admit that we've lost?"

Jake's expression turned to stone. "What about the civilians, Sawyer? The people you'd leave behind. What would happen to them?"

"I don't know, Dad." He gave an angry shake of his head. "I don't have any ready answers. But I'm doing everything I can to put things back the way they used to be. This is about more than just our family or the Storm Pack. None of our wolf allies trust us anymore. The ones that aren't openly hostile won't even cooperate."

Jake stared at him. "Hell, I know that better than anyone. Last week, Charles Redmond's people over in San Diego got into it with the local pack, right in the middle of a vamp attack."

Sawyer experienced a surge of elation, feeling like his father was finally getting it. "It's a cluster fuck. It has to stop."

"And that's what this meeting is about?"

"Yeah, that's exactly what this is." Sawyer had a sketchy plan for putting things back the way they used to be. First, he had to end the hostility between the hunters and wolves. Not all of the pieces were clear yet, but this detente was the start.

Jake's eyes narrowed. "Then why'd you call Andy Chart and ask for ten bricks of plastic explosives?"

Damn Chart and his big mouth. Sawyer stiffened,

angered by the implicit accusation in his father's words. "I'm planning on going after a vampire."

"Ten bricks for just one vampire?" Jake said in a skeptical tone. "Because I'm wondering if you're planning an encore of your performance in Montana. You rigged that warehouse to explode while trying to ambush Victoria's pack, and you almost got yourself killed in the process."

His jaw dropped. "Two minutes ago you were saying I'd fallen under Victoria's influence. Now I'm setting a trap to take her down. Which is it?"

"I came prepared for both possibilities. Sawyer, you haven't been yourself for months," Jake continued, implacable as he made his argument. "Two good men followed you into that warehouse, and they both paid with their lives."

His temper spiked, making it difficult to remain rational. He swung away from his father and paced the porch before he turned back. "Damn it, Dad. Don't you think I know that?"

Jake nodded. "Hell yeah, I think you know it. Sawyer, you haven't been in your right mind since your brother passed, and the guilt of all that death is eating at you."

At a total loss for words, he stared at his old man. Fuck. *Just fucking perfect.* His father considered him too far gone to be rational, and his hot temper reinforced the impression of mental instability. And the worst part— Sawyer doubted himself too.

Striving for calm, Sawyer drew a deep breath and lowered his voice. "I intend to go after the vampire that murdered Daniel. The explosives are a precaution."

Deadly determination glimmered in his father's eyes. He rubbed his lower jaw, short nails scraping over the bristled beard. "Do you really believe her explanation that a vampire murdered your brother? That it's the same one who tried to kill you last night?"

"Yeah." Sawyer's hand covered his recently attached fingers. Phantom pain lingered in the digits. He swallowed hard, choking on emotion. "He bragged about Daniel's death, Dad. I—"

Primordial magic surged through Jake. Ancient pulsating runes flashed beneath his skin. His pupils eclipsed the irises and the whites, and his eyes became sunken orbs of eternal blackness. His voice hollowed and deepened. "Tell me about him."

Sawyer looked upon his father's true face without flinching and found solace in the certainty that his brother's death would be avenged. "He was tall. At least ten feet, and his limbs were long and thin as though he was stretched on a rack. He had brown skin, covered in chalky white tattoos, so he appeared to be wearing his bones outside of his body. He was bald and had a tongue like a whip, covered in barbs."

"Good." Jake nodded. Contemplativeness replaced the threat on his father's countenance. "Did he give his name?"

"No, but he had a stiff, formal way of speaking and a Spanish accent. Not Mexican or South American. I believe he's a Spaniard," Sawyer said, scouring his old man's face for any hint of recognition. His father was a walking library of esoteric knowledge. "Does any of this ring a bell?"

"Maybe." Jake's gaze strayed to the horizon, canvassing the mysterious depths of his wisdom. He rubbed his finger across the bridge of his nose. "I know stories of ancient Mayan death gods. Without my books, I can't say whether any of them were Spaniards."

Sawyer snorted. With dry sarcasm, he said, "If only there were devices for accessing information across vast distances."

Those penetrating eyes locked on him. Jake Barrett didn't trust computers, and he only relied on the types of technology that blew things away or up. "Cut the sarcasm, Son."

"Yezzir." Sawyer dropped a sloppy, mock salute.

Jake bit back a grin before settling into complete seriousness again. "Whether it's true or not this vampire murdered your brother, he has to be destroyed. He attacked you. I have to assume he's a threat to your brothers..."

Sawyer nodded. "We're in total agreement."

The corner of his father's mouth tugged. "Well, that's a novelty."

"Dad," Sawyer said, but the approach of footsteps caused him to fall silent.

"What is it, Chart?" Jake asked.

"Sir, the men are getting restless," Chart said, glaring daggers at Sawyer. The hunter was tall and lean with a face composed of sharp angles set in a sour expression. He stank of Cuban cigars.

Sawyer's dislike of the man skyrocketed to outright distrust.

Jake's voice rose to a rolling boom that carried clear to the edges of the yard. "Tell the men to secure the area and to stop their damn complaining. They sound like a bunch of old women. I've worked with tougher grannies."

Shouts of laughter came from the men, and a couple snapped off smart remarks. All in all, the crew seemed to be in high spirits.

"What are you waiting for, Chart? Get off my porch." Jake pinned his subordinate with a pointed stare.

"Yes, sir." Ears reddened, Chart saluted and departed.

Sawyer glared at his father. "Are you going to shoot or talk?"

Jake cocked his head. "We'll try it your way, for all the good it'll do."

"So long as you're willing to sit down, that's all that matters," Sawyer said, dismissing his father's diffidence.

Once he got Jake and Victoria together, he would work it out even if he had to force them to hammer out their differences.

"I'll talk." Jake inclined his head in a slight nod. "I'll meet Victoria down beside the grain silo next to the parking lot. It's out in the open, so she shouldn't feel like we're trying to pin her in. But I'll bring my men, and I'll bring my guns. Wolves never set down their fangs or their claws. That's something you shouldn't forget."

As if forgetting was even possible. "Fine. I'll go out to meet her unarmed as a sign of good faith." Laying down his arms made his skin crawl, but he'd do it for the sake of assuring the peace.

A tic worked in Jake's face, pulling at the corner of his mouth. "I don't like this one bit."

"I'll second that," Sawyer said and walked away, bringing the tense conversation to an abrupt end.

CHAPTER SEVEN

Sessrúmnir, Freya's hall in Fólkvangr

"You mean your new stallion."

Freya ignored Loki's ugly sneer. "I have honored our deal. I am no Oathbreaker."

"That's more than I can say for any other Aesir."

She looked down her nose at him. "I am Vanir, as is my twin, Freyr."

He chuckled, and his chin dipped to touch his chest. "That's right. Let's not ever forget how you and your brother are hostages against future wars. It's been so long since you came to live in Asgard that most of them have forgotten, haven't they?"

"I never forget."

"No, I don't expect you would. You're as much a prisoner as I, but in less obvious ways..."

Freya threw up her hands. Disgust edged her voice. "You are not even consistent in your lies. You say you were not captured, and then you describe the event in vivid detail. Which is it, Loki? Or is the truth such a foreign concept that you cannot even recognize it?"

He snickered and paced, following the curved edge of the spa. "Thor captured one salmon in a river full of fish. One fish is only part of me. I'm the entire school. I am the water in the river, the rocks on the bank, and the air in the sky."

She gaped in dismay, mouth open despite her determination to show him no weakness. "You lie. I'll grant your ability to shift shape is impressive, but no one is so powerful. Not even Odin."

Loki sighed and exhaled. "Fine, I'm given to exaggeration, but it makes for better stories. Thor captured a portion of me. The rest remains free."

"Impossible! Odin must know of your treachery."

Midgard

"This is a trap. It feels like a trap. It smells like a trap. It's gotta be a trap." Morena's arms swung wide as she chased circles about Victoria, raising a cloud of dust from the dirt road.

"Morena, calm down." Victoria shot the teenager a sharp glance and sent a cooling wave of power over her, soothing her wolf. The pack bond formed the foundation of their magic, connecting each member to the others. As Alpha, Victoria possessed the ability to command the Omega's beast.

As they approached the dairy farm, the need to remain vigilant against an ambush increased with every step. Morena's agitation made Victoria second-guess her decision to bring the girl along.

The dirt road sloped up to where a dozen or so buildings dotted the hilltop, lush and green with spring growth. The odor of cattle permeated the air along with the scents of fresh grass, squirrels, and field mice. A quarter mile ahead, stockyards full of black and white dairy cattle were visible. A couple miles behind, their SUV was parked on an access road blockaded by a padlocked gate.

Morena stopped in her tracks, eyes wide with worry. "I heard what you said to Sylvie about Jake Barrett.

Do you really expect an ambush?"

With a sigh, Victoria also halted. "I'm not a seer. I can't predict the future."

"But—"

"Morena." Victoria's voice contained a distinct note of warning.

The teen's mouth snapped shut.

Victoria continued, "If it's an ambush, then I'll deal with it when it happens."

The girl looked away, casting a sullen glance downward. She reeked of fear and anger, both justifiable reactions, but they caught Victoria unprepared. Morena's skill at hiding her true feelings seemed to be unraveling at the worst possible time.

"Are you angry with the hunters, or with me for failing to protect so many members of the pack?" Victoria wasn't surprised the girl doubted her, but she wanted to hear the accusation stated aloud. Silent recrimination served no useful function.

Morena's head jerked up, face marked with dismay. "The hunters!" she said too fast.

Victoria's teeth clenched, but her Omega's doubt reinforced her conviction. Do or die. She *would* emerge victorious from the negotiations with the hunters.

"Look at me." Victoria imbued her voice with power, creating resonance, commanding obedience.

Unable to resist her Alpha's command, the teenager met Victoria's gaze. "I'm sorry," Morena apologized, shamefaced. "I'm afraid of dying. I'm a coward. I'm not worthy."

Victoria's gaze and tone gentled. She laid a reassuring hand on the girl's arm. "You're not a coward, Morena. You're young. But I'd do anything to protect you. That includes dying for you. I'm asking you to have faith in me. Can you do that?"

Eyes wide, Morena gave a frantic nod. "Yes, of course. I'm just worried about the hunters."

"I don't know what's in Jake Barrett's heart, but I do trust Sawyer," Victoria said. "He wouldn't allow his father to ambush us. Not after everything we've been through."

Morena's lips parted, an expression of surprised disbelief, a glimmer of hurt. "You trust him? For real?"

"Absolutely," Victoria said, speaking with forced confidence.

Morena needed her Alpha to be strong. Her stubborn heart dictated that Daniel's brother must be trustworthy, but private doubts twisted her insides. Was she making a terrible mistake?

Morena's front teeth worried her lower lip. Her gaze flickered toward the outbuildings visible at the crest of the rise. "I'd still like to kill him."

Victoria threw back her head and laughed. "I'm familiar with the feeling, but your last try didn't go so well."

The teenager grinned. "I flubbed the attack on purpose. Next time, he'll underestimate me. He won't know what hit him."

The girl's easy confidence made Victoria shake her head. "Next time, go straight for the throat."

Surprise shot Morena's eyebrows to her hairline. "You think I should try again?"

"No, I think that would be a bad idea. Sawyer is as dangerous as any wolf, Morie. Don't underestimate him."

"But he's only human," Morena protested on a faint breath.

"Many great heroes were 'only human'," Victoria said. "Do not forget. There are men who are the sons of Thor and the sons of Odin, with the blood of the gods flowing through their veins. Humans are the most dangerous predator of all because they outnumber us by the millions. You must not take them lightly."

"I won't." Morena smirked. "Are you sure you're not

saying this because you want to boink Sawyer?"

Boink? *Sawyer?* Victoria's mind went blank. She opened her mouth to issue a rebuke, but Morena's incessant chatter drowned her out.

"Granted, he's hot if you like that redneck Jedi vibe. Just because I noticed doesn't mean I don't hate him. But he is your type..." The teen slipped her a sly sideways glance, a smile that implied secrets.

"Don't be ridiculous." Victoria aimed a playful swat at Morena, but the girl danced away.

"It's a trap," Morena muttered. "I wouldn't put anything past that guy, but I hope you're right."

"Tell you what. If I'm wrong and this is a trap, you can say 'I told you so' as many times as you like."

Morena grinned. "Deal. What do you need me to do?"

"I have to be sure you're going to follow my lead. You can't be out of control like you were at the motel." Victoria held Morena's gaze and smiled in encouragement to bolster the girl's confidence. "I need for you to have my back. I'm counting on you. Can you do that?"

Morena stood straighter, squaring her shoulders. "Yes."

The women resumed walking in companionable silence until they neared the stockyards and the stink of dung worsened. The pens were packed with dozens of white and black dairy cows behind red metal fences. As the wolves drew closer, a restless stir passed among the herd and a chorus of nervous braying went up.

Morena smirked. "Beef. It's what's for dinner."

Victoria chuckled. "Not today."

Morena shaded her eyes against the afternoon sun and scanned the horizon. In the distance, the frightened cattle call alerted dogs and men to intruders. The sounds of barking and voices filled the air.

"We should've approached from downwind," Morena said.

"The main road comes in from that direction. If we have to run, the hunters will have a harder time tracking us over rough terrain." Victoria made a sweeping gesture that encompassed the forest beyond the cleared farmland.

"Unless they've got a helicopter. Hey, do you remember the time Rand swatted that helicopter out of the sky like it was a fly?"

Victoria's mouth turned up in an involuntary grin. "You weren't even there when it happened."

"Yeah, but I like hearing you talk about it," Morena said in a wistful voice.

"I'll tell it later." Distracted by a commotion from the buildings, Victoria stared into the distance. She could make out a white country farmhouse with a front porch and an enormous metal structure made of corrugated metal located closest to the pens. It had the look of an industrial barn. A large gray silo with a curved white cap was the tallest structure for miles around.

They came upon a dirt parking lot full of pickup trucks and SUVs. One vehicle in particular snared Victoria's attention. Her heart skipped, and her world dropped out from under her. *Daniel had loved that car.*

"Is that the Chevelle?" Morena asked in a breathy voice.

The bitter tang of sorrow filled Victoria's mouth. "Yes, that's it."

The top was down on the two-door convertible. The red paint and polished chrome shone in the brilliant sunlight. The black wall tires looked new and clean. The muscle car had been parked outside Sawyer's hotel room, and her reaction had been the same then. The overwhelming tide of memories threatened to drown her. She shook her head to clear her mind.

Priorities. Keep 'em straight. Her head had to be in the game.

"Look, puppies," Morena said in a lighthearted tone.

A pack of mixed breed dogs appeared on the far end of the dirt lot. They charged nearer but then skidded to a frightened halt once they caught the scent of wolves. Voices raised in shouts of alert, three, then five men gathered in the yard, all carrying firearms. A few wore military gear.

Victoria's mouth went dry. She spotted Skinner, Jake's second-in-command and a deadly hunter, and her stomach sank. From their bearing, these were seasoned hunters, not novices. More than she and Morena could handle alone. "Damn. You were right."

"Are we gonna run?" Morena took a step backward, already retreating in the direction they'd come from.

"Wait. I want to see what they do." Victoria held her ground. She licked her upper lip, considering while the orderly group assumed defensive positions. At least they didn't take cover alongside buildings and fence posts. Her sensitive hearing picked up fragments of conversation.

The man closest to Victoria addressed his companion in Spanish. "*Ella es la loba.*"

"*She is the wolf,*" Morena translated. "I was right. It's a trap."

"Maybe." Victoria's adrenaline surged, causing her muscles to bunch in anticipation of an upcoming confrontation. Turning her head, she scanned the area once again. Where the hell was Sawyer?

"There's no maybe about it! Shouldn't we run?"

"They'll start shooting if we turn and run. Stay calm."

"Calm?" Morena squawked.

"Cool." Victoria cast a worried glance toward the girl, praying to Freya the teenager retained her self-control. A terrified werewolf rampaging through cattle and armed men spelled disaster.

"I'm calm. I'm cool. Ice." Morena's throat contracted as she swallowed convulsively. Her breathing and heart rate shot through the roof. "I'm ice."

"Hold your positions!" Moving at a jog, Sawyer appeared up ahead. He deported himself with the easy confidence of a natural-born leader, and the men around him responded to his authority. Even Skinner's body language altered, demonstrating deference in posture and gaze to the Hunter King's son.

Sawyer wore a blue shirt that clung to his muscular torso like a second skin. The short sleeves revealed well-defined arms and a stylized dagger done in black ink on his right bicep. Daniel had the same symbol. The hunters employed the tattoo as a badge of brotherhood and belonging.

As Sawyer drew closer, his pace dropped to a jog and he smiled as he called out a greeting. "Hey."

"Hi." Her hand rose and then fell. Victoria breathed a sigh of relief. A crazy tumble of emotions suffused her: excitement, relief, and pleasure. She turned toward Morena who stood three paces behind her.

"Whoa." Morena stared at her in astonishment. "You really do have a thing for him! I was kidding."

Victoria frowned. "I do *not* have a thing for him. I don't even like him." *Much.*

"Oh, really?" The teen's brow lifted.

Victoria huffed. "He tried to kill me! More than once."

"Some boys throw rocks."

"Sawyer throws hand grenades."

The dirt crunched beneath Sawyer's feet as he neared. He stopped a couple paces from her. "It was one time."

"Once is all it takes." Victoria shot him a challenging glance and stepped close to Morena so she could protect the teenager if things took a violent turn. Her voice dropped to a whisper for the girl's ears alone, "We're going with him because I can't walk away from this. I need you to stay close and follow my lead. Can you do that for me?"

Bright-eyed, Morena nodded. "Yes."

"Is everything all right?" Sawyer's impatient demand intruded on their conversation.

"Yeah, we're fine." Victoria swung toward him and met his gaze. She got caught up in the warm chocolate-brown of his eyes. Her breath caught in her throat, and her heart hit a staccato beat. Her involuntary reaction to his physical presence made her uncomfortable. He exhibited the traits of a strong Alpha: authority, confidence, courage, and leadership. She already admired him as a skilled enemy. Further entanglements with an inappropriate male were the last thing she wanted or needed.

He cleared his throat. "What's wrong then?"

"Morena doesn't trust you."

"Better to be feared than loved, I guess." Sawyer almost smiled. His mouth turned up at the corners, and his nostrils flared as his head cocked. A strand of blond bangs fell over his eye.

Her finger twitched, and she quelled the impulse to reach for that irritating piece of hair. She adopted a taunting tone. "What's with all of the hunters, Sawyer? Were you feeling insecure? Is one she-wolf more than you can handle?"

His smile vanished. "My father brought them."

Her mouth went dry. "I see. Should I feel flattered?"

"They're his men, and he's feeling paranoid. I can't say I blame him for being cautious, all things considered." Sawyer offered more information than was requested. From his tone, he wasn't much happier about it than she was.

Victoria shifted her stance, glancing uneasily toward the silent audience of hunters. "You have to understand, I have mixed feelings about just walking into what looks like an obvious trap. If you still want me dead, you should have to work for it."

He scowled. "It isn't a trap."

"Easy for you to say," she said in a distinctly sour tone. Too many competing odors filled the area, and she doubted her ability to catch him in a lie over the stench of cattle.

"I'm not armed." Sawyer held up his hands to make his point.

"No, but everyone else is." She cast a pointed glance toward the hunters.

He sighed, and his head jerked toward the large main building. "Are you gonna come up and talk to my father? He's waiting over by the grain silo."

She stepped nearer to him. The top of her head came to the middle of his chest, but she was close enough to rip out his throat, to feel the warmth radiating off his skin, to scent the rush of his adrenaline, and hear the throb of his heart. Still, she scented no fear from him, only intense excitement. He took hold of her elbow.

She laid one hand on his forearm and stroked her fingertips across the rough hair on the back of his arms. Power spilled from her, creating an electrostatic crackle where they touched.

Gooseflesh rose on his forearms and Sawyer sucked in a sharp breath. He bent to whisper in her ear. "Are you coming onto me? Because I usually hold out until at least the second date."

She rolled her eyes. "Slut."

He smiled, showing teeth. "I'm a guy."

"Ah yes, one of the simple people."

Fire lit his eyes. "You're a tease."

She chuckled. "And you're an easy target."

He stared at her intently. "It's not a trap. You have my word."

She stood on her toes and tugged him down to her. He obliged and bent. Mouth close to his ear, she exhaled so her breath stirred his hair. His jaw worked, and he swallowed, Adam's apple bobbing. A tremor traveled the length of his body.

"Say it so I can smell the truth."

"It's not a trap." His heart rate, respiration, and scent remained constant, indicating he spoke the truth. No human, no matter how skilled a liar, could have deceived her without some minor fluctuation in physical response betraying them. There were too many tells.

She believed him. Common sense told her to release him, to end the ridiculous, reckless flirtation. But his earthy odor reminded her so much of Daniel, her heart ached. All she wanted to do was close her eyes and get lost in the illusion. To pretend for just a few minutes her lover still lived.

Using him would be wrong. Unfair. With an act of will, she released him and stepped back. "Let's go."

"Right," Sawyer muttered and then headed away with ground eating strides. After a second, Victoria hurried to catch up with Morena on her heels.

"My father's men will maintain a distance of two hundred feet at all times," Sawyer said. "We're meeting in the open yard near the silo."

Still within easy range of a scoped rifle, but there was no point in arguing. The concession was the best deal she'd get. Swallowing an instinctive protest, she asked, "You'll be present?"

"Yeah, I'll be there." The tightness in Sawyer's voice served to ratchet up the tension instead of alleviating it.

Walking together in a loose group, they approached the towering grain silo and the adjacent open area. A wooden pen packed full of cattle bordered the pathway which led to an industrial barn. The odor of cow manure and the buzz of flies hung over the entire area.

"It stinks," Morena complained. "I'm going to puke."

"Don't," Victoria said. "If you can't handle the smell, then please go wait by the cars."

Grumbling, Morena stuck with her Alpha.

As they neared, the cattle grew restless, perhaps detecting the wolves in their midst. The herd brayed, creating a noisy din. The heavy animals stomped about within their enclosures, colliding with the fences so hard the wood groaned.

The imposing figure of Jake Barrett waited in the silo's shade.

Standing with one boot propped on the lowest ladder rung, he cradled a double-barreled rifle with a black walnut stock in his arms. The older man bore a marked resemblance to his son. The Arizona sun had weathered his skin to tanned leather. His short hair and scruffy beard were salt-and-pepper. His broad shoulders and powerful arms matched the rest of his stout build.

The Hunter King. Master of the Hunt. He had many nicknames, not all of them polite.

Across the yard, the man pinned her with his penetrating stare, and a shadow fell over her soul. Rumors purported him to be invincible. He suffered fatal injuries but didn't die. Victoria's mother once said Jake Barrett must be blessed or cursed by the gods. Either way, men pledged their undying loyalty to him. Monsters feared him. To underestimate him meant certain death.

The sight of her sworn enemy made her stop in her tracks. A low growl trembled in her throat. Conflicting emotions ripped through her—anger, hatred, and hurt. So many people were dead because of him. Just a few months ago, she'd sworn to kill the man. Her most soulful desire involved ripping open his ribcage with her bare claws and tearing out his still beating heart.

"Victoria." Jake dropped his foot to the ground and shouldered his rifle with its carrying strap.

"Barrett." Victoria choked on the growl and struggled to achieve an even tone. Behind her, Morena produced a faint whimper and crowded closer to her Alpha.

"I wasn't expecting you to show." His stance remained relaxed but alert. He radiated supreme confidence, power so potent his aura presented as a slate gray wall.

"I almost didn't," Victoria said with an uneasy glance at Sawyer. He stood beside her, not touching, but close enough that she took a measure of comfort from his presence. If for no other reason, he could serve as a convenient shield.

An unsettled expression crossed Jake's countenance. His clear eyes saw far too much. "You look good. You've got a glow about you."

"Thanks." Victoria aborted a reflexive gesture to cross protective arms over her stomach. Death did not scare her. Jake Barrett terrified her. Abruptly, she realized the extent of her arrogance, having placed her unborn child in danger.

Brittle silence descended. She stared into Jake's implacable face, trying to discern any hint of the man's disposition. His impenetrable guise gave away nothing, and she refused to show weakness by making the first move.

"Fuck," Sawyer muttered. He paced closer to his father, restless and abrupt. "Damn it, Dad. I didn't drag the two of you out here to have a staring contest."

Jake's brow knit, and he glanced at his son. "Since you're always so quick to ask first, shoot later, where do you suggest we start, Son?"

Flushing, Sawyer's mouth dropped open, and he looked like he'd just swallowed a wasp.

Despite the dire circumstances, Victoria choked on a chuckle. Sawyer's ability to provoke an incendiary reaction from his father struck her as incredibly funny. Fathers and sons. Mothers and daughters. Apparently, some things were common to all families.

"Let's start with the dead," Victoria said. "It's why we're here."

Both hunters turned to her.

"Victoria," Morena whispered, tugging at her Alpha's shirt.

Frowning, Victoria waved her hand behind her back to shush the girl.

An indefinable glimmer shone in Jake's eyes. "Fair enough. My boy is dead, and you're the only one with the answers."

Victoria's lips curled in a silent snarl. "I could say the same. Jasper was only fifteen years old. You took him hostage and murdered him. You're a monster, Jake Barrett."

Sawyer flinched, and his shoulders slumped. His reaction aroused her curiosity, but Victoria didn't dare divert her attention from Jake.

A flush stained Jake's throat and crept toward his face. "I didn't mean that boy harm. I realized too damn late the mistake I'd made in nabbing him."

"Is that how you apologize for a dead child?" Victoria snapped her jaws together, gnashing her teeth in anger.

"I'm sorry about the boy." Unflinching, Jake held her gaze. "I shouldn't have taken him. I only wanted the truth about how Daniel died, and it was the only sure way of gaining your cooperation."

She thought his words rang true. Her face twisted as she fought the sting of a guilty conscience and a broken heart. Dredging up the past made her relive the excruciating loss, but some truths needed to be spoken. "I wanted to tell you in Albuquerque. All you had to do was ask. Instead, you took a boy hostage, and his death is on you."

Jake took an aggressive step. His tone contained sharp accusation. "Let's not forget my son is dead."

Grief suffused her, threatening her ragged composure. A hand closed on her throat, and her heart ached in her breast. For Jasper, for Rand, for Daniel, for Arik, for everyone else she loved and lost.

"True enough," Victoria said. "Daniel's death is on

me."

"You freely admit it." His hands flexed. He looked angry enough to kill her where she stood. The set of the hunter's head and shoulders brought to mind a gun-slinging outlaw from the Old West. Her imagination supplied a missing cowboy hat and dusty leather chaps.

Behind Victoria, Morena quivered. The teen's voice hissed in her ear. "Victoria!"

Victoria reached behind her and caught Morena's hands in her own. She held tight to her Omega, willing the girl to be quiet through the pack bond. "Yes, I freely admit it. I blame myself for failing to save Daniel. I blame you for failing to protect Jasper when you should have."

"It sounds like there's no shortage of blame to go around." Jake's tone contained bitter finality. "I want to know how my son died."

Victoria's blood ran cold. Jake Barrett had said the exact same thing to her, word for word, in Albuquerque when he'd taken Jasper hostage. For the first time, she realized the demand wasn't an accusation of murder. Suddenly, the conflict took on a whole new light, including connotations she'd never considered before.

She stared at him. "You knew Daniel and I were seeing each other."

Eyes narrowed, he shook his head. "I suspected Daniel had a girl. He was disappearing over weekends, refusing to talk about where he was spending his time. He was a grown man, so I stayed out of his business. But no, I didn't know it was you."

Victoria bristled. "We were keeping our affair a secret but not from my parents or my pack. They knew I was dating a hunter. No, we had to be sneaky lest the vaunted Jake Barrett find out his son was dating a she-wolf."

The Hunter King imposed a strict mandate on his people—no socializing with the Storm Pack outside business. As allies, they hunted together, fought side by side in defense of their overlapping territory, but fraternization was forbidden. There were no BBQs, no holiday picnics, and absolutely no dating. That was until Victoria and Daniel had broken all of the rules.

Jake scowled, and his voice grated like gravel. "Is it true a vampire murdered Daniel?"

"Yes." Victoria's shoulders slumped, and her heart ached with the bitterness of her failure to protect her lover. "We went after a vamp nest. We thought we'd killed all of them, but there was one hiding. He attacked Daniel and then ran."

"Was my son bitten?"

The question cut Victoria to the quick. She blinked, fighting to suppress the hot tears which threatened to drown her. The crushing pressure on her chest increased until she wanted to scream. "Yes. His throat wasn't just torn. It was gone. Given a lesser injury or the help of my pack, I might've healed him."

"Sawyer said you were covered head to toe in dried blood when you brought his body home," Jake said in a gentle voice that scared her worse than any angry outburst.

"*Victoria!*" Morena hissed.

Victoria winched and ignored the girl. Later, she would have strong words with Morena about inappropriate interruptions, but for the moment, the man before her demanded her undivided attention. She met his steely gaze even as her stomach roiled. "Daniel died in my arms."

"Why did you decapitate my son's corpse, Victoria? Why were there claw marks on his throat and chest?" Jake's mouth curled around a snarl, and at last, his deadly predatory nature peered past the facade. "You mutilated Daniel's body. It's no wonder Sawyer tried to kill you."

Anger ripped through Victoria, and she bared her

teeth, allowing her wolf to surface so golden light spilled from her eyes. "You know why!"

"Say it," Jake demanded. "I want to hear the words."

"Dad, take it easy," Sawyer interrupted, but his warning went unheeded.

Victoria shot forward and grabbed the front of Jake's shirt, hauling him to her. She roared in his face. "He turned. I tried to heal him and failed. After his heart stopped, I sat there holding him, rocking, praying."

Jake's big hands seized her shoulders, and his strong fingers dug in with a punishing force. His furious gaze contained hatred and accusation. "You failed my son twice. You didn't have his back during a hunt. Then you allowed him to rise as one of *them*."

In the face of his condemnation, Victoria flinched and released her grip on his shirt. Her anger wilted, and her guilt rose. "Yes, that's true. I should have used a machete to remove his head, but I waited too long. He rose as a vampire and went for my throat. I had to use my claws to behead him."

The gruesome memory of ripping apart her lover's corpse with her bare hands filled her mind, eclipsing all else. Her gorge rose, threatening to spew the contents of her stomach. Jake must have seen the nausea, because he released her shoulders and took a hasty step back. The rasp of heavy breathing filled the air. They stood across from each other, panting hard, unsure of what came next.

Eventually, Victoria released a shaky breath. "It happened because I loved him too much, not because I was careless. I realized my failure. I brought Daniel's body home. I intended to explain, but Sawyer started shooting, and I had no choice but to run."

Jake exhaled with a long, low hiss. His shoulders slumped in an expression of defeat difficult to look upon in such a fierce man. "Sawyer was in the grip of a blind rage following his brother's death. There was no reasoning with him..." He shook his head. "I thought there had to be a credible explanation for what had happened, but then the explosions went off at the airfield, and everything spiraled out of control—"

Victoria blinked. "Explosions? There was more than one?"

Shouting, Morena cut through their discussion. "Does anyone smell that? I mean, aside from the cow shit?"

Victoria swung on her Omega. "Smell what?"

Morena took a quick, startled step back. "Bitter. Like almonds. Maybe it's cyanide?"

"Shit." Sawyer's bellow contained fear and urgency. "There's a bomb."

Victoria spun to the hunter in time to catch the concerned exchange between father and son. Just the sight of alarm on Jake's face sent her pulse skyrocketing as adrenaline surged through her body.

"Clear the area!" Sawyer shouted, waving his arm toward the other hunters who immediately acted on his orders. He lurched into a sprint, heading toward the parking lot.

"Run!" Lunging, Victoria smacked the middle of Morena's back. Her strength of will enforced the command through the pack bond.

The long-legged teenager bolted. In a heartbeat, she passed Sawyer and reached the edge of the parking lot.

Victoria hesitated. Her head twisted as she glanced toward Jake. He stood close to the silo, as still and calm as the eye of the storm. His hand pressed against his chest, covered his heart.

Glassy eyes. Parted lips.

Wrong, wrong, wrong. Everything about him screamed wrongness. Right down to his absolute stillness. Her gaze locked on his chest. Then she noticed the blossom of red staining his shirt.

He staggered backward and collided with the silo.

She hadn't heard a gunshot, but her gut said Jake Barrett had been shot. Victoria ducked her head in case the sniper fired on another target. Her sense of self-preservation clashed with her instinct to protect those weaker than herself.

The earth shook, and the sky caught fire.

A fireball burst through the side of the silo at the base. A burning plume of flame exploded outward, licking at Victoria's head. She threw up her arms to protect her face. The blistering heat seared her skin and stung her eyes, and she inhaled thick, black smoke. A coughing fit convulsed her lungs. The boom blasted her eardrums. She threw herself to the ground and landed face down in the dirt.

The air burned.

As swiftly as the blaze expanded, the broad swath of flame retreated into the main body. A thick column of dark smoke rose into the sky. The flaming tower cast an orange-red glow beneath the afternoon sun.

Victoria turned onto her side. She blinked while her vision cleared. No second explosion followed. Her accelerated healing kicked in, and the ringing in her ears receded so she could hear more than the roar of the conflagration.

From nearby corrals, the air rang with the bellows of wounded cattle and the stamping of hooves hammering the ground. Fences groaned as the massive beasts collided with railings. Farther away, men shouted indistinct words to one another.

Twenty feet from her, Sawyer lay face down, unmoving, in the dirt. Heart in her throat, Victoria crawled toward him. The scent of fresh blood pricked her nostrils. She turned him over. A red splotch stained the shoulder of his shirt.

She grasped the material on both sides of the wound, intending to rip fabric and expose the wound for inspection. "Sawyer, you're hurt."

Sawyer caught her wrist. His eyes were glassy, a thousand-yard stare. His voice rasped, "I'm fine."

Victoria rolled her eyes heavenward. "Freya, save me from stupid males."

Freya's golden voice filled her mind, the silky caress of divine laughter. *A feat beyond even my powers, Priestess.*

"Ha ha, very funny," Victoria muttered.

"Where's my father?"

"There." She pointed to where Jake lay close to the fire, his rifle a couple inches from his hand.

Sawyer grimaced as he lifted his head to look toward the silo.

A sharp *crack* split the air as wooden railings busted under the mass of terrified cattle. The fence toppled and terrified animals burst through the opening. Following the herd leader, cattle poured from the enclosure. Their heaving sides were coated in blood and sweat, and their pounding hooves rolled like thunder.

The stampede turned toward Jake.

"Dad!" Crying out, Sawyer lurched to his feet. He ran to his father, straight into the path of danger.

"Down the rabbit hole." Summoning her wolf, Victoria charged after the hunter and shifted while in motion. Snow-white fur sprang up across her skin, her ears elongated to points, and her teeth sharpened to deadly canines. Her lower face pushed into a muzzle. The forced transformation caused bone-jarring pain while her torso and limbs lengthened and thickened, and the reforming bones distended her skin. She acquired extra height and weight. Her clothing ripped apart, and her claws shredded her shoes. To retain the use of her hands and rudimentary speech, she halted the change midway.

As Sawyer reached his father, she shot past him and placed herself between the hunters and the herd, stopping in the path of the lead animal. Lowering her head, she roared her dominance, focusing her attention on the frontrunner.

She smacked the key steer on the side of the head, and her claws left deep gouges. The forceful blow knocked the animal over. Squalling, he crashed to the ground and was trampled beneath the hooves of other cattle. Several reared and toppled. Further frightened, the stampede parted in the center and diverted about them.

Tilting her head back, Victoria released the fierce howl of a hunting wolf. Flanks heaving, the herd fled faster. The animals stank of panic, and an excited quiver passed through her body. Predatory instincts aroused, her wolf leapt with excitement, wanting to give chase.

The black and white cows were a mouthwatering temptation. Tasty, easy kills. Steak tartare. Cheeseburgers on the hoof.

"Victoria!" Sawyer shouted.

Stomach rumbling, she cast a final longing glance at the retreating flank steaks and heaved a regretful sigh before she swung back to Sawyer.

Sawyer knelt with open hands pressed to his father's chest, covering a gaping wound. "My father is dying. Can you heal him?"

CHAPTER EIGHT

Sessrúmnir, Freya's hall in Fólkvangr

"Impossible! Odin must know of your treachery."

Loki shrugged. "So what if Odin knows. He doesn't seem to care so long as the Aesir can point to their scapegoat and boast of how the defiant Trickster has been punished. It's all politics and appearances, smoke and mirrors."

He spoke casually of his own torture, but Freya understood the horrific nature of his punishment. The longer she considered, the more her revulsion with him blossomed. She had not forgotten or forgiven his involvement in the murder of Odin's son, Baldur, so long ago. The crime was the reason he had been punished. For all of his ability to present a beautiful facade, Loki remained the ugliest, most vile creature known to her.

She sneered. "You are mad."

He *tsked*. "So judgmental. I'm not mad. Of course, I've never been exactly sane, but calling me a stark raving lunatic is harsh."

"That tormented aspect is warping the whole. I perceive the changes within you even if you cannot. Darkness consumes you, Loki. You are fooling only yourself."

He blinked, and then his gaze went out of focus as if staring inward. A moment later, those sharp eyes locked on her face. His smile sent chills down her spine. "I'm nobody's fool."

Midgard

They said the Hunter King couldn't be killed, and Victoria had always believed it. Could the rumors be lies? Was the man mortal after all?

Uncertain, she approached the two men, father and son, while the inferno raged a short distance away. The sooty smoke stung her eyes and clogged her nose, and the unpleasant recollection of fighting Sawyer in a burning building in Montana filled her memory.

Despite her monstrous appearance, Sawyer's face held calm acceptance. No disgust. No fear. Only relief and gratitude. Sharp teeth made speech difficult, so she undertook a rapid shift to human that left her nude. Mentally, she cursed the decision to leave her change of clothing in the SUV.

As she approached the two men, Freya's voice issued a dark warning. *Take care, my priestess. This is a dangerous man who goes to great lengths to protect his secrets.*

Victoria faltered mid-stride, frozen with one foot suspended midair. *Are you saying I shouldn't help him, Goddess?*

Skinner jostled Victoria aside in his haste to get to the Barretts. Breathing hard, he skidded to a halt and directed a question to Sawyer. "How bad is he?"

"Bad." Sawyer bent with open hands pressed to his father's chest, covering a gaping wound over the breastbone. "I can't tell if he's breathing, and I can't find a pulse."

"Is his heart damaged?" Skinner asked.

Sawyer shook his head. "I can't tell."

"We need to get him away from the silo before the whole damn thing comes down," Skinner said.

"Give me a hand." Sawyer shot to his feet and secured a hold on his father's shoulders while Skinner took Jake's feet. Together, the two men carried him farther from the burning structure and then laid him down again.

Goddess? Why are you silent?

Skinner's proximity filled Victoria with hesitation and doubt. In Albuquerque, she had healed his severe injury and saved his life. Seeing the two men working together left her wondering. Had Skinner murdered Jasper? Was he the man Sawyer was protecting?

Two other men joined Skinner. They had the look of veteran hunters—scars and gristle, flinty stares and not a hint of fear. Hands locked on their rifles, they regarded the she-wolf with suspicious gazes. The combined aroma of aggression and hostility were noticeable even over the manure and smoke.

Victoria retreated but allowed her perception to slip into the spiritual plane, seeking a glimpse of Jake's soul. His body retained a dull aura—affirmation his soul remained within his body. Without a pack bond, she was too far away to tell how severe his injuries were or if he still lived.

She moved to get a better look at her potential patient. Watching while a man died went against her every instinct as a healer. Shouting in her mind, Victoria reached for her divine connection with Freya. *Goddess, please. Grant me your wisdom. I am your priestess.*

"Damn it, let her pass," Sawyer snapped. When the two men still hesitated, he shot to his feet, eyes blazing. "That's an order."

As quick as a whip, the hunters stepped aside. Following a blink of surprise, even Skinner moved out of the way to clear a path to Jake Barrett.

Skinner edged closer to Sawyer. "Do you trust her?"

"She saved your life in Albuquerque and reattached my severed fingers," Sawyer answered in a low voice. "Yes, I trust her."

"Hell." Skinner spoke in a way that sounded like a cross between an exclamation and a prayer.

Fine. If you're not going to answer me, then I'll do what I think is best. Fuming over Freya's uncharacteristic silence, Victoria stomped past the men and knelt beside the downed hunter. The exposed skin of his face and arms was burned and his entire shirt scorched.

Relying first on traditional measures, Victoria confirmed that Jake had no discernible pulse or respiration. She stripped away his burnt, bloody shirt, ripping the fabric rather than wrestling with the garment. He had a heavy build, a muscular torso and thick limbs, as strong and as fit as a man half his age. Silvery lines with raised ridges and blotches from old gunshot wounds covered his bare chest. A canvas for a lifetime of injuries, he had more damaged skin than unmarred.

Interestingly enough, three tattoos remained intact despite the surrounding damage to his hide, and she suspected magic protected the symbols. One was the stylized dagger hunters wore on their bicep as a badge of brotherhood. The second were two words over his heart: *Absit omen.* It was a protective invocation, translated — *May what is said not come true.*

The final tattoo, a double-sided dagger with a straight blade, stood apart from the others. A larger version of the membership symbol, it ran the length of his forearm. The image had a raised textured surface, and the surrounding flesh puckered and burned as if molten metal had seared his skin. She'd seen the weapon drawn once before. In Jake Barrett's hand, the tattoo became a physical weapon, a knife with a molten blade.

Rumors abounded regarding the dagger's nature. Some said it had once belonged to a giant, others a demon. Once drawn, the knife couldn't be sheathed until it was used to kill. Once the Hunter King chose a target, the Fates cut that creature's life thread before combat even commenced.

Fresh shrapnel injuries riddled his chest, but a severe wound over his heart concerned her the most. Placing her palm over his breast, she tried for the spiritual connection that allowed her to utilize her healing magic and evaluate the extent of his injuries. She reached and found... *Nothing*.

Skinner's deep voice cut through the thick din of background noise. His voice held an undercurrent of pointed accusation. "Sawyer, did you set that bomb?"

Sawyer barked out a reply. "What the fuck? No! How crazy do you think I am? Never mind. Don't answer that."

Victoria blinked and lifted her hand, giving it an experimental shake. A shower of sparks rose into the air, and the radiant aura of her healing powers poured from her palm. But when she reached for her patient again, the halo dimmed.

"Was anyone else hurt?" Sawyer asked.

"No, only Jake. Everyone else was clear," Skinner said. "This had to be another assassination attempt on your father."

"We've definitely been set up. Who had access to the farm prior to the meeting? Who knew we were coming?" Sawyer asked.

Silence.

Then Skinner growled. "Andy Chart. Goddamn son of a bitch. He came up early this morning ahead of everyone else."

"Where the hell is Chart?" Sawyer's boots stomped in the dirt. "Skinner, go find that bastard and bring him back. I want him alive."

"We'll get him," Skinner's voice grew distant as he joined the men in the yard. "Everyone, gather round."

Despite his tanned complexion, Jake's flesh acquired a translucent texture, and ancient runes rose and writhed just below the surface of his skin. A mystical barrier kept Victoria from connecting with Jake. As she channeled more power into her magic, the resistance increased as if the arcane magic fed off her efforts.

A repulsive jolt slammed into her, and Victoria's entire body convulsed. Skin crawling, she jerked her hand away and rocked back onto her haunches. A panicked feeling of wrongness filled her. She'd never encountered anything like this before. Panting, she ceased her attempts to heal him, so the magic emanating from her hand faded.

His soul remained, but his body was dead. How was it even possible? She'd witnessed the like once before but understood it no better than now.

"Victoria? How is he?" Sawyer asked in a voice brittle with stress. He returned to a crouch across from her. His brow knit, his lips peeled back over his teeth in a grimace. His gaze swept her body, and for the first time he appeared to register her nudity. Without a word, he took off his T-shirt and offered it to her.

"Thanks." Victoria accepted and pulled the garment over her head. It fell to mid-thigh, far more modest than a nightshirt. "I can't detect a heartbeat or respiration, but his aura indicates his soul hasn't departed his body. I'm not even sure why he's still alive, but I suspect it's due to sheer cussedness."

"Can you help him?"

Victoria pinned Sawyer with an accusing scowl. With a quick sweep of her hand, she indicated the runes. "Your father is warded with runic magic I've only seen practiced one place—the halls of Valhalla."

Sawyer shut down. His eyes shuttered, and his lips compressed. "What about his heart? Is it damaged?"

His evasion annoyed her to no end. "What happens if his heart is damaged, Sawyer? Is that what kills him permanently?"

Stubborn silence greeted her.

"Fine. Keep your secrets. If you get him to a medical center, the doctors may be able to help him. Good luck convincing them that a legally dead patient needs a heart transplant." Victoria rose to her feet and stepped back. She glanced around for Morena, but the teenager wasn't within sight. After that explosion, she wouldn't be surprised if the girl had run all of the way home.

Sawyer surged to his feet, and his hand lashed out and caught her wrist. "You have to heal him."

Her blue eyes shone with anger and her mouth formed a flat line. She squared her shoulders. "No."

Sawyer looked mad enough to spit bullets. His grip constricted, and the hot musk of testosterone exuded danger. A violent storm raged across his aura, and his voice dropped to a deadly soft pitch. "No?"

Who are you to deny me, wolf?

Startled, Victoria blinked. Not Freya's voice. A man's assertive, mesmerizing baritone. Authoritative and compelling. She shuttered her expression, attempting to disguise her unease.

"Why?" Sawyer asked.

She scowled and yanked her arm from his grip. "We're at war, so I have no obligation here to aid an ally. Your father is responsible for the death of a boy who was under my protection, and even my goddess is advising me to be careful. Healing outsiders violates my people's customs, customs that I've already ignored once to repair your hand. Now you're refusing to answer even the simplest questions. I'm done."

Fists unclenching as though an act of will, he lowered his arms. His father's blood covered his hands. Agony filled those rich brown eyes, so much like his brother's. Pleading gentled his voice. "Heal him. Please. I'm begging you."

Victoria cringed at having to witness such a proud adversary humbled. The extent of his suffering tore at her heart, and made holding onto her conviction extremely difficult. Glancing down, she noticed the blood on her hands for the first time. Her resolve to walk away faltered.

He used her silence to press his advantage. He caught her hands, and that tenuous empathic bond between them flared to life. "I'm sorry. This is my fault. All of it from the first shot fired to the boy's death. If my father dies because of me—"

The unexpected assault of his guilt and anguish overwhelmed her but not nearly as much as his ability to evoke pack magic. Not even Daniel had possessed such a talent. Seeking to sever the connection, Victoria allowed power to touch her voice. "Sawyer, stop."

He released her and fell silent. From the look on his face, he wanted to argue. As usual, he refused to give up. A word tripped off his tongue. "*Einvigi.*"

Incredulous, Victoria's eyes widened. "You want to engage me in single combat?"

He huffed in surprise. "No, that's not the right term. Damn it all to hell—"

She chuckled. "You just might if you keep tossing words about without knowing their meanings. What are you trying to say? Try using English."

His embarrassed grumble resembled a growl. "I'll pay blood price. Whatever it takes to satisfy your honor. Just agree to heal my father before it's too late."

Victoria eyed him. She had to give him credit for his resourcefulness. "Blood price hasn't been practiced for centuries, Sawyer. Besides, I don't want your life, and I doubt you have the requisite livestock. How many goats *do* you own?"

He stared as if trying to figure out whether she was kidding. "Name your price."

The grinding of his teeth grated on her nerves. She sighed, and her head rolled. She rubbed her neck with one hand, closing her eyes, suddenly weary. Composing a prayer, she made one more attempt to reach

Freya. *Goddess? Do you forbid me to heal Jake Barrett?*

Following a brief, brittle silence, Freya replied, *Do what you must, Victoria.*

Victoria opened her eyes and focused on him. "My price for healing your father is the Chevelle."

Sawyer winced. "My father just might kill me."

"Not if he's dead."

With an abrupt motion, Sawyer extended his hand. "Deal."

They shook, and then Victoria returned to where Jake rested on his back. She sank onto her knees beside him, and studied the canvas of runes. The arcane symbols of power produced a bone-deep resonance, a powerful warding spell that repelled her on a primal level. Without the help of her goddess, she had no chance of breaking through. Even with it... Maybe not.

"There's no guarantee I'll succeed," she said.

"Try. You've got to try."

"Tell me what happens if I can't repair his heart."

He exhaled so his nostrils flared, and the column of his throat worked as he swallowed. "He dies," he said, voice rough and raw with emotion. "Without his heart, he won't heal."

Jake Barrett had an actual vulnerability. No wonder his son guarded the secret with such dogged determination.

"There, that wasn't so hard now, was it?" Victoria muttered. "Now, how am I going to get past the warding?"

She raked her patient with a critical gaze again. Her attention caught on the dagger tattoo on Jake's forearm and then shifted to the smaller version on his bicep the hunters used as a badge of membership. Sawyer bore the mark, as had Daniel. In combat, the symbol glowed, providing the hunter with augmented strength and stamina, not as powerful as a wolf, but greater than that of a normal man.

"Your tattoo." She extended her hand.

He glanced down, hesitating. "What about it?"

"It connects you to your father, right? Like an Alpha to the rest of the pack."

His brow knit. "We're not wolves."

She blew a strand of hair out of her eyes and waved her arm with pointed impatience. "That's a technicality and also irrelevant since the functionality is basically the same."

Sawyer surrendered his arm. "Did Daniel tell you about it?"

"Just a little. I think this may be my way around your father's wards. I'll bond with you and then follow your connection through to him." Grasping his forearm, she placed her other hand over the tattoo, and white light caressed his skin. The dormant magic inherent within the symbol activated, and heat rose against her palm. Mystical, spiritual pathways flared to life, creating an opening through Sawyer just as she'd suspected. At the end of a long, dark tunnel shone a blindingly brilliant star.

A monumental decision hung over her head like the blade of a scythe. If Jake Barrett was the source of that immense power, then the man was more dangerous than she'd ever imagined. Victoria hesitated, once again questioning the wisdom of what she was about to do. Did she really want to take such a huge risk? Freya's warning fed her uncertainty.

"What do you mean bond with me?"

"You'll be joined to me like the rest of my pack." The pack bond was intimate and substantial. Not necessarily unbreakable, but darn close. The idea of adding a hunter to their ranks, even temporarily, made her question her own judgment. But not as much as it should have, and that bothered her more. However, she thought the current circumstances were too urgent for further contemplation.

"What?" Sawyer demanded. His voice over-flowed with outrage. In the sunshine, his blond hair shone in a disarray of straight silk, falling about his face and shoulders. He had a smudge of soot across his fore-head and another on his cheek.

"It should only be temporary." Victoria bit her lower lip, adding a silent *I hope.* She doubted a tempo-rary bond would possess the resilience necessary to endure, and she was counting on their vehement dislike of one another to foster impermanence. After all, Sawyer despised her, and she disliked him. Somewhat.

He pinned her with his gaze. "What if it's not?"

She looked him straight in the eyes. "Do you want me to save your father or not? I'm not any happier with the prospect of having a hotheaded hunter join my pack. You're not even remotely suitable."

His mouth opened, and he looked like he wanted to argue. Then his mouth snapped shut, and he gave a sharp nod. "Do it."

"Goddess, forgive me. Here goes nothing." Victo-ria's hand slipped from Sawyer's arm and rested on his solid pectoral. She tried to ignore the rock hard muscles beneath his warm skin and dropped her other hand, palm down, onto Jake's breast. The steady throb of the son's heart provided a sharp contrast to the father's still corpse.

Concentrating, she summoned her magic and ini-tiated an empathic connection with him. She plunged headlong into an oppressive quicksand of guilt and grief. Shocked, she threw back her head, gasping for air. The blue eternity of sky filled her vision, and she strug-gled to get her bearings. She caught a brief glimpse into Sawyer's soul and recoiled from the torment he carried within. He mourned his brother's death and regretted the war, but his suffering surpassed her expectations.

Determined not to examine his spirit too closely, she located the mystical connection to his father and hurried along her journey. She sped down the long, narrow tunnel. Darkness pressed in upon her from all sides, and she would have lost her way if not for the bright beacon glowing on the other end.

Victoria emerged on a verdant carpet beneath cheerful morning sunshine. Blades bent and broke beneath her bare feet, releasing the sweet scent of grass. Blinking, she tilted her head to gaze up at the sparsely spaced trees which were thick of trunk, wide of limb, and dressed in the light-green foliage of early spring. Bird song animated the leaves, filling the meadow with a melody vibrant and joyful.

Nature's cathedral.

A shrill scream split the air, and the songbirds hushed. The deafening sound caused the earth to tremble and the trees to shake so a shower of leaves descended to the ground.

Hands cupped to the sides of her head, she pivoted on her heel and came face-to-face with Jake Barrett. He stood a few paces from her. Far too close for comfort, so she fell back, stumbling in her haste. Their gazes locked, and they stared.

The cry repeated twice more, then silence followed.

Victoria lowered her hands and waited for her ears to stop ringing. "What in Hel's name was that?"

Jake's lips twisted into an ironic smile that did nothing to settle her nerves. "Damn rooster won't stop crowing."

"Point me to it. I'll solve your chicken problem." Victoria snapped her teeth together to make her point.

He chuckled. "If only it were that easy."

"What is this place?"

"A dream." He sighed with longing. "A memory of a place I used to love."

"It's lovely." Victoria glanced around as an excuse to look elsewhere while she wondered how to broach the most sensitive and immediate issue—his damaged heart. "Do you have any sense of urgency at all?"

He chuckled. "Not at my age."

Her mouth was bone dry. Her fear remained active and vital. Who was he? A giant? Or a powerful sorcerer? Or maybe even a god? Mentally, she ruled out Thor, who lacked both the wit and the will to engage in such games. Not Loki. The game-playing certainly fit, but she'd have expected more cocky arrogance from the Trickster and also better fashion sense.

Jake chuckled as if he were privy to her thoughts. "You're pregnant."

The way he regarded her sent chills coursing down her spine, but Victoria refused to retreat any farther. She squared her shoulders and held her head high. "Yes."

He stepped closer, hand extended toward her abdomen. He came within millimeters of touching her as a vibrant orange glow emanated from his palm and washed across her stomach. Pleasant warmth formed deep in her belly.

"Daniel's not the father."

"I took a mate." His proximity made her maternal instincts scream. Her chills worsened to tremors. Through an act of will, she quelled the instinctive desire to knock his arm aside.

His eyes narrowed, and he frowned. "You claim to have loved my son, and yet you're mated to another within six months of his death?"

She stared him straight in the eyes and replied without apology. "My duty is to those under my protection and my bloodline. I must provide an heir. I would have loved to have had Daniel's child, but we weren't even engaged. I will do whatever I must to ensure the welfare of my pack."

He looked at her with an odd mix of curiosity

and speculation. "Such pragmatism is rare."

Offended, Victoria arched her brow. "In women?"

He withdrew his hand. "In anyone."

She cocked her head, staring at him. She tired of the games, the obvious skirting of the real issue—his true nature. If he intended to kill her to keep his secret, she was already dead. Marshalling her resolve, she went at him point blank. "Why haven't you used your power to heal yourself?"

His eyelids hooded. He said nothing.

She rolled her eyes. "Answering me isn't telling me anything I haven't figured out."

His jaw worked. "While I'm mortal, I'm limited to the abilities of my incarnate form. Healing isn't one of those gifts."

She nodded, thinking. "An avatar. Are you cut off, or have you chosen this?"

"Everything is a choice."

She smiled. "Niiice. Noncommittal, but still profound. Is the reason you didn't lower your wards the same as why you won't repair your own heart?"

He exuded absolute calm, complete focus. "My wards are still intact, so I know you didn't break them. How is it you're even here, wolf?"

Victoria took an involuntary step back. Her throat worked. "Sawyer."

"You used *my son* to get past my protections. Clever." The way he grated the words left no doubt, the man was furious beneath his impervious exterior.

She edged further from him even though she had nowhere to run. The dark tunnel had closed behind her. "Sawyer begged me to help. I couldn't have circumvented your wards without his cooperation."

His hand rose, fingers splayed, and his voice softened. "Relax, Victoria. I'm not angry with you."

"Coulda fooled me." She refused to lower her

guard on his word. The man's reputation as a merciless and unstoppable slayer preceded him.

"Today, we were set up in a manner similar to the day your parents died," he said. "After the attack at the air field, I thought the ambush might have been arranged by one of my enemies. I have many. Only no one knew about the meeting today except for a select handful of my people."

Following in the wake of Daniel's death and Sawyer's attack on her, Victoria's father had arranged to meet with Barrett at a private airstrip outside Phoenix. Most of her pack and a large number of hunters had attended. Ironically, both Victoria and Sawyer had been excluded from the event but for radically different reasons.

Victoria remained silent for a moment, putting two and two together, arriving at the logical explanation. Bile left a sour taste in her mouth. "You have a traitor in your organization."

From the look on Jake's face, he had already reached the same conclusion. "Yes, I reckon so. Someone wanted to break the alliance and put us at each other's throats."

"They succeeded," she said. "Sawyer thinks Andy Chart is your traitor. They're hunting him now."

"Chart." His face hardened. Those penetrating eyes gleamed like diamonds set in a stone mask. Somewhere, a Norn snipped a man's life thread short.

"Did he have access to the airfield prior to the meeting last December?"

Jake's nostrils flared. "Yeah, he did."

"So you really had nothing to do with the ambush?"

"On my honor, I had nothing to do with the explosions at the airfield that day." Jake's gaze remained steady, his scent strong with truthfulness.

"How many were there?"

"Three vehicles went up simultaneously, so they must have been on timers. They were loaded with silver scattershot. Your parents and members of your pack were hit, but just as many of my people were injured or killed."

"My parents were only injured. Not killed in the explosion." She glared, daring him to deny it. "They were killed by hunters with silver ammunition."

Anger suffused his face, a dark flush. "That's right, but it wasn't under my orders—" He bit off his sentence and then said, "Shooting started, and the violence spun out of control on both sides. I don't know who fired the first shot."

She arched a skeptical brow, challenging him. "I'm supposed to believe that the vaunted Hunter King lost control of his people?"

He bristled, but for once, she received the impression it wasn't directed at her. "Your father and I hunted together for thirty years. I wouldn't have attacked without provocation."

Her chin lifted. "When I visited Valhalla, my father defended you."

He smiled, showing teeth. "But not your mother?"

Victoria remained diplomatically quiet.

Jake chuckled. "Your mother never did like me."

Victoria ran a hand through her hair, pacing a circle. How far did this go? Had the attack on her and Daniel also been premeditated or an unfortunate coincidence? "This is a lot to take in all at once. Could Chart have been working alone?"

"Unlikely. The scope is too big for one man." From his expression, he looked deep in thought. "Besides, Chart isn't smart enough to pull off something like this alone."

"Do you think these bombs were assassination attempts?" The death of her parents had crippled her pack.

She imagined if Jake died today, his organization would be weakened and thrown into chaos.

"Yes, I do." He crossed his arms over his powerful chest. "This sordid affair has hurt my organization on multiple levels aside from the hunters who died," Jake admitted in a heavy voice. "Your father negotiated the original treaty and was instrumental in organizing the packs. The attack has devastated our defenses. When we went to war with the Storm Pack, we lost the help of *all* the packs."

She exhaled, a soft gust of surprise, and her eyes widened. Granted, she'd been out of touch with politics but— "All of them?"

He stared, scrutinizing her face as if trying to read her mind. "All of them."

She nodded, hesitant to ask her next question. But she had to know. "What happened to my parents' bodies?"

Regret crossed his face. "I had all of your peoples' bodies burned in accordance with your customs."

Victoria gulped. Her throat hurt, her heart ached. "Thank you for that."

"You're welcome." He squared his shoulders as if bracing for something.

She inhaled a sharp breath and held it.

"How's Daniel doing?" Jake asked. "While I'm mortal, I'm cut off—"

Terrible dread filled her, and she stuttered. "W-w-what do you mean?"

Holding infinity, those implacable eyes locked on her. He inhaled a huge draught of air, and the wind picked up, beating down on their heads. Leaves shook in the swaying branches. "My son's soul. It was your duty to escort Daniel to Valhalla, Valkyrie."

Victoria staggered as if struck. Her heart thundered in her ears. All of the blood drained from her face. "No."

Jake's brow drew together like twin swords. His voice acquired the rumble of thunder, and the forest shook. "What do you mean, *no*?"

Her hands gripped her head to stop it from flying off. "I had no way of knowing. He never said— He never even hinted—"

The sky darkened, and lightning flashed overhead. "No way of knowing what?"

Horrified, she shook her head, and hot tears coursed down her cheeks as the missing puzzle pieces fell into place. Her nightmare, the prophecy, Daniel's request that she go to his father. It all made sense.

"You didn't know he belonged in Valhalla because he never told you," Jake said, tone grim. "Because he was keeping my secrets."

She drew a soggy breath and scrubbed at her tears, humiliated by the display of weakness before her enemy. "I didn't know. When the light came after his death, I allowed his soul to be taken. At the time I thought he was going to his god, but now I know—he was stolen."

The harsh wind stole her tears. Gasping, her starved lungs failed to draw enough, leaving her feeling as if she were suffocating. "I've failed in my duty—"

As if seized by a sudden realization, Jake turned his face aside. "Your sister Valkyries wouldn't have come for him because you were present. It was the perfect trap."

"Daniel came to me in a dream the night before last. He told me his soul is imprisoned by the vampire who killed him. He said to go to you. I wasn't sure it was real, but I agreed to this meeting anyway." Shame clawed at her insides. The magnitude of her screw up left her stunned. A Valkyrie who failed to deliver a fallen warrior to Valhalla... If the gods stripped her of her title and cast her into the underworld, it would be precisely what she deserved.

The Hunter King focused on her. He glowed with wrath. "The loathsome creature dares use my son as bait."

"This is my fault." Horrible guilt consumed Victoria.

"No. This is no one's fault but the vile vampire who has manipulated, deceived, and attacked us." His voice surrounded her, the air and the earth speaking. The storm worsened, and lightning lanced from the sky in a bright arc that split a nearby tree.

Burning rage replaced Victoria's self-loathing, and her blood boiled. Her wolf rose, swift and sure, and peered out of her eyes. Her elongated canines pressed to the insides of her cheeks. A growl rumbled in her throat.

Jake's humanity fell away, revealing his true face. The terrible, glorious visage stared at her with a single, solid black eye. It spanned eternity, defined life and death.

"Sigföðr," she gasped in awe. She dropped to one knee before him, bowing her head out of respect and reverence.

His hand caught her elbow and drew her upright before him. His face appeared human again. "In this life, I am a man. Whether I'm your ally or your enemy, Victoria Storm, I wish to be treated with the respect due Jake Barrett. Nothing more, nothing less."

Victoria stared at him hard, wondering if he was serious, or if this was the sort of joke deities cracked right before they incinerated the hapless mortal who fell for it. Jake Barrett was known as a man of honor, and second-guessing him struck her as dangerous. Her practical side preferred to take him at his word.

She nodded. "Fine. Then you and I still have a matter of honor to settle between us, Hunter King. We can set our differences aside until Daniel's soul is safe, but I'm not done with you. Not by a long shot."

He flashed a feral, toothy grin. "I wouldn't have

it any other way. Now heal my heart, Valkyrie. We're going to war."

Incanting, Jake spoke the ancient runes which lowered his wards. The world around them transformed. The forest became a rocky isle at the center of a stormy gray sea. White crested swells like snow-capped mountains towered overhead. Forked lightning lanced across the sky. Thunder shook the world. Frozen sleet pounded down upon their heads, slicking her blonde hair against her skull and soaking her to the skin.

Awe-inspiring.

The real world returned—the heat of the sun and fire, the beat of her heart and the press of her hands upon his bloody chest. Concentrating, Victoria extended her awareness to his body's life pattern. Her stomach dropped at the extensive amount of shrapnel embedded within his torso, including the bullet buried in his heart.

"Is it bad?" Jake's voice carried through her mind as if he shouted across a great distance.

She swallowed. "Yes. The aorta is severed, and the muscle is destroyed. Death should have been instantaneous."

"Can you fix it?"

She licked her dry lips. "On my own? Maybe. If my pack was here, or we were within my territory..."

"Call on your goddess," Jake commanded.

Was it her imagination or did he sound disgruntled? Victoria sighed and reached through divine channels for Freya. "My Lady of the Vanir, I pray for your blessing. Please, heal this man."

She waited but no answer was forthcoming. Brittle tension filled the air, growing more uncomfortable with each passing second. All too aware of Jake's silent, condemning presence, she tried again. "Freya, please—"

"I can't say I'm surprised with her refusal." He made the matter-of-fact observation with an odd fatalism.

On the surface, Jake appeared cool and detached, but Victoria detected the deadly fury building beneath the surface. She looked up and met his chocolate-brown eyes, seeing the son instead of the father.

Her heart held an imperative—*Daniel*. She must save him.

Without Jake, she didn't know how to go about locating or freeing Daniel's soul from an eternity of torment. Freya's refusal to help when Victoria needed her goddess most struck her as a grave and capricious injustice. It was a betrayal, and her heart railed against the cruelty. And her own bitter anger shocked Victoria to her very soul.

Quicksilver rage rushed through her. Cold ruthlessness took the place of her disappointment and hurt over Freya's indifference. At her core, Victoria possessed a sense of practicality that overrode all else. If her goddess refused to help, then she'd find some other way to accomplish the resurrection. She *needed* divine power to bring a man back from the dead. Ultimately, the source of the blessing didn't matter. Any god would do in a pinch.

Reaching out, she seized Jake's hand. She grabbed for the raw well of infinite capacity and took what she required. A startled cry escaped him, genuine surprise at her audacity. He offered no resistance, and the power flowed. The nova lit her entire soul, eradicating every shadow so she stood at the center of the sun. She wasn't simply connected to a god—she *was* a goddess.

For a full minute, she gloried in the ecstasy, simply existing, until she remembered her mission. With just a flicker of her hand, she healed all of the damage to the hunter's body. Mission accomplished, she asserted her will and released his hand. It required every last iota of discipline she possessed, but she severed the spiritual connection and fell into the darkness of mortality.

CHAPTER NINE

Sessrúmnir, Freya's hall in Fólkvangr

"I'm nobody's fool."

"Debatable." Her lips bowed in a sneer. "All these centuries—you've lived among mortals?" His speech and clothing were contemporary, and she suspected Loki fit perfectly into the modern world. A deceitful, dishonorable creature such as he would prosper in the current age of man.

His grin conveyed secret knowledge. "I've traveled the world, Freya. You'd be amazed at the wonders I've seen. I'm worshipped on every continent, in every culture. I'm known by more names than I can cite." His smile widened. "I've been a rock 'n roll legend and a movie star."

"How nice for you." Freya sneered. She didn't want to admit it but envy smoldered in her belly. Like most ancient deities, the rapidly changing culture and sophisticated technology of the present day eluded her comprehension. She clung to the old ways, grasping at the fading remnants of her power even as her followers dwindled in number with each passing day.

"Hell." He scoffed. "They make films about me... Although, I wonder why I'm always the villain."

She sniffed. "I can't begin to imagine why. You're *so*

sympathetic."

His head lolled. "Ain't I though?"

Midgard

"911 Emergency Response. Do you need police, fire, or medical?"

"Fire," Sawyer said.

"What's on fire?"

"A silo at 4600 Sorenson Road in Truckee, Nevada," Sawyer supplied the full address since the dispatch computer would be unable to pull up a physical location on his cell phone.

"Is anyone in the silo?"

"No."

"Is anyone injured?"

Sawyer hesitated, glancing at Victoria who crouched over his father's body with both of her hands pressed to his chest. The statue still she-wolf had held the same position for the last ten minutes. He had no idea what the hell was happening and the frustration of being helpless ate at him.

Worry churned his gut, leaving the bitter taste of bile in his mouth. The prospect of losing his father scared him to death. His mother's death a couple years before had left an awful void in his life. He couldn't stand to go through it again. Not so soon, maybe not ever. His father wasn't supposed to die. His father was fucking Superman. Invulnerable except for a single, fatal flaw—a blow to the heart could kill him.

"Sir, is anyone injured?" the dispatcher asked again.

"No, just some cattle." He turned away to watch the black column of smoke billowing from the fire. Skinner and his fellow hunters had departed in pursuit of Andy Chart. Sawyer gripped his father's rifle in his hands and absently stroked the black walnut stock as he stood watch over Victoria and Jake.

Sawyer concluded the phone call and checked the time again. The minute hand on his cell phone advanced, officially marking what had been the longest fifteen minutes of his life. The lack of obvious progress or hell, even incremental improvement on any front threatened to drive him nuts.

Movement caught the corner of his eye and triggered a jolt of adrenaline that kicked him to reflexively shoulder his rifle. He spun, aiming the gun at Morena who crept closer along the edge of the yard, less than a hundred feet distant.

The teenager hunched and froze, one foot in the air. Her chin jutted as she shot him a defiant glare. "If Victoria's trying to heal your father, then she needs my help."

He lowered the gun and gestured her closer. "Can you tell what's happening?"

At his signal, Morena scurried to her Alpha's side and knelt. "Something's weird. I've never seen anything like this."

"Like what?" Intensely curious and also concerned, Sawyer dropped to one knee beside his father, across from Victoria and Morena.

"Like... Like... There's something wrong... But I don't know what." Frowning, the tip of the teen's tongue stuck out past her lips, and her eyebrows knit. Without warning, she seized hold of Sawyer's hand and dragged his arm toward her.

Muscles tense, Sawyer curbed the impulse to go for his knife. Taking a chance, he delayed for a second. He opened his mouth to question her, but a surge of pure emotion caught him unprepared. The chilling force cut to the bone, a bitter wind howling down the sides of snow-capped mountains in the dead of winter. Crisp air and sleet pelted his face, blasting back his hair. His humanity recoiled and he struggled to retain a separate identity, even as the current reversed and drew him into the irresistible communion with wolves.

"*Fy faen!*" Morena shouted. "When did *you* join my pack?"

"Is *this* the pack bond?" Sawyer rocked back, a sharp note of astonishment resonating throughout his being. It took him a few seconds to recognize the emotion belonged to the teenager.

"Yes. Not that the likes of *you* should ever experience it." Morena shot him a sharp glance full of irritation and disgust. Snatching her hand away from his arm, she wiped it on her jeans as if he had leprosy.

The girl's melodramatic lament did nothing to improve his mood, especially since the empathic bond continued to hum between them even without the benefit of physical contact. Sawyer sucked in a deep breath, strove for patience. The injury on his shoulder was superficial. His ribcage ached all over, but a sharp jabbing in the left side made him suspect a previously unnoticed injury sustained during the explosion or the cattle stampede.

Moaning, Morena ran her hands over her face. "How did this horrible thing happen?"

"Victoria did it. She said she needed to bond to me to help my father. It's only supposed to be temporary." *Fingers crossed.*

"Maybe, but I doubt it," Morena said. "I can feel you."

To his chagrin, his awareness expanded to encompass Morena—quick and clever, jester and thief. She presented a cheerful, clownish disguise to the world, hiding an intense core of loneliness and hurt. He received no words, only feelings and fleeting impressions like still photos of family, friends, and events past. He knew her in a way no human ever knew another. Not lovers. Not mother and child.

Cross-armed, Morena hugged herself and rocked in a self-comforting gesture. Her resentful stare centered on his chest. "I hope she knows what she's doing. I can't believe she's willing to bring a hunter into the pack, even as an Omega—"

Sawyer took immediate offense. "I'm not an Omega."

She eyed him, and then an insufferable smirk curved her lips. "Right now I know more about being a werewolf than you, so according to our laws, I rank you."

Sawyer bared his teeth in a non-smile. "In your dreams, Foxy."

The teenager averted her gaze, a dark blush creeping up her throat. "Two unmated young males in the same pack is such a bad idea. If you refuse to submit, you're going to have to fight Logan for rank."

His curiosity pricked. It had been his impression that Victoria headed an all-female wolf pack. "Who's Logan?"

"Unless, of course, Victoria claims you as a concubine."

"What?" Sawyer's mind went blank. Had he heard right? *Concubine?*

"Then it would probably be okay." Morena cast him a sly sideways glance, devilish humor glinting in her dark eyes, a smirk on her lips.

Belatedly, he realized that she'd gotten his goat. His mouth tugged into an involuntary grin, and he tipped his imaginary hat to her. "*Touché.*"

The teenager laughed and offered a real smile. "Just because you're funny doesn't mean I like you, asshole."

"Right." She hated him, and he didn't blame her. It was a shame. He and Morena could have been friends under better circumstances. Ironically, he liked the smart-mouthed teenager.

How much longer until the fire department arrived? Weary, Sawyer cracked his neck, noticing how the afternoon suddenly grew dimmer.

As if to echo his thoughts, Morena tilted her head back. "Looks like it might rain."

Sawyer opened his mouth to reply when a sudden flash of lightning, followed by the clash of thunder, roared over their heads. The sky, bright and clear just seconds before, filled with dark, rolling storm clouds. The wind howled, whipping his hair and blowing smoke and dust everywhere.

A familiar jolt of power set his blood to burning. Heart pounding, mouth and eyes wide open, Sawyer rose and walked away from Victoria and his father. His searching gaze scanned the sky for the riders of the Wild Hunt who followed the tempest. For as long as he could remember, his mind echoed with the stomp of hooves and the braying of hounds whenever storms brewed. A fat drop of water struck his cheek, but the towering thunderheads remained empty of warriors and beasts.

A brilliant nova of light and heat radiated forth from Victoria, enveloping the she-wolf in a white-blue halo that obscured her features. The nimbus expanded and swallowed Jake's prone form. Electricity sparked the air, lanced in deadly arcs to strike the ground. The lightning storm enveloped both the hunter and wolf, concealing them from view.

Reflexively, Sawyer threw up his hand to shield his eyes, turning his face to the side. A strangled cry escaped his throat, and he blindly charged toward the pair. He caught a glimpse of Morena, reaching for her Alpha, before his foot hit a rock. He stumbled and then slid in the dirt.

The radiant aura vanished.

Before he fell, Sawyer recovered his equilibrium but wound up balanced on one foot. Still skidding, he blinked repeatedly to normalize his vision. As abruptly as the storm had begun, it faded. The dark clouds receded, leaving clear skies and sunshine.

Jake sat upright as Victoria pitched into his arms.

He inhaled deeply and looked about, obviously recovering his orientation.

"Let her go!" Morena grabbed for her Alpha's leg.

Sawyer slid to a halt. "Dad, are you all right? What just happened?"

"I died." Jake gathered Victoria in his arms and rose in a smooth motion, hefting the she-wolf without any visible sign of exertion.

"Let me carry her. I should carry her." Morena tugged frantically on Victoria's leg.

"Take it easy or you'll dislocate her hip." Sawyer placed a hand on the girl's elbow.

At his touch, a tremor passed through Morena's entire body, but she slowly eased her death grip on Victoria. Her voice was frantic, her eyes full of tears. "Why did she pass out? She's never passed out from healing someone before! What's wrong with her?"

"She's going to be fine. You don't need to worry," Jake said to Morena. "She needs to sleep it off."

"Let me carry her." Arms spread, Morena crowded closer. The teenager had a tall, whip thin stature, but wolves possessed superior strength to that of normal people. Victoria's weight would be nothing to her.

"Take her into the main farm house." Jake passed the unconscious blonde to the girl. "There's a bedroom off the kitchen."

Morena murmured an agreement and headed toward the house. She vanished down the path in a blink, moving with the speed of a cheetah and leaving a trail of dust in her wake.

"The girl is fast. Let's catch up before she decides to just keep going," Jake's voice held a note of admiration. At a measured pace, he strode after her. As he walked, he extended his hand toward Sawyer.

After a second, Sawyer passed Jake the rifle. "You dropped this."

"Likely story." Jake chuckled and slung the strap

over his shoulder.

As accustomed as he was to his father's dramatic recoveries from severe injuries, things were happening too fast for Sawyer to process. He lunged and caught Jake's shoulder. Lowering his voice, he asked, "What was with the storm, Dad? Was that you?"

Jake stopped and turned his head slightly to the side. His eyes contained broody reticence. "Later."

"Okay, later." Sawyer knew that look too well. His father wouldn't speak on the matter until he was damn well ready.

"Where are Skinner and the men?" Jake asked.

"I sent them after Andy Chart." Sawyer burned with suppressed anger and restlessness. More than anything, he wanted to be with his comrades, hunting the traitor who'd tried to kill his father. It was hard staying behind, sitting on the sidelines while others did the hard work.

His father's gaze burned with fury but none of the impatience Sawyer felt. Jake never jumped to conclusions, never rushed into battle without knowing his opponent's strengths and weaknesses inside and out. He never made impulsive decisions based on passion or instinct.

Father and son were polar opposites.

"Trust Skinner to do his job," Jake said. "He's a seasoned huntsman."

"I'm here," Sawyer grated out. "Aren't I?"

Side by side, the two men walked toward the main house where Morena waited on the front porch. The teenager sat on the porch swing with the unconscious Victoria cradled in her arms. She tapped her toes on the wooden planks and regarded them with suspicion. "Is this your farm? I didn't think the Barretts were cow people."

"Actually, Grandpa John was a Texas cattleman," Sawyer drawled. "The farm belongs to a family friend." He shot the burning silo a glance, took in the thick black smoke, and shook his head. "Thom's going—"

"To shit kittens," Jake finished for him, also staring at the silo. "He made me swear not to break anything."

Sawyer chuckled. "Glad I'm not you."

Jake heaved a sigh. "Did you call the fire department?"

"Yeah, a few minutes ago."

Jake turned back toward the farm's access road. "Someone should meet them when they get here. I'll wait." He tipped his head toward the women. "Get them settled."

"I'll do that." Watching his father, Sawyer bit back a grin. His old man was a scary sight—his face, arms, and chest covered in soot and dried blood. "Dad."

The older man glanced over his shoulder, brow arched in inquiry.

"Put on a shirt."

"I've got one in the truck." Amusement sparked in Jake's eyes. "You might take your own advice."

Sawyer looked down at himself, registered his bare chest, and blinked. It took him a second to recall that he'd given his shirt to Victoria. "I didn't bring a change of clothes."

"Lucky for you, I brought several." Jake continued on his way.

Considering the matter settled, Sawyer turned back to the women. Sitting with Victoria on her lap, Morena continued to rock the porch swing. The teenager hugged her Alpha close. The pack bond carried the girl's paralyzing anxiety and worry.

Swathed in his too-big shirt, Victoria looked small enough to be a child. Her features, relaxed in sleep, accentuated the impression of innocence. Sawyer found the image incongruent with his mental perception of her. In his mind, she was a force to be reckoned with, a formidable and wily opponent sporting snowy white fur, fangs and claws. Not this petite creature.

"Let's get her inside." He opened the front door and held it for them.

Morena carried Victoria inside, and he showed them through the kitchen to the downstairs bedroom. The room had big windows dressed in canary yellow drapes, a double four-post bed, and a six-drawer dresser. As the teenager tucked Victoria beneath the antique comforter, the blonde stirred, eyes fluttering open.

Victoria murmured and struggled beneath the covers. "What's going on?"

"Shh, you need to rest." The girl kicked off her shoes and slipped into the bed beside her Alpha.

Uncomfortable, Sawyer drew the curtains closed and beat a hasty retreat from the room. His hand closed on the knob, but soft feminine whispering stopped him in his tracks.

"Is the baby okay?" Morena asked.

"The baby's fine," Victoria answered on a yawn. "Goddess, but I'm tired."

"Get some sleep, Victory. I'll watch over you."

Shocked, Sawyer pulled the door shut with a solid tug. Mouth open, he stood in the hallway for a time, staring at the dull wooden surface while his mind raced. Was Victoria pregnant? He did the mental math and realized in short order that the child couldn't possibly belong to his brother or she'd be showing. Daniel had died in early December of the prior year, and it was already April.

He'd known she'd taken a mate. He even met the guy, briefly. As inappropriate as it was, Sawyer experienced a sharp sting of outrage on his brother's behalf. Even the acknowledgement it was none of his damn business failed to assuage his wounded pride.

On silent feet, he retreated down the hallway, away from the bedroom, letting sleeping wolves lie.

Hours passed.

The emergency response team extinguished the fire, took their reports, and departed. The sun dipped in the sky, and Jake prepared a light supper that father and son ate without exchanging a word.

Sawyer waited in tense anticipation. Half of the time, he expected Victoria would burst through the downstairs bedroom door. The remainder, he worried the she-wolves would flee through the window into the night.

He checked on them twice, cracking the door wide enough to peek through and assess the motionless figures on the bed. Both times, a pair of glowing golden eyes swung toward him, warily watching his every movement. Hastily, he shut the door and returned to the main room.

Seated in a leather chair in front of the fireplace, Jake looked up from his cell phone. "Relax, Sawyer. You're as antsy as a green recruit. Victoria will come around when she's good and ready."

"Want a beer?" Sawyer asked, ignoring the jibe. His injuries had been tended to, but his entire body ached. The physical pain didn't begin to compete with the leaden guilt he bore. He'd never atone for his sins, no matter what amends he made.

"Sure."

He retrieved two chilled bottles from the fridge and passed one to his father. He busied himself with stacking logs in the fireplace. April evenings still tended to be nippy, and so far the spring had been a cool one.

Rare, companionable silence endured between the two men.

"Skinner texted," Jake said eventually. "They caught up with Chart at a gas station. He's heading south toward Arizona."

Sawyer twitched. "Did they take him alive?"

"They hid a tracking device on his vehicle and let him go." Jake took a short pull from his beer. "With some luck and a bit of patience, he'll lead us straight to our real enemy."

Nodding, Sawyer extracted a lighter from his pocket and ignited the kindling. He sat back on his haunches to watch the fire grow. "What I can't get over is how Andy Chart betrayed you."

"I admit, it surprised me too," Jake said gruffly.

He shot his father a dark look. "I'm not shocked that weasel betrayed you. What amazes me is that he had the balls to do it and think he could get away with it."

"We don't know what he's thinking," Jake said, tone reasonable. "Not until we catch up with him and ask."

Sawyer grunted. With the iron poker, he took a stab at the young fire to move a log to a better position. A shower of sparks flew into the air. His beer sat on the stone hearth, untouched.

"What's troubling you, Son?"

His brow knit, and his body tensed. His father's evasive tendencies, although familiar, always wore at his patience. Sawyer preferred straight answers without second-guessing. He placed the tool in the wrought iron stand and sat on the couch. "I miss mom."

Sarah Barrett had possessed uncanny insight when it came to her family. She always clarified and explained Jake's motives and actions. She had been their bridge, and without her, the gap between father and son grew wider every day.

"So do I." Jake's voice contained a forlorn note, alluding to underlying pain. The old man's taciturn nature made such demonstrations a rarity. He seldom showed affection or vulnerability even to those closest to him.

Unsure of how to respond, Sawyer fell silent. He had more blood on his hands than he'd ever imagined possible, and yet his brother's death remained unavenged. Deep-seated guilt gnawed at him, but fear of appearing weak in his father's eyes kept him from talking.

Jake's mood remained expansive, a rare condition for the solitary hunter, and he continued speaking in a mellow baritone. "I love your mother like I've never loved anyone. I always knew someday she'd die, but—"

Jake's voice cracked, and he paused.

Sawyer filled in the unspoken words, *I always assumed I'd go first.*

"You almost died today, Dad. Was that real?" Even though Jake always maintained his mortal life would end one day, Sawyer never believed it. In his mind, the Hunter King was too big, too powerful. Larger than life. Yet today's events rammed home the real possibility.

"Yes, absolutely. Granted, I'm harder to kill than most men, but I came damn close today." His father exhaled before continuing. "My heart was damaged beyond my natural ability to repair it. Without Victoria's intervention, I'd be dead. She really did save my life."

"You don't sound too concerned with the prospect." Glowering, Sawyer hid his fear beneath a belligerent mask. His father spoke far too easily of his own death, without a hint of alarm or aversion.

His old man looked at him with surprise from beneath a furrowed brow. "It's true. I have no fear of death, and I look forward to being reunited with Sarah. Every day that passes without her pains me."

"Why the hell are you staying then?" Chills shot through Sawyer's body. His dad's nonchalance disturbed him on so many levels. The death of his body wasn't the end, but one thing was certain—everything would change beyond recognition if he died.

Jake's flinty gaze never wavered. "Your brothers are still minors. I promised your mother on her deathbed that I'd watch over them until they become ready to stand on their own as men."

Sawyer's heart ached. He desperately wanted to tell his father—*I need you too.* But his throat constricted tight, and his tongue was as thick as cotton. His mouth never opened. No words emerged.

Jake continued, "I've made commitments to the mortals under my protection, too, which I intend to keep. It used to be that I didn't care. Human life didn't matter much. But your mother changed me in profound ways. Sometimes, it shocks me how much."

"I hate it when you talk about dying so casually," Sawyer said. "Life and death aren't a game."

Jake flashed white, even teeth. "That really depends on who you ask."

Troubled, Sawyer turned his gaze toward the fire, seeking comfort in the dancing flames. Heat and light. On a primal level, the siren song of the Wild Hunt beckoned him to join. In combat, the rhythm and pulse compelled him to violence, a battle cry on his lips and the fiery haze of anger immolating reason.

Åsgårdsreien: the Wild Hunt, the manifestation of his legacy.

The silence endured. Stretched. No longer comfortable, it boomed with discontent. Unable to sit still, Sawyer stood and added another log. He used the poker to position it, stirring up more sparks.

"You still haven't said what's really bugging you," Jake said.

The muscles in his back jerked. "Victoria knows you're a god." Maybe not the most tactful opening, but he made his point.

Jake's lips curved into an amused smile. "Of course she does. She's stubborn, not stupid. I suspect she's sensed something different about us all along. Your brother's strength must have attracted her."

"What are you going to do?"

Jake took a long swig, perhaps using the action as

an opportunity to consider. At a glance he appeared re-laxed, but vibrant tension lurked beneath the composed exterior. "Victoria has acquitted herself with honor. When it came down to it, she healed your hand and my heart despite her grievances."

Sawyer shifted his position, more than a little un-easy. The question remained unanswered in spite of his father's response. The evasion told him his father didn't want to answer, which meant one of two things. Either he didn't know what to do with Victoria, or he'd already decided and didn't want to tell Sawyer.

"Once she saw the protective runes, she refused to heal you. I had to pay blood price to get her to cooper-ate." Sawyer expected his old man to be displeased.

Sure enough, Jake sat straighter, brow knit. "What did you give her?"

"The Chevelle." Sawyer braced, anticipating another storm.

"The Chevelle?" The high note in his father's voice contained surprise. Scowling, he lapsed into silence.

The lack of reaction worried him more than an an-gry outburst. The uncomfortable silence got to be too much, drove Sawyer to offer further explanation. "The treaty's not in effect anymore, and she's still wrongly blaming you for that boy's death. Frankly, I think the power of the warding scared her. I made the deal be-cause your life is worth more than that damn car."

Jake cleared his throat, a gruff rumble. "I'm not criti-cizing you, Sawyer. I'm sure you did what you had to do. I'm simply surprised at how pragmatic she is. She has a lot of her father in her."

"You still haven't answered my question." Sawyer returned the iron to the stand and assumed a seat in the opposing armchair. He took a quick swing of his beer.

Jake harrumphed. "About Victoria?

"Do you think she'll keep your secret?" Sawyer asked, changing tactics. He took another jab at the fire, stirring the flames and raising more embers.

The muscles in Jake's face tightened, signaling uncertainty. His wide-set nostrils flared as he inhaled. "Her father took my secret to his grave, so yes, I believe she can be trusted. The problem isn't with her. It's with us."

His blood roared in his ears. Heart throbbing, Sawyer's fists clenched so hard his knuckles ached. Pressure built. "You mean me," he grated out. "The problem is me."

Jake's chair creaked beneath his shifting weight as he rose to his feet. "I meant what I said, Sawyer. I'm your father. I've got your back no matter what. But Victoria can't ever find out who murdered Jasper."

"I know that. I'm not stupid or suicidal," Sawyer snapped. "She'd kill me." The guilty weight on his shoulders threatened to crush him. *I deserve to die.*

Apparently satisfied, Jake eased into his seat. His hands gripped the arms of the chair. "I don't like deceiving her, Sawyer. It does our honor no credit, and if she ever finds out, she'll regard it as a betrayal."

"Rightly so." Renewed resolve fueled Sawyer's determination to find some way to make amends for the boy's death. He'd start by putting things right between hunters and wolves. Restoring the alliance wouldn't repay his debt, not by a long shot, but at least it put him on the road to making amends.

"Your ingenuity has given me an idea."

Sawyer blinked and turned his attention outward to focus on his father. "What do you mean?"

Face turned toward the fire, Jake settled deeper into the armchair. "You've reminded me that Victoria's people retain their cultural traditions. In the old days, before there were prisons, there were other ways of keeping the peace. Blood feuds are costly, and the Storm Pack can't afford to remain at war with us."

Sawyer swallowed so his Adam's apple bobbed. After consideration, he realized what his father meant to do. "You're going to offer to pay blood price for the boy's death."

Jake nodded. "It's the right thing to do. As part of the conditions, she'll have to forswear her pursuit of vengeance."

Ashamed, he looked away. Only a small, worthless man depended on his father to pay his debts. Sawyer owed the people he'd wronged. He should pay. His voice blistered with restrained anger. "I don't want you settling my obligations."

His father's head jerked toward him. "You don't have to like it, Sawyer. You just have to find a way to live with it. We can't win against the undead without the packs as our allies. More than that, we *need* Victoria."

The urgency, the fear in Jake's voice turned Sawyer's blood to ice. "What's happened?"

Taking a deep breath, his dad stood and placed his hands upon Sawyer's shoulders. "There's something I need to tell you, Sawyer. I only just learned about this, so I don't want you concluding that I've been keeping secrets from you. But I need to know that you'll stay calm and focused."

"I'll keep my cool. What is it?"

Jake's grip tightened as if to brace his son. "Your brother's soul isn't in Valhalla. He's captive and controlled by the monster that killed him, this *Vildivia*."

The shock sent a pulse of cold through his core. His father's steadfast presence kept him anchored. Once he processed the revelation, he asked, "How do you know?"

Jake lowered his chin, and he locked gazes with his son. Wrath burned in his dark eyes, the destructive force of a world destroyer. "Victoria had a vision. The vampire has used your brother's soul as a puppet to manipulate you and her. He's hurt you, and I'm concerned he'll go after your brothers. I don't know what his endgame is, and I don't give a shit. When I get hold of him, Vildivia is going to pay."

Sawyer took a deep breath. Rescuing Daniel superseded every other priority and became the single thing that mattered. "We're going after him?"

Jake nodded. "First thing in the morning. We'll free Daniel and send this carrion eater back to the deepest, coldest region of the underworld. I promise you."

CHAPTER TEN

Sessrúmnir, Freya's hall in Fólkvangr

Freya breathed deeply, filling her lungs, bracing to verbalize the question she had thus far avoided. The current direction of the conversation left her with no choice. "What do you want from me, Loki?"

His pacing grew restless, swifter, directionless. "Your priestess, Victoria Storm, wields the enchanted dagger, the only weapon that can slice Fenrir's bindings."

"You're surprised." Freya's hands settled at her sides. She longed to throttle Loki's slimy throat but sensed guile and seduction served her best against the Trickster. He put such stock in his cleverness. His enormous ego blinded him to his own tactics being employed against him.

"Yes." Expression inscrutable, he regarded her for a long time before he spoke again. "That dagger is your guarantee against my treachery. Yet you entrust one of my wolves with possession of it."

She stood straighter. "Victoria is my priestess, as was her mother, and her mother's mother, going back for centuries. She is loyal only to me."

Midgard

"He's a dominant male without kinship to the pack. *Human and a hunter.*" Bursting with hyper energy, Morena bounced in the passenger seat of the black SUV as they rolled to a halt at a stop sign.

Victoria's teeth produced an impatient click. "Thank you so much for pointing it out, because I hadn't noticed."

She used the opportunity to glance in the rear view mirror and confirm that Sawyer was still behind her in the Chevelle. With the top down and one arm resting on the driver side door, he looked like a badass with his windswept blond hair and aviator sunglasses.

He must've noticed her watching him since he tipped his chin toward her. She couldn't see his eyes, but his hot and intense attention focused on her like a spotlight through the pack bond. She picked up on the hunter's irritation and agitation—he wasn't any more comfortable than she was.

Rolling her eyes, Morena sucked in her cheeks. "So you weren't just checking him out?"

Victoria heaved a heavy sigh. "Not in a million years."

Sawyer's discomfort mirrored her mood precisely. Foolishly, she'd hoped the connection she'd forged with Sawyer to save his father would collapse once the resurrection was completed. By her reckoning, it should have fallen like a house of cards under the weight of their mutual distrust. Instead, the tie appeared to be holding fast.

Goddess... Before she completed the prayer, Victoria stumbled to a stuttering halt. Freya wasn't speaking to her. Receiving the silent treatment drove her up the wall. Anything else would have been preferable—angry recriminations or accusations of disloyalty. Guilt ate at her, but she knew in her heart that given the same set of circumstances, she'd have done the same thing again.

The whole situation made her head hurt. Her temples throbbed with the onset of a tension headache and nausea swam in her gut like a bowlful of goldfish. At least she wore clean clothing, thanks to the emergency go-bag she kept stashed in the back of her vehicle.

"Slug bug!" Waving a pointed finger, Morena's other hand shot out and tagged Victoria's upper arm.

Scowling, Victoria forced her attention back to the road, noting the vehicle which approached the four-way intersection from the opposite direction. Annoyed with herself for the lapse, she took her foot off the brake and punched the gas before she forfeited her turn to go.

"That's three to one," Morie bragged.

"No fair! That's a New Beetle," Victoria protested as they passed the oncoming VW. She noted that Sawyer didn't bother with a full and proper stop. He rolled right through the sign.

"Still counts. Rand and I modified the rules while we were on the run. Old Bugs are getting harder to find." With a cheeky grin, Morena stuck out her tongue. "You would've seen it, except you were too busy checking out the asshole hunter."

"You'd better not let Sylvie hear you talking like that," Victoria muttered, eyeing the girl.

Morena huffed. "I'm not stupid. Besides, I bet right now I could cuss up a storm and Sylvie wouldn't even notice. Cause she's gonna be too busy lecturing you about allowing a hunter to join our pack." The girl's voice grew stern as she did a good impression of the older woman. "*Victoria, are you sure this is wise?*"

There were moments when Victoria regretted her lax approach to discipline. Larger packs tended to have stricter rules, rigid social structure, and formal etiquette. Lower ranked members addressed the Alpha with the utmost respect. War bands were the equivalent of military units.

"I do hope you're not considering taking Sawyer Barrett as a mate. He's entirely unsuitable, and he'll upset our dynamic." Blowing out her cheeks, Morena ruined her Sylvie-impression by succumbing to a fit of giggles halfway through.

Victoria scowled to hide the grin which threatened to split her face. "You're getting good at that. You sound just like Sylvie."

"Thanks," Morena chirped. "I've been practicing. How am I doing?"

"Pretty good." Victoria turned off the highway onto the exit that took them home. The Chevelle continued to shadow them.

"Should I keep going?" Morena asked, obviously eager to show off.

Victoria hesitated, debating the wisdom of encouraging her, but the opportunity to bond with Morena trumped everything else. "Sure, go ahead."

Morena made a show of crossing her arms and tilting her head back to adopt a comically thoughtful posture. She resumed impersonating Sylvie. "On the other hand, perhaps I'm being too hasty. After all, the Barrett family is powerful and a smart political marriage would cement the new alliance."

Victoria blinked, then cast the teenager a sharp glance. Was Morena serious or was this still part of her satire? She opened her mouth to ask but hesitated, policing her choice of words. Familiarity with the teenager's sense of humor cautioned her against speaking too readily or freely, lest she wind up being the real target of her wicked wit.

Unfazed, Morena continued her verbal volley, still performing a Sylvie-voiceover. "At least with Sawyer, you'd be getting a male who's not too smart, so he'd be easy to manage. And he's not *too* ugly."

"Oh, you're mean. And I mean that in the best possible way." Choking on laughter, Victoria leaned over and hugged Morena. They traded jibes and cracked jokes for the next half hour, many but not all at Sawyer's expense. Her mood took an immediate and marked upward turn, and both her headache and morning sickness abated. They clowned around until they turned onto a two-lane Main Street which bisected a picturesque downtown lined with shops, businesses, restaurants, the library, and a cluster of government buildings.

Sierra Pines, California, located within the heart of the Sierra Nevada Mountains, had a small-town, big-money feel. The exclusive alpine community clung to the western shore of Echo Lake and boasted country clubs, million-dollar homes, and a ski resort. Miles of pristine alpine forest full of deer and elk and other small prey extended in every direction, including the remote and rugged Desolation Wilderness. Fallen Leaf Lake and Lake Tahoe lay to the north.

"It's good to be home," Morena said in a breathy voice. Her contentment traversed the pack bond. Her aura was a restful forest green.

"Yeah." Victoria heaved a deep sigh of relief, feeling some of her tension drain away. While her territory extended for miles to the north, including all of Desolation Wilderness, and to the east, encompassing the whole of Lake Echo, the most familiar areas were those close to the town.

Across the miles, she sensed the pack's worry and fear. No member of her little family would truly feel safe until they were reunited. That morning, she had called Sylvie to offer assurances she and Morena were okay. The lengthy conversation that followed brought Sylvie up to speed on *almost* everything that had happened. She'd kept Jake's secret, not just for his sake but for the safety of everyone she cared for. She hadn't talked about her rift with Freya yet.

Ironically, Morena had pegged Sylvie's reaction to a T. "Excuse me a moment, but it seems my hearing is failing. I thought you said Sawyer Barrett is a member of the pack now."

Victoria winced and ground her teeth. "That's what I said."

Dead silence followed and then Sylvie moaned. "In the name of the goddess, Victoria. What were you thinking?"

"I wasn't. I had to forge a connection with Jake before I could heal him, because his wards blocked me." Grimly, she enshrouded her thoughts and emotions, using all her self-discipline to hide the truth. Becoming Alpha had improved her skill at subterfuge.

As she turned into the driveway of the lake house, she noticed the front lawn was overgrown. Mentally, she made a note to cut it next weekend. Before she turned off the engine, Morena released her seatbelt and bolted from the vehicle. The front door flew open, and Sylvie and the rest of the Storm Pack bounded down the front walk to greet them.

Sawyer, she noted, parked the Chevelle along the side of the road a few hundred feet from the house. It was the smart, cautious choice. She stood so he remained in her line of sight at all times. Despite joking with Morena, she respected the hunter for his cunning and skill. During their brief association, he'd spent more time trying to kill her than not. In a weird way, she'd gotten to know Daniel's brother between the shotgun blasts and burning buildings.

Sylvie hugged Victoria and then Morena. "Thank the goddess you're both home and unharmed. I swear, you've taken years off my life over the last couple days."

"I'm sorry, Sylvie." Victoria adopted a contrite expression, putting on her angel face. "I didn't intent to cause you undue distress."

"Oh you, so full of it," Sylvie said, chuckling. "I tire of saying it, but you're going to put this old woman in her grave someday. Was all of that danger exciting?"

"Nonstop thrills." Victoria stooped to greet the pack's four non-shifter members with open arms. The gray wolves, Sophia and her three pups, welcomed her with wet tongues and wagging tails.

"Victoria had all the fun. As usual, I got stuck on the sidelines," Morena said with complaint in her tone. She yelped when Mick, the largest and most rambunctious of the young wolves, reared back to rest his front paws on her chest, almost knocking her over. He licked her face while she laughed.

"I wouldn't have gotten out of there alive if it wasn't for Morena's sharp nose." Victoria delivered the praise with a proud smile for the teenager.

"I smelled the bomb," Morena bragged, preening under the approving gaze of her elders. "I called it. It was definitely a trap."

The sound of a car door opening and then closing came from down the street. All heads reflexively turned in Sawyer's direction as he walked around the front of the vehicle. He leaned against the fender, arms crossed, long legs stretched before him. The man wore menace like a cloak even without a 12-gauge shotgun in his hands.

The older woman crossed her arms. "Speak of the devil..."

"Sawyer's not *the devil*."

"But he's *a* devil," Morena said with a quick grin.

Victoria pointedly ignored the sarcastic jibe.

Sylvie harrumphed. Then she spread her arms to herd the bounding gray wolves toward the house. "The lot of you inside. Move along."

"Hey." Morena squawked as she got caught up in the sweep, but she headed in the direction of the front door anyway. In a blink, she shot to the head of the pack, racing across the overgrown front lawn with the rest of the young wolves hot on her heels.

"She makes me feel old," Victoria said, watching the teenager go with a fond smile. "Was I ever that hyper?"

"Twenty-four isn't old, sweetheart. And yes. Once."

"I'll be twenty-five next month." *And a mother before the year is out.* "When?"

"When what?" Sylvie asked, distracted as she cast a worried glance toward Sawyer. "What about him?"

"When was I hyper?" Victoria patted her friend's elbow as they progressed along the paved walkway toward the front porch. "He can wait out here. He knows I'm going with him."

Sylvie's hazel gaze swung toward her Alpha. "When you were three you were as jittery as a grasshopper, but at least you let your mother dress you up in pretty outfits. By the time you were fourteen, it became obvious that you'd never grow those final two inches to reach five feet. You turned into a late blooming tomboy. You had a chip the size of Thor's Hammer on your shoulder, and you went around just daring anyone and everyone to knock it off."

Unchastised, Victoria bit back a grin. She recognized herself in the depiction. "Maybe I had something to prove."

"*Had?*" Sylvie snorted as she crossed the threshold. "That's rich."

Grinning, Victoria wrapped her arms about Sylvie's waist and hugged her. "He's not going to try to hurt anyone, I promise. Let's go inside so we can talk. I have a lot to explain and not much time."

With the pad of his thumb, Sawyer stroked the pebble resting on his palm. Assessing it for weight and smoothness, he found no rough patches, but the shape was more oval than round. Still, he deemed it sufficient. He studied the lake's glossy dark surface, as still as the afternoon air. Conditions were perfect, if he could find the right stone.

He enjoyed the basic physics of the sport—

hydrodynamics, momentum, and gravity. The mental exercise calmed and focused his thoughts while the physical exercise gave him an outlet for pent up energy. As boys, he and his brothers had competed at everything, including stone skipping.

Gripping the edges, he turned and drew his arm back for a throw that sent the projectile skimming across the water. He counted seven skips before the lake swallowed the stone. Before the ripples faded, he resumed his search by shuffling the rounded cobblestones with the edge of his boot.

The manmade river-rock beach covered a quarter mile along Lake Echo's western shore. The backyard of the sprawling craftsman style house led directly to the water. No fences or hedges marked the property line, and there weren't any neighbors visible for as far as the eye could see. A large covered pool and pool house were at his back, a dock and boathouse to his left. The buildings and grounds were well maintained, although the lawns were overgrown. He wondered if any of the women in Victoria's all female pack knew how to operate a mower.

Maybe he could earn an ounce of forgiveness if he offered to cut it for them.

A stand of pine trees provided some shade from the overhead sun, but the temperature climbed steadily toward the mid-seventies. He shed his coat and draped it over a pier pylon to keep it clean. Underneath, he wore a short-sleeve T-shirt and jeans. He had left his firearms in the Chevelle because he didn't want another confrontation with the Storm Pack. Being unarmed made him antsy, but trust had to start somewhere.

After a moment's hesitation, he unfastened the straps of his forearm sheath and placed the silver dagger on top of his jacket. That left him with the bayonet on his belt and the hunting knife tucked into his boot.

Practically naked.

Staring out across the glossy lake, Sawyer absently rubbed his right hand. He tugged at each of his fingers in turn to be sure they remained firmly attached. His ego still smarted over having allowed those three vampires to get the drop on him. Remembered pain continued to haunt him despite Victoria's quick repair of the severed digits. *Shit.* Talk about close calls.

Had he thanked her for saving his hand? He thought he'd done so, but his memory of the attack and what followed blurred together. Just in case, he determined to express his gratitude again at the next appropriate opportunity. Victoria had saved him and saved his father. He owed her.

Sawyer might just offer to do her gardening indefinitely.

He dug into the gravel, kicking the top layer aside, shifting the cobble as he searched for the next skipping stone. Most of the rocks were a couple inches wide, but few possessed the flat, round profile he desired.

Over the crunch of tumbling stones came the crisp *snap* of a branch split underfoot.

Tensed to combat readiness, Sawyer jerked toward the sound, reflexively reaching for his .45. His hand closed on air. The holster was empty. He'd left the handgun in the car along with his shotgun. His hand dropped to the hilt of the bayonet sheathed on his belt.

A gray wolf stood beside the trunk of a pine tree. From its size, the animal was an adolescent, perhaps a few months old, and its stance was friendly—ears pointed, tail held high, tongue lolling.

Exhaling, Sawyer released his grip on the knife and moved his hand from the weapon. He tried to relax, well aware of how scent affected wolves. "Hey, boy," he said, pitching his voice to a soothing tone. "I don't want any trouble. What's your name?"

The gray wolf tilted its head to the side. The bushy tail thumped and the puppy walked toward Sawyer.

Magic crackled in the air, a single, perfectly pitched note, an intense feeling of familiarity. Nearing the hunter, the pup extended an inquisitive nose.

Sawyer's mouth opened in a silent *oh*. Pack bond. He recognized the powerful empathic connection this time from having experienced it before and also from Morena's explanation. *Of course.* The puppy accepted the presence of a stranger in his territory because the magic connected them.

Overcome with awe, Sawyer dropped to a crouch and extended his open hand. The wolf's breath blew past his hand in a hot puff, and then the warm, wet nose touched the center of his palm. Friendship and trust emanated from the pup.

The pounding footsteps of someone or something coming toward them crashed through the forest. Startled, Sawyer yanked his hand back just as the wolf spun toward the sound.

CHAPTER ELEVEN

Sessrúmnir, Freya's hall in Fólkvangr

"She is loyal only to me."

"Are you sure about that?" He mocked her with his stare and his smirk.

Fear whispered through her soul, and Freya hesitated. Deep down, she had doubts, not only about Victoria's loyalty but also about her own worthiness. After all, she consorted with Loki, the vilest of creatures, out of cowardly self-preservation and an unwillingness to accept her inevitable demise. Could it be Victoria sensed Freya's deadly flaw? All too recently, her priestess had chosen practicality over her unquestioning devotion.

Silent, she regarded Loki with hard suspicion. Did the Trickster know something she didn't? She could always ask... But no. She refused to show weakness.

Summoning an aura of confidence, she found her own smirk. "Victoria worships me, whereas she speaks your name with distrust and disdain."

"She loves you." He eyed her with misgiving.

The goddess arched her brow. Her tone became sweet. "I am her goddess. Of course she loves me."

Midgard

Morena barged into the open. Breathing hard, the teenager skidded to a halt, shouting at the top of her lungs. "Mick! Get away from him!"

A tremor of uncertainty rippled through the puppy, and his tail tucked between his legs. Mick shot Sawyer a quick glance, no longer as trusting or welcoming.

The hunter's mouth tugged, and a hard lump of regret formed in his gut. He acknowledged the wisdom of the teenager's distrust. The youngest members of the Storm Pack should be taught to regard him with suspicion. He deserved no better.

Morena snapped her fingers and pointed, still speaking loudly. "Mick, now! I mean it! He's dangerous."

Sawyer rose and directed a nonchalant smile at the girl. "Hey, there, Foxy. Sorry, I didn't mean to scare you."

Her narrow face jerked toward him. She flushed, then her eyes narrowed and her chin assumed a belligerent tilt. "I'm not afraid of you, redneck."

Her choice of slurs irritated the hell out of him, but he refused to let it show. The girl had the potential to become a serious pain in the neck if she figured out how to get under his skin. Showing teeth, he adopted a slow drawl. "Course you're not, darlin'."

With a jerky step, she glared murder at him. "What're you doing out here?"

"Walking. I needed to stretch my legs."

"Did Victoria give you permission to leave the car?"

He smirked. "I don't need permission. I'm a member of the pack now."

A second of stunned silence followed. Then Morena let loose a string of curses, most in Spanish, some in ancient Norse. She insulted everything from his intelligence to his looks to his ancestry, employing surprising creativity and an admirable vocabulary.

He bore the verbal assault with a grin, and once her

rant ran down, he tipped an imaginary hat and winked. "That's some language for a lady to be using, ma'am."

"I'd love to wring your neck," she hissed, fuming.

"I'm sure you would."

Sawyer nudged aside a pile of gravel with the side of his boot. Spotting a promising looking stone, he swooped to pick it up while keeping one eye on the teenager. Turning his back on her would have been a stupid risk, especially since she'd already tried, and failed, to take him out. Even though she ranked low in the Storm Pack, all wolves harbored intensely territorial instincts. Plus, Morena blamed him, with good reason, for the deaths of people she cared about.

Impulsively, Sawyer turned, drew back his arm, and heaved the stone toward the lake. It skipped once, twice, and then sank. Displeased with his performance, he exhaled and dropped his hands to his sides.

Morena blew air in disgust. "You throw like a girl."

"That's sexist. Some of the best throwers I've known have been women. My mother could make a baseball fly in loops. It was uncanny." The fond memory of his mom evoked a deep pang of bittersweet sorrow. Sarah Barrett would be ashamed of the man her second son had become.

Grumbling, Morena kicked over a pile of rocks and snatched one from the ground. "Let me show you how it's done."

Her stone traveled five bounces.

"Not bad," Sawyer drawled. He allowed the proclamation to hang before adding, "For a girl."

"Asshole..."

He snickered and located another skipping stone. He and Morena settled into a semi-friendly competition. After a while, the silence resembled something comfortable. When the wolf puppy and two of his siblings returned to watch them, Morena didn't chase them away. A full-grown female gray wolf shadowed the three youngsters.

"Are they shifters?" Sawyer ventured to ask, making a vague motion with his hand toward the trio of puppies. He counted nine ripples from his last throw — far from his personal best, but not bad. Good enough to top Morena's best throw of eight skips.

A breeze kicked up and created vigorous waves on the lake's surface. The teenager squinted at the water and then huffed in resignation. She tossed aside a handful of rocks that hit the cobblestone bed with a clatter.

Morena pushed her shoulders back and regarded him with an expression best characterized as wily. "Information isn't free."

Caution filled him. "What do you want?"

She crossed her arms. "Tit for tat. For every question I answer, you answer one."

Dubious, he eyed her. On the surface, the exchange sounded fair, and he stood to learn as much from the questions she asked as the answers provided. "Okay, but some topics are off-limits."

Her brow arched. "Such as?"

He jerked his head to indicate negative. "Can't say."

The corners of her mouth turned down. She rolled her eyes heavenward. "Fine, I reserve the same right of refusal."

He grinned. Damn, the girl had brains. His admiration of her continued to deepen. "Explain how the pups fit into the pack."

Morena took a deep breath. "Non-shifter wolves and humans are considered members of the pack so long as they're blood relatives or mated to a shifter. With the pups, Sophia, their mom, is a gray wolf, but she carries our genes. Their dad was a full wolf shifter. He died in Phoenix at the airstrip... Along with my parents."

Morena slanted an accusatory glance his way, but her dark eyes held more grief than hatred. Tentative hopefulness edged her voice. "You really weren't there?"

The massacre in Phoenix was one of the few sins not on his conscience. Guilt churned his gut, hard fists pounding away at his soul. He had plenty more to atone for, if such a thing were even possible. With each passing day, his desperation to identify a path to redemption grew more compelling and elusive. The depths of his pit kept growing deeper, the sides slicker, and the light dimmer.

"I wasn't at the airstrip that day." Staring across the water, Sawyer spoke softly, hoping she'd scent the truth and believe him. No matter what else he'd done, he didn't want Morena believing he might be the hunter who'd killed her parents.

"My turn," Morena said as if she hadn't heard him. Or as if she refused to listen.

He swallowed, shoving nervousness down deep before it showed. "Shoot."

She shot him a fast grin. "Are you like your father?"

Sawyer reared back. *Whoa!* Not what he'd expected at all. "What do you mean?"

"I mean..." Her hands opened and closed, perhaps mirroring her inner struggle as she attempted to grasp thoughts and suspicions. "Are you like him? Magic? Unkillable?"

Tension eased from his body, and he flashed a predatory smile. "Why, are you planning to jump me again?"

Morena's face flushed dark red, and anger sparked in her eyes.

Sawyer chuckled. "No, I'm not like my father. I can die, I think. I haven't actually done it yet."

Satisfied, she nodded. "Your turn."

He licked his dry lips. The whole concept of the genetics of mystical creatures as well as the prospect of a wolf-born werewolf struck him as inexplicably fascinating. Was lycanthropy a recessive or dominant trait? He'd love to lay his hands on some real data and construct a model of the genetics. "So what are the odds those pups will grow up to be shifters, and when will you know?"

"The Change happens after we hit adolescence, but no one knows for sure when, or even if a child will grow up to be a shapechanger." She rolled her shoulders. "We'll know when it happens. Victoria says any one of the pups has a chance. Even if they don't, then their offspring in future generations may produce a wolf shifter."

Sawyer's eyebrows drew together so sharply his brow furrowed. The whole, illogical thing gave him fits. Did the adolescent wolf become a full grown adult with severely retarded language skills? How were they socialized? He opened his mouth to ask, but Morena kept talking.

"Victoria calls them *the future of the pack*." The teenager spoke in a flat, resigned voice, devoid of hope. A poignant pang of depression rang through the girl's soul, echoing like a bell toll.

Sawyer's lips compressed. His conscience laid the blame for her despair squarely on his shoulders. His mind raced, full of words—of comfort, sympathy, assurances, self-recrimination, and a confession that would get him killed.

A good man owned responsibility for his crimes. A good man accepted the consequences. Sawyer wasn't a good man. Even mired in guilt and self-loathing, his desire to live trumped any impulse to make suicidal confessions.

"You don't have much faith in the future," he said, making his words a statement, not a question.

Morena turned toward the lake to avoid his face. The teenager hugged herself and rocked on her heels. She remained stubbornly silent, refusing him an answer.

Respecting her privacy, Sawyer mirrored her

posture. He looked out across the water and watched the white-capped waves the wind kicked shoreward. Sunlight glinted on the broken surface, creating a dazzling display.

"I'm sorry for what happened," he said in a voice rife with sorrow.

"Sorry doesn't make anything better." Morena's tone held bitterness and anger. "It doesn't bring back the dead."

Nothing he ever did would bring back the dead.

"I know that, but I need to say it anyway." He wanted her to know the apology was genuine, so he made his first attempt to control the pack bond, flattening barriers and pushing his regret without any way of knowing what he was doing. "This war between hunters and wolves is over, Morena. For what it's worth, you can believe in the future again."

A gasp escaped the girl, and she swung toward him. "How did you do that?"

"I don't know what I did." He shook his head, hating how uncomfortable this entire pack business thing made him feel. He didn't belong, not in the least.

"You're asserting yourself like—" Morena bit off the rest of her sentence.

Sawyer's brow furrowed while he puzzled over *that*. He had no idea what to say, and then an anomalous movement far out on the lake caught his attention. The thought vanished, and his alarm skyrocketed. Squinting, his hand rose to shield his eyes.

The distant figure of a dark-haired man thrashed about, clearly struggling to keep his head above water.

"Fuck. There's someone out there." Lifting his leg, he grabbed hold of his boot and hopped on one foot while he yanked it off.

Morena charged toward the water but then skidded to a sudden halt. "Where? I don't see anyone."

"Right there! As plain as day!" Sawyer removed his

other boot and tossed it aside. Wasting precious seconds, he thrust his arm toward the water and pointed at the man. The action forced his attention to the distressed swimmer, who reared up out of the water and waved his arms.

The wind swallowed the man's words and carried only an indecipherable cry.

"Where? Where?" Morena pivoted, shouting as she scanned the lake.

Striding forward, Sawyer seized her shoulder and positioned his arm beside her face. "There!"

Mouth agape, Morena scoured the distance and then tilted her head up to search his face. "Sawyer, there's no one there."

A switch flipped in his brain. Recognition slammed him.

Frantic, Sawyer shoved Morena aside and charged toward the water, determined to save the swimmer at any cost. "That's Daniel! I have to get to him!"

"What? No! Dammit, Sawyer!" Morena's hands locked on his elbow and dragged him back. "You're *loco!* There's no one there!"

Acting on reflex, Sawyer twisted and broke her hold on his arm. The maneuver forced her backward, leaving him free to resume his rescue. Frigid water bit at his bare feet and soaked the denim of his jeans as he waded to his waist in the chilly lake. Then he dove, briefly submerging his head below the surface. The cold blanketed his entire body, a rude shock that punched a hole in the adrenaline surge which drove him. Fear formed a leaden weight in his gut. Nothing scared him more than drowning. Nothing.

He settled into a powerful freestyle stroke, swimming for all he was worth. The compulsion to reach his brother overwhelmed all else. No thought, no reason, only primal instinct pulsed through his being. After a couple minutes, he lifted his head from the water in order to get his bearings.

Fifty feet away, Daniel broke the surface, his dark head visible for a moment amid flailing arms. A shout tore from his throat, and then he disappeared under the water.

Sawyer inhaled a huge lungful of air and dove, swimming toward where his brother had gone down. At first, sunlight filtered through the murky water, permitting limited visibility. Bubbles drifted past his face as he went deep, searching desperately for any sign of Daniel.

Without warning, his hair pulled taut, and his head jerked back. Startled, Sawyer lost a burst of air. Hands seized him from behind. They locked about his waist and forced him upward. He twisted, attempting to break the other swimmer's hold, but his assailant clung fast.

As they broke the surface, Sawyer automatically gasped, dragging deep breaths into his strained lungs. Wet hair clung to his face and obscured his vision. Blinking, he ran his hand across his eyes and found Morena treading water in front of him.

"Sawyer, you're hallucinating! There's no one—"

Hands together, he tucked his head and shoulders and submerged again. Her gurgled voice followed him as if she'd stuck her face underwater to keep shouting at him. Kicking hard, he propelled his body downward into the cold, dark depths. A single imperative ruled him—he had to save his brother.

His angled arms spearheaded his dive. Using his legs for propulsion, he sank, releasing a steady stream of bubbles to aid with his descent. Visibility constricted to no more than a few inches in front of his face. The absolute blackness made blindness his reality. Instead, he used his hands to search for Daniel.

He struck an impossibly hard, jagged object head on. Pain lanced through his cranium and shoulder, and he drifted into a tumbling spiral. His groggy mind struggled to regain his bearings, but it only got darker.

The pressure in his chest built. His lungs burned. As he neared the upper limit of his capacity to hold his breath, a sense of urgency impinged on his single-minded determination to rescue his brother. He needed to go up for air, but the lack of visual cues rendered him disoriented. He no longer knew up from down.

Stupid.

Evading Morena's attempts to help him had been pure foolishness. Distantly, he wondered if the teenager had given up or lost him in the gloomy water. If she quit, he wouldn't blame her.

Hanging on by a whisper of reason, he fought the instinct to struggle, aware that strenuous physical exertion used up his remaining air faster. Sawyer slid through the water, hoping his body's natural buoyance would float him toward the surface before he drowned.

Dreamlike images of childhood memories filled his mind.

The summer Sawyer turned six, Arizona's stifling August heat, over a hundred degrees in the shade, made life unbearable. Long days of summer boredom stretched behind him, and the imminent threat of school starting the next week loomed like the hangman's gallows. In those days, Jake was absent more often than home, always away on hunting trips.

"I'm bored!" Sawyer shouted at Daniel, trying to obtain his attention.

His older brother never looked up from his video game. "Go play outside."

"It's hot. I want to go swimming."

"Well, you can't. Not till mom gets back from the store."

Something seized his hand. Startled, Sawyer jerked away but failed to break the grip. He reached for his belt knife, but when he opened his eyes, an eerie orb, haloed in a greenish light, filled his vision. His brother's visage came into rapid, close-up focus, the rest of his body obfuscated by the absolute darkness that surrounded them.

The sight of Daniel's floating head sent a jagged bolt of uneasiness lancing through Sawyer. His entire body convulsed. The jolt set him to tumbling through the dark water. It was a nightmarish memory that was only too fresh in his mind.

Early on a December evening of the prior year, Victoria drove up to the Barrett residence in the Chevelle. Sawyer was home alone, and he recalled being curious and concerned at her arrival, but he recognized her as Adair Storm's daughter. Tearful and incoherent, she offered a garbled explanation, but he no longer remembered exactly what she'd said as she dragged him toward the vehicle.

What he recalled with perfect clarity was his blank horror when he laid uncomprehending eyes on what she had wrapped in an old pattered blanket—his brother's decapitated corpse. What followed remained hazy, a blur of violence and fury. He'd pursued her halfway across the country with unthinking rage, trying to avenge Daniel's death.

Sawyer's gaze locked with Daniel's. He stared deep into his brother's eyes, perceiving awful torment and anguish. Love and loyalty washed through him, reinforcing his determination to help at any price. His grip tightened. He wouldn't let go, not for anything.

Wishing he possessed the ability to share his thoughts, Sawyer verbalized his commitment, *I'm here. I've got you. I won't ever let go, no matter what...*

Sawyer's oxygen-starved lungs burned.

Daniel's lips formed words. As if crossing a great distance, his voice carried, but the words were indecipherable. The sound echoed to another decade, another time of great duress. At six-years-old, Sawyer had been a know-it-all with no sense of his own mortality.

"But I wanna!"

"No! You know the rules!" Daniel growled, still focused entirely on his video game. "No swimming till Mom gets home."

"Fuck the rules!" The F-bomb was the first dirty word Sawyer ever learned, and he loved the forbidden sound. "Fuck, fuck, fuck. Fuck the rules. Fuck everything and everyone."

"Mom hears you talkin' like that, she'll make you eat soap."

"Yeah, fuck the rules."

The Arizona sun blazed white-hot overhead, and the pool was as warm as a bath as he slid into the deep end off the side. He swam for a while, laps at first, working off some of his excess energy. Then he floated on his back, staring at the clear blue sky. Sucking in a deep breath, he sank beneath the surface, releasing a steady stream of bubbles as he drifted downward. At the eight-foot mark, he struck concrete.

"Sawyer!" Daniel's voice was full of frantic fear and urgency.

Hands seized his shoulders and attempted to turn him. Doggedly, Sawyer tightened his hold on his brother's hand. No one would tear them apart, never again. He stared into Daniel's face, needing his brother to see the promise.

Objects, wavering tendrils like tentacles all adjoined at the base, sliced through his brother's head and disrupted the vision so it disintegrated into a swirl of dark energy. *A monster? Magic?* Before he decided, Morena's foxlike face appeared in his peripheral vision. Her hands locked on his forearm, and she tugged, trying to separate him from Daniel.

Convulsing, Sawyer expelled the last of his air. Through an act of sheer will, he aborted the reflexive inhalation that would suck water into his lungs. Instead, he clamped his eyes and mouth shut. Suffocation was by far preferable to drowning. He refused to release his hand clasp with his brother.

Daniel's shout grew fainter but more coherent,

"Sawyer, let…"

He floated on the bottom of the pool until the burn in his lungs reached the point where he had to go up for air. He pushed off only to discover the sluggish response of his body. Head thick, limbs leaden, he felt as if his insides were filled with sand and weighing him down.

With a panicked effort, he worked his arms and kicked for all he was worth. Flailing, he broke the surface long enough to gasp a lungful of air, and then he submerged again. He managed to come up one more time before the strength to fight deserted him. He floated for a time, panted his final breaths, and then silently slid beneath the clear water.

Fingers pinched the tops of his ears hard. His eyes popped open just as Morena jerked his head toward her. Her mouth covered his own, lips pressed together to create a seal. She forced him to open and blew air into his lungs. His starved body latched onto the lifeline. His free hand molded to the back of her head, his fingers grasping for her short hair.

"Sawyer, let go!"

Sawyer's entire body thrashed. Turning Morena with him, he twisted to look for Daniel. Instead, he saw the enormous bulk of the submerged tree trunk sprawled on its side like a felled giant. His hand was grasping the stump of a branch, anchoring him to the bottom of the lake.

He opened his hand and let go.

Morena released his ears and yanked her mouth away. Strong, small hands grasped his arms, and he grabbed hold of her in return. Together, they pushed off the bottom and kicked in unison. Precious seconds later, their heads broke the surface. Water streamed from his long hair and down the sides of his face as he looked upward toward the sun.

Clean, blessed air flooded Sawyer's lungs as he floated on his back. He lacked the energy necessary to do anything else. He gazed up at the infinite blue sky overhead, breathing heavily while his body replenished its depleted oxygen reserves. Confusion and curiosity about what had happened thrummed in the back of his mind, but for the moment, he was thrilled to be alive.

A short distance away, Morena floated beside him. The teenager recovered first. He could tell because he heard her muttering beneath her breath. "Idiot hunter..."

Sawyer tilted his head toward her. "No argument here."

Not this time anyway.

Convulsions wracked Sawyer's young body as he expelled pool water from his lungs. The blistering pavement baked his bare skin, and his brother's hands pressed hard against his back, an additional layer of abuse. Daniel's voice shouted recriminations in his ears long before his vision resolved.

"You idiot! I told you, Sawyer, no swimming till mom gets home! Oh man, you're in a shitload of trouble. You're gonna get a whipping when dad hears about this stunt."

Female voices carried across the lake. Wolves echoed the calls, voices raised in plaintive howls. Treading water, he turned toward the cacophony. He spotted Victoria's white-blonde head as the she-wolf swam steadily toward them. The Native American woman, Sylvie, watched from the shore along with the mother wolf and three pups.

"What happened?" Victoria asked once she reached them.

"Sawyer tried to kill himself," Morena snapped out, jerking her head toward the hunter. She added something in Spanish and lifted her arm out of the water to gesticulate.

His tired mind struggled to translate. She was pretty much calling him an idiot again. He had to love a woman who could curse him as a fool in three distinct tongues, although the names she called him in Old Norse were usually far cruder.

Victoria's dubious gaze swung toward him. "If you

wanted to drown yourself, you coulda just said so. I've got some burlap sacks in the shed."

"I did not try to drown myself." Irritation pricked at him despite his fatigue. Being cursed with the company of smartass werewolves must be the price fate had determined he should pay.

"Let's get to shore and then discuss this." Victoria's tongue clicked against the roof of her mouth, and she grabbed for Sawyer's arm.

Even exhausted, Sawyer evaded her attempts to help him. He set out at a slow but steady sidestroke aimed at the shore. He might not arrive fast, but he'd arrive under his own power.

"Idiot," Victoria muttered. The she-wolf followed, effectively hovering by swimming circles around him.

"That's what I said." Ever impatient, Morena shot off through the water, splashing the adults behind her with a couple kicks undoubtedly designed to throw up a wave.

Closer to shore, the depth became shallow enough for Sawyer to stand. Sharp rocks bit into the bottoms of his feet as he trudged onto land. He slicked back his wet hair, and dropped to his knees on the cobblestone. Bending over, a sense of detachment swept him even as he experienced the heaving of his lungs and the throb of his heart with increased awareness.

He'd almost drowned. His worst nightmare manifested as reality.

Victoria walked to hug Morena. "Are you all right?"

"I'm fine." Morena mustered a smile.

"Let's get everyone inside right away." Like a matriarchal hammer, Sylvie took command of the situation. They were rounded up and herded to the house. Following imperious commands, Sawyer stripped naked, donned a towel, and then was shoved into a seat in the kitchen. While his wet clothing was whisked away, allegedly destined for the dryer, he sipped tea. The hot liquid spread from his belly, warming his core.

Sylvie dropped a quilt over his shoulders, and one of the pups lay across his bare feet like a giant furry slipper. A comforting aura of belonging suffused him— *home.*

A chair's legs scraped on the tile as Victoria sat across from him. She leaned toward him, her blonde hair slicked against her skull. Her blue eyes were intense. "Sawyer, what happened? Morena says you imagined someone drowning and charged out into the lake."

He took a slow, deep breath. Discomfort pinched at his insides, an uneasy sense of humiliation over how he'd acted. "I didn't hallucinate anything. I know what I saw. There was a distressed swimmer signaling for help. A man with dark hair."

Her lovely face contorted into a frown. "Dark hair?"

"Yeah." He nodded, unable to confess that he had believed it to be Daniel.

"I believe you." Victoria lurched to her feet. She swung toward Morena and caught the teenager in an embrace. "Thank you for going after him, Morie. We've lost enough lives already to that damn lake."

"Victoria—" With a distraught undertone to her voice, Sylvie cut off whatever she'd been about to say. The older woman and Victoria exchanged a loaded glance.

Victoria charged from the kitchen, leaving her pack behind in anxious silence. After a moment, Sylvie followed the Alpha from the room. The atmosphere of hominess vanished.

Sawyer dared break the brittle quiet first. "What just happened?"

Morena swung on him. "Arik drowned. They never found his body."

Arik. Victoria's brown-haired mate. *Shit, no wonder she looked upset.*

"Oh." Deflated, Sawyer exhaled.

After a short pause, Morena asked, "So, did he beat you?"

"Huh?" His thoughts were elsewhere, so it took him a second to process her question. He'd forgotten the pack bond worked two ways.

"Your father. Did he beat you?"

Sawyer sat upright in alarm. "How much did you see?"

Morena smirked. "Enough."

His chair creaked when he rocked back. His hands dropped to his lap. "No, my father never laid a finger on us. When one of us got a whippin', my mom did it. My ass still hurts to this day."

Snickering, Morena ducked her head.

Desperately desiring to restore the comforting aura, he extended his hand and touched Morena's elbow.

Fine eyebrows drawn together, she tilted her face and looked at him. "What?"

"You saved my life. Thank you."

With a rough yank, she pulled her arm free. "You're a member of the pack. I was obligated. This doesn't change anything."

Except to increase exponentially what he owed her.

"I still hate you!" Morena glared at him.

He smiled. "I know."

Victoria joined Sawyer an hour later as he leaned against the Chevelle's hood. He snapped his math textbook shut. Reaching through the open window, he dropped his book onto the front seat and used one finger to shove his sunglasses into place.

"Ready to go?" He noted the strap bisecting her breasts, the bulk of the duffle slung behind her. His gaze lingered longer than appropriate. Flushing, he looked away.

She snickered. "Almost." Opening the passenger

side door, she slung the bag over her head and stowed it in the backseat. "Before we go, there's something I wanted to ask you..."

She trailed off into uncertainty, so he waited. When the normally plainspoken Victoria failed to elaborate, Sawyer rounded the car and stood beside the open door. She chewed on her lower lip, hands closed to fists. Her pensive expression unsettled him. Not a good feeling, considering recent events had left him downright spooked. His clumsy attempt to use the empathic connection to read her hit a brick wall, and he sensed her blocking him.

"Spit it out," he grated. "I'm not in the mood for any more surprises."

Her regard focused on him, blue and belligerent. She snapped, "Me either."

They glared at one another, grim-faced, jaws jutting. Tension stretched, silk drawn taut, fine and thin. Sawyer wasn't sure who cracked the first smile, but he found himself grinning stupidly.

"What's your question?"

She swallowed a smile. "Out on the lake, when you thought you saw Daniel, was there anything..."

A serpent coiled in his gut. "Yeah?"

"Odd?" She bit the word in half.

He huffed in exasperation and ran a hand through his hair. "The whole damn thing was odd. Can you be more specific?"

Nodding, she eased around the car door separating them. "Did you sense anything that felt like magic, like someone was controlling your mind or influencing your emotions?"

He blinked. "You mean like your Jedi mind trick?"

Her lips thinned. "Yes, like that."

Sawyer rolled the matter around in his mind. The whole thing had him freaked out, but he didn't recall anything specific. Nothing to make him ascribe the experience to external influences. Eventually, he shook his head. "I don't know. Maybe. I'd swear it was real. Too real."

She nodded. "Okay."

"Why?"

"No reason." Without another word, she climbed into the Chevelle's passenger seat and pulled the door shut with a solid thunk.

He stood rooted in place for several seconds. Arms raised, he allowed his head to loll and gazed skyward. His lips formed a silent word, *Women.* The chirping birds offered no ready explanation, so he climbed in and started the engine.

He drove south toward Arizona for several miles. Victoria stared out the window, perfectly motionless in the manner of a predator. Against his better judgment, he harbored illicit curiosity about her relationship with his brother. There were too many unknowns, too many unanswered questions.

Curiosity got the better of him. Staring straight ahead, he asked, "How did you meet my brother?"

After a hesitation, she answered, "Daniel pulled me over for speeding and wrote me up."

"He must have known who you were," Sawyer said skeptically. The Barrett family and the Storm Pack had been allies for over thirty years prior to the war that now divided them. Hunters and wolves never socialized but often coordinated their efforts to defend the Phoenix area and their mutual, overlapping territories.

"Oh, he knew all right. But he pulled me over in an unmarked vehicle and peacock-strutted alongside my car with his thumbs hooked in his belt, his hands framing that big brass Winchester Repeating Arms belt buckle of his. He tilted his hat and let his sunglasses slip down his nose and he said..." Victoria affected a deep baritone. "'*Miss, do you know how fast you were going?*'"

"Oh yeah, that was Danny." Chuckling, Sawyer

glanced over and found her smiling at him.

"Such bullshit! No one drove faster than your brother." Victoria rolled her eyes. "I tried to change his mind about the ticket."

"Flirting?" A smile tugged at the corner of his mouth. Daniel had been a sucker for gorgeous blondes.

She laughed. "Something like that."

He slanted a side stare at her. Damn, curiosity was killing him, and not asking required all of his self-control.

After a moment, Victoria relented. "After he handed me the citation, he asked for my phone number. So I wrote my phone number on the back of the ticket and gave him a choice." She grinned. "You can probably guess what he chose."

"Yeah, I think so." He laughed, wanting to cry with grief for his brother.

"He was a good man." Sorrow turned her voice watery.

"Yeah, the best. Fuck, I miss him." White-knuckled, Sawyer clutched the steering wheel and choked on the awful emptiness. The one time he would have welcomed the pack bond, silence filled his mind.

Victoria remained cut off from him.

"Yeah," she said, echoing his loneliness and loss. "Me too."

CHAPTER TWELVE

Sessrúmnir, Freya's hall in Fólkvangr

Scowling, Loki sneered. "Love is worthless."

"Love is everything. Only one who is unloved would dismiss it so."

His mouth opened, but for once, the talkative Trickster offered no witty insults, no ready retorts. He looked lost and sad.

Seeing an opportunity to press her advantage, Freya smirked. "It's been centuries since you ordered your wolf children to pledge fealty to the Aesir, Loki. Even among the wolf shifters, your name is spoken with derision. You are hated by your own blood."

"I did what I had to do to protect them from Odin's wrath," he said. "Their fealty was false. Their loyalty a lie."

"Ah, but where have you been?" Freya asked, deliberately taunting him. "You have been a neglectful father. All those who knew it was supposed to be a false promise are dead. Without a reminder, their descendants have forgotten their god."

Freya smiled and savored his bitter realization. How it must sting!

"So Victoria loves you." A slow, wicked smile spread on the Trickster's lips. "Ah, but do you love her?

Because you do realize that you're going to have to command her to cut Fenrir's bonds. We have a deal."

The taste of bile replaced the sweet satisfaction in her throat. "There is only one reason you would say such a thing—"

He nodded. "Ragnarök is coming."

Midgard

Fucking werewolves never stopped complicating his life.

A vein throbbed in Jake Barrett's temple, and he imagined the pressure building in his skull until the vessel burst. Weariness and hunger aggravated his irritation, and having a pack of wolves hijack his personal traitor had put him in a less than premium mood. Skinner's news was the cherry on the shit sundae.

Jake squinted to compensate for the glare of the late afternoon sun. "Say that again."

His friend flashed a fierce grin. "Sure thing. Should I talk slower?"

"Don't be an ass."

Skinner chuckled. "Way too late for that."

"Skinner..." A note of warning crept into his voice, a sign of his short-temper.

"It's fucked up beyond all recognition," Skinner said. "We followed Chart to Payson, hanging back so he wouldn't make us. He pulled over for fuel, and a group of werewolves grabbed him. We chased 'em, but they crossed into their territory, so I called off the pursuit."

His nostrils flared as he exhaled. What reason could Fireball Finn and the White Mountains Tribe have for abducting Andy Chart?

"Did I make the wrong call?" Skinner asked.

"Nah, you made the right call. Did the Alpha give a reason for wanting Chart?" Jake shifted his stance and surveyed the hunters scattered throughout their loose convoy of stopped vehicles. His people possessed the equipment and training of an elite para-military unit. Civilians regarded them as an ultra-right-wing private militia, but they operated with the knowledge, sanction, and funding of the federal government.

At a glance, his people looked bored as they cleaned firearms, shot the breeze, and bent their heads over phone screens. At the front end of her Jeep, Crazy Cali Kinkaid carried on a muttered conversation with the hood while she abused the tire with the point of her steel-toed boot. Coiled tension lurked beneath the unit's apparent ennui. One of their own had betrayed them, and they lusted for vengeance.

"Fireball wants to meet with you in person," Skinner said.

"Let's get this over with then."

Skinner scowled. "You going alone?"

Jake bared his teeth and addressed his people. His voice rose. "We go together."

A cheer arose from the ranks, a bloodthirsty furor.

Skinner shouted but then dropped his volume, speaking to Jake in an aside. "You gonna tell Finn to stick it up his ass if he objects?"

He chuckled. "Nah, I'll let you have the honors. Let's move out."

Ten miles outside Show Low, the hunters parked their vehicles. Carrying backpacks and firearms, they hiked into the remote location the werewolves had chosen for the meeting. His unit wasn't at full-strength. Due to losses suffered during the ambush in Tucson, their numbers were down by more than a tenth.

At the prospect of another potentially lethal confrontation, tension soared in the unit. Voices rose along with fiercely competitive banter.

"Smell that? Good, clean nature. That's what you smell."

"All I smell is shit."

"That's 'cause you're walking behind Mendoza. His ma never did teach him how to wipe his ass."

Raucous laughter ripped through the entire unit before Skinner busted their asses. "Buncha fucking sissies," Skinner shouted. "Listen up, men. So long as I'm the Mother Fucker in Charge of this unit, I don't want to hear anymore pansy-assed whining. Makes me think we need to engage in some serious PT once we return to base. Anyone else got anything negative to say about our nature walk?"

"Not a word, sir," Crazy Cali shot back. "I'd like to say that I think it's fucking fantastic that there's nothing mechanical present that might blow the fuck up."

For a second, Skinner's face looked ready to explode. Brow arched, he traded a look with Jake.

"Woman's got a point," Jake muttered.

"Amen to that." Shaking his head, Skinner walked away.

Alpha Finn and what looked to be his entire pack met them at the agreed upon location in the wilderness just beyond the reservation's border. The two groups squared off, a couple hundred feet separating them.

His men were armed with firearms loaded with silver ammunition, but Jake hoped against hope it didn't come to that. Even against automatic rifles, the werewolves had the advantage at close range.

With Skinner at his side, Jake surveyed the wolves.

"This doesn't look good," Skinner muttered. "We're way outnumbered."

"Just the opposite, this is very good." Jake altered his grip on his rifle, stroking the black walnut stock, taking pleasure in the smooth grain of the wood beneath his fingertips. "He's brought females with pups, the lame, and the elderly. He expects to talk, not fight."

Skinner grunted. "Sure hope you're right."

"I'm right. Finn has too much cunning to make the mistake of placing his people in harm's way," Jake said confidently. "No, they're here 'cause he wants them to bear witness."

In terms of total numbers, when non-shifter kinfolk, mates, and children were counted, the White Mountains Tribe was the largest in Arizona. Jake knew the pack boasted close to a hundred werewolves, making it the strongest in several states. To win the war with the undead, he needed to restore the alliance. Gaining the support of Finn and his pack was an essential piece of the bigger puzzle. If Finn threw his support behind a new treaty, smaller packs would follow suit.

With his second-in-command at his side, Jake walked out to the midway point between the two groups. The time-honored ritual of negotiating with the strength of his army at his back dated to antiquity. As a military man who hated the deception and pretense of modern politics, he had a deep appreciation for the traditional practice.

As a human, Finn stood over eight-feet tall. The Alpha had the flaming-ginger hair of a Norseman and the brown skin of a Native American. He fairly represented the blended heritage of his people.

Accompanying Finn was a man known to Jake as Tarak. The muscular werewolf was a full head shorter than the Alpha. He had braided black-hair, brown skin, and Apache tribal tattoos on his bare biceps. By reputation, he was a fierce warrior, bloodthirsty and sadistic, and intolerant of outsiders.

Finn's broad smile displayed a wide swath of teeth. "Jake Barrett, welcome to the territory of the White Mountains Pack. I'm surprised to see you here so soon after our encounter down south. It is intriguing how fate keeps bringing us together."

Jake scowled, curbing the desire to call the Alpha on his bullshit. "Finn, why have you taken Andy Chart hostage?"

"You have a particular interest in this man Chart?"

He scowled, on the edge of losing his temper. Games annoyed him. He had no patience for scheming, and he refused to play. "I think you damn well know who he is."

Finn's head dipped as he traded a sideways glance with Tarak before returning to the hunter. "He is not our hostage. He is a... Guest. I am curious to know why you are so interested in him."

The fuse to Jake's temper ignited at a slow burn. His hands worked, opening and closing, and he nailed the Alpha with a deadly stare. "Are you certain you're not mistaken, Finn? Andy Chart is a traitor, the worst sort of coward. If you insist upon proclaiming friendship with him, you can see how I might conclude that you acted as his co-conspirator."

Finn's mouth opened and surprise flickered across his face before he controlled his reaction. Wariness glinted in the wolf's eyes. A considerate pause ensued, and then he asked, "What has he done?"

"He tried to assassinate me—"

"Then he's a fool," the Alpha said. "It is well known that you cannot die. No matter how many may wish it were so."

Tarak's lips curled, and he glared at the hunter. "Everyone dies. Even the gods."

"Bring it on, Fuzzball." Skinner tightened his grip on the stock of his rifle. The hunter's aggression incited an immediate response from the Beta werewolf.

Tarak snarled, bristling menacingly.

Finn's head turned toward his second. Glaring, a growl rumbled in his throat. "No."

Sullenly, Tarak glared at Skinner, but he stood down.

Jake let the incident pass without remark. "We have reason to believe that Andy Chart is responsible for the explosion that killed Adair and Katherine Storm."

The muscles in Finn's face tightened. "They say Adair's daughter murdered your son."

A tick worked in the hunter's jaw. "*They say* lots of things."

"I do not hear you making denials." Finn's direct gaze challenged him. "They also say you ambushed the Storm Pack, murdering the Alphas and many others in revenge."

Jake met the werewolf's gaze. "On my honor, I wasn't behind those explosions. We were set up. Just as many hunters died that day."

"I sense no deception about you." Finn shrugged his skepticism. "However, you are known to have powerful magic. How am I to know whether you possess the ability to deceive me?"

The insult to Jake's honor offended him, but he masked his displeasure. "What if Victoria Storm vouched for what I'm telling you?"

Finn's head jerked back. A stir passed through his followers, murmurs of astonishment and speculation. "Adair's daughter is still alive?"

No thanks to Sawyer's best efforts.

Jake arched his brow. "Would her word be sufficient?"

The Alpha's eyes hooded, and his voice grew shrewd. "I would listen to what she has to say. For the moment, I notice that she is not here, and so, once again, I have only your word..."

"That's not entirely accurate," Jake replied. "You have Andy Chart. If he confirms what I say, then you would have proof that he is a poor assassin and a traitor."

Snickers passed through the werewolves. A few even dared chuckle until their Alpha's angry glare raked over them.

"Why would this man admit to such a thing?" Finn

asked. "Does he have a death wish?"

"He must. He betrayed me." Jake smiled, a cold, deadly smile that never reached his eyes. "Allow me to speak with him, and he will confess. I can be very convincing. If he speaks the truth, you will know it, since you can smell lies."

Spine ramrod stiff, Tarak's head jerked in silent denial. Behind him, the pack's reaction ranged from curious to furious, but awaited Finn's reaction.

Jake ignored the Beta wolf and stared straight at the Alpha, the center of true power within the tribe. He had the patience of a veteran huntsman. He could wait for as long as it took the Alpha to make up his mind. Fortunately, Finn didn't strike him as the contemplative sort.

"Why not?" Finn's face lit with a huge grin. He punched his Beta on the arm. "Stop scowling, my friend. What do you have against good entertainment?"

"Nothing." Grumbling, Tarak spun and marched off. Members of the pack turned and followed him.

As he watched the others leave, Jake found himself standing shoulder to shoulder beside Finn. The hunter turned his head to address the Alpha. "I hope you're not too attached to your guest. I'm going to carve Chart into pieces and curse him to eternal damnation."

"You are furious. It is good." Finn eyed him shrewdly. "My father often told the tale of how the Hunter King rose from the dead and went on to slay a dragon. He described runes that arose beneath your skin, turning it as black as coal. It is a sight I have waited to see my entire life."

Gruffly, Jake cleared his throat. "It was a small dragon, more of a big fucking lizard."

"You're a funny man." Chortling, Finn clobbered his shoulder with a meaty paw. "I've seen the photographs."

Right. Jake huffed. "Of course you have."

Snickering, Finn strolled away, shaking his head. "Big fucking lizard, my ass!"

The man's hoarse screams rent the midday sky. On a wide rock platform, he lay spread-eagle, chained and naked. Sweat beaded on his skin, forming rivulets that flowed across the raw, branded flesh of his ribcage and mingled with blood before dripping onto the thirsty limestone. The stench of pain and urine punctured the sweet aroma of springtime wilderness.

A pair of ravens perched on the branch of an old tree, witnessing the spectacle.

"*Please, please, please. I confess. No more!*" Almost incomprehensible, he sobbed for mercy. "*I admit to it all.*"

With the back of his hand, Jake wiped perspiration from his brow. He hesitated, staying another downward stroke of the burning dagger in his hand. More than a dozen burn marks delivered by the flat of the blade branded Andy Chart's naked skin.

Forming a loose circle, his fellow hunters and the White Mountains Pack bore silent, fascinated witness to the interrogation.

Turning his head, Jake traded a loaded glance with Skinner. If the wolves refused to accept Chart's confession under duress, then they needed to be prepared for a sudden escalation.

Skinner nodded his understanding, adjusting his grip on the stock of his rifle.

Summoning his power, Jake reached through the mystical connection he shared with his men. He infused the bond with magic, and the dagger tattoo on the arm of every hunter glowed red-hot.

Finn issued a threatening rumble, and the rest of his pack echoed the warning. "Is this treachery, hunter?"

Jake shouted over the din. "This is justice, Alpha. Just as your people have their code, we have ours."

Finn's head lowered, but he ceased growling and so did the other wolves. "Proceed."

Jake leaned over Chart. He brandished the molten

hot dagger over the traitor's face. "What are you confessing to, Andy? Say it so there's no doubt or confusion."

A shudder wracked Chart. "I shot you at the farm. I set the bomb at the silo."

"Why?"

"I was ordered to."

An itch of irritation prickled his already short temper. Jake allowed the point of the blade to dip toward Andy's eye. "I want useful information."

"No, no, wait, wait!" Chart howled his panic, struggling furiously within the iron shackles which bound him to the rock. "I'm working for a necromancer. He wanted you and Victoria Storm killed together in the same explosion!"

Through the magic binding them, Jake believed Chart spoke the truth. But he wanted more information. He needed specifics. "What's the necromancer's name?"

"I don't know."

"Why did he want us killed at the same time?"

The prisoner's taut muscles formed ridges beneath his skin. Sweat poured from his face, and his chest heaved from hard breathing. "I don't know."

"You'd better tell me something you do know, fast, or I'll take it out of your hide," Jake threatened.

A tear leaked from the corner of Chart's eye and trickled along his cheek. "All I know is that he's playing elaborate games, pulling strings and manipulating people through agents. That's the truth. You have to believe me."

"Do you know the names of any more of his agents?"

"No, I don't. I've seen Vildivia, the master vampire who works for him. But he mostly kept me in the dark." Frantically, Andy shook his head.

When the dagger descended toward the side of his face, a fresh flood of information spewed from Chart. "I've only been working for him for six months. At first, I only supplied him with information. I thought that was as far as it would go, but after Vildivia killed Daniel, the Necromancer ordered me to set those bombs at the airfield. They were only supposed to kill werewolves."

Growls erupted from the White Mountains wolves. The entire pack bristled and shifted restlessly. Jake remained focused on his prisoner and trusted Finn to control his people.

"No one else was supposed to get hurt," Chart continued. "You have to believe me."

"I believe you." Sickness formed a vortex in Jake's gut. If one rat had managed to survive in his organization undetected for six months, what were the odds there were others?

"Why did you betray us, Andy?" Skinner demanded. His huge body radiated anger from every pore. The specter of violence rode on his shoulders as he gave voice to the question burning in the hearts of all his fellow hunters.

Chart turned his head and spat out a mouthful of blood and bile. A coughing fit seized him, and he suffered a fit of convulsions before his breathing calmed enough to allow him to speak. "I'm dying. Melanoma. It's spread throughout my body. I've got weeks to live, a couple months max."

"This Necromancer, he promised you a cure?" Jake asked.

Chart jerked his head to the side in a gesture neither nod nor shake.

Jake hazarded a guess. "He promised you immortality?"

Chart barked out an abrupt laugh. "Yeah, he promised me I'd live forever if I served him."

"Did you tell the Necromancer that my son and Victoria Storm were lovers?" Jake asked, his tone deceptively mild. Following the revelation, gasps huffed from both his people and the werewolves.

Oddly, he experienced no discomfort or self-consciousness regarding the admission. Through repeated conflicts with the petite blonde Alpha of the Storm Pack, he'd come to admire Victoria's tenacity, courage, and resilience. His son's woman. To Jake's singular regret, Daniel never told him, because multiple tragedies could have been averted.

Sudden anger shone in Chart's eyes. "Yes, I told him. Daniel betrayed you by bedding that bitch—"

His fist slammed into Andy's face, shattering the cheekbone. Burning with fury, Jake wiped the blood from his knuckles. With one hand, he grasped Chart's face and immobilized his head.

"You'll never speak my son's name again, traitor." A swift precision strike of the dagger's blade sliced Andy's mouth wide open at the corners and severed the root of his tongue.

While Chart screamed and flailed, blood gushed from the injury.

Grasping the piece of muscle, Jake tossed the chunk to the dirt. An enormous raven swooped from the sky and snatched the morsel up in his shiny beak. Head cocked, black eyes gleaming, the bird swallowed the meat whole.

Stepping back, Jake planted his feet far apart. Deliberately, he wrapped both hands about the hilt of his dagger and held it over his head, aimed at Chart's chest. Primal magic throbbed through his body. Runes ascended from his core and appeared beneath his tanned skin as distinct ciphers that vibrated with power. They expanded until the writhing symbols interlocked and blackened his complexion.

Clouds rolled out of the clear sky, so close to the ground they formed a stairway to heaven. Lightning arcs struck the stone above Chart's head, and then thunder swallowed his screams.

"You betrayed me. You betrayed your hunter brothers, Andy Chart." Jake boomed like the thunder. "Since you seek immortality, I grant you eternal life. For your part in the murder of my son, you'll suffer until the world ends."

The Hunter King plunged the dagger deep into the traitor's chest, striking the sternum. Bone cracked and flesh sizzled. Gritting his teeth in a savage smile, Jake cleaved Chart's sternum in half from top to bottom. Then he willed the dagger to return to his arm as a tattoo.

With his bare hands, Jake pried apart the traitor's ribcage, spreading the two halves wide to expose the internal organs. An awful stench filled the air. He smeared his face with his enemy's blood and then scooped out the insides. He placed the beating heart, the breathing lungs, and other internal organs upon the rock table.

Overhead, ravens released triumphant *crraas* while Chart screamed in agony. The hunters shouted with the bloodthirsty desire to see the man who had betrayed them suffer, and wolves howled their approval.

Grim-faced, Jake finished his work and stepped back to survey what he'd done. It was good. He'd emblazoned his name upon Andy Chart's soul. The curse would endure for the rest of time—however long or short that happened to be.

Satisfied, he faced his men. Power blazed, unifying them in their resolve and reinforcing their solidarity. "My son's death, our brotherhood's honor, isn't fully avenged. But I promise you, we're going to destroy all who oppose us."

His men shouted at the tops of their lungs, a cheer embodying their support and loyalty.

Jake addressed Finn, staring at the werewolf from behind his blood mask. "Are you satisfied? Have I proven that Chart is a traitor?"

Yellow eyes glowing, the Alpha grinned. His voice was silky smooth. "It was everything I'd hoped it to be. I am convinced. Let's go somewhere more comfortable to continue our negotiations."

Jake turned to the ravens watching overhead. *Watch over Chart. See to it he is never set free.*

A raucous *craa* answered his command.

They reconvened in a tiny community a few miles from Andy Chart's crucible. Finn and Tarak invited Jake and Skinner into a small adobe building to continue their negotiations. The rest of the hunters waited outside, seeking shade beneath a grove of trees in the courtyard of the village's library. The furnishings were sparse, but luxury didn't concern Jake. It never had.

"You had an agenda when you brought Chart here," Jake said. "You wanted me here, so I came. All you've done is play games."

Finn's head tilted to the side, and he studied Tarak with a sideways glance. His nostrils flared as he exhaled. "I would prefer to speak with you alone, Jake Barrett."

Tarak stiffened, and he barked out a protest. "Alpha!"

"Silence. Leave us."

Under the Alpha's watchful gaze, the recalcitrant Tarak stood and headed toward the door. Skinner's brow rose, and he grinned. He traded a pointed look with Jake and then headed for the door without a word.

Just as Tarak reached the exit, Finn rumbled a command. "Tarak, send in Bodaway and Lenna."

Anger crossed Tarak's face. He held Finn's gaze and then dropped his eyes in submission. "Yes, Alpha."

Tarak departed.

Skinner left, shutting the door behind him.

Silence reigned. To make his point, Jake locked gazes with the Alpha and refused to look away. "How is it that your war party came to be in the Santa Catalina Mountains in the first place, Finn? It's a long way from your territory..."

Finn leaned closer, intense energy animating his hulking form. He exuded the aura of power associated with Alpha wolves. "Thor sent me a vision."

Jake stroked his beard. "Thor?"

"I am his follower." Revealing his bicep, Finn proudly displayed a tattoo, *Mjölnir*, Thor's hammer.

He studied the symbol and nodded acceptance. "Who are Bodaway and Lenna?"

Finn's mouth puckered as if he'd sucked on sour lemons. His yellow eyes shone with gemstone hardness. "Bodaway is a priest of Heimdallr."

Heimdallr, Guardian of the Rainbow Bridge.

Jake nodded. "And the woman?"

Giving the impression that he might burst, Finn stilled and then slowly exhaled. "Lenna is the she-wolf who was slain in the battle at the mine."

"Ah." Jake crossed his arms and waited. As he anticipated, his forbearance won out over Finn's limited patience.

"Bodaway is insisting that Lenna's soul was rejected by the Valkyries. He says she was passed over for entry to Valhalla and cursed to return to this wretched existence. Her life thread was cut by the Norns, so she is doomed."

Floored by surprise, Jake failed to retain control over his demeanor. His anger percolated to the surface. "That's the most self-serving bullshit..."

Eyes gleaming, Finn crossed his arms over his chest. The redhead cocked his head. "I saw what transpired with my own *two* eyes."

Jake tensed. His fingers flexed, but he aborted the automatic grab for his dagger. "What do you think you saw, Finn?"

The Alpha chuckled. "I know old One-Eye when I see him."

The hunter stilled. His brow arched, he held the wolf's gaze and waited.

"The affairs of the gods are none of my concern." Finn's tone remained low, demonstrating circumspection at odds with his blunt demeanor. He leaned closer and talked faster. "The fact is that I'm eager to serve, should the opportunity present itself. However, there are politics, even within my own pack..."

Within seconds of ruining a lifetime of secrecy for the sake of cementing a new alliance, Jake opened his mouth, but an inopportune pounding on the door of Finn's office prevented him from saying anything.

Snarling, Finn swung toward the entryway. "What is it?"

After a measureable delay, the door swung inward and revealed a tall, thin man of Native American descent. His face, throat, and hands bore extensive burn marks which disappeared beneath his long sleeve shirt. Gray hair grew in scraggly patches from his scored scalp.

The man's gaze snaked through the room before he looked down and slithered into the room. His voice was oily and obsequious. "You wished to speak with me, Alpha?"

A slender young woman followed him, walking with her head bowed and her hands clasped before her. She had light brown hair and skin. She hunched as if trying to take up as little space as possible, and her gaze remained firmly fixed on the ground.

Tarak stood behind the pair but remained in the doorway as if obeying the letter of his Alpha's command. Jake made note of the division between the two highest ranked wolves of the White Mountains Tribe. The information might prove useful.

"This is Bodaway, my priest of Heimdallr," Finn informed Jake. "Bodaway, please repeat what you told me."

Bodaway arched his pencil thin brow. "All of it, Alpha?"

"All of it."

Bodaway shot Jake a conniving glance before reciting his speech. "These are trying, perilous times we live in, Alpha. A long winter is coming, and we must choose our path with great care. Those who align with the Hunter King have been shown to endure misfortune because it is not the will of the gods that our people should be his ally."

Jake snorted. "Which gods would those be?"

Bodaway's mouth opened and then closed. "I serve Heimdallr. He is the guardian—"

"I know who Heimdallr is," Jake interrupted.

Turned so Bodaway couldn't see, Finn rolled his eyes.

"Then why do you ask?" The priest addressed him in a facetious manner.

"I've heard enough of your lies."

Jake's proclamation elicited exclamations from Bodaway and Tarak. Their growls rolled through the office. Shame-faced, Lenna remained silent and cowered in the corner.

"How dare you!" Spittle flew from Tarak's curled lips. "How dare you denounce our gods!"

Bodaway directed his challenge to Finn. "Alpha, this is an outrage."

Finn's booming voice drowned out Bodaway. "Enough."

Silence swept the room. All eyes turned to the Alpha.

"I brought you here because you have the right to hear these accusations, Jake Barrett. Bodaway is a powerful and influential priest within my pack. Many listen to him. He has the ear of my second." Finn's mouth curled in a sly non-smile. "I wanted you to know the opposition I would face should I consider allying with you."

"Alpha," Bodaway protested. "Surely you can't

mean to align yourself with this man!"

Fiery mustache and beard bristling, Finn swung on the much smaller man and advanced, intimidating him with sheer brawn. "You have said your piece. Now you will listen."

Seething, Bodaway dropped his gaze. "Yes, Alpha."

Finn swung to the hunter. "I'd like to hear your position."

Brow furrowed, Jake strove to remain impassive. "The undead are attacking across southern Arizona with overwhelming numbers. We're fighting losing battles in Nogales and Tucson. Without the support of the packs, we don't have the manpower necessary to hold out much longer."

Finn's solemnness belied the jut of his jaw. "My pack defends its territory. What happens beyond our borders—"

"Isn't your problem," Jake finished for him. The Alpha's challenge left him unfazed. He admired Finn's cleverness in playing Devil's advocate for the sake of their audience. "That is until all of your neighbors have fallen and the enemy arrives on your doorstep. *Then* it's your problem."

Tarak snarled, revealing glistening fangs. Every head in the room turned toward the Beta wolf. "Then we shall fight and die in glorious combat, honorable deaths befitting true warriors. Our deaths will honor Odin, and we will join him in Valhalla."

Finn smiled, spreading his hands. "See what I must deal with?"

Jake's breath escaped in an exasperated huff. *Idiotic fucking fruit loop.* Striving for patience, he tilted his head back and rolled his eyes heavenward. "Have you considered the possibility that Odin doesn't appreciate senseless deaths?"

Sputtering, Bodaway choked on his outrage while Finn grinned wide enough to swallow worlds. Behind raised hands, Lenna giggled.

Silence reigned, and then Tarak choked out a challenge. "How *dare* you!"

Finn's snort diffused the buildup of outrage. "Tarak, you're going to rupture something. Relax." The Alpha addressed Jake. "Go on. I'd like to hear your proposal for unity."

"Cooperation among the packs has dissolved into chaos," Jake said. "Petty rivalries and infighting are taking priority over defeating the real enemy. While your people bicker, the undead threat is growing. A strong Alpha must step up and unite the packs again before it's too late."

Finn's lips compressed. "You want someone to fill Adair Storm's shoes."

The hunter rocked on his heels. "A tall order, I know."

"He was a great hero." Finn's gaze strayed to where Tarak and Bodaway stood united in open opposition. "You have your work cut out for you, Jake Barrett."

Jake walked over to face the Beta wolf and the priest, holding the gazes of each in turn. He looked them in the eyes and spoke with quiet determination. "Make no mistake. Those who choose to fight with me will be triumphant. Stand aside or get out of my way. If you oppose me, then you'll be destroyed and your soul won't be receiving the E-ticket to Valhalla. You'll wind up somewhere dark and deep, suffering eternal hunger and endless thirst. Hel's hounds will dismember your body, the pieces used to reinforce the walls of Hel's mansion."

Stupid Tarak fumed in silence, but real fear crossed the priest's face. His eyes widened, and he took a step backward.

Finn chuckled, spreading his hands wide. While he spoke in an amiable tone, his gaze contained forbearance. "Well, it sounds like we have much to discuss. It is too bad the hour grows so late. Perhaps we should re-convene this discussion when circumstances are more favorable."

"Another time then." Casting a glance over his shoulder, Jake regarded Finn with a newfound respect. The Alpha possessed unexpected cunning.

"Yes, another time. But soon. We must not allow too much time to pass between our visits." Finn clapped his hands together. "I don't know about you, but this has been very informative."

Jake strode from the suffocating hot room, breathing easier once he stood outside beneath the open sky. He headed toward his people who greeted him with monocyclic words and tense stares.

"We done?" Skinner asked.

He nodded. "We're done. Let's get the hell out of here."

"Jake Barrett!" Finn bellowed from across the yard.

Jake swung around to face the Alpha, his brow lifted in question.

Grasping Lenna's arm, Finn marched the young woman toward the hunters. "You have forgotten something."

"Oh?" Jake regarded the downtrodden young woman. He pitied her. She'd committed no crime, merely had the misfortune of being in the wrong place at the wrong time. Thanks to a misplaced dagger stroke, she was his responsibility.

"Lenna belongs to you now." With a gentle shove, Finn sent her stumbling toward him, and she advanced a couple steps before she stopped. "You should take her, for her own protection. Here she is in great danger."

Anger crashed through Jake. He glanced down at Lenna's bent head, and pity tempered his fury. Bending, he extended his arm and offered her an open hand.

He waited.

After a full minute, she looked up to meet his gaze, her expression full of reverence. Her trembling arm rose, and she closed his fingers around his palm. She smiled, trusting, like a child with wonder in her eyes.

Guilt pinched his conscience for how inexorably he'd altered her life with a single careless knife thrust. Exiled from her home, stripped of everything she'd ever known. As they walked away, he dropped his voice to a gentle pitch. "Your place in Valhalla is eternally assured."

She humbly lowered her face. "Thank you, my king. I am your wolf."

Long shadows stretched, providing a welcome shade from the sun's beating rays. Gripping the brim of his baseball cap, Jake adjusted the tilt to better shield his eyes while his thick fingers swiped sweat from his brow. In a few hours, he was supposed to rendezvous with Victoria and Sawyer. It would be tight, but he'd make the meeting.

His men marched ahead. Skinner strode at the front of the unit as they tracked through the forest. Flush with springtime growth, the slopes were bedecked in orange and yellow wildflowers and speckled in violet blossoms.

Lenna trailed the unit, walking apart from the hunters. Her chin hugged her chest, and her shoulders hunched. Her path ran parallel to Jake's, and he remained acutely aware of her terrible isolation.

Rejected by her people, not a member of his. She stood alone. Her plight engendered a deep tug of pity at his heartstrings. He wanted to find some way to help her, but he lacked a clear plan. Even introducing her to Victoria carried inherent risk. Wolves were territorial and rarely accepted outsiders.

The hunters neared the dirt turnoff where they'd parked the vehicles. At the head of the unit, Skinner shortened his stride and dropped back through the ranks until he walked beside Jake. Staring straight ahead, he spoke from the side of his mouth. "Are *we* going hunting?"

"We'll discuss it." Teeth bared, Jake shot his friend a knowing glance. The not so subtle emphasis wasn't lost on him.

Skinner's brown eyes were hard and bright, polished agates. "Good."

"Gather round, we need to talk." His voice rose over the unit's banter. With a wave of his arm, Jake convened an informal roadside meeting.

With Skinner at his side, he waited for his people to settle down. Contemplatively, he surveyed their faces. All total, his organization numbered in the thousands, spread to the far flung corners of the globe. However, the select group of people who served with him and fought beside him on a daily basis occupied a special place in his esteem. He loved each and every one of them.

They fell quiet. Eyes turned to him in pregnant expectation. Hidden in the branches of a nearby tree, a raven let rip with a raucous *craa*. Biding his words, Jake remained silent a moment too long.

Crazy Cali toed the line. "With all due respect, sir, I need to take a piss. So if you're going to give a speech, get on with it."

Laughter rocked the unit. An anonymous male voice called boldly from the rear of the crowd. "And keep it short."

"That's enough. Quiet down." Jake affected a scowl, enjoying their easy camaraderie.

His men's rollicking amusement continued unabated.

"Shut the fuck up!" Skinner shouted at the top of his lungs. "Or I'm gonna kick some ass."

A sudden hush descended.

Jake tipped his hand to his second-in-command, then addressed his people. "Today, you've witnessed the truth behind our conflict with the Storm Pack. My son and Adair Storm's daughter enacted their own version of Romeo and Juliet. Our enemies exploited the situation. Killed my son. Framed Victoria for his murder. Set us at our allies' throats."

Among his followers, Jake sensed troubled minds and hearts, even in those like Skinner, self-disciplined enough to conceal their turmoil. With the exception of Sawyer, his people weren't accustomed to his sons blatantly disobeying him. Daniel had always been a model son. Focused and disciplined.

Voices rose in a concerned murmur. Jake's hands rose and slowly lowered, soothing the disquiet. "I'm not interested in recrimination or casting blame. Victoria isn't a murderer. Daniel acted within his rights as a grown man. What matters is my son is dead. Our alliance is broken. We've been manipulated and infiltrated. Betrayed by one of our own."

A spark flickered, igniting murderous anger in the core of their community. Jake's grasp of the fire exceeded simple empathy. Their shock and rage were *known* to him. Chart's treachery wouldn't be soon forgotten or forgiven.

"The traitor in our ranks is dead. Cursed. That's not the end of this matter. Far from it. I've learned Daniel's soul has been imprisoned by the vampire who murdered him. Behind it all is an individual we only know as 'the necromancer'."

He hesitated, parsing his words while he allowed them time to absorb the news. Gasps accompanied shock, followed by exclamations and curses. A turbulent riptide sundered his people, and voices swelled to shouts.

He employed magic to reach out to them, perceiving each individual as a distinct thread. Gathering the chaotic strands, Jake pulled them closer, restoring the unity. He refused to allow their enemies to destroy them. Soothed, they quieted.

"I'm going to rescue my son," he said in a voice like gravel, "and destroy anything and everyone who gets in my way, starting with the vampire, Vildivia, and ending with the necromancer."

The eyes of every man and woman present riveted upon him.

Outwardly, he exuded cool confidence, but a volcano brooded at his core. His vengeance would not be an impulsive act of uncontrolled rage but a conscious act of absolute destruction. "This ain't a noble quest to protect humanity. It's personal. It's probably a trap. It's definitely dangerous."

He waited to hear their response. Skinner spoke first. "We're talking about the diversion of resources from the defense of civilian targets. People are going to die."

Cali snorted. "People gonna die, regardless of what we do."

"More people will die." Skinner shot her a narrowed-eyed glance. "Than would've otherwise."

Jake tipped his head. "That's exactly right. For that reason, I'm going alone. Skinner, you'll take the unit and return to Tucson to defend the civilian population."

Dead silence greeted his announcement.

In a deliberate display of defiance, Skinner stepped from his side and joined the rest of the unit. A brick wall of mutinous faces stared back at him. The men drew together, adopting a tight shoulder to shoulder formation.

Skinner folded his arms across his barrel-shaped chest. "Fuck that. We ain't going anywhere."

The men rumbled their agreement.

"We look after our own," Cali said. "Daniel was one of us. We owe him."

He scanned their faces. "It's your choice."

"We appreciate you asking, Jake," Skinner intoned. "But we're with you."

"To hell and back," Jose Ortiz pledged, tone fervent.

"Whatever it takes."

Echoing his sentiment, a cheer went up among his men, embodying their unity, loyalty, and support.

His heart warmed, and he smiled upon his family. "Let's go to work then."

CHAPTER THIRTEEN

Sessrúmnir, Freya's hall in Fólkvangr

"Ragnarök is coming."

Panicked, Freya sought to deny the world-end even though Odin predicted the inevitable outcome. "Loki, why must this be? So much time has passed. It sounds like you have been successful on your own. Why must you seek to end the world and destroy—"

Seething, he cut her off with a violent wave of his arms. "No matter how many times I say it, no one ever hears me. I have no desire to end the world. For all of their flaws and weaknesses, I prefer the company of mortals. They are ever-changing. Unlike stuffy, stagnant immortals, humans explore, destroy, and adapt the world to themselves and themselves to their world. They evolve. I love popcorn. Chocolate and peanut butter. Rock 'n' roll. Action movies. I'm not ready for this world to end. There's so much I haven't seen or done. I want to walk on the moon. Be there when humanity sets foot on another planet."

He spread his hands. His ironic voice boomed throughout the chamber. "I'm not ashamed to admit that I'm a huge George R.R. Martin fanboy. What do you suppose the odds are that I can save him from perishing when Ragnarök arrives?"

Freya sniffed in disdain. What a raving lunatic!

Most of what he said was utter nonsense, but she believed him. Desperation pinched the corners of his eyes and mouth. "Then why?" she asked. "Why orchestrate the end of everything if you like it so much?"

Midgard

"Oh, Daniel. I'm so sorry..."

Glass crunched beneath Victoria's flip-flops. She crouched on a filthy tile floor between two rows of busted metal shelving in the abandoned gas station. The skeleton of the rundown building remained, steel beams and decaying red brick walls, and all of the windows were smashed.

Dozens of restless spirits, spectral blurs suffering in torment, wandered through the area. Fortunately, none of the ghosts were aware of her presence, and she preferred to keep it that way. Vampires had once used the structure as a haven, and she suspected those who remained were their murdered victims, souls trapped in the veil between the physical world and the afterlife. The metaphysical realm had many names, but Victoria's mother, Katherine, had always called it the Shadowlands, and it was the word Victoria liked best.

Her fingertips touched a dark, crusty stain on the floor. She lifted her hand to her nose and inhaled the musty scent of old dried blood and mold. Her throat ached as tightness centered deep in her chest. She blinked, and tears ran down her cheeks. Flowing fast and free, they dripped from her face and landed in the dust.

Her tears reconstituted the blood in the place where she and Daniel had fought and slain a dozen vampires. In the exact spot where her lover had died.

Chocolate-brown eyes stared at her, wide with shock, confusion, and pleading. His mouth opened and closed as he attempted and failed to form words. His hands grasped at his torn jugular, trying to staunch the bleeding from the gaping wound.

Daniel crashed to his knees.

She rushed to him and reached for his throat. A spurt of hot blood hit her cheek and upper torso, splattering her T-shirt. Tears flowed down her cheeks, becoming lost in the rivulets of blood running down her face. Her hands covered his, and she made a clumsy, panicked grab for her magic.

"Oh, Goddess, help me." Light sputtered from her hands, flickering before emanating as a steady glow. She connected with him spiritually and perceived his slowing heart and plummeting blood pressure. She poured energy into a spell and attempted to stop the bleeding. The injury was too massive.

His heart beat for the last time.

"*No, no, no...*" Sobbing, she clung to his body, still trying to knit the severed vein. Slick blood coated her hands and face. Overwhelming pain crushed her, so all she could do was crouch on the cold ground, drowning in tears.

"Victoria, don't cry." Strong hands gripped her shoulders.

"It was my fault. I should have saved him." Tears dripped down her face. She'd held Daniel for an hour after his heart stopped. She'd witnessed the departure of his soul from his body, doing nothing to interfere because his soul belonged elsewhere than Valhalla. Or so she'd believed...

"It was no one's fault but the bastard who murdered him." Kneeling beside her, Sawyer pulled her into his arms. He held her close, her face pressed to his shoulder, her body cradled against his chest. The empathic pack bond flared between them. His guilt and sorrow mirrored her suffering.

Sawyer smelled like her pack. He also smelled like her enemy.

"I wish that were true." For a moment, she succumbed to temptation and melted against him, taking comfort in his strength. The savory scent of a cinnamon aftershave overlay his earthy arousal. He desired her, but he didn't want to. His posture remained stiff. His arms and back were just a little too tight.

"We'll avenge my brother." Sawyer turned the words into a vow, the place where he channeled his darker emotions. His single-mindedness and bloodthirsty rage rivaled that of any wolf. He locked onto his target and pursued it with fanatical determination.

Having been the focus of his obsession, she could honestly say she never wanted to get on that side of him again.

She had to get away from him before the situation escalated into sex or violence. Or both. Gulping air, Victoria reigned in her wildcatting emotions. She seldom cried, even in front of members of her own pack, certainly *not* in front of an enemy. An Alpha never showed weakness or demonstrated vulnerability, especially not before a man she hardly trusted.

"Revenge isn't everything, Sawyer." Straightening, she placed her hands on his chest and pushed him away. Fortunately, he didn't test her resolve.

At her slight prompting, he stepped back. "I know that. I want to rescue my brother's soul."

"I agree with that."

"*Then* I want to rain hell and destruction on his captors, this Vildivia and Necromancer. They both have to die."

Despite her best effort to remain somber, a smile split her face. "That's a plan I can get behind."

He flashed a grin as he ran his hand through his unkempt hair and pushed it out of his face. His long bangs flopped into his face, concealing his right eye. "Do you smell anything?"

Dirt. Mold. Dried blood. Grief, guilt, and desire.

Her gaze locked on those dirty blond strands, and her fingers twitched. Pursing her lips, she hid behind her irritation and adopted a fierce scowl. "I smell lots of stuff, but aside from us, none of the scents are fresh."

"Did you find any evidence of vampires?"

Startled, Victoria's heart surged and throbbed against her breastbone. Beside her, Sawyer also stiffened. Like guilty teenagers caught groping on the couch, they jerked around and faced Jake Barrett.

Hands braced against the steel frame of the doorway, the veteran hunter stood in the store entrance amid rocks and rubble. The late afternoon sun cast him in silhouette, haloing his form. His penetrating gaze swept over them, silently judging even though his face maintained a impassive mask. While she and Sawyer inspected the interior of the abandoned gas station, Jake had excused himself with the stated intention of performing a perimeter sweep.

She wondered nervously how long he had been standing there and how much he had seen. Her hand lifted to scrub the evidence of tears from her face, but she aborted the telling gesture. Her reddened eyes and flushed face must be proof enough of her faults without giving him *carte blanche* to the susceptibilities of her heart.

Sawyer edged around her and strode toward his father. "Nada. You?"

"I found a pile of human bones in a ditch on the south side."

Sawyer stopped in his tracks. "A body dump?"

Jake nodded. "From the looks of it, the oldest remains are several months old."

"I'm gonna go have a look for myself." Without looking back, Sawyer passed his father and departed the decrepit building, leaving Victoria alone with Jake.

They stared at one another in strained silence. Standing tall, she squared her shoulders and thrust her jaw out at a stubborn tilt. They stood in the place where Daniel had died. She expected a harsh condemnation or angry accusation, and she wouldn't have blamed him either.

"Hmm." Jake rumbled deep in his throat. "This is a tough situation."

"Yeah." She released a long held breath, blowing a stream of air through her mouth. "What do you want to do about it?"

"This location looks like it's a wash. If the vampires have a new base of operations in the area, we'll find it. First thing in the morning, I'll bring in my men, and we'll search the area. We'll overturn every stone between here and the border. If they're hiding, we'll find them. If they run, we'll hunt them to the ends of the earth."

The corners of her mouth turned down. "Not exactly what I was asking, but it'll do."

Jake broke eye contact and glanced toward the dark stain on the ground at her feet. "Is this where Daniel died?"

A tremor passed through Victoria. Her mouth was bone dry, but she swallowed convulsively. She blinked, refusing to succumb to tears again. "Yes."

"You're shaking."

She looked down. To her surprise, she realized it was true. Her hands were trembling. Her emotions congealed in a messy knot, sickening nausea in her gut. She wanted to chalk her queasy stomach up to morning sickness, but rage and fear ruled her heart.

"Yeah, well, I'm upset." Her shoulders rose and fell in a careless shrug.

"We're overdue to talk." Walking on broken glass, he approached her with measured steps, not a hint of menace in his manner.

She wasn't fooled. The man was dangerous. Lifting her head, she looked him straight in the eyes and arched her brow. "What do we have to say that hasn't been said already?"

He chuckled low, the rusty sound of a man who'd forgotten how to laugh. "My experience with women is there's always something more to be said. Tell me what you're thinking, and we'll go from there."

With an effort, Victoria tried to relax. "I'm scared." *Terrified to the depths of my soul.* "And angry. And confused. And alone."

"At least you're not at a loss for the right words." His inflection reminded her precisely of Daniel's dry sarcasm.

Temper surging, her hands formed fists. "Freya refuses to speak with me because I consorted with some asshole god of the hunt who blames me for his son's death. The same asshole is responsible for the murder of an incredibly sweet adolescent boy who was under my protection. My mate is dead, along with my parents and most of my pack. Oh, and the Norns have predicted the tragic death of my daughter in early childhood."

Sides heaving, she bit her tongue. She hadn't meant to tell him about the prophecy. Tears threatened, and she banished them. *Goddess forbid he should ever learn the rest.* She reached instinctively for her wolf, embracing her primal nature which chose anger over fear.

"I don't blame you for Daniel's death. I did for a long time, but I don't anymore." Sorrow pinched Jake's face and shadowed his voice. "I know you'd have done anything to save my son."

"Oh." Stunned, she stared at him, and her anger drained away, leaving her confused. "Thank you."

His teeth ground together, creating an unpleasant crunch like bones breaking. "I've accepted responsibility for the boy's death and expressed regret. I'd bring him back if I was able, but that's beyond my power. So I'm going to do the only honorable thing I can do. Allow me to make reparations and pay Jasper's blood price."

Jake demonstrated a familiarity with her heritage few humans possessed. Blood price, sometimes called *were gild*, was the historical practice of compensating the relatives of a murder victim for the loss. For centuries, her people had used the method of reparation to prevent blood feuds and settle debts. It was archaic.

She opened her mouth to reject the offer but then stopped and actually considered the suggestion. It was crazy, completely insane, yet it made a twisted sort of sense. The unrelenting violence and bloodshed left her soul weary. She wanted, *no, she needed* peace. For the good of her pack, for the good of her unborn child. And yes, for her own good as well.

"Did you get the idea from Sawyer?" she asked.

"Yes."

She nodded. "I don't like this place. It's haunted."

"This world is full of lost souls. It's a wonder you can find peace anywhere."

She shot him a sharp glance. "Can you see them?"

"Only when I choose to look," Jake said. "Shall we speak outside?"

"Yes, I'd be more comfortable there."

Jake led the way outside. He strolled to the broken-asphalt parking lot where the Chevelle and his SUV were parked close together. The sun hung just over the distant mountains, like a great orange ball about to drop, and the near-full moon already occupied the opposite half of the sky. Not even a breeze stirred the red earth of the butte.

About a half mile distant, Sawyer followed a dirt path, walking uphill toward them.

Jake stopped beside the open driver's side window of his vehicle and tossed his baseball cap inside. Then he leaned against the front fender of his vehicle with his arms crossed.

Victoria leaned against the Chevelle's right front door, a position that allowed her to track Sawyer's approach. "All right," she said. "I'm listening. What do you suggest is a fair blood price?"

He pinned her with his gaze. "What do you want?"

Her lips pulled taut over a glistening snarl. "The head of the man who murdered Jasper."

Jake's face froze in a harsh mask. His voice grated. "That's not going to happen. Choose something else."

She smiled grimly. She'd opened with an impossible demand so her next request would sound more reasonable. From the look on Jake's face, he suspected as much, but there were certain negotiation conventions that had to be followed. She had to be careful because she knew he held the superior position. Her pack presented no threat to the hunters, but they were a real and present danger to hers.

Her interest in forging a new treaty trumped all else. Peace meant everything. They could stop looking over their shoulders and living on the run. Putting down permanent roots in Sierra Pines meant Morena would graduate from high school, and Victoria could obtain a job as a registered nurse. The miles of pristine wilderness surrounding Lake Echo were an ideal environment for Sophia's pups once they reached adulthood. If none of them turned out to be wolf-shifters, they'd live out their lives in the wild.

"This war has weakened my pack. All of our adult males are dead. In another couple years, Jasper would have come of age. His loss is devastating. I have to bring new blood into the pack or we're doomed. So in reparation, I want one of your sons as a potential mate."

Holding her breath, she hung on his response, afraid he'd mention her inappropriate physical attraction to Sawyer. Yes, a part of her wanted his second son, but she considered him too inconvenient and darned inappropriate. In her heart, she suspected she desired

Sawyer because he reminded her so much of her beloved Daniel, even down to his earthy aroma. Sure, they shared sexual chemistry, but also a violent and volatile history. In the past, her fascination to rebellious guys had brought her nothing but trouble, so from here on out, she intended to be a staunch supporter of Bad Boys Anonymous.

Jake chuckled. "I'll admit, you keep surprising me, Victoria. For the sake of discussion, let's pretend I'm willing to consider this. Which of my sons are we discussing? And what would this marriage of convenience be to you?"

She jerked her head in a sharp, instinctive shake. Daniel's death had eviscerated her soul. Before she'd even finished grieving, she'd taken another chance on Arik Koenig and gotten hurt yet again when he'd fallen in battle. She secured her heart from within and sealed the key behind the lock. Forever off limits.

"No. I don't want another mate," she said. "It's too soon. Besides, I have to keep my options open. Pack politics can be brutal." Her mouth puckered due to the bitter knowledge that the men she cared for seemed doomed to die. She couldn't help thinking the best way to be rid of a future rival for her territory might just be to marry him.

Jake's dark eyes glimmered. "This isn't the Dark Ages. You can't really expect that I'd coerce one of my sons into an arranged marriage."

"I'm not suggesting that," she hastened to explain. "What I'd like is for my pack's unmated females to have an opportunity to meet your sons in a social setting."

Jake's youngest sons, Gage and JD, were fraternal twins and seniors in high school. They were slightly older than Morena, and they would be strong, attractive men, like their father and brothers. The right marriage would strengthen the pack and reinforce the peace they were brokering. As Alpha, she'd never force Morie to marry, but she wasn't above making the suggestion.

Jake said nothing, apparently giving the matter serious consideration.

The fact this was really happening struck her as incredibly surreal. Huffing, Victoria threw in her final condition before it was too late. "What I demand is your word that you'll give your blessing should such a pairing occur."

A look of astute understanding crossed Jake's face, and he smiled. "You have my word."

"It's a deal." She stuck out her hand before she could change her mind.

"Done." Jake's big hand engulfed hers in a solid grip and they shook.

Touching him, her isolation dissipated. No longer lonely. The hair on her arms rose, her eyes widened. Spooked, she bit her lip and squashed her reaction before weird, uncontrolled emotions—no doubt the product of her rollercoaster pregnancy hormones—got the better of her.

"Good to see you two getting along," Sawyer said, sounding perfectly self-satisfied.

Startled, Victoria jerked from Jake's grip and twisted to face Sawyer. She hated that he'd managed to take her unaware. Flushing with anger, she glared and arched her brow. "I suppose you're going to take credit?"

"Hell yeah." Sawyer smiled immodestly.

Jake grunted. "Don't be smug, Son. No one likes an asshole."

Sawyer chuckled. "What were you shaking on?"

"I just traded you as chattel to the Storm Pack," Jake said, tone bland, expression deadpan. "You'll be marrying one of their women at Victoria's discretion."

With a startled squawk, Sawyer rocked on his heels and almost toppled over backward. While his father and Victoria dissolved into laughter, he frantically windmilled his arms to keep his balance. He barely recovered before he went over.

"Very funny." Stiff-backed, Sawyer straightened and smoothed out an imaginary wrinkle on his sleeve. "Ha, ha, you're hilarious."

"If you could have seen the look on your face, boy..." Grinning, Jake waved his hand in an emphatic gesture.

"That was pretty damn funny." Tears threatening, Victoria held her sides. Lightness swept through her, mirth alleviating the worst of her tension. Her mood improved even more when Sawyer joined them, finding laughter even at his own expense. She liked him a little bit better for his ability to be self-effacing.

By unspoken agreement, the three of them assumed new positions between the cars, an uneven triangle. Sawyer sat beside Victoria on the Chevelle's broad hood, and Jake stood across from them.

Jake's serious demeanor set a new mood. "I want to finish this negotiation, Victoria, before we meet up with my men to go after Vildivia and the Necromancer. We need to figure out how to restore the treaty and cooperation between my organization and the packs. Nothing should be left hanging or open to interpretation."

Wary, she eyed him. "I agree, but I don't know what more you want from me. I'm pregnant. I can't and I won't endanger the life of my child. If you bring your wounded to me, I'll help them as much as I'm able. But as a wartime ally, the Storm Pack has nothing left to offer."

Both men stirred. Jake shook his head.

Displeasure rolled off Sawyer, tainting both his aura and odor. His silent protest traversed the pack bond. His mouth opened and then snapped shut. His head dipped to the side as he ran an agitated hand through his unruly hair.

Undeterred, Victoria crossed her arms over her chest. "You should speak with the other Alphas. Have you tried the White Mountains Tribe?"

Jake grunted. "I've tried that. Finn is receptive, but his second is an idiot."

Victoria choked on laughter. In an attempt to hide her amusement, she feigned a sudden interest in the distant horizon. Sucking in her cheeks, she intoned, "Tarak is a difficult man."

The metal hood of the Chevelle creaked beneath Sawyer's shifting weight. "I take it you know him?"

Victoria assumed her angel face. "A couple years ago, he sought to win me as his mate. Of course, he had rivals. Flat-out refusal would have caused political awkwardness for my parents, so I made it a contest. I agreed to become the mate of the man who brought me *Sleipnir*, Odin's eight-legged horse."

The Hunter King's mouth hung open. The expression on Jake's face was priceless. The man looked like he didn't know whether to laugh or bellow.

With hindsight, her arrogance in setting the challenge was even more outrageous than it had been at the time. However, she couldn't bring herself to regret it. If anything, in retrospect, she savored the irony now more than ever.

Sawyer shook his head with a wry grin. "Man, you've got balls."

"The challenge is still open as a matter of fact." Smiling, she shrugged. "Most of the males went away immediately. A few tried and failed. Tarak was the last to give up. I think he's still holding a grudge against me to this day."

"I didn't like his arrogance or his presumption," Jake grumbled.

Sawyer leaned toward her. His voice dropped, and he winked. "Tarak presumed to know the will of Odin."

A snort of laughter rocked her. "Ha, lovely. Well, it's a shame the All-Father's priesthood has fallen so out of favor. Rumor has it that Odin no longer speaks to his priests."

With a playful nudge of his elbow, Sawyer jostled her side. "It's so damn difficult not to laugh when Dad tells these sort of stories. I miss Daniel. He was the perfect straight man."

Tears stung her eyes, and her chest tightened. No longer amused, she looked away and stared into the past. "I remember."

Sawyer opened his mouth as if to apologize.

Jake cut him off. "You're both hilarious, but this is a matter of life and death."

Victoria considered Jake. His seriousness made her uneasy. "What about the Vail Pack? My father always said Ventana was a reasonable man."

Jake hunched slightly. "Vamps destroyed the Vail Pack three months ago."

"Oh." The news hit her like a ton of bricks. She sat back, struggling to absorb the implications. She'd known many of the members, men, women, children... Wide-eyed, she stared at the older hunter. "All dead?"

"So far as I know. I'm sorry." Jake stared at her in silent expectation.

She sighed, sensing he demanded more from her. She wanted to help, but she also resented the feeling of being pressured. With each passing moment, she grew tenser. "Tell me what you're thinking, Jake. Stop making me guess."

Beside her, Sawyer fidgeted, radiating edgy aggression.

"I need to be able to present you to the packs as proof we were deceived and set at each other's throats by a common enemy seeking to undermine our alliance." Jake pushed away from the SUV and approached her.

She narrowed her eyes and bared her teeth, bracing for conflict. "Like a trophy? A prize show dog?"

So help him, if he dared call her *bitch* again...

"As an ally." The Hunter King snarled right back at her. Without warning, he laid his hand on her shoulder and squeezed firmly. A vast reservoir of magic opened to her, no shields or warding, nothing to prevent her from tapping his personal power. His brown eyes held an unspoken offer and the mysteries of eternity.

Shock rocked the foundation of her world. Confused, Victoria gazed into his face. Warmth and welcome, nothing threatening or suspicious. He embodied paternity. Protectiveness. Everything she'd so poignantly missed since her own father's death.

Point blank, she asked, "Do you understand what you're doing? A pack bond goes far deeper than a handshake. This isn't something that just goes away if you change your mind. Unlike a mate bond, a pack bond can be broken, but both parties have to physically and emotionally sever all ties."

"I know what I'm doing." Jake's regard never wavered. The invitation remained unspoken but unmistakable. Strength without strings, free for the taking. Perhaps sensing her reluctance, Jake addressed her doubts. "Victoria, when your father and I forged the alliance thirty years ago, we realized that the pack bond was the inevitable product of hunters and wolves associating closely in stressful situations. At the time, I didn't trust Adair enough to risk it, so I forbade all hunters who followed me from fraternizing with your people outside of the hunt."

Her injured pride stung. Jake Barrett's authoritarian rules were the reason she and Daniel had kept their relationship a secret. Arguably, the entire war between wolves and hunters could have been averted, but now the man was suggesting reconciliation as if no one had died.

Jake continued talking in that philosophical tone that drove her nuts. "I understand now that I was complacent in allowing the status quo to persist for decades, even when I knew the restrictions were unnecessary. When you're as old as I am, change is difficult."

She arched her brow. "So, you're admitting you were wrong?"

Jake' flashed an easy smile, and he chuckled. "Never admit you're wrong—"

"It's a sign of weakness," Victoria and Sawyer finished in unison.

She'd forgotten Sawyer. Again. She shot the hunter a sideways glance, uncomfortable with how accustomed she'd grown to him. His presence at her side was natural. Pedestrian. Much like having Morena or Sylvia along.

Dear goddess, help me.

Frowning, she focused on Jake. "What's in it for you?"

Jake answered without hesitation. "A means of ensuring our enemy can never divide us again, a path to uniting all of the packs in a peace treaty with all hunters. We're at war with these undead, and yet we're still fighting each other."

War.

His choice of words sent chills down her spine, but he was right. She found his logic to be sound and his argument convincing. The vampires had declared war. Hunters and wolves needed to present a united front against their adversaries.

Guilt and doubt assailed her. Was this a test?

The Norns' prophecy echoed from the depths of her memory. "*The final days are upon us. To save your daughter, you will side with Loki against the Aesir. You will use your enchanted dagger to cut the binding of the great wolf, Fenrir. You will be responsible for freeing the beast that kills Odin.*"

Her teeth sank into her lower lip until it drew a ruby drop of blood which tasted salty on her tongue. Conflicting desires and loyalties battled for dominance in her heart. As Alpha and a mother, duty dictated she act in the best interests of her pack. As a priestess, she owed fidelity to Freya. As a Valkyrie, she'd taken vows to serve Odin.

Doubts crumbling, Victoria's suspicions and mistrust charged to the forefront of her mind as if sensing they were about to be abandoned forever. Before she committed to anything, she needed to remove all doubt. "You sound like you've thought this through."

He tipped his head. "I have. My son has already joined your pack. This is the next logical step."

She exhaled, taking time to consider.

Silence fell.

Thankfully, Jake waited for her to decide without pressuring or hurrying her decision. Sucking in a deep, slow breath, she opened herself to Freya. *Goddess, what should I do? What is your will? Command me.*

The Norns whispered, predicting her inevitable betrayal. "*You will be responsible for freeing the beast that kills Odin.*"

No, never.

"This is the right thing to do." Victoria reached out and accepted him into her life, her heart, and her soul. The ultimate proof of her loyalty.

His callused palm was rough against her skin. He met her gaze, never wavering in intention or commitment, steadfast in character, insurmountable in will. The bond flowed through Victoria like molten lava, slow but unstoppable in its advance which forged new pathways through her soul. The searing intensity hurt, but she bore the pain with a stiffened back and welcomed the newest addition to the Storm Pack with an open heart. He brought strength, stability, and stamina to her little family, all traits she sought and needed in new members.

"This isn't what I expected," Jake murmured. His surprise communicated on an empathic level, and at long last, she glimpsed past the complex layers of wards he maintained to hide his true nature. She sensed immense power, primal passion, and restless energy. But also single-minded focus, fatherly devotion, courage, and competence mixed with a whole lot of authoritarian arrogance.

"What were you expecting?" Victoria arched her brow.

"Not sure." Jake grinned, a slash of white teeth, completely unapologetic, but skilled enough in controlling his outward demeanor that she had no hope of discerning his real thoughts. She suspected he was more than capable of shutting her out if he desired.

She hoped he wouldn't.

Unexpected heat seared the skin of her upper arm, the same pleasurable-pain she associated with shape changing. Surprised, she glanced down just as the red flare faded and revealed the stylized dagger tattoo all hunters had on their arm, but hers wasn't black like Jake's or Sawyer's.

Oh, for the love of irony. He'd marked her as a hunter.

Her breath expelled on a huff of outrage. "Hot pink?"

"I don't choose the color," Jake deadpanned. "You do."

Sawyer snickered. "It's cute."

"Such BS." Rolling her eyes, she released Jake's hand to test the new union. The bond held fast. The thread binding him to the body of the pack wobbled because the dynamic was too new to be static. Eventually, they would achieve stability, once she and Jake worked out the particulars of their relationship. The uncertainty scared her even as thrills of excitement traveled her spine. She realized too well Jake might seize the role of Alpha from her. Time would tell.

Victoria held Jake's gaze and smiled. She spoke with the truth of a joyful heart. "Welcome to the Storm Pack."

"Congratulations on becoming a hunter, Victoria Storm," Jake drawled. Then the most dangerous man in the world hugged her.

CHAPTER FOURTEEN

Sessrúmnir, Freya's hall in Fólkvangr

"Why orchestrate the end of everything if you like it so much?"

He rolled his eyes. "Ragnarök is what Odin wants, what he insists must and should be. It is the will of the All-Father."

With a sigh, Freya fell silent. She knew better than to argue. Loki clung to the same stubborn insistence, attempting to shift all blame onto Odin. Instead of wasting her energy in pointless pursuits, she preferred to do whatever was necessary to ensure her survival, even if it meant cooperating with this maniac.

"How much longer do we have?" Freya asked.

Loki exhaled, and his gaze dropped. The normally self-important Trickster deflated before her wary gaze. He spoke, voice heavy. "This will be the last summer the world knows. Three years of winter will follow. *Brothers will fight and kill each other. Blood relatives will defile kinship. It is harsh in the world, whoredom rife. An axe age, a sword age. Shields are riven. A wind age, a wolf age. Before the world goes headlong, no man will have mercy on another.*"

Midgard

His fingers lovingly caressed the curve of the Chevelle's steering wheel, and then his hand dropped to stroke the butter soft leather. The poignant ache of loss throbbed deep in his gut, in sync with the rev of the engine. He savored every stolen moment since it was likely the last time he'd ever drive her. "I'm gonna miss you, baby."

"Would you like a moment alone?" Victoria asked with dry sarcasm. "To say goodbye?"

Sawyer glanced at his passenger. "I thought you were asleep."

The blonde she-wolf curled in her seat, legs tucked against her abdomen. She covered her mouth over a wide yawn. "I was."

Her yawn triggered the reflexive response, but he fought the impulse. Exhaustion rode him. The night before, they'd driven from Sierra Pines to Arizona to rendezvous with his father. Sawyer slept in the car on the way down, but Victoria had refused to nap. He suspected she hadn't trusted him enough to let down her guard.

He didn't ask.

The trip to check out the abandoned gas station where Daniel died had proven to be a bust, and the experience left Sawyer unsettled. Agitation roiled at his core. Tired and irritable, they had broken off their search and agreed to retire to the Red Butte compound, rest for the night, and resume the hunt in the morning.

Jake drove alone. Victoria and Sawyer rode together in the Chevelle.

Near sundown, Sawyer stopped for gas at an antiquated Shell station with a line of old-fashioned canary yellow pumps out front. A modern-day Rip Van Winkle dozed behind the register, so he left a handful of bills on the counter and skipped asking for change. At the neighboring convenience store, he bought two large coffees.

"I don't know how you drink your coffee," Sawyer explained to Victoria as he handed her a cup along with a handful of powdered creamer and sugar packets.

"Black." Her face skewed into a grimace. "I'm heading for the Worst Mother of the Year award," she muttered before downing the coffee.

He chuckled and drove.

The sun dipped below the horizon. The almost full moon came up, casting a brilliant halo in the clear sky. Near Red Butte, he got off the highway and slowed the car to accommodate for the uneven, pothole-marked roads. They passed through the decaying remains of an old mining town, a handful of battered buildings left over from a 1930's boom and bust gold rush.

Victoria nudged his arm with her elbow. "Have you ever wondered why moonlight doesn't kill vampires? It's reflected sunlight, so it should. At least, you'd think it would."

He opened his mouth but remained silent, thinking. Then he smiled and posed a rhetorical question. "Why do werewolves have to shift in the full moon?"

"We don't."

"Bad reasoning skills on the part of horror fiction writers."

Victoria grunted and glared. "How much longer till we're there?"

"We're here. The compound is at the top of this butte."

Steadily gaining in elevation, they drove the next several miles in silence. Sawyer negotiated the rough terrain until they reached the dirt access road. Darkness hung over the compound northwest of the Phoenix metropolitan area. Squat, rectangular concrete buildings crouched low on the top of the mesa. The facility had solar panels and drew on well water. The underground bunker stocked emergency supplies of fresh food and water. There were no fences, so they relied on the remote location and difficult terrain to discourage unwanted guests.

"Fences attract attention," Jake always said. *"Fences make people think you've got something to hide, and they wouldn't even slow the creatures we'd want to keep out."*

Sawyer parked alongside his father's SUV. Their vehicles were the only ones on the lot. The main building sat at the top of the hill at the end of the long walkway. Releasing his seat belt, he climbed from the car and stretched his arms and back to work out the kinks. Victoria recovered her duffle bag from the back seat and lingered beside the car.

"I'll be along in a sec." Victoria held up her cell phone. "I'm going to check in with Sylvie and let her know we arrived."

"Okay." Sawyer left her beside the car and strode away to give her privacy.

Approaching from the main compound, Jake walked out to meet him. A young woman unknown to Sawyer trailed behind his father.

"Who's she?" Sawyer asked, glancing toward the stranger. Her unexpected presence unsettled him. The woman appeared to be in her late teens or early twenties. Loose, straight black hair obscured her features. She had brown skin, and the curves beneath her loose clothing hinted at a pleasing figure.

"This is Lenna," Jake said. "Lenna, this is my son, Sawyer."

She looked up quickly and stared at him with wide eyes. Her dulcet voice was breathy. "Hi. You're... "

"Sawyer." He offered his hand.

She glanced at his father who nodded. Lenna shook Sawyer's hand only after receiving tacit permission. She said, "It is an honor to meet you."

"Pleasure to meet you too." Confounded, Sawyer dipped his chin, squinting slightly. Her starry-eyed gaze threw him. Women often flirted with him, and he did okay with the ladies, but that was about it. His last serious relationship had gone down in flames when he'd dropped school and his lover to hunt Victoria.

Lenna giggled like a school girl and offered no other reply.

Lifting his brow, he cast a pointed glance at his father.

Jake's stoic facade gave away nothing.

Sawyer's lips compressed. Fine, if that was how the old man wanted to play it. Too tired for guessing games, he opted to wait for the explanation. Stretching, he dug into the aching muscles at the juncture of his neck and shoulder with one hand. "Is anyone else here?"

His father shook his head. "I sent everyone home and gave my crew the night off too. They have instructions to check back first thing in the morning."

Sawyer rocked back in astonishment. He'd never seen the main compound evacuated. Protocol demanded a 24/7 year round staff, even on holidays.

Hair rose on the back of his neck. "*Everyone's* gone? As in the whole facility has been evacuated? Why? Did you see something?"

His father's mouth tugged into a grim smile, and his volume dropped precipitously. "I didn't want a situation where Victoria felt trapped, and I sure as hell don't need some hothead escalating the situation before I've had a chance to make it clear to everyone the conflict with the Storm Pack has been resolved."

Hothead. Sawyer's lips compressed. Whether intentional or not, the implied criticism stung. He turned away to hide his reaction. At the same time, the explanation rang hollow. He didn't believe that was all there was to it.

Not for a second.

Jake sighed. "We're all tired. We should head inside and grab some shut-eye."

Eager to end the conversation, Sawyer agreed. "I'm bushed."

The distinctive *flop-flop* sound of Victoria's thongs striking her heels announced her approach. The she-wolf carried her bag slung over her shoulder. She cleared her throat and said, "It should go without saying. Whispering hunters make me nervous."

Jake swung around to face Victoria. He adopted a purposeful stance, squared shoulders and wide-set legs. His powerful frame thrummed with pent-up tension.

From his father's body language, Sawyer immediately realized something was wrong. Hairs rose on his neck, and a surge of adrenaline kicked him to alertness. His hand dipped, fingers brushing the familiar stock of his shotgun.

Victoria's gaze slipped past Jake and riveted upon Lenna. The blonde's mouth fell open, revealing the flash of fang. Primal energy surged over her, and gold glimmered in her eyes. The skin of her forearms rippled over contracting muscles.

A growl rumbled in Lenna's throat. Her eyes flashed, and she bristled.

"Shit." Realization bitch-slapped Sawyer upside the head. "She's a wolf."

"Nice grasp of the obvious." Jake's big hand gripped Sawyer's elbow, and he dragged his son to the side. "Best to stay out of their way 'til they sort this out."

He opened his mouth to argue but then thought better of it.

Silent, Victoria marched toward the other woman. She halted once they stood toe-to-toe, and their proximity served to contrast the marked difference in their heights. Lenna was a full foot taller and also heavier. Clearly threatened, she sank to a crouch and conveyed the clear impression of laid back ears and a tucked tail.

The she-wolves locked gazes. A stare down ensued, the specter of violence looming greater with each passing second. Thick, oppressive tension blanketed the atmosphere. Sweat trickled down Sawyer's spine. Restless, he adjusted his stance and bit his tongue to keep quiet.

"I'm Victoria Storm, Alpha of the Storm Pack."

Lenna's growl stuttered and died. She whimpered. Her head and shoulders dropped, posture altering to signal submission. "I'm Lenna."

Surprise flickered across Victoria's face. "What pack do you belong to?"

Shame-faced, Lenna hid behind her hair. "No pack." Her hands crafted a vague gesture toward Jake. "I'm his."

Sawyer choked. His father's elbow dug into his ribs. With a huff, he glanced over into Jake's forbidding scowl and swallowed the smart-ass remark he'd been about to make.

From beneath a knit brow, Victoria shot Jake a puzzled frown.

The Hunter King spread his hands. "It's a long, complicated story."

"Isn't it always?" Victoria's voice lilted, rich with amusement. She extended her hand to Lenna. "It's a pleasure to meet you."

While the she-wolves became acquainted, Jake pulled his son aside. "That went a hell of a lot better than I expected."

"What did you think was gonna happen?" Sawyer demanded. Fatigue served to ramp up his irritation. Off hand, he couldn't name a worse time or place to stage a werewolf meet-and-greet.

"Stow the attitude, Son." Jake's obsidian eyes glimmered, potent with command. "My decisions are never random or cavalier. Despite what you might think, I have my reasons."

Anger crashed over Sawyer. Seething, he ground his teeth. Always the same old shtick. Don't ask. Don't argue. Do as you're told. His father's authoritative mandates got really fucking old, really fast. Still, the last thing he wanted was to engage in another pointless argument, so he kept his mouth shut.

"Victoria doesn't look well." Jake's gaze flitted to the blonde.

Sawyer followed his father's regard. "Yeah, it's the first time I've ever seen a green werewolf."

"What are you saying about me?" Victoria asked over her shoulder.

"I was just saying that shade of shamrock looks lovely on you." Sawyer dazzled her with the most ingratiating smile he could muster. "It brings out the blue in your eyes."

Jake deadpanned, "It's a fetching color."

Victoria's glare sent energy coursing across his skin. Her glare was as hot as the desert sun. She spoke in a low voice. "I'm tired and thirsty. My stomach hurts, my head feels like it's about to explode, and I need to pee. The next *man* that gives me grief is going to wind up with my foot so far up his ass he'll taste my shoe."

From beneath her curtain of hair, Lenna giggled.

"I doubt she can kick that high." Sawyer traded a glance with his father.

Jake's mouth curled up at the corners. "That may be a tall order."

"Maybe out of her reach." Through an act of pure will, Sawyer kept his face straight.

"You'd be shocked by how high I can kick." Victoria glared daggers at the father and son. "Say one more word."

Dead silence greeted her dare.

With an audible huff, Victoria turned on her heel and marched up the hill toward the compound. The way she failed to slow down or glance back made it clear the Barrett men could follow... or not.

Sawyer's gaze skimmed the line of her spine down her straight back and clung to her tight little backside.

Her gait rocked her ass as she walked. He stared after her in longing, and then guilt sucker-punched him. *Fuck.* He desired her. He didn't want her to be as sexy as sin, and he sure as hell didn't want to want her.

"You're heading down a dangerous path, Son."

Sawyer flushed, but refused to acknowledge his father's dig. "Are we going to go over our plans for tomorrow, tonight?"

Intelligence glittered in the older man's eyes. "No. Victoria's wound tight. It's always smart to give a wolf or a pregnant woman a wide leeway. Either is as volatile as TNT when pushed."

Sawyer grunted. "In this case, that's TNT cubed."

"She seems nice." Lenna's soft voice came from behind them. "Most pregnant Alphas are serious bitches."

Startled, Sawyer shot a quick look over his shoulder. Lenna flashed him a sassy smile. She trailed a couple paces behind him and his father. With her inconspicuous demeanor, he'd missed her proximity. Her submissive deportment made him uncomfortable. He didn't understand why she persisted in walking behind them. Was there some strange aspect of pack life beyond his grasp?

"How do you know she's pregnant?" Sawyer blurted without thinking.

Smiling sheepishly, Lenna ducked her head and tapped a finger to her nose. "The nose knows."

"I suppose so." He chuckled, and his father echoed the sound. Ahead, Victoria showed no sign of slowing, so Sawyer sped his pace. Footsteps thudding on the concrete, they followed her along the pathway leading to the compound. As they neared the top, a chorus of howls rose from the mesa's hillside. Victoria stopped in her tracks, head turning toward the sound. Jake also halted, so Sawyer followed suit.

Nervously, Lenna edged closer to Sawyer.

Her fear aroused his protective instincts. His unaccountable reaction triggered a quiver of discordance in his mind. Technically, any grown werewolf, even a female, was physically stronger than a human. His instinctive response made no sense.

Coyote song filled the night. Making an uneducated guess, Sawyer estimated the band to have at least a dozen members who were no more than a half mile distant. The cacophony continued for over a minute.

"What's happening?" Sawyer asked, impatience threading his voice when his companions failed to volunteer an explanation.

"Listen and learn, Sawyer." Jake addressed Victoria. "What are they talking about?"

Victoria stood turned away from them so her face showed in profile. The corner of her mouth tugged into a smile. "Rabbits."

An involuntary exclamation of skepticism escaped Sawyer. "You're both giving me shit. She doesn't speak coyote."

"Do so." Victoria's teeth clicked together with a sharp *snap*. "My people have been taking mates from among Native Americans for centuries. I've got a bunch of second and third cousins on my father's side who are Navajo shifters. At least half are coyotes."

"It's true," Lenna said softly. "They're discussing rabbits."

"Huh." Sawyer still suspected the trio of pulling his leg, but he lacked the knowledge necessary to prove it. He shut his mouth before he said anything further to reveal his ignorance.

Tilting her head back, Victoria exposed the slender column of her throat and released a full-bodied howl. The chorus ceased, and her wolf's song soared into the night. The power touching her voice sent shivers coursing along his spine.

Without understanding why, Sawyer moved to a flanking position alongside the she-wolf. At Victoria's other side, Jake also adopted into a defensive stance.

Lenna formed the last leg. Back to back, the four of them formed a fort.

Victoria fell silent, and a jumble of yips and yowls rose from the coyotes. She listened with her head cocked. A golden glow emanated from her eyes.

Adrenaline surging, Sawyer's pulse raced. In the brush, a branch snapped. His hand snapped to the butt of his shotgun, and he shouldered the firearm. He swung about, senses straining to penetrate the light-devouring blackness. The darkness was filled with things darker still. Half-formed shapes dissolved before his mind fully grasped their form, mysterious and terrifying to the imagination.

For a time, dead silence reigned. Even the band of coyotes ceased howling. His companions stood statue still, bodies drawn to bowstring readiness. The suffocating smog of dread hung over their heads.

Sawyer adjusted his hold on his shotgun. "What's happening?"

Victoria explained in a soft voice. "The coyotes want to know if I'm here for the vampires."

"He's here." Jake's lips barely moved, and the words came out almost indecipherable.

Comprehension dawned in a blinding flash.

"Shit." Sawyer's heart slammed against his breast. On his arm, his dagger tattoo throbbed.

"My sentiments exactly," Jake drawled.

Down the hillside, Sawyer spotted movement in the desert brush. First one, then another. Distant darting bipedal forms emerged from the shrubs, advancing with unnatural swiftness upon stilt-like legs. Their profiles stretched long and thin like pulled taffy. Their spindly limbs bloated and dipped with undulating curves.

The entire hillside popped with undead.

Jake shouldered his rifle and took aim down the hill. He fired a single shot. One of the charging figures fell and then surged back to its feet.

Standing shoulder to shoulder with his father, Sawyer fired into the oncoming horde and scored a headshot. The vampire fell and didn't rise. The others didn't slow their approach. Not a single one swerved or ducked. He hastily reloaded.

"There's too many to fight in the open. We need to get to cover," Sawyer said.

Jake grunted in agreement. "You're right."

Sawyer lurched into a run toward the compound, and his father fell into stride beside him. There would be an arsenal within. Not just knives and guns, but hand grenades and flamethrowers. When he realized the she-wolves had fallen behind, he dragged his feet and looked over his shoulder.

Victoria's hands smacked against the middle of his back. Her shout filled his ears. "Go! We're right behind you."

He ran.

Ahead, a spindly creature dropped from the compound's roof and landed directly in his path. Dark gray skin dappled in oozing sores covered the vampire's face. His open mouth revealed serrated fangs and a barbed tongue.

Nosferatu, a Romanian species.

Unable to avoid the collision, Sawyer dropped his shoulder, rammed the revenant, and knocked him aside. A tug on his shotgun's sling brought the weapon into the hunter's hands. He wielded the firearm like a club and used the stock to catch the creature square on the jaw.

The *Nosferatu* staggered, then lunged straight at Sawyer with his long arms extended. Ice-cold hands seized the sides of his head. The gaping mouth yawned in his face. Lips stretched grotesquely to expose double rows of canines. The fat, thorny tongue lashed toward his face.

The song of the Wild Hunt raged through Sawyer's

soul. Lightning blazed. Thunder rumbled. Frenzy grabbed ahold, obliterating rational thought. He forgot everything—pain, fear, companions.

Vicious desire ruled him.

Swinging the shotgun, he shoved the double-barrel straight into the monster's face. The thrusting tongue collided with steel. He pushed until he met resistance and pulled the trigger.

The gun roared.

The back of the *Nosferatu's* skull exploded. Bits of bone and brain splattered the concrete. The body dropped but didn't disintegrate.

Sawyer yanked out his belt knife and dropped to one knee. He plunged the bayonet into the revenant's throat and sawed through the thick flesh. The putrid stench flooded his nostrils. He gagged and spat to be rid of the taint. While he worked the blade, coagulated blood squished from the cut. Finally, the steel edge hit the spinal column and wedged in dense bones. Focusing his strength, he bore down until the vertebrae severed with a sickening *crunch.*

The *Nosferatu* turned to ash.

Another thick-barrel vampire dropped from the roof and landed on her back, her beetle-thin limbs milling furiously. Alarmed, Sawyer plunged forward and swung in an overhanded thrust. The blade embedded in the vamp's forehead to the hilt.

With a serpentine hiss, the revenant rolled, wrenching the knife from his hands. The hideous visage loomed over his face. From the corner of his eye, Sawyer spied a swift blur. He ducked, but the fist caught his chin and knocked his teeth together. Head swimming, he staggered and almost went over.

His hand closed on the pommel of his boot knife. Cool steel kissed his palm. He yanked the weapon free of its sheath and thrust, puncturing the undead's tough hide. He drove deep into the abdomen, straight to the heart until the revenant keened.

Excited by the sound, Sawyer stabbed over and over. He sliced at the desiccated corpse until the last fleshy bits supporting the heart were severed. The *Nosferatu's* flesh turned to liquid, sloshing into a rancid pool.

Heart thundering, Sawyer sprinted up the driveway and across the concrete courtyard before colliding with the solid metal door. He stabbed at the keypad, fumbling to enter the combo—his mother's birthday—and shoved his face against the retinal scanner. His eyes watered for the precious seconds the computer required to identify him.

The locking mechanism clicked open. He grabbed the handle and yanked the door open. Complete darkness hung over the interior of the building due to the shuttered security windows.

Recalling his companions, he looked around but wasn't able to find them amongst the sea of undead. A stiletto of guilt stabbed at his insides. His father could take care of himself, but he worried about the wolves. The best way to help them now was to continue with his mission and obtain the more effective weapons before he searched for them.

With the blade of his boot knife, he propped open the door so the wolves would be able to enter without dealing with the security system. He went for weapons first, planning to go after them as soon as he was armed.

As soon as he crossed the threshold, motion detectors turned on the lights. Illumination flooded the inside of the main armory, a large open room that contained bare concrete floors, sparse furnishings, and steel vaults. Enough weapons and guns to arm a platoon lined the walls. Sawyer dashed toward the nearest rack and grabbed for the closest armament, a battle axe with a short haft designed for throwing.

Tucking the axe beneath his arm, he fed fresh cartridges into the shotgun. A clatter caught his attention, and he looked up.

Four *Nosferatu* crowded the doorway. The harsh florescent light illuminated their dull gray flesh. They sprinted on spindle legs, their movements fluid and swift. One turned right, the other left. They scuttled along the sides of the room, flanking him. The other two charged straight at him.

The hunt raged in his mind, hounds braying, the riders on the storm. He'd known his entire life he was meant to become one of them. Shouting at the top of his lungs, Sawyer heaved the axe. The blade embedded square in the middle of his target's forehead.

The vampire fell.

Hastily, Sawyer brought up his shotgun. The firearm nestled into his hands, the steel barrel and wooden stock intimately familiar, a part of him. He braced and fired from the hip at the closest oncoming enemy. The double blast hit the vamp dead center in the chest, knocking him back.

The other two kept coming at Sawyer from either side.

CHAPTER FIFTEEN

Sessrúmnir, Freya's hall in Fólkvangr

Ragnarök: the twilight of the gods.

A shudder wracked the goddess to hear the dreaded prophecy fall from the lips of the Trickster, the Destroyer of the Nine Worlds. She knew the prediction by heart, but knowing didn't compare to confronting the reality of the end. As a goddess of war, Freya held no fear of battle, but she also didn't harbor a death wish. She desperately desired to live, and if survival meant throwing in her lot with Loki, then so be it. When it was over, she would bathe and scrub her skin raw.

"You still have a secret that will allow you to endure the end and escape to the new world or you wouldn't be undertaking this campaign," she said severely. "You are a selfish creature. You must have a plan to ensure your own survival."

Loki fell silent, and his expression transformed to a scowl. He looked down, heaved a sigh, and then looked up with a grim smile. "Of course I have an exit strategy, Freya. After all, as you've pointed out, Ragnarök is but the product of my capricious whims."

Satisfied, she nodded. "Our deal endures. I will protect your wolf children who reside in my hall, and in return, you shall guarantee my survival and a place in the new world."

Midgard

The molten dagger descended in a flowing arc toward a vampire's nodding head and sliced through the neck grown brittle with the passage of decades. The spine shattered, and the grotesque body dissolved to dust. The seeds of soil rained to the ground.

"I'm more than capable of bringing up the rear," Jake snapped over his shoulder to Victoria who protected his back.

"I never said you weren't," Victoria shot back.

"Then why are you still here?" He wanted her with Sawyer and Lenna, headed for the shelter and safety of the fortified compound. Not here on the mesa's precipice. Taking on armies was his job.

"I don't leave pack mates behind."

Jake craned his head to check on her. From his peripheral vision, he glimpsed the shimmer of a moonshine blade. Wind swift, feather light.

Vanadium: The forbidden blade.

Surprise kicked him in the teeth. Pivoting, he jerked instinctively away from her, creating a dangerous separation in their defense. Anger erupted, magma hot. His skin turned translucent, and runes arose from the magic secreted within the murky depths of his soul. His flesh metastasized to glittering obsidian. With a lonely moan, the wind kicked up, and dust rose in thick clouds.

Prophecy predicted the dagger would someday cut Fenrir's bindings, freeing the slavering wolf to seek his revenge on the one who'd enslaved him. The weapon's appearance shouldn't have taken him by surprise, but it did. Victoria's mother had carried the dagger at the time of her death. He'd had no idea Katherine had passed it on to her daughter.

A *Nosferatu* charged straight at Victoria. For a shameful second, Jake did nothing and contemplated worse. The grim thoughts demonstrated a weakness of character that reflected poorly upon his honor.

Compared to the brutish vampire, Victoria had the lithe build of a dancer. Taking advantage of the size disparity, she ducked beneath her attacker's outstretched arms. In motion, *Vanadium* produced a sound like the buzz of a hummingbird's wings. An even stroke sliced clean through her opponent's knees. Another took his head.

Two more *Nosferatu* rushed her, latched onto her arms, and dragged her to the ground. She lost her grip on the enchanted dagger. The weapon floated, rocked on air currents, and vanished before it touched down. Victoria underwent a swift partial transformation, growing fangs and claws, and resorted to brawling. She shredded skin and sent chunks of carcass flying.

A hunk of rancid meat plopped on the point of his boot.

Cursing, Jake led with a kick to a vampire's gut. He threw himself into the melee, kicking and stomping the corpses' gray limbs. He stayed his blade, but he despised the constraint. He didn't dare employ the tattoo dagger in close quarter combat, not with Victoria so near. He refused to risk a repeat of what had happened to Lenna.

His already hot temper soared. Fuming, he ground his teeth and questioned why Victoria wasn't with Sawyer or protecting Lenna, the weakest of their number. He already had enough to deal with—the world in panic, masses of people perishing horrible deaths, and destruction all around them. The entire cosmos was about to be consumed in flames.

Yet one stubborn werewolf was his vexation.

"You need to go inside. Right now. You're a thorn in my side." He asserted his bulk between Victoria and a revenant. The vampire seized his arm, and he shouldered it aside. He pressed the dagger's point to the un-dead's throat so the burning steel melted flesh and bone and then severed the head with a sharp thrust.

"Thanks, I try." Blue eyes glared at him as she flashed fang, a wolf's smile. A long gash from her elbow to her wrist wept blood.

Despite his grumbling, she was a solid partner in battle. Swift. Precise. Had it only been the two of them, he'd have welcomed her companionship.

As soon as one undead fell, another vampire imme-diately sprang from the wall of undead pressing toward them. The undead army appeared to be consolidating, and Jake sensed dark, powerful forces at work.

Necromancy.

His gut churned, and he reached down deep. The wind blew hard, creating a raging tempest that beat down on their heads. The sky darkened as if a great hand had strung byzantium lace before the moon. Thick layered clouds gathered, a stairway descending toward the plateau, rumbling with short bursts of thunder.

Stillness fell over the battlefield. The vampires stopped, heads tilted to stare up into the storm. Victoria cocked her head to listen, gnawing her lower lip. In the distance, dogs wailed and the pounding of hundreds of hooves announced the arrival of the mounted troops.

Riders on the storm.

An ancient curse fell from Jake's lips. The Wild Hunt was coming, and there was nothing he could do to stop it. He'd over-extended and called on too much of his magic, invoked the runes too often in too short a time. There were consequences to the flagrant abuse of power, even for him.

The heavens opened, and pellet-sized raindrops pummeled their heads. Frost clung to his eyebrows and beard. Rivulets seeped down his face and arms. Frozen water hit the molten metal of his dagger and sizzled, creating wisps of steam.

While the vampires remained still, he seized the opportunity to scan the area. He spotted Sawyer close the compound, and his son looked to be holding his own. Heaving a sigh of relief, he searched for Lenna but failed to find her among the many Nosferatu.

"What's happening?" Victoria cut a quick path to his side. Her small hand closed on his wrist, holding fast as if seeking reassurance.

"The hunt. It's coming." He captured her gaze and her forearm. "Listen to me. Go to Sawyer. Both of you need to get inside. Seal the doors and stay there."

She stared at him. Wonder and fear edged her face, and flowing rain slicked her blonde hair against her scalp. "What about you?"

Jerking his wrist free of her grip, he released her and stepped away.

"I am the Lord of the Storm." He hefted his dagger skyward. A lightning strike lanced from the dark thundercaps and struck the blade. The bolt snapped and sizzled, its white hot energy imprisoned. His voice resounded in the storm: "I am the Master of the Wild Hunt. Hunter King. Wodan. Knecht Ruprecht. Berchtold."

Victoria's chin jutted. Fear made her angry, and anger made her ornery. "I was just getting comfortable calling you Jake."

Delighted with her sassiness, he threw back his head and laughed. Overhead, thunder clapped—*boom, boom, boom*—Thor pounding his drums. Hearing his son, Jake grinned. What the boy lacked in rhythm, he made up for in enthusiasm.

Holding the dagger level, he swept the weapon in a smooth arc and released the captured lightning into a wall of vampires. Thick smoke mixed with the rain, and the stench of extra crispy corpse permeated the area.

The previously dumbfounded vampires lurched into motion, most charging toward him while a few retreated.

Chuckling, he waved his arm. "Go!"

"A simple 'No thanks' would've sufficed," Victoria tossed over her shoulder before she sprinted away.

Lenna's panicked yowl rent the air and his gut wrenched in dread. He spun toward the sound and located the grizzled gray wolf close to one of the compound's outlying buildings. The she-wolf had her back to the concrete wall. Fighting claw and fang, she was boxed in and beset by vampires.

Shouting his fury, he charged. His dagger cut wide swaths through the corpses. Heads rolled, undead clawed at him from all sides, but their sharp nails glanced off his stony flesh. Dozens of hands caught his clothing, dead weight that slowed his progress to a crawl.

Grasping the hilt of his dagger in both hands, Jake dropped to one knee. Without regard for consequences, he summoned all of his magic. A tsunami swept through him, obliterating the shields he maintained to block out his second sight. Shouting the runes, he plunged the molten blade into the asphalt, and it melted into a viscous, sticky fluid. Tar fumes singed his nostrils.

Arcane energy coalesced about Jake and formed a compact, cracking bubble. Pressure built in his eardrums until they threatened to rupture. He released the force all at once, and the wave exploded forth, flattening everything in its path. Nosferatu were blasted off their feet and blown backward.

A pair of eagle-sized ravens glided overhead. Braying hounds ran on the cusp of the hunt. Riders carried swords, axes, bows, and spears, although a handful brandished firearms. The nostrils of great horses flared orange, and hooves threw sparks.

The ground quaked with their approach. They were a legion.

Åsgårdsreien.

Jake resumed his advance, running for all he was worth. He rejected his foresight which showed him his efforts were doomed to failure before he even reached her. Ahead, a swirl of black energy crackled into existence, cutting Jake off from Lenna. Bellowing his anger, he veered and started around it.

The necrotic magic conjured an immense gravitation well. The pull sucked every nearby vampire into an immense sphere of flesh. Faces squished together. The grotesque abomination spun, supported on a forest of protruding arms and legs, a vision his mind rejected. It stank like a hideous fester of rotted corpses.

Spinning at cyclone velocity, the writhing mass pulsated, grew ever larger and denser. No new vampires joined. Rather, the expansion was fed from within, corpse flesh pulled from the depths of the underworld and infused to the whole.

Seconds before Jake reached her, the sphere rolled over Lenna and engulfed her. Her anguished wail soared over the growls and moans. The cry for help punched a hole in his soul.

Roaring, he plunged into the sphere. His arm worked as a piston, rising and falling with wild energy. He hacked at the wall of dead flesh, slicing off limbs and cleaving hunks. He experienced her terror and agony as the clammy mass crushed her. Bony hands grasped her limbs, yanking her in all directions.

She howled, and he howled with her. Her front leg separated from her torso. Bones broke, tendons ripped, and sinew tore. A ruptured hind leg brought another paroxysm of bright, blinding agony. Her body stretched and pulled apart. Her decapitation came as a stale blessing, a sudden ending to the awful torment.

Lenna's death eviscerated him. With his second sight fully open, he died with her, suffering every excruciating sensation.

The swirling sphere imploded. With a *pop*, it was

gone.

Jake simply stopped. Stopped moving, stopped fighting. He wished desperately for the freedom to stop caring. Failure tasted bitter in his mouth, and the blessed relief of emotional numbness, total apathy, beckoned.

His molten dagger faded from his hand.

The hunt stormed through the parking lot, pulverizing undead beneath their stomping hooves. Bent over the flanks of raging mounts, riders leaned wide and seized the few remaining vampires who were summarily dragged off to eternal service in that furious army.

Hounds pressed against Jake's legs. Warm, rolling tongues licked his fingers. A great sable steed pranced to a halt before him.

The great brute of a rider dismounted. The Swedish warrior sported a wild tangle of golden hair and a fierce beard of a darker shade. He bent his head to Jake in a show of respect. "Lord, you summoned us?"

"So it would seem, Bjorn. So it would seem." He gazed past his Lieutenant, watching the circling riders. All of the undead were destroyed or claimed. Without prey to pursue, turmoil ruled those restless souls.

Jake strode toward the compound, and Bjorn tagged along on his heels.

"I have issued orders that the Chevelle is protected from damage." Tension edged Bjorn's voice as he referenced events a decade past. The last time Jake had summoned the hunt, several of the riders had galloped their steeds across the Chevy's roof.

He might have been amused if not for the hollow emptiness in his heart. Still, Jake offered assurances. "You have done well."

"My lord, your horse is here." An ancient warrior known as Gron rode past on his trotting roan pony.

A stallion blew hot spittle, a resounding huff. Eight clomping hooves generated a cannonade. The ranks of riders split to make way for the horse's massive bulk.

One of the eagle-sized ravens clung to the empty saddle with inky talons.

Despite his sorrow, Jake strode to meet his horse. Arm raised, he rested his hand upon the heavy muzzle and stroked the velvety skin. The stallion's coat, full mane and thick tail were snow-white.

"Hello, old son."

Sleipnir nuzzled his fingers. *I have missed you.*

"We have been without your companionship for a long time, Lord," Bjorn said, echoing the sentiment. "The men have missed you."

"I've missed them also." Stroking Sleipnir's wide neck, he considered. Was it time to leave and rejoin the eternal hunt he was born to lead?

Even as temptation beckoned, Jake thought of his sons who still needed him. The horrific vision of the world's doom, too soon coming, loomed in his mind's eye. He exhaled in a long, thin stream.

"No, not yet. My job here isn't done." He placed a final, fond pat of farewell on his mount's forehead and relayed a poignant apology. *I'm sorry. Our reunion will come soon. Just not today.*

Don't delay too long. Dark eyes gleaming, the horse's massive head dipped and struck his chest. The force of the blow staggered Jake. Grinning, he watched as his steed rounded and tromped away.

"As you will, my lord." Sounding distinctly disgruntled, Bjorn delivered the orders to depart to the legion hunters. The hounds took up the call and sprang to the forefront, leading the charge toward the dark stairway of thundercaps ascending to the heavens. Mounted riders followed on fiery steeds.

As swiftly as the storm had struck, the clouds rolled back. Overhead, a twilight pall enshrouded the moon. Shades of sorrow haunted him. He was alone again. Only seconds had passed, and already he ached for their camaraderie.

Heartsick, Jake walked to where Lenna's body lay scattered in pieces upon the ground. Her blood-soaked torso rested in a puddle not too far from a torn leg. The jagged, exposed bones dripped marrow. A short distance further, her severed head rested on its side. Her glassy eye stared up at him, full of agony and accusation.

So much power at his command, yet he couldn't save a single life. The one creature he'd sought to protect, and he'd failed her. How then was he supposed to save the world?

"I'm sorry." He bent to retrieve her spirit, intending to escort her personally to Valhalla. His fingers brushed the soaked fur of her shoulder, and he found the corpse empty of a soul.

A shadow crossed over him.

An old woman occupied the space where the physical and spiritual worlds intersected. Her essence ruled destiny. Paper thin lips were drawn taut over yellowed-teeth. The tip of her tongue poked through a gaping hole.

Bony fingers formed grasping talons. "I claimed the she-wolf's soul, Deceiver. My shades dragged her to eternal damnation."

He towered, rage erupting. Magma flowed from his lips. "How dare you, Crone! She is mine!"

"You missed your chance." Her cackle shrilled across his nerves, terminating in tiny sharp pops.

His roar rocked the earth and sky. Infuriated, he summoned his dagger. Brandishing the blade overhead, he cleaved a long arc from the top of her head through her torso.

Screeching, she dissolved to a tangled mass of strings and then bled away into nothingness. The gloomy past. Unforgotten, always haunting him.

A snarl came from his right.

No time to reload. Sawyer reversed the shotgun and bludgeoned the vampire with the stock. Definitely not a killing blow.

A *Nosferatu* blindsided him. Ice-cold arms wrapped around his throat, choking off his air supply. A chilling hiss filled his ear, and the rot of a decaying corpse was suddenly overpowering.

Sawyer locked his hands around the arms strangling him and strove to insert his fingers between his throat and that dead flesh garrote. His vision blurred. The ashen face of another vampire loomed closer. Struggling to dislodge the assailant choking him, he bucked and twisted. Stinging pain blossomed in his shoulder. *Breathe, breathe, breathe, breathe, breathe...*

Can't.

Lungs burning, head spinning, he staggered. He lost his grip on the shotgun, and collapsed beneath the revenant's weight. His knees smashed against concrete, and jarring pain seared through his joints and shins.

The revenant was still locked about his throat.

Desperate, Sawyer let go of the tongue wrapped around his neck and grabbed for the dagger strapped to his wrist. Like a silken whisper, the knife slid into his hand. His recent close association with werewolves had made him feel rude for carrying the silver blade, but now he was relieved his survival instincts had overruled the niggling impulse to be polite.

Taking a blind stab, Sawyer thrust the weapon over his shoulder into the creature's face. A wet squish and a snarl rewarded his effort when the silver blade sank to the hilt and fluids gushed over his fingers.

Teeth bared in a snarl, Sawyer retracted, then plunged the dagger home again and again until congealed blood coated his hand and arm. A chunk of brain splattered the floor.

The vampire choking him disintegrated.

Oh, but that first breathe of air was fucking spectacular. *So damn good.* Gasping, Sawyer crouched on all fours while ash rained down around him. His irritated eyes watered, and the grit clogged his nose and throat. Coughing, he struggled to clear his abused airways.

A ferocious growl came from nearby, then a loud collision. *Oh shit.* Too close for comfort, he scrambled and scooted away until his back hit the wall.

The pack bond shimmered with Victoria's distinct psychic energy.

More growls. The thud of blows. A battle cry arose from the Alpha, a bone-chilling triumph expressed on a primal level. Something deep and visceral awakened within Sawyer, a kinship that echoed through his soul and filled him with the primitive desire to tilt his head back and howl at the moon.

As his head cleared, he struggled to regain his feet but lost his balance and dropped to his knees again. When his eyes focused, a gaping mouthful of serrated fangs filled his vision. The vampire lunged, his teeth snapping. Ducking, the hunter slashed the revenant across the cheek and opened a deep gash.

From behind, Victoria caught the vampire's head between her hands. She wore the visage of a wolf, more monster than human. Her face twisted with exertion, and corded muscles bulged beneath her skin. A nasty gash encrusted in dried blood marred her forearm.

The tips of her index fingers pierced his eyeballs, sinking into the gelatinous orbs. Hot fluids sprayed. The revenant shrieked and thrashed as Victoria's hands shifted to claws, and her thickening fingers expanded within the orbs. Sharp nails penetrated the thickset nose and cheeks, ripping open his face.

With a sharp *crack,* bone shattered. Victoria's wrists

disappeared into the skull, and the entire carcass decayed to a pile of rotted meat.

"Gross." She shook goop off her hands. Her mouth curled down with disgust.

"Why didn't you use your dagger?" Panting, Sawyer hauled himself to his feet.

Victoria ducked her head in a sheepish evasion. "Sometimes I get caught up in the heat of the moment. I forget I have it."

Sawyer chuckled, wiping his eyes with his forearm. "If I had a magic weapon, I don't think I'd forget about it."

"I haven't actually had it all that long." Behind Victoria, the vampire he'd shot in the chest rose and focused on her.

Sawyer shouted a warning. "Look out!"

Snarling, Victoria turned as the *Nosferatu* slammed into her. As she fell, she lashed out and grabbed hold of the vampire's wrist. Her weight wrenched the damaged arm out of the socket.

Fetid blood gushed from the wound. Stringy pieces of tendon and cartilage dangled from the exposed joint. Shrieking, the revenant toppled.

"You've been disarmed." Smirking, the smart-mouthed werewolf tossed the limb aside and bent to finish the mutilated vampire.

A groan ripped from Sawyer. "You've got to be kidding."

"Sawyer, behind you!"

An icy grip latched onto his calf. Frost burned his skin through his jeans. A female vampire with an axe embedded in her forehead grasped at his legs. Her mouth hung wide open as she struggled to bite through his boot. The axe's haft wedged between his leg and her face, preventing her from reaching him. The harder she tried, the deeper the blade sank.

With a muffled curse, Sawyer jerked his leg from

her grasp. He grabbed hold of the haft with both hands, yanked it free, and placed his foot on top of her skull. Hefting the axe, he swung overhead and delivered a decapitating blow.

The revenant dissolved into a gory mess.

Outside, the storm raged. Blood called to blood.

A chill of realization traversed his spine. Fear curled in his belly. "Oh fuck. He's summoned the hunt."

Victoria's fine brow arched. "The what?"

"No time." At a dead run, Sawyer went for the security door he'd left propped open with the knife blade. Outside, black clouds hugged the earth. The wind cut like a whip, and sleet pelted his face. Within the thunder, hounds brayed, men shouted, and horse hooves stomped.

He kicked the knife blade out from beneath the door's edge and pulled hard on the handle to shut it, but the forceful gale resisted his efforts. Half a dozen vampires rushed toward the entrance, seeking escape from the riders.

Craning his head toward Victoria, he shouted. "Help me!"

Victoria rushed to his aid. She grabbed the door, and together, they pulled until a sudden surge of resistance stopped their progress. Muscles strained, Sawyer threw all of his weight into the effort.

An arm wedged between the door and the frame. The ghoulish hand waved wildly, the long fingers opening and closing, searching for something to grab.

Victoria's blade descended and sliced through the elbow.

The door slammed shut, and the automatic locks clicked into place.

Sides heaving, Sawyer slumped heavily against the wall. Lightness swamped his head, and his shoulder burned like a sonofabitch. "That should hold them."

"I've never seen so many vampires in one place.

Where do you think they all came from?" Victoria hovered close to the entrance as if expecting the vampire horde to burst through at any moment.

"No idea." He assumed his father had a clue, but he kept his mouth shut. He wasn't going to speculate aloud without solid evidence to support his conclusions. Otherwise, his suspicions were nothing more than reckless conjecture.

"Your father and Lenna are still outside." Victoria leaned against the doorframe, panting as she caught her breath. "We should help them."

"We have to stay inside until the Wild Hunt passes," Sawyer said in a flat tone, hoping she wouldn't argue. He lacked the presence of mind for a battle of wits. He straightened, and a stabbing ache in his shoulder blade caused him to wince. "The *Åsgårdsreien* claims everything in its path."

"What will happen to Lenna?" Her voice was thick with worry.

"I don't know. Maybe Dad can protect her." He had his doubts.

Dragging the edge of his boot across the floor, Sawyer scraped blood and tissue into a pile, revealing the blood-soaked cement underneath. The armory floor was covered in gruesome, gory remains. Newly-turned vampires decayed messily. A vamp had to be at least a decade old before the insides desiccated enough to turn to ash.

The jabbing pain in his shoulder worsened, so he reached back to touch the injury. His fingers came away wet with fresh blood. His head ached as if it were about to split open.

"Give me a sec, and I'll heal you," Victoria murmured from her spot beside the door. "I'm tired."

"No rush. I'm fine." He wasn't, but he'd be damned before he'd admit it.

Her pointed snort spoke volumes.

An indeterminate time passed. He wasn't watching a clock, but his physical symptoms took a turn for the worse. The lightheadedness increased. Fever flushed his skin, and sweat soaked him.

Sawyer opened his mouth, on the verge of asking for help when the door to the armory swung open. Bright moonlight filled the doorway, haloing the Hunter King.

Jake strode into the room. *Alone.* The set of his shoulders angled at a slight slump, and his face was a grim front. Sawyer took one look at his father's expression and felt his stomach drop.

"I lost Lenna," Jake announced in a neutral voice.

Victoria looked away. "I'm sorry."

"Me too." Unexpected weakness collapsed Sawyer's knees out from under him. He slid down the wall and landed in a heap.

"Have you been bitten?" Jake asked with sudden concern.

"I can't tell." Sawyer shrugged. Lancing pain radiated throughout his neck and back. Moving more gingerly, he eased off his leather duster.

His father stepped behind him to inspect the injury. His voice was sharp with concern. "That's a bite."

"Well, fuck." Alarmed, Sawyer reached back again, twisting in a futile effort to get a look at his back. His self-discipline asserted itself, squashing his rising panic. A bite wound meant an excruciating death followed by reanimation as a vampire. He might be okay if they purified the bite with holy water before the poison spread. If they didn't, then he'd suffer the same horrible fate as Daniel.

He'd turn.

Sawyer grabbed his father's arm, gripping with white knuckled desperation. "Dad, promise me you'll kill me before you let me turn."

Exhaling, Jake grasped his son's forearm in return.

"It's going to be okay, Sawyer. Victoria will purify the bite, and you'll be fine."

Father and son confronted the she-wolf with tense expectation. Victoria stood near the doorway, staring down at her feet. Strands of blonde hair fell into her face, and her complexion was several shades paler than usual.

"Victoria?" Jake edged closer to her, arm extended and hand open in a beseeching gesture. He cautiously kept his distance. "What's wrong?"

Leaden fear coalesced in Sawyer's gut. Her continued silence fed the specter of overshadowing dread. The poison in his shoulder burned, radiating outward like needles beneath his skin. Every beat of his heart drove the blood flowing through his veins, spreading the toxin throughout his body like a cancer.

Face ashen, Victoria looked up. Her lips trembled, and her voice emerged weak. "Freya hasn't spoken to me since I healed you, Jake. Purifying a vampire's bite isn't simply healing the injury. That I could do on my own. I have to channel divine power. I have to deliver my goddess' blessing."

"Then I'm fucked." Resounding disbelief overrode Sawyer's anxiety. He'd done terrible things, committed crimes too heinous to be forgiven. For a while, the grief, hate, and guilt had been too much of a burden. He'd thought he wanted to die, but he really wanted to live.

Karma was a bitch. He *deserved* to die. Maybe the Fates were speaking.

The Hunter King's eyes crystalized to glittering obsidian set in a stone mask. The cruelty of the frozen north frosted his voice. "Tell Freya this is for my son. She'll understand there are consequences to angering me."

Victoria's head jerked back. Gasping, the she-wolf bristled with defiance. Bones cracked and crunched as her hands shifted to claws. She snarled, revealing canines. "I won't threaten my goddess!"

"Then take what you need from me." Jake offered his hand. "Become my priestess, and you'll become more powerful than you ever imagined possible."

Victoria recoiled, horror etched in the lines of her face. Her terror slammed Sawyer through the pack bond, but he also spied her underlying desire. Shaking her head, she retreated from Jake until her back hit the wall. "No, I can't. I'm sworn to Freya's service."

The huntsman advanced, driving her into the corner. "You're also sworn to my service. It makes no sense to remain loyal to a goddess who has forsaken you."

Sawyer lunged. Catching hold of his father's shoulder, he jerked him around. "All right, Dad, that's enough! Can't you see she's terrified?"

Those ferocious eyes bore holes into Sawyer. Then love restored Jake's humanity. He blinked, and his visage returned to normal. "I've already lost one son, Sawyer. I'm not going to lose another."

"Give me five minutes alone with her. Please." Sawyer stepped between his father and Victoria, hoping to give her an opportunity to recover. The throbbing, burning ache in his shoulder made it impossible to concentrate. Heat left him flushed and itchy. His breath rushed in fast pants.

Worry pinched the corners of his father's eyes. Grim-faced, he gave a curt nod. "Five minutes. I'll be in the main kitchen."

"Thank you." Sawyer propped his hand against the wall for support.

"You don't have much time. You're already feverish." Delivering his final warning, Jake backed up three paces and then left the armory.

Absolute silence reigned except for the labored huff of Sawyer's breathing and the thundering of his heart in his ears. He formulated words, but they got muddled in the hazy nightmare of heat and hurt. Pain defined his entire world.

He looked at Victoria, and she stared back at him with wide eyes. He'd seen photos of glaciers in the sunlight that radiated the exact same shade of blue—bright, cool, and clean.

She licked her lips and then squared her shoulders. Her voice hardened with determination. "Take off your shirt. I'm going to purify your shoulder with a blessing."

Sweat poured from his every pore. *Which god did she intend to pray to?* He wanted to ask, but the question was too dangerous. If she intended to forsake her goddess for his sake, he wasn't sure he wanted to know.

In agony, he pulled his shirt over his head, provoking a fresh wave of pain from his shoulder. Once he had it off, he discovered a man standing in front of him where no one had been seconds before.

Startled, Sawyer craned his head back to stare into the ghoulish face. His shocked mind registered a ten-foot-tall skeletal figure with exceedingly long, thin limbs. Chalky white lines formed the design of a skeleton on golden brown skin.

The Spaniard. Vildivia.

"*You.*" Sawyer's breath hissed with shocked realization. "You killed my brother."

"Yes, yes, I murdered the Hunter King's eldest son." The vampire flashed a demonic grin and extended a gnarled hand. His fingers were tipped in pointed nails. "Shall I prepare to die, Idiot Montoya?"

Vildivia's lips parted to reveal serrated dentition. A thick black tentacle covered in wicked barbs coiled within his mouth. Serpent-like, his tongue unfurled and lashed like a striking snake. A sharp *crack* split the air.

Turning his head to the side, Sawyer threw up his arm to shield his face. The adrenaline surge slammed his body and kicked his reflexes into overdrive. His heart raced. The dagger tattoo on his bicep sparked and flared lightning bright. He lunged to the side in a desperate dodge to avoid the whipping tongue.

Too fucking late.

Mid-leap, Victoria snatched the vampire's tongue out of the air. Clinging to the length, she slammed to the ground and landed in a crouch. Thorny spines bit into her hands. Blood spurted on the floor. The blonde werewolf bristled and growled, eyes glowing golden bright.

Complete surprise rendered Sawyer motionless.

For a second, no one moved, and no one said a word.

Vildivia wore an expression of utter shock. He gurgled, "Ub-bub-bub."

"Not again, you son of a bitch." Lips stretched taut over bared teeth, Victoria yanked Vildivia's tongue and jerked him right off his feet.

The Spaniard crashed to his knees.

Rumbling in her throat, Victoria coiled the Spaniard's tongue about her forearm and reeled him in. "This time, you're mine."

CHAPTER SIXTEEN

Sessrúmnir, Freya's hall in Fólkvangr

Loki crossed his arms. "From now on, *all* wolf shifters whose souls are claimed by Valkyries are to come to your domain. No more are to be taken to Valhalla."

Freya paled. "No. I cannot. Odin will notice."

"Odin sits on his throne taking advice from the severed head of a dwarf!" He rushed her and shoved his handsome face, contorted with rage and determination, into hers. His breath huffed hot on her cheek. His lips pulled taut over canine teeth, and the beast roiled beneath his skin. His hands grasped her arms, and his fingers dug into her flesh. "You can, and you will, or our deal is off. You can burn with the rest of the conceited, useless Aesir."

Freya gazed into his eyes and shuddered to see the horrifying depths of his madness. The Loki she had once known was gone, and the monster who wore his skin terrified her. She nodded. "I will instruct the Valkyries to bring them here."

Loki released her and backed away, suddenly all laughter and smiles. "Good. Don't worry. By the time Odin notices, it won't matter anymore."

Midgard

Vildivia's fist nailed Victoria square in the face. His bony knuckles flattened her nose with a sickening squish. Bones broke, and blood squirted from her nostrils. A burst of pain shattered her thoughts. Her body went slack. Falling backward, she lost her grip on the undead's tongue.

Victoria slammed into the wall. She slid to the ground and landed on her back in a boneless heap. The ceiling spun while a haze of red fogged her mind. A glistening skull floated above her, then descended swiftly, growing larger. Those wicked elongated fangs threatened to pierce her eyes.

The stink of carrion clung to him. She gagged, and her stomach heaved.

A growl erupted from deep in her throat. Raising her hands, she raked his chest with her claws, inflicting vicious slashes. She struggled to be free of the monster's grasp.

His strength crushed her.

Pain blossomed throughout her abdomen, inspiring terror within her. She feared desperately for her unborn child.

Angry tears pricked her eyes. *Freya, help me. Please.* Praying, she reached to her goddess for strength.

Another punch pummeled her head, another explosion of pain that destroyed coherent thought. She heard a man's shout, the pounding of feet.

The vampire growled, and Sawyer's shout ended abruptly. A heavy thud signaled the hunter had been knocked out of the fight. The loss sliced clean through her, and she feared the worst.

No time for fear or mourning.

Vildivia's hissing voice filled her ear. "Such a delectable morsel you are, little wolf. I'm going to savor every ounce of your blood."

Icy hands grasped and immobilized her even as the

dead body pressed her to the ground. Vildivia forced her head to the side, nails gouging deep incisions into her skin. Victoria gasped for air. She shoved and clawed but failed to dislodge him. Then he pinned her arms at her sides. She was helpless. Terrified to the depths of her soul, she howled and thrashed.

The vampire's fangs pierced her skin at the juncture of her shoulder and neck, tearing open a deep wound. Dead lips pressed tight against her skin to catch the spurting blood. He drank with noisy gulps. Feeding on more than just the vitae in her veins, he stole her power.

Her enhanced regeneration replaced some of the blood as it was taken, but not fast enough. As she spiraled toward death, her vision shifted to the spiritual plane. Her life force was a radiant, golden light draining into an empty void. Vildivia's soul was a dark flame which flickered deep within his chest and consumed her essence.

A second soul fire blazed close to Vildivia's desiccated heart.

Terrible agony tore through her abdomen. A cry erupted from her throat, and another cramp seized her, worse than the one before. Fear for her baby's life sent her into a blind panic.

Vildivia clamped down on her body, tightening his grip and sucking harder. He drank faster, attempting to empty her entire body faster than she healed.

The voice of self-recrimination hissed through her mind. She was a hothead. She took reckless chances. Sylvie had warned her. *"Don't start any fights while you're pregnant, Victoria. It's too dangerous."*

If she lost Arik's child, she'd never forgive herself.

"Freya." Blood bubbled on her lips. Her voice croaked as she called for her goddess.

Golden light flowed into Victoria, and divine energy coursed through her body. Freya's sweet voice filled her mind: *Heal yourself, Victoria. You have my blessing.*

Tears overflowed her eyes and streamed down her cheeks. She seized hold of the gift and reached into her own body, past layers of skin and muscles, ligaments and tendons. Deeper than bone. She touched marrow and infused the blessed energy to stir the production of blood beyond even the vampire's destructive capacity. Brilliant white light spilled from her eyes and her mouth.

Her blood burned.

Howling, Vildivia wrenched his mouth from her throat. The pain-maddened vampire tore at his face and throat with bony fingers, seeking to be rid of the blessed blood. As he writhed, the skin on his face bubbled and melted as if acid ate away at his insides. Fizzing and popping, his face melted from the bone. Chunks of flesh fell from his cheeks and revealed aged yellow teeth and mandibles. A foot-long lump of black barbed tongue dropped to the floor where it flopped about.

While the laceration on her throat healed, Victoria rolled to her side and crawled away from the vampire. Panting, she prayed aloud. "Thank you, Goddess. Thank you. Why? Why now? I thought you were angry with me."

I was angry when you turned to another god, but not enough to allow you to die. When you embraced him, I was shocked and hurt.

Terrible remorse filled her heart. *I'm so sorry, My Lady. Please forgive me.*

For a split second, the goddess hesitated. *I heard what he said to you. He terrifies me, but he is right. He is my king, and as a Valkyrie, you are sworn to his service.*

Freya's final words hung in the air. *As am I...*

The vampire's decayed face reared into the air. Rising onto all fours, he crawled closer to her. The tattered root of his barbed tongue snaked out of his gaping mouth. The organ's passage through the dissolved cheek produced a wet, squishing sound.

A growl rumbling deep in her chest, Victoria braced for a fight. "Here we go again."

Like an avenging angel, Jake appeared behind the injured vampire, his face a mask of murderous anger. The Hunter King's aura was a storm of red striations and jagged streaks of darkness. Wavy lines of energy crawled across his bare skin, coalescing into runes that blackened his complexion. A monstrous amount of magic emanated from him. With a vicious stomp, Jake drove his boot into the vampire's side. Bones crunched as ribs broke. He delivered another hard kick that sent Vildivia flying across the room and crashing into the wall.

"About fucking time," Victoria snapped. Her wolf lusted for violence and sent energy coursing through her body. Through an act of will, she suppressed the desire to shift, to rush the vampire from the rear and crush his head between her jaws.

Jake grunted a reply. His exact words were unclear, but she caught the gist. "You're welcome."

"Sawyer? Are you all right?" Jake moved to where his son lay in a crumpled heap on the floor.

A cough wracked Sawyer, but he struggled to sit upright. He leaned heavily against the wall for support. His legs shook. Sweat coated his entire body and glistened on his chest. His aura blazed, a bright beacon full of pain, and his agony traversed the pack bond. "Yeah, I'm fine."

Victoria was astonished by the hunter. He looked terrible, battered and feverish, but alive. Vast relief suffused her. Throat tight, she smiled, and her heart soared. *Alive.* She hadn't realized how much she cared until she'd feared him dead.

Movement in her periphery vision grabbed her attention. Terrifyingly fast, Vildivia sprang to his feet, viper-like teeth bared to strike. He charged straight at the veteran hunter.

Jake faced Sawyer with his back to the vampire.

Her mind too chaotic to form words, she shouted at the top of her lungs, a sound that morphed to a growl at the end. She leapt toward the vampire. She couldn't possibly reach him in time, but she had to try.

Without turning, Jake reversed the dagger's blade and impaled Vildivia through the abdomen. He held the weapon level and steady so the Spaniard's momentum drove him further onto the blade. With a neat side step, Jake evaded his enemy's grabbing hands. Powerful arms flexing, he wrenched the weapon and cleaved through the vampire's ribcage.

"Let's cut off the possibility of any more surprises," Jake said, his voice cold. He hefted his dagger, and the weapon transformed into an axe that glowed crimson.

Victoria's jaw dropped in astonishment.

He pinned Vildivia's shoulder beneath his boot. Like a woodsman, he swung the axe overhead. The deadly descent ended with the blade cleaving clean through the vampire's upper arm. The severed limb turned to ash. While the vampire howled, Jake moved onto Vildivia's other arm and then his legs.

In surprise and then growing glee, she watched as the hunter trimmed the vampire's trunk of limbs with the quick efficiency of an arborist. Every time red-hot iron sliced through dead flesh, toxic fumes flooded the air and filled the room with the stench of seared carrion.

Victoria gagged, fighting to not vomit. "If you chop off his head, it's over."

Axe haft resting against his shoulder, Jake glanced at her. "I'm aware of that. Are you okay?"

Pinching her nose, she covered her mouth and swallowed convulsively. "I'm fine. Let's get this over with."

Flopping about on the ground, the vampire retained his head and his trunk. His ruined face lacked lips and cheeks. Scraps of meat clung to his jawbones, and his tongue was a stump. Yet those exposed teeth and mandibles twisted into a horrific parody of a smile, terrible to behold.

"Without lips or a tongue, he can't speak."

"He doesn't need to speak." Staggering, Victoria lunged for the vampire. She grabbed his bald head with her clawed hand. His flesh was icy and hard like a frozen steak beneath her palm. The needle fine points of her nails penetrated his scalp and drew pearls of black, coagulated blood. Hissing, Vildivia jerked at her touch, but Jake's molten dagger prevented him from escaping. Those cold, dead eyes glared at her with pure hatred.

Bow-string tension sung through the hunter's rigid body. Facial muscles rigid, he spoke from the side of his mouth. "Victoria, what the hell are you doing? We need him until we recover Daniel's soul."

"We already have Daniel's soul." Focusing all of her strength, she squeezed until her claws punctured his skull a quarter inch deep. When the vampire growled and struggled, she held on even tighter. "Watch."

"You sure as hell better know what you're doing." Jake conveyed the deadly threat with a simple sentence, the embodiment of vengeance.

"I do." Victoria focused her rage. The beast in her chest was about to burst free. She wanted to scream, to howl. But she was more than an animal. She was a healer and a priestess and a leader.

"Freya, accept this sacrifice. I make it in your name." White-hot light burst from her palms and flared outward to envelop Vildivia's head in a nova. Shrieking, the vampire bucked and writhed in agony, but he failed to throw her. Her hands sank deep through melting flesh that ran like hot wax off his skull.

"Victoria!" Jake's enraged shout roared over the vampire's screams. He seized her shoulder, but he was too late.

The holy inferno consumed Vildivia's skull, incinerating bone and brain matter and reducing everything to ash. The resistance beneath her hands vanished, and slag spilled through her spread fingers to the pile forming on the ground. Decapitated, the vampire's ancient body rapidly decayed, leaving her kneeling in his residue.

"What have you done?" Jake asked in a ragged voice, raw with horror. The hand locked on her arm tightened even further, hurting her.

Expecting fury, Victoria met his eyes, but she found sorrow and despair. A father's face contorted with the agony of having lost a beloved son. Her heart hurt for him. She grieved with him. She longed to offer assurances and comfort, but deep down, a paralyzing doubt niggled at her conscience. What if she was wrong? What if she'd destroyed their only means of freeing Daniel?

Only one way to find out...

"This. I've done this." She groped through the pile of slag, sifting it with her fingers. Her hand touched something hard. She grasped the artifact and lifted it, shaking off the ash. The toxic aura of silver impinged on her soul seconds before the metal scalded her skin. The links of a heavy chain seared her palms, and the scent of burnt flesh wafted into the air.

Agonized, she whimpered but refused to release the amulet. Gritting her teeth, she shook off the last of the ash and revealed an antique necklace. A large, radiant ruby pulsed at the center of the tarnished talisman—the vibrant soul of her murdered lover.

"Daniel's soul is trapped here." Pain coursing through her arm, she offered the item to Jake.

He cast a stunned glance at the necklace and then raised his gaze to her face. His strong hand closed about the talisman, and he lifted it from her grasp. His eyes gleamed, and a smile formed on his lips. He stared at the ruby and then closed his fist, holding it tight.

Relieved, Victoria's breath exhaled in a whoosh. The pain ceased, and her naturally accelerated healing kicked in. Silver injuries took longer to heal than other types of wounds, so she'd bear burn marks on her palms for a few hours to come.

She thought she saw admiration in his eyes, and her heart gladdened. Certainly respect. Doubts banished, she sat straighter and basked in his adulation. It wasn't often she succumbed to vanity or self-pride, but damn it, she intended to enjoy every narcissistic second of her triumph.

"How did you know?" he asked.

"He had two souls. The second was way too bright—" She cut her sentence short, jerking her head to the side. Jake also turned toward the disruption.

Reality shifted. Bifröst, shimmering path of the Aesir, surged through the wall of the armory in a multicolored flash. A beautiful woman stepped off the rainbow bridge, and it closed behind her, leaving the building intact. She had the strong, fierce bearing of a Viking shield maiden, flame-red hair, bright blue eyes, armed with a sword and a shield.

"Hildr," Victoria exclaimed, astonished to see her sister Valkyrie. "Why are you here?"

Hildr opened her mouth but said nothing. Frowning, the Valkyrie looked from Victoria to Jake and back. She passed over the Hunter King without a hint of recognition. Following the hesitation, she said, "I was sent to collect the soul of the warrior fallen this day in combat and escort him to Valhalla, but I see you are already here. Has there been a mistake?"

Mind blank, Victoria blinked. Daniel's soul remained imprisoned in the amulet. Nothing had changed. Why would one of Odin's shield maidens be sent *now*? She traded a glance with Jake, perceiving his confusion. She took a deep breath, and the answer burst upon her as an epiphany—Hildr wasn't here for Daniel's soul at all.

Jake recoiled, mirroring her horrified realization. They spoke as one, "Sawyer."

From a standing leap, Victoria flew across the room

and landed at Sawyer's side. She dropped to a crouch, seized his shoulders, and flipped him over. He turned as dead weight, heavy and limp. His skin had a grayish pallor, and his lips were blue.

"He has to be alive. He has to be," she voiced her desperation as she searched for a pulse and found none. Her head jerked in automatic denial. "I'd have felt him die."

The pack bond.

As Alpha, she should have experienced Sawyer's distress and been compelled to go to his aid. But she hadn't accepted him as a full member of her family, hadn't integrated him into her pack, hadn't wanted to deal with the emotional dilemma. He twisted her insides up into pretzels of doubt and confusion.

"Victoria, can you help him?" Thick with worry, Jake's voice came from behind her.

"I'll heal him." Victoria placed her hands directly over Sawyer's heart. Summoning her power, she reached to establish contact between them. For scary seconds, nothing happened, but then the pack bond whispered across a vast void, a pale shadow of the vital connection she shared with the rest of her wolves.

Radiant light haloed her hands and bathed Sawyer's skin. Her vision altered, allowing her to perceive shifting fields, overlapping auras, and biological patterns. His heart didn't beat, and his lungs drew no air. Dark, necrotic energy swirled through his body—the transformation to a vampire was well underway.

She turned her head toward Jake. "He's dead, but his soul is here."

"Save him," Jake grated the command. "Whatever it takes."

Behind her, a sharp inhalation preceded the shuffle of feet. Hildr protested, "No, you mustn't. This is forbidden."

"Hildr," Jake said. "Stay out of this. The decision

goes well beyond your pay grade."

"His soul has been chosen to enter Valhalla," Hildr argued. "It is my duty to escort him."

Jake barked out a sharp curse and lunged toward the recalcitrant Valkyrie. The sounds of a scuffle blended with their argument and faded to a background din.

Returning her attention to Sawyer, Victoria shut them out. She trusted Jake to handle Hildr. If he couldn't, then no one could. She didn't have time for the distraction. She'd resurrected the dead twice before but always with the aid of a deity. She had no experience with vampires and didn't know if a reversal was even possible.

As she concentrated, her focus shifted to the mystical state of existence where the living and spiritual intersected. She no longer saw or heard the physical plane. An insidious demonic force assailed Sawyer's soul and ate away at his natural radiance, but his body's changes grabbed her attention. As she watched with sick fascination, the necrotic energy advanced through his corpse and reanimated dead cells.

Acting on a wild hunch, she summoned all of the power at her disposal and imposed her aura over Sawyer's body. At best, she hoped to use the regenerative properties of her metabolism to impede the change.

To her shock, it worked. The necrotic advance slowed and then halted.

"Freya," Victoria chanted the prayer. "I pray to you —"

The goddess interrupted. *I'm sorry, Victoria, but I won't help you bring him back. I've made the mistake once already. Your mate gave his life to settle your debt with the Norns, to protect you and his child. What you did for Jake Barrett far exceeds mere mortal concerns, but Sawyer Barrett is human.*

Reeling from shock at Freya's harsh rejection, Victoria gasped and rocked on her heels. She lost her balance but recovered before she fell out of sync with Sawyer. Needing something to hold onto, she dug her fingers into his muscular chest. "Arik begged me to save his son. He would have taken his own life and damned his soul. I did what I had to do."

The goddess offered a stern, swift response. *You always have your reasons, but I'm telling you, do not do this. It is too dangerous. Resurrecting this man violates the will of the Norns who have determined the day of his death and already cut his life thread.*

Resentment flickered in her heart which shamed her greatly because there was no honor in rebellion. A goddess commanded her priestesses and had the right to demand fidelity, obedience, and diligence of them. Did she even deserve to call herself Freya's servant any longer?

Victoria braced to bow her stiff neck and submit to her Lady, but a stubborn, intractable darkness deep in her soul rebelled. She argued, "This is what *he* wants."

Even across the room, the Hunter King exerted an irresistible pull. Victoria turned toward him, blinking so her perception reverted to the physical world.

Hildr skulked in the corner, appearing thoroughly chastised.

Victoria looked into Jake's face. Their gazes locked, and she perceived a father's sorrow and love for his son. His hopes pinned on her, she who had already failed to protect his oldest son's life.

Daniel would beg her to save his brother.

Freya huffed. *This is what you want, Victoria.*

Tears blinded her. Heart in agony, Victoria licked her lips. "Are you telling me to choose, My Lady?"

Freya hesitated. Her essence embodied grief and anger, but caution edged her reply. *I need you too much to renounce you. I will share you with him if I must, but think about this. You do his bidding to demonstrate your loyalty, but do you trust him to protect you when the time comes?*

What will he do when he learns of the prophecy that you will be the one to free the great wolf who will destroy him?

Victoria stopped breathing. Her heart thudded and skipped. Her eyes widened even as Jake's narrowed, but still he held her gaze. His chocolate-brown eyes were Daniel's whom she'd loved more than life itself. She stared deeper and deeper into eternity. He personified wisdom and ancient knowledge.

He smiled.

Uncertainty fell away, and her resolution hardened. To be true to herself, she would do whatever was necessary to defy Fate, even if it meant disappointing Freya or destroying the Norns. No matter the cost.

"He already knows who I am, and what I'm prophesized to do. I love you, My Lady, but in this I must disobey you. I am sorry." Victoria turned from Freya, and a vast void consumed her soul. Pain lanced through her, more agonizing than a severed limb or massive silver burn.

Freya's tearful sob filled her mind. *As you wish.*

Emptiness.

She blinked, and tears fell, splattering her arm and Sawyer's chest. She ached with loneliness. No more than she deserved but excruciating none the less. She hiccupped and then ruthlessly banished her useless weakness.

She repositioned her hand over Sawyer's chest. His flesh was ice cold to the touch. Her vision shifted once again, allowing her to perceive the mystical patterns of life and spirit that she manipulated as a healer. His body remained stuck in a state of stasis, the corrupting malignant energy held at bay by her regenerative aura.

Chest heaving, she reached out and took what she needed without asking permission or praying for the endowment. In her assessment, initiative and resolution mattered. Courage and honor counted. Much like wolves, personal loyalty meant everything, whether the kinship of blood relatives or the brotherhood of one's chosen family. Nothing else appeared to hold weight with the All-Father. Maybe his priesthood had fallen out of favor because they'd grown too timid.

In touch with the ultimate divinity, she died and was reborn.

A brilliant nova of sound and colors blinded her. Immense, unchecked power transformed Victoria. Remotely, she sensed constraints on his influence, restrictions on even the most powerful of the gods. True understanding of his entirety evaded her grasp, and his limitations were no more real than her own mortality. She soared, glorying in the ascension until she glimpsed something awful.

Horrified, she recoiled from the vision of the future.

"My gift, my curse." Jake's voice surrounded her. "Foresight. *This* is the awful, unalterable future. Do you want to see more?"

"No!" Terrified, she turned from the power and the prophecy. Already, her daring exceeded common sense to a dangerous degree. Blind arrogance led inevitably to downfall. She had a task to attend to, and then she must return to her mundane life, once again try to piece together the shattered ruins. She harbored no illusions — Freya would not forgive her infidelity a second time.

Concentrating, she sent healing energy coursing through Sawyer's body. Heat and light blazed where she touched his bare chest, a captive sun held in the palms of her hand. Dead cells revived and reverted to healthy, living tissue. She eradicated the last trace of necrotic energy from his body, and with a flicker of her will, she jumpstarted his heart. He inhaled, the first breath sharp and stuttering, but he swiftly settled into the slow, shallow rhythm of sleep.

Blinking, she brought her vision into focus again. Her surroundings resolved into an ancient primeval forest, vast trees towering overhead. Dappled sunlight filtered through the thick canopy. The sweet scent of fragrant grasses, bent and broken beneath her knees, wafted about her. Hundreds of birds sang in concert, and tall, broad leaf ferns swayed in the warm breeze. She recognized the dreamscape as the same place he had brought her to before, so she experienced no sense of fear at the unaccountable change in setting.

Awed, Victoria tilted her head back and inhaled, drinking in hundreds of distinct scents untainted by even a hint of pollution or synthetic materials. Nothing manmade. Nature at its purest.

Sawyer lay supine flat on his back upon a bed of matted grass before her. He remained sound asleep. She lifted her hand and discovered she'd left a print on his skin directly over his heart. Wincing, she scrubbed at the mark, but it wouldn't rub off.

"Shit." How was she going to explain an indelible brand in the shape of her hand? And why wasn't he awakening? With escalating urgency, she shook him. "Sawyer, wake up."

His mouth fell open, and he snored.

In her peripheral vision, everything shifted and blurred as if the scenery were rushing past at a great speed. Startled, her head jerked up to discover that a dense wood full of dead trees surrounded her. Instead of grass, she knelt in marshy soil that stank of decay and rot. A bog where a virgin forest once stood.

A man crouched opposite her, on Sawyer's other side. He was tall and strong, and the hooded cloak concealed his features except for his mouth. He had thin lips and a narrow, pointed chin. Thick glossy-brown hair cascaded to his throat.

The stranger's sudden proximity alarmed Victoria, so she bristled. In a rush, her wolf surfaced, and a low growl rumbled in her throat. Her eyes flashed a golden strobe, and her teeth elongated to fangs. Caught in an adrenaline rush, her muscles bunched as she prepared to pounce.

"Dust bunnies," he said in a rich, limber baritone.

She blinked and hesitated. "Excuse me?"

"We're all really like dust bunnies, snarled messy clumps that get stuck in dark corners, except when we're exposed. Then we're blown about and torn apart. Although, I suppose you might argue that Kansas said it better, certainly more eloquently."

Victoria scrunched her nose, regarding the madman with reservation. He sounded young, eminently reasonable, and his way of speaking struck her as oddly familiar, but she couldn't quite place him. She took an immediate and passionate disliking to him.

"Who are you?" she asked. "How are you here? And what do you want?"

"So many questions," he drawled. "Which would you like me to answer first?"

Her hands formed fists, and she checked the impulse to bloody his nose. His smugness irritated her like a poison ivy rash, pervasive and unremittingly itchy. She sneered and asked, "Do you have some disability that prevents you from answering them in order?"

He snickered and pushed back the cowl of his cloak. He was hideous to behold, ruddy and gnome-like, features pinched in places, puffy in others. "I have many names, but you'd know me best as Loki."

Surging forward, Victoria straddled Sawyer's chest, hands on one side, feet on the other. A growl reverberated deep in her chest, and quicksilver energy flowed across her skin as she changed. Flicking her hands open, bones crunched, ground, and transformed to claws. White fur erupted across the back of her hands and arms. She stopped midway.

Laughing, Loki stood and retreated out of reach. He held up staying hands. "Take it easy there, Snowball. I don't want to hurt your Barbie-haired boy toy. I only want to talk—

"I'm not interested in anything *you* have to say." She glowered, wanting nothing more than to chase him down and rip him to shreds, but she refused to leave Sawyer unguarded. "How did you get here?"

"There you go. You are interested in something I have to say." Loki snickered at her snarled frustration. He leaned against a blackened tree stump, arms crossed over his chest. His head assumed an arrogant tilt. "I have a talent for slipping through cracks, and reality is more fractured than you'd ever imagine. Even the most impenetrable fortress has minor flaws, tiny holes I can sieve my essence through."

She stared at him in disbelief and then pantomimed a yawn, covering her mouth with her clawed hand. "You're as pedantic as I expected. Now if you're done with your self-important babbling, I have more pressing matters to attend..."

Darkness engulfed Loki's features, and the cavalier jester demeanor flashed. Flames blazed in his eyes as the facade slipped and revealed the true monster lurking beneath. "You're making a huge mistake, Victoria. You should heed Freya's warning. She may be the whore of Asgard, but at least she understands the All-Father's true nature. Odin may appear all good and wise and fatherly, but deep down, the truth is much more insidious."

She flinched as his words struck home, scoring a direct hit on her deepest worries and insecurities. A little voice whispered, *What if he's right?*

Loki mocked her with a cruel tone and smile. "I'm aware you've got daddy issues, little girl, but be careful who you choose to play —"

"Shut up!" Victoria leapt into the air, her fist aimed for his chin.

He smoothly evaded the attack. Smirking, he finished, "...your father figure."

Furious, Victoria took a step back, dragging Sawyer

with her. She retreated as a means of checking her hot-headed temper. If she didn't put space between them, she'd go straight for his throat next time. "I won't listen to your lies," she hissed. "It's well known that you are a manipulator and a cowardly villain, Trickster."

Loki glanced down, mouth contorted in a sadistic grin. When at last he looked up, his face relaxed once again into a pleasant smile. "I'm not evil. I'm just drawn that way."

"Leave me alone." Glowering, Victoria enunciated each word as a distinct sentence. "I know what you want from me, and it's never going to happen. I'll never free Fenrir."

"Good, because I'll never ask." Loki shoved away from the tree. He swiped his hands together as if wiping them clean. From beneath hooded lids, he smiled. "Odin will be the one to command you to set Fenrir free, Victoria."

CHAPTER SEVENTEEN

Sessrúmnir, Freya's hall in Fólkvangr

The goddess adopted a rigid stance, and her spear and shield manifested in her hands. "In return for the modification to our agreement, you will assure my brother's survival as well."

Eyes rounded, Loki took a quick step back. "This is ridiculous. Freyr wouldn't even be in danger of perishing in Ragnarök if the fool hadn't given up his sword for the love of a woman."

She lifted her nose into the air. "Do not dare mock my brother's sacrifice. He chose true love over a weapon. It was a noble deed, and love is something the likes of *you* will never understand."

Loki rolled his eyes. "Yeah, I'm sure a whore's love is worth a *magic* sword that fought on its own. True love shouldn't require a man to cut off his nuts for the sake of dipping his—"

Freya interrupted, cutting short his lewd words. "That is how you will save him. Recover his sword."

Loki spread his hands in a display of outrage and shouted so his voice filled her hall. "How the hell am I supposed to do that?"

Freya offered him a grim smile. "You are the clever one, Trickster. Figure it out."

"But—"

"Be gone." With a wave of her hand, Freya expelled the loathsome creature from her hall.

Midgard

"Liar," Victoria hissed, hatred blazing in her heart.

A grim smile twisted Loki's lips. "So they say."

She shook her head hard. "You can't expect me to believe such an absurd—"

Loki vanished.

Lies! Shocked, Victoria was frozen in place, denial screaming through her mind. Lies. They had to be. The Trickster sought to sow dissension and suspicion. He desired to drive wedges and to undermine untested alliances. He must possess some uncanny knowledge of her secret doubts which enabled him to precisely target her fears.

The dead forest dissolved into a dizzying multi-colored swirl like TV snow, and Victoria's stomach lurched. Hands clutched over her queasy abdomen, she bent as reality reorganized itself once again. The armory reappeared.

"I'm really starting to hate this." A wave of nausea hit her, so she bent and tucked her knees against her chest. "Ugh."

On the ground, Sawyer performed a quick sit-up. His hands closed on her shoulders and offered her support. "Are you okay?"

"Yeah. You?" She looked up into his face and smiled, amazed and grateful he lived. She tentatively touched his cheek, fingertips grazing his bristled beard growth. Those unruly bangs that hung over his eye were as annoying as the man himself. Succumbing to temptation, she brushed the dirty-blond locks aside. Right then and there, she swore a silent vow. She'd learn to accept him into her pack, no matter how weird or uncomfortable.

"I'm alive." He spoke casually, but then a spark of startled realization gleamed in his eyes. Lips parted, he released a long sigh and squeezed her shoulders tighter. "I'm alive. *Thank you.*"

"You're welcome." She smiled and turned her head aside, blinking to rid the sudden sting of tears. A pair of jean-clad legs entered her field of vision. She looked up and made eye contact with Jake. Stillness overcame her, the nervous anticipation of waiting on a parent's approval or rejection.

"Nice job, Victoria." Jake's lips pulled over even white teeth.

She flushed with pleasure. "Thanks."

Jake offered a hand up to Sawyer. "I'm glad you're okay, Son."

Sawyer cleared his throat and accepted his father's help to his feet. "Thanks."

They grasped each other's forearms, interlocking limbs in a restrained demonstration of their devotion to one another. Delineated muscles bulged beneath their tanned skin as the two men slapped one another on the back in an abbreviated version of the man hug.

"What happened to Hildr?" Victoria asked, glancing around the room. The armory looked like the middle of a war zone with piles of slag, pools of blood, and dropped weapons and shell casings. Cleaning it up would take forever. Thankfully, Jake had plenty of minions, presumably ones who knew how to use mops in addition to assault rifles.

"I told her to wait in the other room," Jake said. "Are you feeling okay?"

"My stomach hates me." Grimacing, she stayed seated to be on the safe side. She inhaled, held her breath, and then exhaled slowly. "I can't believe it's finally over."

"Not quite yet," Jake said in a serious tone, capturing their immediate attention. He lifted his hand, the glowing ruby pendant in his palm, the heavy silver chain treaded between his splayed fingers.

Sawyer hitched. "Is that..."

"Your brother's soul." Jake gripped the amulet in a white knuckled fist. The corded muscles of his forearm bulged. The bones in his wrists stood out, and his knuckles whitened from exertion. "It's time to set Daniel free."

Victoria opened her mouth to protest before he damaged the gemstone, but a sharp crack split the air. Her heart leapt in her throat. *Too late!* Reflexively, she lunged to her feet and suppressed the impulse to grab Jake's arm.

"Dad, what the hell?" Sawyer demanded in alarm, stepping closer.

Jake's fingers uncurled and revealed a handful of sparkling powder. With a flick of his wrist, he cast the gemstone dust into the air. A ruby whirlwind swirled through the room, bellowing further outward with each graceful rotation. Following a rapid expansion, the entire cloud condensed into the shape of a man.

A pair of familiar black, steel-toed boots, worn and muddy, appeared before Victoria. Her breath exited her lungs in a sudden huff, leaving her winded, and her heart slammed against her breastbone, thundering in her ears. Swiftly, the figure coalesced from a blurry shimmer into a solid form, rugged good looks to go with his athletic build.

Daniel flashed his bad boy smirk, and his chocolate-brown eyes gleamed with mischief. He glanced down, performing a quick inspection of his body. "Nice job. I knew you'd get that bastard. But *damn*, Dad. It took you long enough."

She shot toward him, but the Barrett family came together in a collision closer to a rugby tackle than a hug. The three men were all talking at once, creating so much noise she only caught fragments of the conversation. Shouting, laughing, and pounding, their roughhousing effectively locked her out. Frustrated, Victoria circled, looking for an opening to Daniel. Spotting her opportunity, she rushed forward and jostled Sawyer aside with a well-placed elbow to the ribs. "Let me through."

"Ouch." Exaggerating the severity of his injury, Sawyer positioned a protective arm over his ribcage. He vacated the area, muttering, "...chopped liver..." But he wore a genuine smile, free of tension and anger, and he looked years younger.

"Daniel." She came face to face with his chest, blue cotton stretched taut across ripped muscles. Beneath her fingertips, the material was downy soft over hard as steel muscles. She tried not to let it get to her that he wore the shirt he'd died in, but the knowledge rendered perfect happiness impossible.

"I've missed you, baby," Daniel said, choking on the words. "So damn much."

"I've missed you too." Tears of joy threatened. Within a heartbeat, the walls erected about her heart in the months since his death, tumbled. Unconditional love ruled her. She wrapped her arms about his trim waist and enjoyed his embrace. Her nostrils flared as she drank in his earthy male scent.

Tucking his hand against the back of her skull, Daniel bent and pressed warm lips against her mouth. Hot. Wet. His flavor, an aromatic bouquet of cardamom and burgundy, tasted rich on her tongue. Strong fingers caressed her shoulder, stroked along her back, and cupped the curve of her ass. His body thrummed with energy, crackled where they connected, and she sensed the enormous effort he channeled into maintaining a solid form.

Sawyer cleared his throat. "Would you two get a room?"

"Maybe we should clear out," Jake rumbled.

Breathing hard, they broke apart.

Aware of their audience, Victoria stepped back. She wanted nothing more than to drag Daniel off and have her way with him, to hold him and love him, to surrender to uninhibited ecstasy in his arms. They deserved to celebrate their reunion.

Her heavy heart guarded against the knowledge his return was temporary. Jake had commanded Hildr to remain for a reason. The Valkyrie would escort a soul to Valhalla. It simply wouldn't be Sawyer's.

Daniel eyed his father and brother and said sardonically, "Yeah, this isn't awkward."

"Weird doesn't begin—" Sawyer stopped.

Electricity cracked and arced across Daniel's skin, and he became transparent. He looked down, and a soft cry of alarm escaped his lips. "Damn it."

Victoria stepped closer, grabbing his arm. "Your pattern is unstable. What can I do to help?"

"What's wrong? Why can I see through you?" Sawyer barked out a sharp demand and extended his hand.

"I can't manifest like this for long." Daniel's gaze tracked his brother's fingers as they passed straight through his forearm. "Damn."

"What's happening?" Jake demanded, practical and to the point.

"Daniel's using a lot of energy to remain solid." As a priestess, Victoria communicated with and touched spirits, but most people couldn't perceive the spiritual realm. She had no idea of Jake's capacity or limitations, but Sawyer didn't possess second sight.

Daniel turned to his father, exuding calm and focus, but ripples traveled the length of his body, creating visual static like an interrupted signal. "Dad, I need to talk to you. It's important."

"You need a host," Victoria surmised. "I can do it."

"I'll do it." Insistent, Sawyer stepped closer.

"I'm better qualified," Victoria argued. "You don't know the first thing about channeling a spirit."

Sawyer glanced at her, brow knit, defiance in his eyes. "Yeah, well, I've got a dick."

Victoria's mouth dropped open. "You are a dick! That's asinine, and it's not even a real reason."

Sawyer snorted. "Yeah, well, ask Daniel which body he'd rather take up residence in, yours or mine?"

Jake snorted, suppressed laughter. "Children, stop fighting."

"Are they always like this?" Daniel asked, slanting a glance at his father.

"When they're not trying to kill each other," Jake said. "Daniel, what's your preference?"

Rocking back, his gaze shifted between Victoria and Sawyer. His eyes locked with hers, and he offered her an apologetic smile. "Sorry, baby, but I plan to kiss you goodbye, not my brother."

Warmth fluttered in her stomach. She glanced away to conceal her sudden involuntary smile. Affecting irritation, she grumbled. "Don't make assumptions, *baby*. You lied to me. We have things to discuss."

"I never lied. I omitted." Daniel seized her shoulders and covered her mouth, stealing a hard kiss, crushing her lips.

Quicksilver arousal quickened her core. Electricity sparked. Victoria clung to him, rising onto her toes to close the distance between them. Her fingertips pressed into his muscular chest. Passion and competition had always defined their relationship. Right from the start, it had been a contest of one-upmanship and coming out ahead.

In her heart, she'd already forgiven him. She'd always forgive him any transgression, but he didn't need to know that. He deserved to be sorry for a time. She damn well intended to make him work to earn the pardon.

Panting, they separated.

"Enough with the chick flick already," Sawyer complained, thrusting his arm toward his brother. "Here."

"Thanks, man." Daniel accepted Sawyer's hand. As soon as they touched, he disappeared from the physical world.

His ghost remained visible to Victoria's spirit sight. She witnessed the transition as Daniel entered his brother's body. Their spirits overlapped, one image atop the other like a double exposure. The blending worried her, left her wondering if they shared memories as well. She wasn't sure she wanted her deceased lover privy to all that his brother knew.

Or vice versa.

He performed a curious self-inspection and then ran his hands over his head, pushing his hair back. "I need a damn haircut."

"Been saying that for years," Jake rumbled.

Victoria took one look at that mischievous grin, and she knew Daniel had taken the driver's seat. Sawyer never smiled like that—a cat with canary feathers dripping off his whiskers. *This* was Daniel, the man she had fallen in love with.

Daniel traded a long look with her, tilting his head toward his father. His brow arched. "Give me a few minutes?"

She nodded. "Of course."

He turned to his father, indicating the exit. "Dad, let's talk."

The men left her alone in the ruined armory. Suddenly starving, Victoria went in search of food. She'd heard Jake mention a kitchen. If she couldn't find it, she'd shift and go rabbit hunting, although she craved pickles and potato chips.

Freya's laughter filled her mind. *What are the odds of finding junk food in a kitchen stocked by men?*

Startled, Victoria missed a step. Relief flooded her,

and then a joyful smile curved her lips. "My guess is pretty darn good, Goddess."

Hildr is standing alone in the common area. Please go and speak with her and offer reassurances. Freya's voice carried more than a hint of insistence. It was a command.

A test. Or maybe just a peace offering.

"Of course, My Lady." Victoria hurried her steps. Her relationship might never be the same between her and Freya again, but she intended to do everything in her power to make the matter right no matter how long it took. Restitution would probably take years, but she'd already sworn her life in service to her goddess.

From the perimeter of an immense common room, Victoria gazed across dozens of long tables equipped to seat a hundred men. Beyond those, an entrance of double stainless steel doors presumably led to the galley. The dining area flowed into a recreation zone full of couches and chairs, all arranged before pool tables, dart boards, and wall-mounted flat screens.

In the far corner, a man's ghost bent over a pinball machine, seemingly oblivious to the Valkyrie behind him. His spectral form lacked definition, blurry about the edges, aura tinted a dull gray. He radiated dissatisfaction in jagged waves as he tried and failed to touch the buttons that flipped the paddles.

Hildr stood a couple feet behind the man, pleading with him. "Please, won't you speak with me? It is obvious your spirit is tormented..."

Curiosity whetted, Victoria crept up behind the pair. She halted a couple yards from them, observing their interaction in silence. Closer inspection revealed the ghost to be a middle-aged, Hispanic man who had been of average height and somewhat obese at the time of his death.

Primarily red, white and blue, the pinball table was themed Evel Knievel with a leather-wearing rider popping a wheelie on the back glass. Silver duct tape secured a handwritten *Out of Order* sign across the coin slots.

Hildr's voice sharpened with impatience as she tried to attract the spirit's attention again. "Sir, if you'll explain the circumstances of your death, I may be able to assist you in crossing over."

The man failed to respond. His clubbed fingers stabbed at the flipper buttons, passing through and penetrating the sides. A rumbled snarl of frustration tore from his throat. His anger infused his form with a sudden burst of energy. For a couple seconds, he appeared completely solid in a pair of camouflage army surplus pants tucked into short black boots and a tan T-shirt with the sleeves torn off. A stylized dagger shone bright on his bicep, marking him as a hunter.

Self-conscious, Victoria rubbed her hand across the tattoo on her own arm. The uncomfortable reminder of her new connection to Jake's organization created a deep pang of dissonance. Any sort of new responsibilities made her uneasy, especially since she had no clue what they might be. She barely managed to juggle all of her current duties as Alpha, priestess, and Valkyrie. On top of that, she was about to become a mother. What new obligations did joining the hunters entail?

Edging closer, Hildr shuffled her feet and extended her hand toward the spirit. "As a Valkyrie, it is my duty to help you."

A crimson riptide ripped through the spirit's aura. Ignoring the Valkyrie, he kicked the front leg of the machine, but his foot passed right through the support. He shouted at the top of his lungs. "God damn, mother fucking, son of a bitch!"

As the litany continued, the hopping-mad spirit launched another attack upon the pinball table. His thick fists sank into the main body of the machine. With a sudden clash that disrupted the nether, the ghost dissolved into a thick gray column of smoke that was then sucked through the handwritten sign and into the steel front housing the coin slots.

Victoria blinked and spoke without thinking. "Wow. Talk about a Daffy Duck temper."

Huffing, Hildr spun to face her. The redhead's arm rose to a guard position, and her hand flew to the hilt of the dagger sheathed on her leather belt. Her curly tresses fell in tumbled disarray about her shoulders, appearing artfully disheveled.

Victoria held up her open hands to show she presented no threat. "Hildr, Freya directed me to see to your comfort until Jake is able to speak with you."

"Jake." Face scrunched, Hildr's lips puckered as if the name left a sour taste. Her confusion pinched her face into a worried frown. A distressed litany poured from her. "I don't understand what's going on. Why is *he* here? Playing mortal? He has *sons* with a mortal woman. I don't understand what any of this means. It just doesn't make sense." Hildr's troubled gaze locked with Victoria's. "Do you know what's going on?"

Her brow furrowed. "I don't have to understand the how or why, and it's not our place to question."

Hildr's eyes widened, lips parting. "But he has sons."

Victoria sucked down a deep breath. If she thought about it, *really thought about it,* the potential ramifications left her staggered, but opened up many questions. Had her father and mother known the truth about Jake? How deep did the conspiracy of silence go? She shared all of Hildr's questions and concerns, but an overwhelming sense of caution silenced her. There were too many dangers, too many unknowns.

"You're here to escort one of his sons to Valhalla," Victoria said even as her heart ached within her breast and tears pricked at her eyes. *Daniel.* Finally getting her beloved back only to lose him again so soon was destroying her.

The redhead's face closed up, growing guarded. "Yes, it is a great honor."

"A great honor," Victoria echoed dully. They were talking about the soul of the man she loved. Overcome with sorrow, she cleared her throat. Reaching out, she took Hildr's elbow. "Come into the kitchen, and I'll try to find us some tea."

Hildr stiffened, offering initial resistance, but then she submitted and followed Victoria through the dining area and through the swinging double doors. Together, they entered a galley full of stainless steel cabinetry and appliances. A massive walk-in freezer stood alongside an equally enormous fridge, opposite a pantry the size of a bedroom. In full swing, it probably took a staff of twenty to keep the entire operation running smoothly.

Inside the pantry, Victoria flipped on the light switch and gazed at the floor to ceiling shelves that were loaded with enough canned and dried food to feed an army. She released a long whistle. "Wow. It looks like they're ready for the end of the world."

"From what I'm hearing, that may be coming sooner than we all expect." Hildr's low voice contained a distinct tone of doom 'n gloom.

Abandoning her search for tea, Victoria swiveled on her heel. Her chest constricted, and she automatically crossed her arms over her breasts. She took a breath and asked, "Why are you here, Hildr?"

Hildr blinked, and then answered by rote. "I'm here to gather the soul of the warrior slain in combat and escort him to Valhalla."

The corners of her mouth tugged in displeasure. She lacked patience with games like 20 Questions, and her sister Valkyrie struck her as either willfully dense or evasive. "Yes, yes," Victoria said. "But why were you sent when I'm already here?"

The redhead's eyes widened. "I didn't know you were here. I was only following orders..."

"Whose orders then?"

"Ráðgríðr sent me. She offered no explanations, and I did not ask. She does not appreciate it when her orders are questioned."

Victoria's face pinched. "I understand."

"Good." Hildr nodded.

Ráðgríðr was the High Valkyrie in charge of all others who reported directly to Freya. Victoria seldom interacted with the autocratic woman, and she preferred to keep it that way.

Victoria returned to the pantry and used the act of searching to disguise her disquiet. While she looked, her mind churned the matter. Was Hildr's presence evidence of Freya's doubt in her priestess-Valkyrie? Or did it indicate something more sinister going on behind the scenes?

At long last, she located a small box of assorted teas smashed between mega-sized containers of coffee beans and instant coffee. "What's your preference?" she asked, strolling out of the pantry as she sorted through the bags. "We've got Earl Gray, green, Lipton—"

Hildr offered her a tense smile. "Just black tea, please."

"Of course." Schooling her features to a polite front, Victoria fished out the appropriate bags and set about finding a pot for warming water. The next hour or so promised to be awkward and left her wondering just how long the men would be.

"Another three inches." Signaling with his hand, Jake indicated Daniel to continue backing the Chevelle into the compound's vehicle maintenance bay. Once the muscle car reached the correct position, he reversed the gesture to signal his son to stop. "That's it."

A Humvee slated for routine maintenance occupied the next bay over. The retractable steel-plated doors of the garage remained open to allow exhaust fumes to escape.

Daniel set the emergency brake and left the engine idling. He climbed from the vehicle, circling around to meet his father at the front end. Reaching under the hood, he popped it manually. Hefty springs kept the lid propped up.

"Do you hear that? The timing's off." Cocking his head, Daniel listened intently to the engine rev. His hand caressed the gleaming red fender. "What the hell has Sawyer been doing to you, baby?"

Jake chuckled. "He signed the pink slip over to Victoria."

His son's head jerked to the side. His eyes widened, and his lips parted. "You're kidding."

"I'm not. It's a long story, but the Chevelle rightfully belongs to her now. Is that a problem?" Jake watched his oldest son, curious about his reaction to the news.

Daniel huffed his outrage. "No, it's not a problem. I like the idea of her having the Chevelle. We had a hell of a lot of good times in this car. But damn it, Dad, Victoria knows less about maintaining a fine machine than Sawyer."

His chest shook. Through intense self-control, Jake suppressed his laughter. "I'll drop by to perform regular maintenance checks."

"You do that." Daniel's hooded stare conveyed layered meanings. He stepped away to open the drawer of the large red toolbox against the wall and returned with a wrench. "I think the distributor has come loose."

"Might be a plug wire." Savoring their last moments together, Jake watched while his son leaned over the engine. They'd never work on a classic car again, or talk sports. Not in this lifetime...

Jake went to the garage's refrigerator and retrieved two beers. Returning, he uncapped both and offered one to his son. "Tell me about the bastard who imprisoned your soul in that ruby."

Daniel finished adjusting the distributor. He took a long pull from his bottle before he answered. "There's a master pulling the strings from behind the scenes. Vildivia worked for him."

"The Necromancer?" Jake asked.

"Yeah, that's what he called himself." His gaze distant, Daniel stared down at the engine, and his knuckles turned white on the bottle. "I never got a good look at him, but I'll never forget his voice. He spent a lot of time jerking me around."

Jake stroked the bristle along his jawline, rubbing the four days of growth that had accumulated since the last time he'd had a moment to shave. "What'd he do?"

Daniel's lips compressed, and he remained silent for an indeterminate time. "Whatever he could to fuck with me. He let me out long enough to stop Victoria from killing Sawyer, but then he turned around and threatened to make me beg her to kill him. He had absolute control over everything I said or did while I was out of the gemstone. The rest of the time he left me to rot in that hellhole."

Jake tensed, disliking the turn the conversation had taken. "Did he hurt you?"

Daniel's face froze, and he took a steadying breath. "Nah. He screwed with my head. He wanted information about you and about your organization. He tried to break me..."

Jake opened his mouth and then closed it again. His son's murder and the imprisonment infuriated him. That Daniel preferred lying to admitting to having been hurt—it broke his heart. Molten lava rage built within, far beneath the obsidian exterior he showed to the world.

"I didn't tell him anything, Dad."

"I know you didn't, Daniel." He placed his hand on his son's shoulder, offering support. Silently, he vowed revenge, but vengeance talk wasn't what his son needed to hear.

Following a couple more adjustments, the Chevelle's engine settled into a contented purr. Daniel lowered the hood and ran a loving hand over the driver's side fender. His voice dropped to a murmur. "Feeling better now, baby?"

Heart aching, Jake chuckled.

Daniel set the beer aside. Leaning into the driver's side window, he switched off the ignition. "We need to discuss Victoria."

Jake deemed a diplomatic approach best, so he nodded. "I'm listening."

Daniel's stance shifted, openly aggressive. "Funny. I thought you'd have something to say after you discovered I'd broken your rules about fraternization with the Storm Pack."

"I'd say it went a hell of a lot further than fraternization." An involuntary smile tugged at Jake's mouth. His sons were trained in the art of combat and exposed to battle at an early age. As the eldest, Daniel had always been out front, leading the pack. He confronted every challenge head on, and yet father and son seldom disagreed on anything. In contrast, headstrong Sawyer had always been more of a lone wolf than a team player, and he challenged Jake at every turn.

Yet, it was Daniel who broke the biggest rule of all.

"That's your reaction?" Daniel arched his brow.

"I'll admit, I was shocked once I realized who your girl was," Jake drawled. "Unlike your brother, you bent the rules from time to time but never outright broke them."

Daniel inhaled sharply. "The first time I laid eyes on

Victoria, I knew she was the one, and I intended to claim her no matter what. You know I have nothing but respect for you, Dad..."

Despite himself, Jake smiled. "But?"

"But there are times when you're dead wrong and no one can tell you anything."

Jake sighed. "Now you sound like Sawyer."

"Yeah, well this is one hundred percent me," Daniel insisted. "I hope you know that."

"I do." Jake's heart ached. "Why didn't you confront me outright instead of sneaking around with her for almost a year?"

"Because I needed time to convince her that we belonged together. We were almost there when I got—" Voice cracking, Daniel cut off whatever he'd been about to say. Swallowing, he looked away and then resumed after a moment. "I planned to ask her to marry me over the Christmas holiday. I had two weeks of vacation coming. I wanted to take her down to Baja and propose on the beach."

Hurting for his son, he nodded. "I guessed as much. At first I blamed her for your death—"

"Well, you shouldn't," Daniel interrupted. "She did everything in her power to save me."

"I worked through that," Jake continued evenly. "I've done my best to do right by her. I've paid blood price for the wrongful death of that boy."

"I can't believe how fucked-up things got after I died." Head down, Daniel stared at the Chevelle, perhaps using the car as a window into his boyhood when things had been simpler.

Jake hated pushing, but certain things had to be cleared up. "I'm worried about Sawyer. Guilt is eating him alive, and he can't let it go."

"I'm worried too." Daniel looked nauseated.

"You can't tell your girl," Jake said. "Even with the debt settled, there's no telling what she might do."

Daniel's dark eyes flashed. "I know that. The whole situation just makes me sick..."

Relieved to have his son's cooperation, Jake nodded. "I don't like deceiving Victoria, but I have to protect your brother. I've tried to make things right by solidifying the ties between the Storm Pack and my organization."

"Those are political choices designed to make your position stronger." His son's tone carried accusation and anger.

A severe reprimand on the tip of his tongue, Jake opened his mouth to bark out a sharp rebuke. But the way his son looked at him made him hesitate. Daniel's words had the ring of truth. Ultimately, Jake put the best interests of himself, his family, and his people first. It just so happened his plans also benefitted Victoria and her wolves.

He had enemies on all sides, closing in like hungry wolves hot on the scent of blood. The identity of the unknown necromancer troubled him most. Not many creatures were powerful enough to open portals to the underworld and pull through revenants, or to steal a man's soul and enchant it into a gemstone.

Was his greatest enemy at play?

As much as he longed to confide in Daniel regarding his troubles, Jake remained silent. His son would have duties in Valhalla which would exceed mortal concerns. Burdening him with knowledge he couldn't act on would be cruel.

As a loving and faithful father, his first duty was to fulfill his oldest son's final wishes. "What would you have me do?" Jake asked Daniel. "Ask, and it is done."

Daniel calmed, acquiring focus. "I want you to remember this is the woman I love, the woman I intended to marry. She should have been the mother of my children. I need to know that you're looking out for her, because I won't be able to."

"Does Victoria know all this?" Jake hedged, weighing the full implications. His son had pulled out all the stops and made it a family matter. An ocean lay between *ally* and *daughter-in-law*, and it sounded like Daniel wanted him to cross it.

"No, and I'm not going to tell her. It wouldn't be fair," Daniel said, tone serious. "She has her entire life in front of her. Mine is over."

"I see." The boy's decision was half-assed and pathetically noble, and also completely wrong. However, Jake kept his opinion to himself. If it made things easier for Daniel, then his son was entitled to whatever rationalization he needed to make.

"This way she won't always be looking back. She'll get over me and move on." Shoulders squared, Daniel looked down, swallowing convulsively. "Maybe someday we'll be reunited, and I'll tell her everything then."

In a flash, the prophecy of his own death loomed in Jake's mind. A great black wolf howled, a maddened wail of ferocity and fury, mouth gaping wide enough to swallow worlds. He died between those slavering jaws, and a woman cried, tears falling from her cool blue eyes. The future, unchanging and inevitable.

Heart breaking, Jake hugged his son. "You have my word, Daniel. I'll watch over her."

Hot tears dashed down Daniel's cheeks, and he croaked. "Thanks, Dad."

CHAPTER EIGHTEEN

Sessrúmnir, Freya's hall in Fólkvangr

"Dirty little lying miscreant," Freya swore, curses falling from her lips like petals from the rose. Marching ahead at full tilt, she pushed aside the heavy velvet curtains separating the bath from her sleeping chambers and plowed straight into her new general.

Arik Koenig stood just beyond the drapery, arms crossed over his broad chest. Startled, Freya released a cry and twisted so her shoulder smacked his sternum. Even so, her full weight failed to move him.

In an undignified display, the goddess reeled backward, hands raised in a defensive gesture. Seconds later, she recovered. Anger replaced her surprise and covered a thick sludge of her underlying fear. Hot spots appeared in her cheeks, and her thoughts raced. She wondered how much of her conversation with Loki he had overheard.

Fuming, Freya damned Loki for the inopportune timing and inconvenient venue of his visit. The Trickster's lack of common sense was appalling. Arik Koenig was more than just another gorgeous body she'd taken to her bed. The Alpha werewolf possessed a keen, deadly intellect. Perhaps she'd made a dangerous mistake in allowing him to gain so much power so swiftly. She didn't know him well enough to predict his loyalties when the conflict finally came to a confrontation.

"I'm sorry, Goddess. I didn't mean to startle you." Arik's voice flowed rich and golden like his honey-colored irises. "You seem upset. May I ask what's happened?"

"Nothing of consequence. I apologize for having awoken you." Smoothing her hair, Freya searched his handsome face for any trace of anger or malice. She found his expression to be pleasant and neutral, but the scrutiny of those penetrating eyes unsettled her.

"It's time for me to inspect the troops and see that all is in order. With your leave..." Arik offered a flourished bow, remarkably eloquent for a man of the modern era.

Freya dismissed her worries as Loki-induced paranoia. Obviously, Arik hadn't witnessed anything untoward. "Of course, but one thing…"

Arik's brow arched in silent inquiry.

The goddess smiled coyly. "I might suggest you don a pair of pants."

"As you will, My Lady."

Midgard

Perched on the edge of a stainless steel credenza, Victoria nodded her head and smiled while Hildr paced a trough in the galley's polished cement floor. The red-head weaved a seemingly endless web of pointless chatter. She carried the entire conversation without any apparent expectation of input aside from the occasional nod or smile.

An hour later, Victoria's frustration had grown to the point where she was seriously contemplating pummeling Hildr into silence. Where ruthless hunters, wicked witches, and evil vampires failed to destroy the final vestiges of her sanity, the other Valkyrie's incessant talking threatened to be her undoing.

"I've never seen Sif so angry." Hildr's expansive hand and arm gestures served to emphasize the portrayed outrage of Thor's wife.

On cue, Victoria mustered a strangled chuckle, forcing her lips into a polite smile. Thank the goddess, Hildr lacked a nose sensitive enough to detect lies as well as the perceptiveness necessary to interpret body language. She seldom encountered anyone as dense. Cutting the neophyte Valkyrie some slack was the kind and appropriate thing to do, but Victoria detested gossip.

Freya's laughter chimed through her mind. *Victoria, be nice. Hildr is your sister Valkyrie. She is worthy of your patience.*

Yes, My Lady.

Exhaling so her nostrils flared, Victoria mustered more interest in Hildr's monologue as she moved on to regaling the epic extent of Sif's tantrum. The woman shrieked and bounced, gesticulating wildly as she pantomimed Thor's wife in a highly unflattering light.

Victoria's lower lip curled down. She *liked* Sif. The goddess was sweet and kind, and *good*.

A visceral tug from deep in her gut set Victoria to squirming atop the credenza. Instinctively resisting the unknown pull, she tuned Hildr out and focused her attention inward. It took a couple seconds to identify the source of her discomfort—a summons through the pack bond.

Sawyer.

Shoving off the cabinet top, Victoria dropped and landed squarely on her feet. At the sudden movement, Hildr stopped talking and walking. She stared with her eyes wide and her mouth hanging open.

"Sorry, I've got to take this." Joyous for the out, Victoria offered no further explanation. She darted past the redhead and headed toward the communal dining area. Hildr's footsteps thudded behind her.

Pushing open one of the swinging doors, Victoria hesitated before entering the other room. She studied the two hunters waiting there. Jake stood closer to the kitchen entrance, but her gaze slid past, barely registering the dangerous man. Her attention riveted on his son. Sawyer leaned against a metal frame chair just beyond his father. She blinked, peeking into the Shadowlands. Daniel's soul still occupied his brother's body, auras blended as two spirits in one shared vessel.

A deep sigh of relief escaped her. Daniel hadn't departed for the afterlife yet. She sensed Sawyer through the pack bond because the connection tied one soul to another. His ability to summon her shocked her. He had no training or experience, and yet he acted with the competence of a dominant wolf.

Maybe the challenge to her status as Alpha would come from Sawyer instead of Jake Barrett.

"It is time for you to come with me," Hildr proclaimed, advancing past the swinging door toward Daniel. "We have been too long already."

"Hold up." Daniel's hands rose in a staying gesture. "I'm not ready yet."

Hildr released an imperious huff. "That is not for you to determine."

Fierce anger blazed through Victoria. A low growl rumbled in her throat, and she released her hold on the door. Reaching overhead for the hilt of *Vanadium*, she lunged toward Hildr, determined to protect her lover.

A yelp escaped the redhead, and she spun to face the onslaught. She wore patent disbelief plain on her face as if she were unable to accept that her sister Valkyrie would shed blood over a man's soul.

"All right, ladies, all's good. Let's not fight like dogs over a bone." A second before Victoria's hand locked on the hilt of her mystic dagger, Jake's arm wrapped around her waist and hauled her right off her feet. An undignified squawk escaped Victoria and forced the air from her lungs. He spun her around and released her straight into Daniel's arms.

"That's characterization I take issue with." She landed against the solid, muscular expanse of Daniel's chest. The bittersweet knowledge that they only had stolen moments together ruined the perfection, but for the moment, she was safe in his embrace. She wrapped her legs around his waist and gripped his hips with her knees. She clung to his shoulders, wanting more, so much more.

Daniel snickered. His hands cupped her backside, and his fingers flexed. "He's baiting you."

"I know." Beaming, she tilted her head back and gazed into his face. For a second, her vision flickered out of focus, and Sawyer's likeness appeared before her. The transition startled her, and she rocked back. Disgruntled, she blinked and brought her lover's soul firmly into focus. Unfortunately, the restoration of her perception came too late for comfort. Her emotional disquietude lingered along with unaccountable guilt.

"This is weird." She placed a loving kiss on his cheek and loosened her hold so she slid along his body.

"Yeah, it is." Still cupping her bottom, he lowered her until she landed on her feet.

Jake's stern voice came from behind Victoria. "Hildr," he said. "I'd like to have a word with you about how a prince of Asgard should be treated."

An audible gulp came from the Valkyrie, and her voice quavered. "Yes, my lord."

Victoria sneered, punching his bicep lightly. "*Prince.*"

"That's 'Your Highness' to you, missy." A huge, shit-eating grin lit his entire face.

"In your dreams," she snapped, thrilled with his audacity beneath her deliberately grumpy exterior.

Daniel's voice dropped to a whisper, and he tugged her hand. "C'mon, let's go for a walk. We need to talk."

Breathing quickened, heart racing, Victoria cast a guilty glance over her shoulder. Jake and Hildr sat across from one another and appeared to be deep in conversation. Excitement pulsed through her, the feeling of being led astray into an adventure, deliciously dangerous and sexy and *wrong*.

She relished the way Daniel seduced her into temptation. Always.

No matter what, this time she must not succumb. Nothing lay on the other side of desire but heartbreak. The trauma and stress of the months since Daniel's death had changed her. Exacting duties and obligations crushed her spirit, leaving her sober and serious, a shadow of the carefree young woman she'd been a year before.

"Let's go." Clasping his hand, she walked, rather than ran as her heart longed to, beside him. Somberness resonated between them, an echoing boom in an empty canyon.

Together, they crossed the room, following a long corridor lined with opposing doors. Daniel's long, fast stride verged on a flat out run, and she scurried to keep up with him. Without warning, he swerved right and led her around a corner. They passed through sterile hallways, a complex labyrinth that included frequent stairwells marked with *Emergency Bunker Entrance* which were barred by reinforced steel doors.

The size of the facility astonished her, and the vast emptiness disturbed her, especially since the spiritual plane echoed with the memory of numerous absent voices. "How many people is this place designed to accommodate?"

"Upward of a thousand. It's our southwestern stronghold. Our fallback location if everything should go to hell."

"Who paid for it?"

"The government funded it. They don't know how

to deal with dad, so they throw money at him and call him an 'independent contractor'." His deep baritone was rife with amusement.

"Where is everyone?" Aside from the Barrett men and Hildr, she hadn't encountered another living soul, except for the pinball ghost. Of course, she had her suspicions regarding the reason for the vacancy.

"Dad sent everyone home." He chose an entrance, twisted the knob, and used his shoulder to shove it open.

"Because of me?" When he turned sideways, holding the door for her, Victoria walked through into the dark room. A golden glimmer radiated from her eyes, permitting her to make out a cavernous roomful of vehicles. A garage.

"He didn't want another altercation." Daniel flipped a switch, activating recessed lights that revealed row after row of cavernous mechanical bays. The enormous lifts were large enough to service the military vehicles. Sound carried within the confines and bounced off concrete and steel, making their voices boom.

As she surveyed their surroundings, Victoria grumbled. "I don't exactly go around picking fights—" Her vision landed on a behemoth tucked away in the far corner of the garage, and her jaw dropped. "Fuck me, is that a tank?"

Chuckling, Daniel took her hand. "It's an M4 Sherman from World War II. Dad picked it up on auction. He can't resist an old war machine. I think he feels a sense of kinship."

Refusing to be led, Victoria dug in her heels. She couldn't go any further without discussing his death and imprisonment. Guilt weighed on her, and pressure throbbed within.

When their arms grew snug, he looked back with mixed curiosity and caution on his face. "What's wrong?"

"I'm sorry." The apology burst from her.

"Hey." He frowned and turned fully back to her. His hand tightened about hers. "For what?"

She sucked air between her teeth, creating a slurry sound. "I failed you, failed my duty."

"Victoria, no."

Determined to speak her piece, she released his hand. "Your father said it. If I'd had your back, I'd have stopped the vampire before he got to you. If I'd done my job as a Valkyrie, I'd have taken you to Valhalla instead of allowing that abomination to abduct you..."

His jaw jutted in stubborn disagreement, and he adopted a fighter's stance as he prepared to tackle opposition head on. "You don't have anything to apologize for."

"Daniel, I do."

"My dying wasn't your fault."

"You forgive me?" Shivers coursed through her body. Her heart hurt and threatened to crack in half. Blinking, she gulped air, overcome not with sorrow but blinding relief, a sweet rush of release. Following his death, she had blamed herself, as had his family. Daniel's absolution freed her to forgive herself. She could finally grieve.

"Of course I forgive you. There's nothing to forgive. *I lied.*" Two fingers thumped his breastbone to add emphasis. "Me, not you. We both know you did everything in your power to save me. If anyone should be apologizing, it's me."

Her eyes narrowed, and her hands fisted. Anger crackling, a surge of adrenaline quickened her entire body. She tilted her head back to stare up at him and settled her fists on her hips. "So apologize."

He looked at her, hesitated, and then chuckled. "I'm sorry."

She grinned. "I'm sorry too."

"C'mere, spitfire." He reached for her.

She stepped backward but failed to evade his reach. He grasped her hips and pulled her into his embrace. His strong arms enveloped her. His head dipped, and his marauding lips covered her mouth. He tasted earthy, strong, and a little bitter.

The tip of her tongue flickered against his palette as she struggled to place the flavor. Her grip on his arms tightened as he bent, pressing closer so their bodies ground together.

Ah… *Beer.*

He and Jake must have shared a drink during their talk. For some odd reason the trivial detail delighted her. The knowledge that father and son were reunited, thanks in part to her efforts, brought her a sense of joy.

Smiling, Victoria turned her face slightly, breaking the kiss. Panting, she clung to him and struggled to regain control of her wolf before she succumbed to instinctual desires and dragged him to the ground. Her she-wolf urged her to claim him in the most primal act.

"I wanted to tell you. So much it hurt." Daniel gasped, sides heaving. He held her tight as if afraid to let go. "So damn much. But I had to keep dad's secret."

Her spirits lifted, carried aloft on an overwhelming sense of peace. Any residual anger she harbored over his deception dissolved along with her desire to make him squirm. Their final moments together were too precious to waste. Pressing her palm to his, she interlaced their fingers. "What was it you wanted to show me?"

Daniel flashed a cocky grin. "Are you through dragging your stubborn heels?"

"For the moment, yeah."

"You're more like a weremule than a wolf." He tugged her toward him and urged her forward into his arms.

She snorted, following him around a parked Humvee. The shining red Chevelle occupied the next bay. Her breath caught, and she came to a sudden halt.

A smile touched her lips, and her gaze flitted to Daniel.

"Are we gonna make a run for it?" Victoria kept her tone lilting, but her heart leapt in anticipation. A part of her was ready to say, "Screw everything," and follow him to the ends of the earth. She loved him that damn much.

"I'd love to run away with you, baby. More than anything." Gripping her hand, he flashed a boyish smirk, but tightness about the corners of his eyes alluded to sorrow. Stress sharpened his underlying scent, echoing the aggression thrumming through his body.

Hands held fast, they gazed into one another's eyes, but perception went further—soul deep. Her heart twisted in her chest, hurting like a creature caught in a snare. For every precious second they stole, she faced a lifetime without him.

Between one heartbeat and the next, she realized a simple and irrevocable truth. They'd never say, "damn the consequences," and take off together. For one, Daniel wouldn't ever abscond with his brother's body. As for her, she had responsibilities. People counted on her, and she refused to fail them.

"I'm sorry." His grimace made it clear he shared her conclusion and her disappointment.

A sad smile twisted her lips. "Yeah, me too."

Raising her face, his warm hands cupped the sides of her head, and he swooped to capture her mouth. His lips feathered across hers in a touch that tasted of bittersweet regret. He suckled her upper lip and then caressed her with a tender kiss.

Shivers coursed through her body, a scorching desire burned in her core. She clung to his waist, standing on her toes to close the gap between them. When he lifted his face and placed his lips against her forehead, she blinked back tears.

"I love you," she whispered, stroking his sides through the soft cotton of the T-shirt. Her fingers hooked on the waistband of his jeans and wedged between the skintight denim and his smooth skin.

His lips moved, the beginning of the reply she expected, but he froze and pulled away from her. Shoulders dipping, he turned and staggered toward the car with his arms outstretched. His palms landed on the Chevelle's gleaming red fender as if seeking to draw strength from the classic muscle car. His intimate connection to the vehicle extended to the spiritual plane.

A jealous twinge pinched her ego.

Stung by his rejection, Victoria forced her lips into a sardonic smirk. She sunk her hurt into the vast well of pain she already carried inside. After a while, individual injuries would lessen and become part of her substantial overall trauma. Like some girl in a song, she had issues, but she didn't want him to pay.

Daniel didn't want to break her heart, so he chose to close her out. Despite his rambunctious energy and cavalier attitude, he embodied the honor and courage of a true protector. When it came down to his deepest emotions, he became taciturn. The Barrett men shared several defining characteristics, including the determination to never show weakness.

Still, she clung to the stubborn hope that they could find some way to defy death and be together. Without thinking, words spilled from her lips. "We could send Hildr away. I can escort you to Valhalla. Here you're only a ghost, but there you'll have a physical body."

"Victoria."

"You'll feel like you're alive again once you're within Odin's halls," Victoria continued, unable to cease babbling. Fear, nervousness, terrible grief, the gamut of emotions overwhelmed her.

"Victoria."

"We can be together." She stopped talking and stared at him, all the while wondering if her offer was a lie. She couldn't give up her mortal obligations, so any effort to continue their relationship would involve great distances and time spent apart. Her commitments were many. How much time away from Midgard could she spare?

"No." The vehement denial burst from him.

Shocked and hurt, Victoria rocked on her heels. Her mouth opened, and then her teeth sank hard into her lower lip. She tasted the salt and heat of fresh blood in her mouth.

Face contorted in agony, Daniel grabbed her hands. He rushed his words, speaking too fast and without his prior harshness. "Victoria, there's nothing I want more than to be with you, but this is something that can't happen. You're alive, and I'm..." His throat worked convulsively. "...dead."

She blinked. "Daniel..." she whispered in denial. He was right. As much as she loved him, she had to let him go.

Steel threaded his voice. "You have to live your life."

Eyes stinging, Victoria stared into his face, perceiving the terrible tension he carried within his body and soul. She opened her mouth to argue, but understanding dawned on her with the suddenness of a shooting star. His stubborn, unreasoning insistence was as much for his own sake as hers.

She pressed her face against his breastbone, trapping their locked hands between their bodies. His heart throbbed rhythmically against her cheek. "This is the last time we'll be together."

He swallowed audibly so his Adam's apple bobbed. He grunted, a rough, "Yeah."

For his sake, she had to be strong enough to endure without him. Easing away, she squared her shoulders. Her gaze fastened on the Chevelle's red hood, and she latched onto inspiration.

"Don't worry," Victoria said, affecting a teasing tone. "I'll take good care of her. I'll check the oil every fifty-thousand miles and rotate the tires every couple years."

His head jerked around. Open-mouthed, outrage shone on his face as he barked out a sharp reply, "You'll burn out the engine!"

Victoria flashed a wolf's smile to let him know he'd been had. Her sorrow easily mimicked mirth, so she laughed because it was easier than crying.

Chagrined, Daniel bit off whatever else he'd been about to say. He smiled in acknowledgement, tipping his chin. His voice emerged as a husky growl. "Come here, you, and I'll show you how to check the oil."

Her father taught her how to check a vehicle's oil when she was a girl. As he damn well knew. Swallowing an instinctive protest, she sashayed alongside him. Her fingers hooked in the crook of his elbow, and she suggestively stroked the hard bulge of his bicep. For his sake, she would put on a brave front and hide her pain.

Tilting up her chin, she fluttered her lashes and said in a sultry murmur, "I don't know much about classic cars. You'd better show me... Everything."

A wicked light lit his eyes. "That sounds like the smart thing to do. Let's start with the back seat."

"Oh, is that important?" With a teasing pout, Victoria allowed him to lead her.

His chuckle ignited her passion. "It's vital."

Dawn was born on the eastern horizon as a band of light which steadily brightened the desert sky. Overlooking the vast vista, they stood outside the hunter's complex on the edge of Red Butte. Tears and laughter threatening, Victoria stroked Daniel's chest with her palms, wishing gone the layer of cotton that separated them.

"I never imagined saying goodbye to you with an audience," she whispered, casting a glance to where Jake and Hildr stood together. The Valkyrie held open a shimmering portal to the rainbow bridge in preparation for their departure.

Daniel chuckled. "I think they're afraid we'll make a break for it."

He caught a strand of her hair and pushed it behind her ear. His firm lips pressed against her forehead, and his strong fingers stroked her jawline. He trailed kisses across her face, lips encountering the salty tears in his path. He whispered against her skin. "Don't give up on love because of what happened to me. Promise me."

"Maybe," Victoria said, evasive because she was unwilling, incapable even, of making such a promise, and she refused to lie to him.

Daniel's arms tightened. No doubt, he understood her well enough to interpret the single, stubborn word. "Consider it. Please."

"I'll try." The concession was the absolute best she could do. She hadn't told him about Arik or her unborn child. If he knew, he said nothing, and she was grateful. Their last minutes together wouldn't be spent on messy issues.

Daniel pulled away to look into her eyes. He hesitated. "Sweetheart—"

Victoria interrupted. "You want something from me."

Surprise crossed his handsome face. "How did you know?"

"Because you only call me sweetheart when you're about to ask for something. The rest of the time it's 'baby'."

He snickered. "I guess you know me, huh?"

"Yeah, I do." Her hand settled palm flat on his chest so she could feel the pulse of his heart, and she imagined her own beat in rhythm with his. "What do you need?"

Daniel's hands closed on her wrist. His tongue darted out to wet his lips. Tiny nuances in his body language communicated some sort of internal conflict. Was he at odds with his brother?

"Tell me." Dread filled her belly, and gooseflesh prickled her arms. What could be so awful Daniel would hesitate to even ask? Worried, she scanned his face, and her vision shifted between the two souls sharing Sawyer's body. She read a muddled double aura ripe with contention.

His nostrils flared, and he spat the words out with a suddenness that startled her. "Victoria, you have to forgive Sawyer."

She flinched as if he had struck her and then stared with open disbelief. She desperately tried to keep her feelings of hurt from turning into betrayal. She jerked her hand from his grasp. His request knocked her into a free fall. How dare he take advantage of her feelings to even ask such a thing?

Deep within her soul, a flare of unreasoning anger burned. She struggled to keep her tone even. "I can't. What he's done is unforgiveable."

Yet, Victoria couldn't dismiss or forget the terrible sorrow engulfing her just hours before when she believed Sawyer dead. When he was dead. Was she being uncharitable? So many people found it in their hearts to forgive her myriad of mistakes and failures.

"Please," Daniel pleaded. "This is me, and I'm begging. He's my brother. If you can't forgive him, then he'll pursue redemption at any cost. It'll lead him down a dangerous, self-destructive path. Do it for me."

A crushing weight squeezed her throat and chest. She fought tears, not wanting him to remember her crying. "For you, I'll try, Daniel. I love you. If I could have given my life so you could live, I would have in a heartbeat."

"I wouldn't let you make that sacrifice." He stepped closer, arms wide open, leaving the choice to her. "I won't be able to visit again. Kiss me goodbye?"

"Don't think you're getting away without it." Victoria cast aside everything else. Nothing mattered but him. Longing for a tender goodbye, she eased into his embrace and savored every precious second.

"Watch over my family for me." Daniel leaned, pausing just shy of her lips. Their breaths mingled, and he cradled her in his arms.

Her body tingled with the sweet ache of longing. Her hands caressed the firm wall of muscle underneath his soft cotton shirt. "I will. I promise."

Feather soft, their lips brushed and then clung with gentle pressure. His arms slipped around her, and his hands slid down her back. Fingers splayed, he gripped her buttocks and pulled her closer so their bodies rubbed together with delicious friction.

Wanting to feel everything, Victoria held back to savor the smallest sensations and commit them to memory for the years to come. He tasted of warmth and light, her sun god, and she adored him with every ounce of her being. She leaned into him as the kiss grew more demanding. Her hands rose, stroked his hair, her fingers threading the silky strands. Energy sparked between them, dancing arcs which hinted at the storm. Intoxicating. She wanted more, so much more, to become one with him in body and soul.

Goodbye, my love. Daniel's parting words whispered through her mind as his soul departed.

Goodbye, Daniel. Beneath closed lids, her tears fell, streaming down her cheeks. She sensed the exact moment his soul transitioned from his body. A brilliant flash of light signaled her lover's departure with Hildr and the closing of Bifröst.

Sawyer's lips covered hers with primal hunger, and he lifted her off the ground. Their bodies ground together, his solid chest agitating her nipples and crushing her small breasts. Her groin pressed against his crotch, and her knees clung to his hips. Her wolf urged her to tear through his pants and claim him in the most fundamental way. She ached to feel him inside her.

Sawyer hesitated and broke the kiss. "Victoria."

Confusion penetrated her lustful haze, and she stared into his brown eyes. Seeing his desire and his doubt, Victoria's common sense slammed her back to reality. She pushed away from him and dropped to her feet. Her departure shoved him off balance, so he took a step backward. Heart pounding, she retreated from him.

His breathing was an audible rasp. For a full minute, they stared at each other, gazes locked in astonishment. Finally, unable to handle anymore, Victoria turned and walked away.

Hours later, Victoria hesitated with her hand on the knob of the compound's door. She cast a quick glance at Sawyer who sat on the sofa cleaning a shotgun. The hunter's head bent, causing long blond hair to fall into his face. He appeared intent at his task, but she sensed his awareness. He tracked her every movement.

Gathering her nerve, she cleared her throat. "I'm going to do my best to forgive you because Daniel asked. The rest of my pack may take longer to accept you, but I'll talk to them."

Sawyer's head swiveled toward her. His face was blank with surprise, his mouth open in question. He didn't speak, but hope flared in his eyes.

She held up a staying hand. "Give me a good reason."

His Adam's apple bobbed, and he nodded. "I will. I swear it."

Without another word, Victoria fled the tense room. She left the compound and approached the parking lot. The sun hung in the position of early morning in the sky. She leaned against the Chevelle's fender. Arms crossed and legs extended, she stared into the horizon. The scent of soil and desert plants flooded her nostrils, creating a perpetual itch.

Waiting was torture. Anxiety played whack-a-mole with her confidence. Jake had requested that she wait outside for him because he had something they needed to discuss before she left. She wondered why he wanted to see her alone. What more was left to say? Fortunately, the hunter wasn't long.

Boots crunching on dry dirt, footsteps approached from behind. Based on the man's weight and manner of moving, she identified Jake Barrett without bothering to look. A second later, the pack bond crackled to life, and the seasoned hunter rounded the car. He stopped a short distance from her and mirrored her pose, resting against the fender, arms crossed and boots stretched out alongside hers. His legs extended much farther.

She inhaled, drinking in the dusty air. She chased words through her mind, and her lips parted, but she preferred to employ the patience of a predator. The man had something on his mind, so she decided to wait for him to speak.

He huffed. "Helluva a thing."

Her mouth tried to push into a smile which she struggled to repress by biting down. "Yep."

Jake grunted. "How is this pack thing supposed to work?"

Victoria gulped and choked on laughter that sounded like a cough. She shook her head and rolled her shoulders. "We've broken all of the rules, so I figure we're going to have to make up new ones as we go."

"Fair enough." He raked a hand through his hair, a sign that his thoughts remained troubled.

Victoria allowed her gaze to drop to his boots and then lifted her eyes, appraising him. She arched her brow and flashed a feral grin. "Do you intend to challenge me for Alpha?"

With a startled sound, Jake threw back his head, and then a guffaw of laughter erupted from him. "I'm not a wolf, and I've already got my hands full with my own people. I suppose you can remain the official figurehead."

"Gee, thanks." She kept her tone sour, but her grin was genuine. "This is absolutely impossible, you know. It can't work."

He nodded, acknowledging the absurdity of the arrangement, and yet the unspoken agreement resonated between them. Damn convention, screw tradition. Come hell or high water, they were going to try.

A companionable mood prevailed. She got the impression he still hadn't broached what troubled him, so she waited. An alternative topic popped into her head, something she had wondered about often. "Can I ask you a question?"

"Sure."

"What became of Michael, the little boy we rescued in Albuquerque?"

Jake smiled. "I adopted him and that mangy Rottweiler too. Damn dog follows him everywhere."

She blinked, and surprise delayed her reaction. Unexpected pleasure warmed her heart, and her lips curved into a smile. "So he's being raised by hunters after all."

"Better than wolves."

They shared a laugh, and she decided he wanted her to ask. "What's really on your mind?"

"My organization is being overwhelmed," Jake said. "Hunters are being slaughtered *en masse*. The other packs have stopped cooperating with us because of what happened in Phoenix. A restoration of the alliance is necessary if we're to have a snowball's chance in hell of coming out of this war intact."

Victoria nodded. "I'll convene a gathering of the packs."

His brow jumped. "That hasn't been done in thirty years."

"No, not since you and my father negotiated the original alliance," Victoria agreed. "But that's what it'll take to put everyone back on the same page. You'll have to attend."

"I'll be there." He paused for a beat and then asked, "Will the other Alphas accept a female?"

Victoria's face set in an expression of pure determination. "They will if they know what's good for them."

If any Alpha male refused, she'd ram it down his stubborn throat.

Jake grinned and chuckled. He fell silent. Long moments ticked past.

Victoria sighed. "Is there more?"

He scowled. His eyes held too much dangerous emotion. "Victoria, there's something I need to say, but I'm not a man of words."

She gulped. "Just spit it out then."

Jake reached into the pocket of his coat and removed a handkerchief which fell open in his hand. Reaching out, he pressed a small metal object against her palm. "A week before he died, Daniel asked me for his mother's wedding ring. He told me there was a woman I had to meet. The woman he intended to marry."

Shocked, she looked down. A ring in an antique white gold setting lay in her palm. The diamond shone with the brilliance of the Arizona sun, breaking apart the white light and casting a spray of colors. Her mouth opened, and her lips worked, forming nonsensical words. Her heart stopped for an eternity before the beat resumed.

Her brow furrowed, and she looked up at Jake. Studying his grizzled face hard, she tried to discern his meaning. She licked her lips, strove to appear unaffected when his revelation had just rocked the foundation of her world. The knowledge compounded her sorrow and reminded her just how much she lost when Daniel died.

"My son loved you."

Tears filled her eyes. The shredded remnant of her heart ached in her chest. "I loved him more than anything. A part of me died with him."

Jake's throat constricted as he swallowed. "The way I see things, you were meant to be my daughter. The baby you're carrying should've been my grandchild. I figure, we're family now."

Tears overflowed her eyes. She sprang and wrapped both arms around his waist in a fierce hug. The momentum was enough to stagger Jake upon impact. The union burned intense between them, as strong as any other kinship bond Victoria had ever known.

The hunter remained ramrod stiff. He cleared his throat and rumbled with choked emotions. His arms rose around her, formed an awkward circle, and then at last, he returned her hug. She squeezed her eyelids shut, and the tears soaked into his shirt.

"Shit, don't start bawling." Jake whomped her on the back with his fist. "I hate weepy women."

"Yeah, me too." Grinning, she pulled away from him and scrubbed the tears from her cheeks. She took a step away from him and stared out into the desert while she got her emotions in check.

Composed, she faced him again and returned the ring to his hand. She had to put the past behind her and maintain momentum. For the good of her pack. "Save it for one of your sons, Jake. Someday, one of them will ask you for it."

He glanced at the glittering diamond, and his hand closed on the ring. With a brusque nod, he shoved it into his front pocket.

The profound silence endured for a full minute until Jake cleared his throat. "So, you'll be heading back to California?" He pronounced it *CAL-a-FORN-ee-a* and sneered.

"Yeah, it's my home now." With a grin, Victoria pushed away from the car and dug the keys from the front pocket of her jeans. "I guess this is it."

His gaze fell on the red Chevelle. Love and pride shone on the hunter's normally aloof face. "You'd better take good care of her or you can forget this alliance. I'll come after you myself."

She turned toward the convertible, running a loving hand over the gleaming fender. Blue eyes dancing, she grinned over her shoulder. "I hear ya, old man. I hear ya."

CHAPTER NINETEEN

Do you remember, Odin, when in bygone days
We mixed our blood and swore oaths?
You promised you would never drink ale
Unless it was brought to both of us.

~*Lokasenna or "Loki's Quarrel", Stanza 9*

Midgard

Sharp talons dug into Jake's shoulder as the bird ducked its head to whisper in his ear. Raising his hand, he stroked his fingers over the jet black plumage upon the sleek breast. Warbling a sweet croon, the raven pecked playfully at the side of his hand, capturing a fold of skin in its keen beak.

Chuckling, he shooed his pet. "Go."

Craa! The raven launched from its perch, strong wings beating the air. The bird's form remained visible for a while against the twilight sky, but darkness inevitably swallowed its swift silhouette.

In springtime, the desert teemed with life, much of it hidden from view. Low creatures crawled, scuttled, and scurried through the hard-packed soil and thick brush. Sensing an intruder, Jake cocked his ear toward the ground and listened to a serpent's scales sliding over cracked earth. His eyes narrowed when he confirmed he wasn't alone.

"Come out, Loki. I know you're here." He waited.

A rattlesnake slithered from beneath a rock, its long form altering as it emerged. While Jake watched, the creature's shape underwent a swift alteration, the solid mass turned to liquid to facilitate the change. Limbs sprouted from the snake's smooth sides, and the head rounded and enlarged. Skin replaced scales, and a young man sprang from the serpent. With a skip and a hop, he pulled ribbon strands of magic from the air and conjured clothing from nothing to cover his nudity.

Resting his chin on his chest, Loki's lips lifted to reveal thick fangs in lieu of his incisors. "It's been a long time, *dear brother*."

Jake scowled. The taunt stung as it was no doubt intended. However, he refused to succumb to anger. The Trickster's tactics were well known to him. "Why are you lurking about?"

Loki's tongue swiped his lips. "I'm always lurking about. It's what I do."

The Hunter King forced his face to a stoic mask and crossed his arms. "You're close enough to endanger your cowardly hide, so you must want something."

A bitter laugh strangled Loki. "Call me a coward? It is you who are paralyzed by paranoia, strangled by stagnation."

"My patience runs thin."

"Is that a threat?" Laughing, Loki sidled closer. "What are you going to do to me? We both know you're not going to kill me. Oh no, I'm fated to die by Heimdallr's hand as foretold by *you*, Prophecy Man."

Jake smiled grimly. "There are worse things than death. As you well know..."

"Your threats are empty. You have already taken everything from me. I have nothing left to lose." Loki rolled his eyes, boldly holding his ground.

"There's always something."

Loki's gaze darted skyward, and he stared at some far off point. Then those bright eyes focused to brilliant pinpoints. His dancing hand wove a rune in the air. "Shall we revisit yet again how you condemned my children to be imprisoned? Punished for crimes you *claimed* they might someday commit? Wrigley Jörmungandr, tossed into the depths of the great ocean. My darling daughter, Hel, condemned to the dreary underworld. Ah, and let's not forget poor Fenris, that happy, eager-to-please pup, chained in bindings so tight that festering wounds cover his body. He has suffered in agony for so long, madness and rage are all that's left of him. *You* made them into monsters."

"Let's not forget your punishment, Loptr." Jake leaned forward, locking gazes with his old rival. Once, he had called the Jötun his closest friend and most trusted ally. His affection for the shapechanger had been boundless. They had mingled their blood and sworn oaths.

Loki, his brother in blood.

Once, long, long ago.

"No, let's not forget that either." The serpent's tail rattled in his hiss. "I made mischief for centuries while you watched and smiled. My antics amused you even when all other Aesir despised me, but we stood united. All this, then you condemned me for the one crime I *didn't* commit."

"You know why you were punished, Loki." Despite Jake's determination to remain detached, a molten core of anger pushed to the surface. His dagger burned on his forearm, pulsating rhythmically. The runes swirled beneath his skin.

"Just not for the reason everyone thinks!" Perceiving his peril, Loki ducked away as a nimble cat. He retreated to a safer distance before he shifted to human. "You know damn well I had nothing to do with Baldur's murder! You allowed the others to assume. Even Thor turned against me. One word from you would have stopped them. Yet you said *nothing*."

"You were complicit in my son's death." His mask slipped. Jake's teeth ground together, crunching like boulders. Runes rose and turned his flesh darker than midnight.

"I overlooked a fucking twig!"

"On purpose."

"No. No. Not on purpose!" Loki stomped his feet, hopping in rage. "Baldur's death gained me nothing! Frigg herself told me not to concern myself with the damned mistletoe."

Primordial magic threatened to consume his mortal vessel in a fiery blaze. Dark, dangerous things, too awful to be named, writhed within his soul. "You knew better than to listen."

"I warned you not to defy the Norns. Fate is a tricky bitch who comes back to bite you every time," Loki shouted, waving his fist. "Frigg had no business trying to make Baldur invincible. She painted a target on his back."

Reaching across his body, Jake drew his enchanted weapon. The tattoo vanished from his arm, and the molten knife appeared in his hands. "We have argued about this more times than I can count." *Words led to words, always the same.* "Say something new or get off my butte."

"Nice subversion." Smiling in pointed admiration, Loki trotted out the consummate charm that served him so well. *Old Silver Tongue.*

"Thanks." Nonplussed, Jake hesitated, but curiosity got the better of him. Sighing, he asked, "Why are you here, Loki?"

"I'm intrigued."

"About me?"

The Trickster's chin dipped. "You're different from

the old man who sits on his throne, day in and day out, apathetic to the world outside his halls."

"How so?" Jake grew guarded. Oftentimes, Loki saw too deeply, perceived too much, deadly insight he employed as a weapon.

"You're like the *Wōden* I remember from the primordial times." Soulful wolf eyes regarded him with sorrow. "Before the days had names, when the world tree was a sapling."

"I am the hunt."

"Riiight." Loki rolled the word around on his tongue for a time. Then his visage hooded. "Why have you cut yourself off from your precious foresight, brother? You gouged out your own eye to attain it. Now I'm to believe you've now turned your back on prophecy?"

"I care not what you believe."

Loki *tsked*. "Then what's with the mortal coil? It's perverse, a god walking among men wearing a meat suit."

Jake grunted. His anger further dissipated, spiraling into resignation. In all the Nine Worlds, he owned no man, creature, or god an explanation. Why then did he find himself playing 20 Questions with the Trickster?

"You do it." Jake willed the dagger to return to his forearm, and it did.

Loki grinned. "I'm perverse. You're not."

He was tired, tired of Loki's games, tired of everything. He had too much to do before the final days descended. Overcome with impatience, he turned his back and headed toward the compound. His boots crunched in the dry desert dirt.

"Hey, where are you going? This is just getting interesting." Loki appeared before him, blocking his path. "Tell me why, and I'll leave."

Exhaling, Jake stopped. To be rid of the clever meddler, he'd entertain the notion of answering one more question. "Tell you what?"

"I've been to Valhalla. I've witnessed the apathetic lump your greater aspect has become. He sits on his throne, whispering secrets with the embalmed head of a long dead dwarf. And they call *me* mad." Loki spoke swiftly, weaving words and hands. "Yet, here you are, an insignificant avatar, still trying to defy the Norns. You tried to save that she-wolf from her death even though you must have known her life thread had been cut."

"Lenna." His voice echoed the emptiness in his soul. He had failed her.

Loki huffed, expanding. "It's the same with Sawyer. His fate has been carved into the trunk of the World Tree, his destiny decided. I get that he's your son, so you want to save him. You're nothing if not predictable. But do you really think you'll get away with it?"

Why? Why did he always make the mistake of engaging Loki? Vein throbbing in his temple, Jake stared at his bitter adversary, allowing centuries of presumption and grievous mistakes to roll like a long line of credits at the end of a film. Sickness worsened inside him as all of the pieces fell into place.

"It was you," Jake said at last, speaking with absolute certainty. "You arranged Daniel's murder, the theft of his soul, these vampire attacks. Vildivia and the Necromancer—"

"Arranged is a strong word," Loki interrupted. "I orchestrated certain events to unfold as I desired. Did you enjoy the *draugar*? I arranged them just for you. A touch of nostalgia. The players in my game always had free will. *I* didn't force Sawyer to shoot that wolf boy in the back. *I* didn't trick you into openly defying the Norns. I only set the stage to see what you'd do."

Incensed, Jake's hand shot out and closed on the Trickster's throat, crushing his airway. Loki choked and writhed in his grasp. With one arm, he lifted the god of lies off his feet and held him high. He roared, "Betrayer!"

Loki dissolved into a thousand mobile specks. Ants swarmed Jake's hand and arm. His skin itched and burned from multiple bites while the colony scurried down his body to form a living pool at his feet. Vengefully, he crushed hundreds of insects beneath his boots, but the massacre didn't prevent the insects from retreating at a rapid pace.

Twenty feet away, Loki reformed, rubbing his throat. He mocked, "Temper, temper. Don't lose yours, dear friend."

On the verge of abandoning his humanity, Jake stopped dead in his tracks. If he pursued Loki, he'd succumb to temptation and leave everything and everyone he loved behind. He had obligations and responsibilities. People were counting on him. His boys, even stubborn Sawyer, *needed* him.

"You're going to pay for what you've done to my family, Loki," Jake vowed, a promise he intended to fulfill by any means necessary. If he had to employ all of the knowledge, magic, and power at his command, he would.

Loki sneered. "I'm your family, *brother*."

"No longer. I'll make you pay for this."

"Is that so?" Loki croaked hoarsely. His eyes glittered, black diamonds in an empty void of a face. "How? Let me hazard a guess. You'll punish my children. Again. Is that why you're setting up that little girl? Seducing her with your glorious power?"

Jake stumbled. His brow knit, and without thinking he defended his actions. "My intentions toward Victoria are honorable."

A bitter smirk twisted the Trickster's lips. "Really? You drove a wedge between Freya and Victoria when you made her your priestess. Are you going to stand by your promises when the time comes for her to fulfill her fate? Or will you turn on her the way you turned on me?"

Before Jake formulated a reply, Loki transformed into a hawk, and the wind caught his wings. He soared high into the sky and disappeared in a flash.

Grunting in disgust, Jake shook his head. "Damn know-it-all always has to have the last word."

Midgard

Throughout the Sierra Pines High School campus, multiple bells clamored in unison. Victoria's palms pressed into the rough textured plaster of a yellow wall. She stood just outside the main office with Morena. A steady stream of students trickled by on their way to their first period classes.

"Are you sure about this?" Victoria scrunched her nose and cast a dubious glance at the sign announcing a basketball game that coming Friday. The billboard proudly displayed the school's mascot, *Mannie the Marmot*, an anamorphic rodent clad in a cap and little red jacket. The varmint's buck teeth were bared in a snarl of aggression.

"Yes! Sure!" Morena bobbed on the balls of her feet, arms swinging. Her entire long, lean body engaged in constant motion, vibrating as if the teenager might fly apart in a thousand directions all at once. "I told you, I'm okay with starting in the middle of the school year. I know it'll be tough, but I can handle it!"

"It's not that, and I know you can handle it." Victoria smiled even though she harbored concerns the Hispanic teenager might have trouble fitting in at the predominantly white school. Just a glance at the expensive automobiles in the student parking lot reinforced her worries, but she concealed them from the girl behind a front of unshakeable confidence. Anyone who didn't adore smart-mouthed Morena wasn't worth the time or effort.

But a cool car would help. She'd have to take a close look at the finances and find a way to swing a sweet ride for the teen, even if it meant letting her borrow the Chevelle.

"What then?" Morena's gaze skittered to the side, and her body followed, sliding toward the thinning crowd of teenagers on their way to class.

"Are you sure you want to attend a school where the mascot is a giant rodent?" Victoria flashed a wolf's smile. "Seriously, the Fighting Marmots?"

Morena grinned. "Aww, marmots are cute."

The teenager took a giant stride backward, creating distance between herself and her Alpha. The wolf rose in her eyes, gleaming bright with laughter. "They taste great too!"

She braced. Here came the hard part, letting go. Waving her hands, Victoria shooed the girl. "Go on. Get going. You're gonna be late."

"Bye!" In a flash, Morena whirled and bolted, darting around the remaining stragglers. Without slowing, she disappeared around a corner.

Shaking her head, Victoria returned to the parked SUV where Sylvie waited in the passenger seat. A skein of yarn rested on the center counsel, feeding the whirling knitting needles clutched in the older woman's hands.

As Victoria climbed into the driver's seat, Sylvie looked up and smiled. "How did it go?"

"Great. She seems genuinely happy to be back in school." Reaching for the keys already in the ignition, Victoria turned on the engine. For a second, she stared at the steering wheel, doubt assailing her. Was she making the right decisions for her pack?

Sylvie's warm hand patted her elbow. "It's tough, I know, but you're doing your best, Victory. No one can ask for more."

She tilted her face to the side to offer her friend a

smile. "I hope so, Sylvie. I hope so." She took a deep breath. "Now that we're alone, we need to go somewhere and have a long talk."

"Sounds ominous." Sucking in her cheeks, Sylvie eyed Victoria.

"It is."

Weary of speaking, Victoria finally wrapped up her story. "So, the three sisters have prophesized that I'll act in service to Loki and use *Vanadium* to cut Fenrir's bonds, freeing him to kill Odin. All to save my daughter from being killed on the eve of her third birthday."

Victoria cast a glance over her shoulder, concerned with her companion's persistent silence throughout the entire recounting of her spirit quest to visit the Norns. Sylvie's face was wan and drawn, her hunched over posture conveyed tension. The older woman had yet to share her opinion.

With a sigh, Victoria bent and placed the bunch of lilies beside the granite headstone. Extending her hand, she traced her fingers over the name inscription—*Arik Koenig*. Explained aloud, her spirit quest to visit the Norse Fates sounded more than a little crazy, but then consultations with the Norns seldom yielded predictable results.

"I promise you, my mate," Victoria whispered. "I'll keep our daughter safe." Her hand fell from the engraving, and she rose to stand beside Sylvie.

The late afternoon weekday yielded a cemetery empty of visitors except for the two women. Victoria chose the graveyard as the venue for her storytelling because it offered relative isolation and privacy from prying ears.

"Arik being buried here doesn't seem right," Sylvie's voice emerged as a rough croak, poignant and powerful.

"Our people aren't meant to be buried in the earth, but to be cremated on a funeral pyre."

"Arik's body isn't here, Sylvie. This grave is merely for show, a memorial for the humans who knew him." Victoria studied her friend, wondering what went on behind Sylvie's thoughtful expression. "He is with Our Lady of the Vanir. He is Freya's chosen general, leading her army."

Sylvie's head bowed. "Yes, of course. I'm having difficulty absorbing the magnitude of what you've told me. It was already difficult just trying to accept hunters as part of our pack without learning that Ragnarök is upon us."

"I'm sorry. I know it's a lot to take in." Victoria's decision to share everything with her friend had been a difficult one. But her ordeal with the hunters had hammered home one undeniable truth—she couldn't bear every burden alone. She not only wanted but needed a dependable confidante. She trusted Sylvie more than anyone.

Sylvie looked at her with bright eyes. "What are you going to do?"

Her gaze focused on the distance as she envisioned the future. "Call for a meeting of the packs and bring this war with the hunters to an end. We need to unify our people against the undead if we're to survive."

The skald's lips tugged into a smile. "I meant regarding the prophecy."

"Oh." Victoria huffed. "*That.*"

Sylvie's head swooped in a nod. "Yes, that."

"I'll do everything in my power to prevent the prophecy from coming to pass, but first and foremost, I'm going to protect my daughter," Victoria said with the determination born of a mother's love.

A contemplative silence ensued before Sylvie spoke again. "Have you considered that such a course of action may be precisely what brings about the end?"

A harsh bark of laughter escaped Victoria. Hollowness echoed within but also the determined flame of hope. She could not, must not, give up before she began.

"Yes, but doing something is better than doing nothing," Victoria said. "I may sit with my hands folded in my lap, and it may still come to pass that I cut Fenrir's bonds, bringing about Odin's death, which makes me responsible for the end of the world. No matter what I do, I'm second-guessing Loki. God of lies."

Sylvie frowned. "Loki is a trickster. If you wish to thwart his desire, then you must be constantly on your guard."

"I know." Victoria's hands crept to her abdomen, protectively crossing over the life growing in her womb. "But I have a plan."

Through narrowed eyes, the skald stared at her Alpha. "What will you do, Victory?"

Victoria's gaze returned to her mate's grave. In her mind's eye, the faces of all the loved ones already lost haunted her. Her heart ached but hardened. Many more would follow. She did not know how much more loss she could bear before she broke.

She inhaled. "I'll do whatever I have to."

Sylvie placed her arm about Victoria's shoulders and hugged her Alpha. "No matter what, know you're not alone, sweetie."

Victoria embraced her best friend. Together, the two women strolled toward the cemetery entrance. "Sylvie?"

"Hmm?" The older woman regarded her with curiosity.

"Will you teach me to knit? I have a pile of Freya's golden hair just begging to be made into a baby blanket."

"Absolutely, Victory. We'll get right on that."

About the Author

Melissa Snark is a paranormal and romance author with a particular interest in werewolves and Norse mythology. Her Loki's Wolves series combines elements of both in a contemporary fantasy setting. She lives in Northern California with her husband, three children and a glaring of cats.

Visit Melissa at:

www.melissasnark.com

or

www.thesnarkology.com

Books by Melissa Snark

A Cat's Tale

Learning to Fly

The Mating Game

Loki's Wolves

The Child Thief (A short story)

A Brother by Choice (A short story)

Valkyrie's Vengeance (Book #0)

Hunger Moon (Book #1)

Battle Cry (Book #2)

Wolf's Cross (Book #3)

Also available

The Mating Game

by

Melissa Snark

ISBN(s):
978-1-62830-378-0 Paperback
978-1-62830-379-7 Digital

Two males…two friends…a competition for the right to claim The Heart of the Iron Stone Pack.

An alpha female at her core, Theresa Sanchez struggles to protect her young daughter, but rivalries and politics create volatility in the pack. As Theresa comes into heat, lust and need rule her body. Her pack demands only the most virile male have her. How can she choose only one mate when her body craves two—the virile beta and the man she loves?

Zachary Hunter will do anything to take Theresa as his mate, even if it means killing his best friend. However, Robert Blane is just as determined to ascend to Alpha. Both their beasts howl to mark her flesh, but only one can survive to claim her.

But with enemies circling, they must fight…for the pack, for Theresa, and for a future together